This season Mills & Boon® Romance brings you

CHRISTMAS TREATS

For an extra-special treat this Christmas
don't look under the Christmas tree or in
your stocking—pick up one of your favourite
Mills & Boon® Romances, curl up and relax!

From presents to proposals, mistletoe to marriage,
we promise to deliver seasonal warmth, wonder,
and of course the unbeatable rush of romance!

*And look out for Christmas extras this month
in Mills & Boon® Romance!*

D0550170

Marion Lennox and Linda Goodnight
introduce two independent women,
on two very different routes to motherhood.
Their fiery, protective natures bring out
the best in their proud, gorgeous men!

Enjoy our new 2-in-1 editions of stories
by your favourite authors—

for double the romance!

CROWNED: THE PALACE NANNY
by Marion Lennox

JINGLE-BELL BABY
by Linda Goodnight

CROWNED: THE PALACE NANNY

BY
MARION LENNOX

MILLS & BOON

All the characters in this book have no existence outside the imagination of the author, and have no relation whatsoever to anyone bearing the same name or names. They are not even distantly inspired by any individual known or unknown to the author, and all the incidents are pure invention.

First published in Great Britain 2009
Harlequin Mills & Boon Limited,
Eton House, 18-24 Paradise Road, Richmond, Surrey TW9 1SR

© Marion Lennox 2009

ISBN: 978 0 263 86976 7

Set in Times Roman 12½ on 13½ pt
02-1109-54155

Harlequin Mills & Boon policy is to use papers that are natural, renewable and recyclable products and made from wood grown in sustainable forests. The logging and manufacturing process conform to the legal environmental regulations of the country of origin.

Printed and bound in Spain
by Litografia Rosés, S.A., Barcelona

Marion Lennox is a country girl, born on an Australian dairy farm. She moved on—mostly because the cows just weren't interested in her stories! Married to a 'very special doctor', Marion writes Mills & Boon® Romance as well as Medical™ Romances. (She used a different name for each category for a while—if you're looking for her past Mills & Boon® Romances, search for author Trisha David as well.) She's now had over 75 romance novels accepted for publication.

In her non-writing life Marion cares for kids, cats, dogs, chooks and goldfish. She travels, and she fights her rampant garden (she's losing) and her house dust (she's lost). Having spun in circles for the first part of her life, she's now stepped back from her 'other' career, which was teaching statistics at her local university. Finally she's reprioritised her life, figured out what's important, and discovered the joys of deep baths, romance and chocolate. Preferably all at the same time!

CHAPTER ONE

DR ELSA LANGHAM disappeared after a car accident four years ago. Mrs Elsa Murdoch took her place.

The invitation had been sitting on the table all day, a taunting reminder of her past.

> The International Coral Society invites Dr Elsa Langham, foremost authority on Coral: Alcyonacea, to submit a paper at this year's symposium in Hawaii.

The ICS hadn't kept up with her change in direction. Eight-year-old Zoe was asleep in the next room, totally dependent on her, and Dr Elsa Langham was no longer an acclaimed authority on anything.

She read the invitation one last time, sighed and finally dumped it in the bin.

'I don't know why they're still sending me invitations,' she told the skinny black cat slinking out from under her chair. 'I'm Mrs Elsa Murdoch, a mother to

Zoe, an occasional student of starfish to keep my scientific hand in, and my cats need feeding.'

She rose and took a bowl of cat food to the back garden. The little cat followed, deeply suspicious but seduced by the smell of supper.

Four more cats were waiting. Elsa explained the terms of their tenancy as she did every night, fed them, then ignored five feline glares as she locked them up for the night. They knew the deal, but they didn't have to like it.

'At least you guys go free every morning,' she told them. 'You can do what you want during the day.'

And so could she, she told herself. She could take Zoe to the beach. She could study starfish. She could be Mrs Elsa Murdoch.

Until a miracle happens, she thought to herself, pausing to look up at the night sky. Not that I need a miracle. I really love Zoe, I don't mind starfish and I'm incredibly lucky to be alive. It's just…I wouldn't mind a bit of magic. Like a rainbow of coral to appear in our cove. Or Prince Charming to wave his wand and take away my debts and Zoe's scars.

Enough. The cats weren't interested in wishes, and neither was anyone else. She smiled ruefully into the night, turned her back on her disgruntled cats and went inside. She needed to fix a blocked sink.

Where was Prince Charming when you needed him?

* * *

The little boy would live.

Prince Stefanos Antoniadis—Dr Steve to his patients—walked out of Theatre savouring a combination of triumph and exhaustion. He'd won.

The boy's mother—a worn-looking woman with no English, but with a smile wide enough to cut through any language barrier—hugged him and cried, and Stefanos hugged her back and felt his exhaustion disappear.

He felt fantastic.

He walked into the scrub room, sorely tempted to punch the air in triumph—and then stopped dead.

This wasn't fantastic. This was trouble.

Two months ago, King Giorgos of the Diamond Isles had died without an heir. Next in line to the throne of the Mediterranean island of Khryseis was Stefanos's cousin, Christos. The only problem was, no one could find Christos. Worse, if Christos couldn't be found, the throne belonged to Stefanos— who wanted the crown like a hole in the head.

In desperation he'd employed a friend who moved in diplomatic circles and whose discretion he trusted absolutely to search internationally for Christos. That his friend was here to tell him the news in person meant there must be a major problem.

'They told me you've been opening a kid's skull, chopping bits out and sticking it back together,' his friend said with easy good humour. 'How hard's that? *Seven hours…*'

'I get paid by the hour,' Stefanos said, grasping his friend's hand. But he couldn't make himself smile. 'What news?'

'From your point of view?' As an investigator this man was the best, and he knew the issues involved. 'You're not Crown Prince of Khryseis.'

'Not!' He closed his eyes. The relief was almost overwhelming.

It hadn't always been like this. As a boy, Stefanos had even dreamed of inheriting the throne that his almost pathologically shy cousin swore he didn't want.

But that was in the past. King Giorgos was bound to have sons, and if not… Christos would just have to wear it. Almost twenty years ago, Stefanos had moved to the States to pursue a medical career. His dream since then had been to perfect and teach surgical techniques, so wounds such as the ones he'd treated today could be repaired in hospitals less specialised than this one, anywhere in the world. 'So you've finally found Christos?' he asked, feeling the weight of the world lift from his shoulders.

'Sort of,' his friend said, but there was something in his face which made Stefanos's jubilation fade. His expression said that whatever was coming wasn't good.

'Christos is dead, Steve,' the man said gently. 'In a car accident in Australia, four years ago. That's why you haven't been able to find him.'

'Dead.' He stared at his friend in horror. 'Christos? My cousin. Why? How?'

'You know he left the island soon after you? Apparently he and his mother emigrated to Australia. Neither of them kept in touch. It seems his mother held his funeral with no fuss, and contacted no one back on Khryseis. Three months after he died, so did she.'

'Dear God.'

'It's the worst of news,' his friend said. He hesitated. 'But there's more.'

Stefanos knew it. He was replaying their conversation in his head. His friend's first words had been, 'You're not Crown Prince of Khryseis.'

Christos had been first in line to the throne, followed by Stefanos. But Christos was dead. Therefore it had to be Stefanos. Unless…

'There's a child,' his friend told him.

'A child,' he said numbly.

'A little girl. Christos married, but his wife was killed in the same accident. Their child survived. She was four when her parents were killed. She's now eight.'

Stefanos didn't respond. He was staring at his friend, but he was seeing nothing.

He was working on groundbreaking surgical techniques. His work here was vital.

A child.

'Her name's Zoe,' his friend said. 'She's still living in Australia with a woman called Mrs Elsa

Murdoch, who seems to be employed as her nanny. But, Steve…'

'Yes?' But he already knew what was coming.

'Christos's death means the child takes the Crown,' he said gently. 'Zoe's now the Crown Princess of Khryseis. That means you're Prince Regent.'

Stefanos still didn't answer. There was a chasm opening before him—a gaping void where his career used to be. He could only listen while his friend told him what he'd learned.

'I've done some preliminary checks. From what I gather of the island's constitution, you'll be in charge until Zoe's twenty-five. The island's rule, and the consequent care of your cousin as Crown Princess, lies squarely on your shoulders. Now… do you want me to find an address for this woman called Elsa?'

CHAPTER TWO

ROYALTY was standing on Elsa's beach.

Sunlight was shimmering from the surface of a turquoise sea. The tide was at its lowest for months. Their beach was a mass of rock pools and there were specimens everywhere.

They'd swum far out to the buoy marking the end of shallow water and a pod of dolphins had nosed in to check them out. They'd dived for starfish. They'd floated lazily in the shallows; floating eased the nagging ache in Elsa's hip as nothing else could. Finally they'd made each other crowns out of seaweed pods, and now Queen Elsa and her consort, Princess Zoe, were marching back to the house for lunch and a nap.

To find royalty waiting for them. Royalty without seaweed.

For a moment Elsa thought she'd been out in the sun too long. The man was dressed like a prince from one of Zoe's picture books. His uniform was black as night, tailored to perfection. His slick-fitting suit was adorned with crimson epaulettes, tassels, braid and medals. His jacket and the top collar of his shirt were unbuttoned, but for some reason that made him look even more princely.

A prince trying to look casual?

Uh-oh. Her hand flew to her seaweed crown and she tugged it off as icy tendrils of fear crept round her heart.

Royalty was fantasy. Not real. Zoe's father had always been afraid of it, but his stories had seemed so far-fetched that Elsa had deemed them ludicrous.

'Look,' Zoe said, puzzled, and the eight-year-old's hand clutched hers. Zoe had only been four when her parents died, but maybe she remembered enough of her father's paranoia to worry.

Or maybe the sight of someone dressed as a prince on a Queensland beach was enough to worry anyone.

'I can see him,' Elsa said. 'Wow. Do you think he's escaped from your *Sleeping Beauty* book?'

'He's gorgeous,' Zoe said, relaxing a little as Elsa deliberately made light of it.

'He must be hot,' Elsa said cautiously.

'Do you think he came in a carriage like in *Cinderella*?'

'If he did, I hope it has air-conditioning,' Elsa retorted and Zoe giggled.

Good. Great. Zoe giggling was far more important than any prince watching them from the sand dunes.

She would not let anything interfere with that giggle.

'Maybe he's looking for us,' Zoe said, worry returning. 'Maybe he's from Khryseis.'

'Maybe he is.' Neither of them had ever been to Khryseis, but the fabulous Mediterranean island was part of Zoe's heritage—home to the father who'd been killed when she was four. According to the Internet, Khryseis was an island paradise in the Mediterranean, ruled up until now by a King who was as corrupt as he was vindictive. Zoe's father, Christos, had spoken occasionally of the old King's malice. Now those stories came flooding back, and Elsa's fears increased accordingly.

The man—the prince?—was walking down the sandy track towards them, tall, tanned and drop-dead gorgeous. Elsa stopped and put down her pail. She held Zoe's hand tighter.

A lesser mortal might look ridiculous in this situation but, despite his uniform, this man looked to be in charge of his world. Strongly built, aquiline features, dark hooded eyes. Cool, authoritative and calm.

And then he smiled. The combination of uniform, body and smile was enough to knock a girl's socks off. If she had any socks that was, she thought, humour reasserting itself as she decided it was ridiculous to be afraid. She wiggled her toes deep into the sand, feeling the need to ground herself.

Oh, but that smile…

Down, she told herself fiercely. Hormonal response was exactly what wasn't wanted right now. Act cool.

She met the man's gaze and deliberately made herself match his smile. Or almost match it. Her smile was carefully that of someone passing a stranger. His smile, on the other hand, was friendly. His gaze dropped to Zoe—and his smile died. That always happened. No one could stop that initial reaction.

Instinctively Elsa tugged Zoe closer but Zoe was already there. They braced together, waiting for the usual response. Try as she might, she couldn't protect Zoe from strangers. Her own scars were more easily hidden, but Zoe's were still all too obvious.

But this wasn't a normal response. 'Zoe,' the man said softly, on a long drawn-out note of discovery. And pleasure. 'You surely must be Zoe. You look just like your father.'

Neither of them knew what to say to that. They stood in the brilliant sunlight while Elsa tried to think straight.

She felt foolish, and that was dumb. She was wearing shorts and an old shirt, and she'd swum in what she was wearing. Her sun-bleached hair had been tied in a ponytail this morning, but her curls had escaped while she swam. She was coated in sand and salt, and her nose was starting to peel.

Ditto for Zoe.

They were at the beach in Australia. They were appropriately dressed, she thought, struggling for defiance. Whereas this man…

'I'm sorry I'm in uniform,' he said, as if guessing her thoughts. 'I know it looks crazy, but I've pulled in some favours trying to find you. Those favours had to be repaid in the form of attending a civic reception as soon as I landed. I left as soon as I could, but the media's staked out my hotel. If I'd stopped to change they might well have followed me here. I don't want Zoe to be inundated by the press yet.'

Whoa. There was way too much in that last statement to take in. First of all… Was he really royal? What was she supposed to do? Bow?

Not on your life.

'So…who are you?' she managed, and Zoe said nothing.

'I'm Stefanos. Prince Regent of Khryseis. Zoe, your grandfather and my grandfather were brothers. Your father and I were cousins. I guess that makes us cousins of sorts too.'

Cousins. That was almost enough to make her knees give way. Zoe had relations?

This man's voice had the resonance of a Greek accent, not strong but unmistakable. That wasn't enough to confirm anything.

'Christos didn't have any cousins,' she said, which was maybe dumb—what would she know? 'Or…he always said there was no one. So did his mother.'

'And I didn't know they'd died,' he said gently. 'Zoe, I'm so sorry. I knew your father and I knew your grandmother, and I loved them both. I'm very sorry I didn't keep in touch. I'm so sorry I wasn't here when you so obviously needed me.'

Elsa was starting to shake. She so didn't want to be shaking when Zoe was holding her hand, but it was happening regardless.

She was all Zoe had. And—she might as well admit it—for the last four years Zoe was all she'd had.

'You can't have her.' It was said before she had a chance to think, before her head even engaged. It was pure panic and it was infectious. Zoe froze.

'I'm not going with you,' she whispered, and then her voice rose in panic to match Elsa's. 'I'm not, I'm not.' And she buried her face against Elsa and sobbed her terror. Elsa swung her up into her arms and held. The little girl was clutching her as if she were drowning.

And Stefanos…or whoever he was…was staring at them both in bemusement. She looked at him over Zoe's head and found his expression was almost quizzical.

'Good one,' he said dryly. 'You don't think you might be overreacting just a little?'

She probably was, she conceded, hugging Zoe tighter, but there was no room for humour here.

'You think we might be a bit over the top?' she managed. 'Prince Charming on a Queensland

beach.' She looked past him and saw a limousine—
a Bentley, no less, with a chauffeur to boot.
Overreaction? She didn't think so. 'You're frightening Zoe. You're frightening me.'

'I didn't come to frighten you.'

'So why did you come?' She heard herself then,
realising she was sounding hysterical. She knew
Zoe's father had come from Khryseis. She knew
he'd been part of the royal family. What could be
more natural than a distant relative, here on official
business, dropping in to see Zoe?

But then there was his statement… *I've pulled
in some favours trying to find you.* He'd deliberately come searching for Zoe.

Prince Regent… That made him Prince in charge
while someone was incapacitated. The old King?

Or when someone was a child.

No.

'Zoe, hush,' she said, catching her breath,
deciding someone had to be mature and it might as
well be her. 'I was silly to panic. Stefanos isn't
here to take you away.' She glared over Zoe's head,
as much to tell him, *Don't you dare say anything
different.* 'He comes from the island where your
papa grew up. I'm sorry I reacted like I did. I was
very rude and very silly. I think it's time to dry our
eyes and meet him properly.'

Zoe hiccuped on a sob, but there'd been worse
things than this to frighten Zoe in her short life, and
she was one brave little girl. She sniffed and wiped

her eyes with the back of her hand and turned within Elsa's arms to face him.

She was a whippet of a child, far too thin, and far too small. The endless operations had taken their toll. It was taking time and painstaking rehabilitation to build her up to anywhere near normal.

'Maybe we both should say sorry and a proper hello,' Elsa said ruefully, and Zoe swallowed manfully and put a thin hand out in greeting. Clinging to Elsa with the other.

'Hello,' she whispered.

'Hello,' Stefanos said and took her hand with all the courtesy of one royal official meeting another. 'I'm very pleased to meet you, Zoe. I've come halfway round the world to meet you.'

And then he turned his attention to Elsa. 'And you must be Mrs Murdoch.'

'She's Elsa,' Zoe corrected him.

'Elsa, then, if that's okay with Elsa,' Stefanos said, meeting her gaze steadily. She had no hand free left to shake and she was glad of it. This man was unsettling enough without touch.

So… She didn't know where to go from here. Did you invite a prince home for a cup of tea? Or for a twelve course luncheon?

'You live here?' he asked, his tone still gentle. There was only one place in sight. Her bungalow—a tired, rundown shack. 'Is this place yours?'

'Yes.'

'Can I come in and talk to you?'

'Your chauffeur…'

'Would it be too much trouble to ask if you could ring for a taxi to take me back into town when we've spoken? I don't like to keep my chauffeur waiting.'

'There's no taxi service out here.'

'Oh.'

Now what? What was a woman to say when a prince didn't want to keep his chauffeur waiting? She needed an instruction manual. Maybe she was still verging on the hysterical.

She gave herself a swift mental shake. 'I'm sorry. A taxi won't come out here but we have a car. It'll only take us fifteen minutes to run you back into town. I'm not normally so…so inhospitable. It's the uniform.'

'I expect it might be,' he said and smiled, and there it was again, that smile—a girl could die and go to heaven in that smile. 'I don't want to put you to trouble.'

'If you can cope with a simple sandwich, you're welcome to lunch,' she managed. 'And…of course we'll drive you into town. After all, you're Christos's cousin.'

'So I can't be all bad?' It was a teasing question and she flushed.

'I loved Christos,' she said, almost defensively. 'And I loved Amy. Zoe's mama and papa were my closest friends.' She managed a shaky smile. 'For their sake…you're welcome.'

* * *

The house was saggy and battered and desperately in need of a paint. A couple of weatherboards had crumbled under the front window and a piece of plywood had been tacked in place to fill the gap. The whole place looked as if it could blow over in the next breeze. Only the garden, fabulous and overgrown, looked as if it was holding the place together.

Stefanos hardly noticed the garden. All he noticed was the woman in front of him.

She was…stunning. Stunning in every sense of the word, he thought. Natural, graceful, free.

Free was maybe a dumb adjective but it was the thought that came to mind. She was wearing nothing but shorts and a faded white blouse, its top three buttons undone so he had a glimpse of beautiful cleavage. Her long slim legs seemed to go on for ever, finally ending in bare feet, tanned and sand coated. This woman lived in bare feet, he thought, and a shiver went through him that he couldn't identify. Was it weird to think bare sandy toes were incredibly sexy? If it was, then count him weird.

But it wasn't just her toes. It wasn't just her body.

Her face was tanned, with wide intelligent eyes, a smattering of freckles and a full generous mouth with a lovely smile. Breathtakingly lovely. Her honey-blonde hair was sun-kissed, bleached to almost translucence by the sun. There was no way those streaks were artificial, for there was nothing artificial about this woman. She wore not a hint of make-up, except the remains of a smear of white suncream over her nose, and her riot of damp, salt-and-sand-laden curls looked as if they hadn't seen a comb for a week.

Quite simply, he'd never seen a woman so beautiful.

'Are you coming in?' Elsa was standing on the veranda, looking at him with the beginnings of amusement. Probably because he was standing with his mouth open.

'Is this a holiday shack?' he managed, forcing his focus to the house—though it was almost impossible to force his focus anywhere but her. The information he'd been given said she lived here. Surely not.

'No,' she said shortly, amusement fading. 'It's our home. I promise it's clean enough inside so you won't get your uniform dirty.'

'I didn't mean…'

'No.' She relented and forced another of her lovely smiles. 'I know you didn't. I'm sorry.'

He came up the veranda steps. Zoe had already disappeared inside, and he heard the sound of running water.

'Zoe gets first turn at the shower while I make lunch,' Elsa explained. 'Then she sets the table while I shower.'

It was said almost defiantly. Like—don't mess with the order of things. She was afraid, he thought.

But… This woman was Zoe's nanny. She was being paid out of Zoe's estate. He'd worried when he'd read that—a stranger making money out of a child.

Now he wasn't so sure. This wasn't a normal nanny-child relationship. Even after knowing them only five minutes, he knew it.

And the fear? She'd be wanting reassurance that he wouldn't take Zoe away. He couldn't give it. He watched her face and he knew his silence was being assessed for what it was.

Why hadn't he found more out about her? His information was that Zoe's parents had died in a car crash four years ago. Since then Zoe had been living with a woman who was being paid out of her parents' estate—an estate consisting mostly of Christos's life insurance.

That information had him hoping things could be handled simply. He could take Zoe back to Khryseis and employ a lovely, warm nanny over there to care for her. Maybe this could even be seen as a rescue mission.

This woman, sunburned, freckled and barefoot, standing with her arms folded across her breasts in a stance of pure defence, said it wasn't simple at all. Mrs Elsa Murdoch was not your normal nanny.

And… Christos and Amy had been her best friends?

'I'm not here to harm Zoe,' he said mildly.

'No.' That was a dumb statement, he conceded. As if she was expecting him to beat the child.

'I just want what's best for her.'

'Good,' she said brusquely. 'You might be able to help me. There are a couple of things I could use some advice over.'

That wasn't what he meant. They both knew it.

'Did you know Zoe's the new Crown Princess of Khryseis?' he asked, and she froze.

'The what?'

'The Crown Princess of Khryseis.'

'I heard you. I don't know what you mean.'

'I think you do,' he said softly. 'Your face when I said it…'

'Doesn't mean a thing,' she whispered. 'I'm tired, confused and hungry, and your uniform is doing my head in. Come in and sit down while I make lunch and take a shower. But if you say one word—one word—of this Crown Princess thing to Zoe before we've discussed it fully, you'll be off my property so fast you'll leave your gold tassels behind. Got it?'

'Um…got it,' he said.

'Right,' she said and turned and marched inside, leaving him to follow if he felt like it. Or go away if he felt like it.

Her body language said the second option was the one she favoured.

The moment he got inside he took his jacket off. He pulled off his tie, undid the next two buttons of his shirt and rolled up his sleeves.

It was a casual gesture of making himself at home and it rendered her almost speechless.

Outside he'd seemed large. Inside, tossing his jacket on the settee, rolling up his sleeves, taking a slow visual sweep of her kitchen-living room, he seemed much larger. It was as if he was filling the room, the space not taken up with his sheer physical size overwhelmed by his sheer masculinity.

He was six one or six two, she thought. Not huge. Just…male. And more good-looking than was proper. And way too sexy.

Sexy. Where had that word come from? She shoved it away in near panic.

'This is great,' he said, and she fought for composure and tried to see the house as he saw it.

It was tumbledown. Of course it was. There was no way she could afford to fix the big things. One day in the not too distant future Zoe might be able to go to school and she could take a proper job again and earn some money. But meanwhile they made do.

'Where did you get this stuff?' he asked, gesturing to the room in general. 'It's amazing.'

'Most of it we found or we made.'

He gazed around at the eclectic mix of brightly coloured cushions and faded crimson curtains, the colourful knotted rugs on the floor, lobster pots hanging from the ceiling with shells threaded through to make them look like proper decorations, a fishing net strung across the length of one wall, filled with old buoys and huge seashells. There were worn pottery jugs filled with flowers from the garden; bird of paradise plants, crimson and deep green.

'You found all this?' he demanded.

'I used to have an apartment at the university,' she told him. 'Small. My parents left me this place and I came here at weekends. I'm a marine biologist and we…I used the cottage as an occasional base for research. Zoe's parents were what you might call itinerant. They had a camper van and most of what they owned was destroyed in the accident. So Zoe and I scrounged what we could find, we made a bit and we filled the rest by beachcombing.' She met his gaze full on, defying him to deny her next assertion. 'Zoe and I are the best beachcombers in the world.'

'I can see you are,' he said. He paused. 'You're a marine biologist?'

'Yes.' She faltered and tried for a recovery. 'Very part-time until Zoe goes to school.'

'Zoe doesn't go to school?'

'I home-school her here at the moment.'

'So meanwhile you're living off Christos's life insurance.'

She'd opened the refrigerator and was lifting out salad ingredients. She froze.

She didn't turn around. She couldn't. If she had he might have got lettuce square in the middle of his face. What was he suggesting?

'That's right,' she said stiffly. 'I'm ripping Zoe off for every cent I can get.'

'I didn't mean…'

'I'm very sure you did mean.' Finally she turned, carefully placing the lettuce out of throwing range. 'What is it you want of us, Mr Whoever-The-Hell-You-Are, because there's no way I'm calling you Prince. I don't know why you're here but don't you dare imply I'm acting dishonestly. Don't you dare.'

'I already did,' he said, holding his hands up as if in surrender. 'I'm sorry.'

'So am I.'

The door swung open. Zoe appeared, looking wary. The little girl was in clean T-shirt and shorts. Her hair was a tangle of dark, wet curls. She was far too thin, Elsa thought, trying to see her dispassionately through Stefanos's eyes.

She was so scarred. The burns had been to almost fifty per cent of her body, and twenty per cent of those had been full thickness. She'd had graft after graft. Thankfully her face was almost untouched but her skinny little legs looked almost like patchwork. Her left arm still needed work—her left hand was missing its little finger—and there was deep scarring under her chin.

She'd protect this child with her life, she thought, but protection could only go so far. This man was part of Zoe's real family. She had to back off a little.

'Okay, it's my turn for the shower, poppet,' she said, trying to make her voice normal.

'You sounded angry,' she said, doubtful.

'I'm crabby 'cos I'm hungry.' She tugged Zoe to her in a swift hug. 'I'll have a shower in world record time. Can you set the table and talk to… Stefanos. He's your papa's cousin. He knows all about Khryseis. Maybe he could show you exactly where he lives on the Internet. We have pictures of Khryseis bookmarked.'

And, with a final warning glance at Stefanos, she whisked herself away. She didn't want to leave at all. She wanted to bring Zoe into the bathroom with her. She wanted to defend her with everything she had.

Zoe, Crown Princess?

Zoe had far too much to deal with already. If Stefanos wanted to take on part of Zoe's life, then he had to contend with her. Zoe's life was her life. She'd sworn that to Zoe's mother, and she wasn't backing down on it now.

She couldn't. She was so afraid…

CHAPTER THREE

ZOE set the table while he watched her. The little girl was watching him out of the corner of her eye, not meeting his gaze directly. Table done, she turned to a corner desk holding a computer. The machine looked like something out of the Dark Ages, big, cumbersome and ugly. She checked the Internet, waiting until the Khryseis information downloaded—seemingly by slow-boat from China.

But finally the websites in Khryseis were on the screen. By the look of the bookmarks, she and Elsa spent a lot of time browsing them.

He tentatively showed her where he lived on the island—or where he'd lived as a child. She reacted with silent politeness.

He checked the other bookmarks for the island. They were marine sites, he saw. Research articles about the island.

Worth noting.

'So you and Elsa spend a lot of time studying…

fish?' he ventured and got a scornful look for his pains.

'Echinoderms.'

Right. Good. What the hell were echinoderms?

And then Elsa was back. Same uniform as before—shorts and faded shirt. She was tugging her curls back into a ponytail. Still she wore no make-up, and without the suncream her freckles were more pronounced. Her nose was peeling and her feet were still bare.

She walked with a slight limp, he noted, but it was very slight. A twisted ankle, maybe? But that was a side issue. He wasn't about to focus on an ankle when he was looking at the whole package.

She was so different from the women in the circles he moved in that her appearance left him stunned. Awed, even.

He'd implied she was dishonest. There was nothing in this place, in her dress, in anything in this house, that said she was taking advantage of Zoe. His investigator had shown him Christos's financial affairs. If they were both living totally on Christos's life insurance…

'How much outside work do you do?' he said, carefully neutral, and Elsa pulled up short.

'You mean how much of my obviously fabulous riches are derived from honest toil and how much by stealing from orphans?'

He had to smile. And, to his relief, she returned

a wry smile herself, as if she was ordering herself to relax.

'I'm not accusing you in any sense of the word,' he assured her. 'What's in front of my eyes is Zoe, in need of your care, and you, providing that care. Christos's life insurance wouldn't come close to paying for your combined expenses.'

'You don't know the half of it.'

'So tell me.'

She shook her head. 'I'm sorry, but Christos never spoke of you, as a cousin or as a friend. As far as I know, neither Christos nor his mother ever wanted to have anything to do with anyone from Khryseis. How can my finances have anything to do with you?'

'I do want to help.'

'Is that right?' she said neutrally. She shook her head. 'I'm sorry. Look, can we eat? I can't think while I'm hungry and after a morning on the beach I could eat a horse.'

She almost did. There was cold meat and salad, and freshly baked bread which she tipped from an ancient bread-maker. She cut doorstop slices of bread and made sandwiches. She poured tumblers of home-made lemonade, sat herself down, checked Zoe had what she needed—the sandwich she'd made for Zoe was much smaller, almost delicate in comparison to the ones she'd made for herself and for him—and then proceeded to eat.

She ate two doorstop sandwiches and drank

three tumblers of lemonade, while Zoe ate half a sandwich and Elsa prodded her to eat more.

'Those legs are never going to get strong if they're hollow,' she teased, and Zoe gave her a shy smile, threw Stefanos a scared glance and nibbled a bit more.

She was trying to eat. He could see that. Was his presence scaring her?

The idea of frightening this child was appalling. The whole situation was appalling. He was starting to have serious qualms about whether his idea of Zoe's future was possible.

Except it must be. He had to get this child back to Khryseis. Oh, but her little body…

It didn't take his medical qualifications to realise how badly this child was damaged. The report he'd read had told him that four years ago Christos, his wife and their four-year-old daughter had been involved in a major car accident. Christos had died instantly. Amy, his wife, had died almost two weeks later and Zoe, their child, had been orphaned. No details.

There was a story behind every story, he thought, and suddenly he had a flash of what must have happened. A camper van crashing. A fire. A death, a woman so badly burned she died two weeks later, and a child. A child burned like her mother.

He knew enough about burns to understand you didn't get these type of scars without months—

years—of medical treatment. Without considerable pain.

He'd arrived here thinking he had an orphaned eight-year-old on his hands. On *his* hands. She'd seemed like one more responsibility to add to his list. Her nanny was listed as one Mrs Elsa Murdoch. He'd had visions of a matronly employee, taking care of a school-aged child in return for cash.

His preconceptions had been so far from the mark that he felt dizzy.

Despite the man-sized sandwich on his plate, he wasn't eating. The official reception had been mid-morning, there'd been canapés, and he'd been watched to see which ones he ate, which chef he'd offend. So he'd eaten far more than he wanted. Elsa's doorstop sandwich was good, but he felt free to leave the second half uneaten. He had a feeling Elsa wasn't a woman who was precious about her cooking.

Actually…was this cooking? He stared down at his sandwich and thought of the delicacies he'd been offered since he'd taken over the throne— and he grinned.

'So what's funny?' Elsa demanded, and he looked up and found she was watching him. Once more she was wearing her assessing expression. He found it penetrating…and disturbing. He didn't like to be read, but he had a feeling that in Elsa Murdoch he'd found someone who could do just that.

'I've had an overload of royal food,' he told her. 'This is great.'

'So you wouldn't be eating…why?'

'I'm full of canapés.'

'I can see that about you,' she said. 'A canapé snacker. Can I have your sandwich, then?'

He handed it over and watched in astonishment as she ate. Where was she putting it? There wasn't an ounce of spare flesh on her. She looked…just about perfect.

Where had that description come from? He thought of the glamorous women he'd had in his life, how appalled they'd be if they could hear the *perfect* adjective applied to this woman, and once more he couldn't help smiling.

'Yep, we're a world away from your world,' she said brusquely.

What the…? 'Will you stop that?'

'What?' she asked, all innocence.

'Mind reading.'

'Not if it works. It's fun.' She rose and started clearing dishes. He noted the limp again but, almost as he noted it, it ceased. Zoe was visibly wilting. 'Zoe, poppet, you go take a nap. Unless…' She paused. 'Unless Stefanos wants us to drive him into town now.'

'I need to talk to you,' he said.

'There you go,' she said equably. 'I mind read that too. So, Zoe, pop into bed and we'll take Stefanos home when you wake up.'

'You won't get angry again?' Zoe asked her, casting an anxious look across at him.

And he got that too. This child's mental state was fragile. She did not need angry voices. She did not need anyone arguing about her future.

This place was perfect for an injured child to heal, he thought. A tropical paradise.

He had another paradise for her, though. He watched with concern as Elsa kissed her soundly, promised her no anger and sent her off to bed.

There was no choice. He just had to make this… nanny…accept it.

She washed.

He wiped.

She protested, but he was on the back foot already—the idea of watching while she worked would make the chasm deeper.

They didn't speak. Maybe the idea of having a prince doing her wiping was intimidating, he thought wryly, and here it was again. Her response before he could voice his thought.

'An apron beats tassels for this job any day. I need a camera,' she said, handing him a sudsy breadboard to wipe. 'No one will believe this.'

'Aren't you supposed to rinse off the suds?'

'You're criticising my washing? I'm more than happy to let you do both.'

'I'm more than happy to do both.'

She paused. She set down her dishcloth and

turned to face him, wiping her sudsy hands on the sides of her shorts.

She looked anxious again. And territorial.

And really, really cute.

'Why the limp?' he asked and she glanced at him as if he was intruding where he wasn't wanted.

'It's hardly a limp. I'm fine. Next question?'

'Where's Mr Murdoch?' he asked, and her face grew another emotion.

'What?' she said dangerously.

Uh-oh. But he couldn't take the question back. It hung between them, waiting for an answer.

'My researchers said Zoe's nanny was a Mrs Elsa Murdoch.'

'Ms,' she said and glared.

'So never a Mrs?'

'What's that to do with the price of eggs?'

'It's merely a polite question.'

'Polite. Okay.' She even managed a…polite… smile. 'So where's your Princess?'

'Sorry?'

'I'm Mrs so there has to be a Mr. I believe I'm simply reversing your question. Is there a matching Princess?'

'Why would you want to know that?'

'Exactly,' she said, and smiled—a smile that confounded him as she turned back to her washing. Only there was nothing left to wash. She let the water out and wiped the sink with care. She waited for him to dry the last glass, then wiped his part of the sink as well, as if it was vital that not a speck of anything remained.

This woman confounded him—but he had to focus on their future. He must.

'Zoe's needed back on Khryseis,' he said, and Elsa's hand stilled mid-wipe. She couldn't disguise the fear sweeping over her face.

'She stays here.'

'I believe I'm her nearest living relative,' he said mildly. 'As such I can challenge your guardianship.'

She didn't move. Her hand seemed suddenly to be locked on the sink. She was staring downward as if there was something riveting in its depths.

'Oh…' He couldn't mistake the distress on her face. 'No!'

But it had to be said. Like it or not, the stakes were too high to allow emotion to hold sway.

'I'm her cousin,' he said, gently but as firm as he needed to be. 'It's obvious you're struggling to care for her. I can…'

'You can't.' She whirled to face him at that. Her voice was low enough not to disturb Zoe, but loud enough to make him feel her fury. And her fear. 'She's been with me for four years. I'm her godmother and her guardian. Her mother was my best friend and I promised Amy I'd care for her. Her father was a colleague and I loved him too. You…did you know any of them?'

'I knew Christos.'

'Yeah, close family,' she mocked. 'He never mentioned you. Not once. He said royalty on Khryseis was a shambles, the King was concerned only with himself, the King controlled all three of the Diamond Isles and the original royal families of each island were helpless. Christos was frightened of the royal family. He came here to escape what he saw as persecution. He hated them.'

Okay, he thought. Stick to facts. Get over this patch of ground as fast as possible and move on.

'King Giorgos gave Christos a dreadful time,' he told her, keeping his voice as neutral as he could. 'Christos and his mother left Khryseis when he was seventeen. Did he tell you he was first in line to the crown of Khryseis's original royal family?'

'No.'

'He was. That's why Giorgos made life hell for him. He made life hard enough for me and I was only second in line. So we both left and made our lives overseas, but when Giorgos died…'

'Giorgos is dead?'

'Without an heir. So Christos should be Crown Prince. It's taken weeks to get this far. To find he was dead. No one on Khryseis knew he'd died.'

'His mother wasn't well when her son died.' He could see facts and emotions swirling, fighting for space as she took in his words. 'I guess… I imagined it was up to her to tell others if she wanted. But she was frail already, and her son's death made things… Well, she died three months later.'

'So Zoe lost her grandmother as well.'

Her eyes flew to his. She hadn't expected that response, he thought, and wondered what she had expected.

'Yes,' she whispered. 'Thank you for recognising that. It did make things much harder.'

'So then you stepped in.'

'There was no one else.'

'And now we have a mess,' he said, choosing his words with care. 'Yes, Christos hated the royal family, but it was King Giorgos he feared and Giorgos's line is finished. The three Diamond Isles have splintered into three principalities. As Christos's only child, Zoe's the new Crown Princess of Khryseis. She'll inherit full sovereign power when she's twenty-five but until then, like it or not, I'm Prince Regent. Whether I want that power or not, the island's desperate for change. The infrastructure's appalling but I only have power for change if Zoe lives on Khryseis for at least three months of every year. Otherwise the power stays with an island council that's as impotent as it is corrupt. Elsa, she has to come home.'

She didn't say a word.

She was a really self-contained woman, he thought. He'd shaken her out of her containment but he'd done it with fear of losing Zoe. She had her self-containment back now, and he had no idea what was going in her head. He wouldn't be privy to it until she decided to speak again.

She poured two tumblers of water. She walked outside—not limping now, he thought, and found he was relieved. He could cope with an injured child—but not an incapacitated nanny as well. There were two ancient deckchairs on the porch. She sank into one of them and left it to him to decide whether to sit on the other.

The chairs were old and stained and the one left vacant looked to be covered in cat fur.

His trousers were jet-black with a slash of crimson up the side. Ceremonial uniform.

'It brushes off,' she said wryly, not looking at him. Gazing out through the palms to the sea beyond.

He sat.

'You have a cat?' he asked, feeling his way.

'Five,' she said, and as he looked around she shook her head.

'They won't come near when you're here. They're feral cats. Cats are a huge problem up here—they decimate the wildlife. Only Zoe loves them. So we've caught every one we can. If they're at all approachable we have them neutered. We feed them really well at dusk and again in the morning. We lock them up overnight where we feed them— in the little enclosure behind the house. That way they don't need to kill wildlife to eat. Apart from our new little black one, they're fat and lazy, and if you weren't here they'd be lined up here snoozing their day away.'

'You can afford to feed five cats?'

Mistake. Once again she froze. 'You're inordinately interested in my financial affairs,' she said flatly. 'Can you tell me why they're you're business?'

'You're spending Zoe's money.'

'And you're responsible for Zoe how? You didn't even know she existed.'

'Now I do know, she's family.'

'Good, then,' she said. 'Go talk to Zoe's lawyers. They'll tell you we put her money in a trust fund and I take out only what's absolutely necessary for us to live.'

'And the cats?'

She sighed. 'We catch fish,' she said. 'I cook the heads and innards with rice. That's my cat food for the week. So yes, I waste rice and some fish heads on our cats. Shoot me now.'

'I'm not criticising.'

'You are,' she said bluntly. 'You said I'm struggling to care for her. Tell me in what way I'm struggling?'

'Look at this place,' he said before he could stop himself—and her simmering anger exploded.

'I'm looking. I can't see a palace, if that's what you mean. I can't see surround-sound theatre rooms and dishwashers and air-conditioning. I can't see wall to wall carpet and granite bench tops. So how does Zoe need those?'

'It's falling down.'

'So if it falls down I'll rebuild. We have isolation, which Zoe needs until she gets her confidence back. We have our own private beach. We have my work—yes, I'm still doing research and I'm being paid a stipend which goes towards Zoe's medical costs, but…'

'You're paying Zoe's medical costs?'

'Your investigator didn't go very far if he didn't find that out. Her parents hadn't taken out medical insurance,' she said. 'In this country the basics are covered but there have been so many small things. The last lot of plastic surgery was on her shoulder. The surgeon was wonderful—that's why we used him—but he only operates on private patients so we had to pay.'

'*You* had to pay.'

'Whatever.'

'You can't keep doing that.'

'Try and stop me,' she said, carefully neutral again. She'd obviously decided it was important to keep a rein on her temper.

'Where does that leave you?'

'Where I am.'

'Stuck in the middle of nowhere, with a damaged child.'

She put her drink carefully down on the packing case that served as their outdoor table. She rose.

'You know, I'm not enjoying myself here and I have work to do. I correct assignments online and

I try to do it while Zoe's asleep. When she wakes we'll drive you back into town. But meanwhile... Meanwhile you go take a walk on the beach, calculate cat food costs, do whatever you want, I don't care. I believe any further dialogue should be through our lawyers.'

And she walked deliberately inside and let the screen door bang closed after her.

CHAPTER FOUR

SHE was true to her word. She wouldn't speak to him until Zoe woke up. He took a walk on the beach, feeling ridiculous in his ridiculous uniform. He came back and talked for a while to a little black cat who deigned to be sociable. Finally Zoe woke, but even then Elsa only spoke when necessary.

'I'll give you the address of my lawyer,' she said.

'I already know who your lawyer is.'

'Of course you do,' she said cordially. 'Silly me.'

'You're being…'

'Obstructive?' she said. 'Yes, I am.'

'What's obstructive?' Zoe asked.

'Not letting your cousin Stefanos have what he wants.'

'What does he want?'

'You might ask him.'

Zoe turned to him, puzzled. 'What do you want?'

'To get to know you,' he said, refusing to be distracted by Elsa's anger. 'Your papa was a very good friend of mine. When he left Khryseis we didn't write—he wanted a clean break. I should have made more of an effort to keep in touch and I'll be sorry for the rest of my life that I didn't. That he married and had a little girl called Zoe… that he died…it breaks my heart that I didn't know.'

'It makes you sad?'

'Very sad.'

But apparently Zoe knew about sad—and she had a cure.

'When I'm in hospital and I'm sad, Elsa tells me about the fish she's seen that day, and shells and starfish. Elsa keeps saying the sea's waiting for me to get well. She brings in pictures of the beach and the house and the cats and she pins them all over the walls so every time I wake up I can see that the sea and this house and our cats are waiting for me.'

His gaze flew to Elsa. She was staring blankly ahead, as if she hadn't heard.

But she had heard, he thought. She surely had.

And he knew then… As he watched her stoical face he realised that he was threatening her foundations. He was threatening to remove a little girl she loved with all her heart.

He'd never thought of this as a possibility. That a nanny could truly love his little cousin.

He'd come here expecting to meet Mrs Elsa Murdoch, paid nanny. Instead he'd met Elsa, marine biologist, friend, protector, mother to Zoe in every sense but name.

After the shock of learning of Zoe's existence, his plan had been to rescue his orphaned cousin, take her back to Khryseis and pay others to continue her care. Or, if Zoe was attached to this particular nanny, then he could continue to employ her to give the kid continuity.

It had to be option two.

Only if he broached it now Elsa might well lock the door and call the authorities to throw him off her land.

So do it when? He had so little time.

'I need to go back to Khryseis tomorrow,' he told Zoe and glanced sideways to see relief flood Elsa's face. 'Elsa's said she'll drive me into town now. But I've upset her. She thought I might want to take you away from her, and I'd never do that. I promise. So if you and Elsa drive me into town now, can I come and visit again tomorrow morning?' He looked ruefully down at his ceremonial trousers—now liberally coated in cat fur. 'If I'm welcome?'

'Is he welcome?' Zoe asked Elsa.

'If you want him to come,' Elsa said neutrally. 'Stefanos is your cousin.'

Zoe thought about it. He was being judged, he thought, and the sensation was weird. Judged by an eight-year-old, with Elsa on the sidelines doing her own judging.

Or…it seemed she'd already judged.

'If you come you should bring your togs,' Zoe said.

'Togs?'

'Your swimming gear—if you own any without tassels and braid,' Elsa said, still obviously forcing herself not to glower. 'As a farewell visit,' she added warningly. 'Because, if you really are Zoe's cousin, then I accept that she should get to know you.'

'That's gracious of you,' he said gravely.

'It is,' she said and managed a half-hearted smile.

The drive back to town started in silence. Elsa's car was an ancient family wagon, filled in the back with—of all things—lobster pots. There was a pile of buoys and nets heaped on the front passenger seat, so he was forced to sit in the rear seat with Zoe.

She could have put the gear in the back, he thought, but she didn't offer and he wasn't pushing it. So she was chauffeur and he and Zoe were passengers.

'You catch lobsters?' he said cautiously.

'We weigh them, sex them, tag then and let them go,' she said briefly from the front.

'You have a boat?'

'The university supplies one. But I only go when Zoe can come with me.'

'It's really fun,' Zoe said. 'I like catching the

little ones. You have to be really careful when you pick them up. If you grab them behind their necks they can't reach and scratch you.'

'We have lobsters on the Diamond Isles,' he told her. 'My friend Nikos is a champion fisherman.'

'Do you fish?' Zoe demanded.

'I did when I was a boy.'

They chatted on. Elsa was left to listen. And fret.

He was good, she conceded. He was wriggling his way into Zoe's trust and that wasn't something lightly achieved. Like her father before her, Zoe was almost excruciatingly shy, and that shyness had been made worse by people's reaction to her scars.

Stefanos hadn't once referred to her scars. To the little girl it must be as if he hadn't noticed them.

The concept, for Zoe, must be huge. Here was someone out of her papa's past, wanting to talk to her about interesting stuff like what he'd done on Khryseis when he was a boy with her papa.

She shouldn't be driving him back into town. She should be asking him to dinner, even asking him to sleep over to give Zoe as much contact as she could get.

Only there were other issues. Like the Crown. Like the fact that he'd said that Zoe had to return to Khryseis. Like crazy stuff that she couldn't consider.

Like asking a prince of the blood whether he'd like to sleep on her living room settee, she thought suddenly, and the idea was so ridiculous she almost smiled.

He was leaving tomorrow. He'd stopped talking about the possibility of Zoe coming with him. Maybe he'd given up.

She glanced into the rear-view mirror and he looked up and met her eyes.

No, she thought, and fear settled back around her heart. Prince Stefanos of Khryseis looked like a man who didn't give up—on anything.

The township of Waratah Cove had two three-star hotels and one luxury six-star resort out on the headland past the town.

Without asking, she turned the car towards the headland and he didn't correct her.

Money, she thought bleakly. If she could have the cost of one night's accommodation in this place…

'Can you stop here?' Stefanos asked and she jammed her foot on the brake and stopped dead. Maybe a bit too suddenly.

'Wow,' Zoe said. 'Are you crabby or something?'

'Or something,' she said neutrally, glancing again at Stefanos in the rear-view mirror.

'Your nanny thinks I spend too much money,' he said, amused, and she flushed. Was she so obvious?

'Elsa's not my nanny,' Zoe said, amused herself.

'What is she?'

'She's just my Elsa.'

My Elsa. It was said with such sureness that he knew he could never break this bond. If he was to take Zoe back to Khryseis, he needed to take them both.

He had to get this right.

'So why did you want me to stop here?' Elsa asked.

'Because the ambassador to the Diamond Isles leaked to the media that I was coming here,' he said bitterly. 'That's why I had to find myself a uniform and attend the reception. I've already had to bribe—heavily—the chauffeur they arranged for me so he wouldn't tell anyone my location. I imagine there'll be cameramen outside my hotel, wanting to know where I've been, and I don't want a media circus descending on Zoe. I can walk the last couple of hundred yards.'

'Maybe you should check your trousers,' Elsa said, and there was suddenly laughter in her voice. 'Cat fur isn't a great look for a Royal Prince.'

'Thanks very much,' he said, and smiled.

And, unaccountably, she smiled back.

Hers was a gorgeous smile. Warm and natural and full of humour. If he'd met this woman under normal circumstances...

Maybe he'd never have noticed her, he thought. She didn't move in the circles he moved in. Plus he liked his women groomed. Sophisticated. Able to hold their own in any company.

She'd be able to hold her own. This was one feisty woman.

He needed to learn more about her. He needed to hit the phones, extend his research, come up with an offer she couldn't refuse.

Unaccountably, he didn't want to get out of the car. The battered family wagon, loaded with lobster pots, smelling faintly—no, more than faintly—of fish, unaccountably seemed a good place to stay.

He thought suddenly of his apartment in Manhattan. Of his consulting suite with its soft grey carpet, its trendy chrome furniture, its soft piped music.

They were worlds apart—he and Mrs Elsa Murdoch.

But now their lives needed to overlap, enough to keep the island safe. The islanders safe.

Zoe safe.

Until today he'd seen Zoe as a problem—a shock, to be muted before the islanders found out.

Now, suddenly that obstacle was human—a little girl with scars, attached to a woman who loved her.

They were waiting for him to get out of the car. If he left it any longer a media vehicle might come this way. One cameraman and Zoe would run, he thought, and it'd be Elsa who ran with her.

Elsa wasn't family. It wasn't her role to care for Zoe.

Forget the roles, he told himself sharply. Now he must protect the pair of them. He climbed from the car and tried to dust himself off. He had ginger cat fur on black trousers.

Suddenly Elsa was out of the car as well, watching as he shrugged on his jacket.

'Do your buttons up,' she said, almost kindly. 'You look much more princely with your buttons done up. And hold still. If a car comes I'll stop, but let's see what we can achieve before that happens.'

And, before he knew what she intended, she'd twisted him round so she could attack the backs of his legs and the seat of his trousers.

With a hairbrush?

'It's actually a brush Zoe uses for her dolls,' she told him, sweeping the cat fur off in long efficient strokes. 'But see—I've rolled sticky tape the wrong way round around its bristles. It's very effective.'

He was so confounded he submitted. He was standing on a headland in the middle of nowhere while a woman called Mrs Elsa Murdoch attacked his trousers with a dolls' hairbrush.

She brushed until she was satisfied. Then she straightened. 'Turn round and let me look at you,' she said.

He turned.

'Very nice,' she said. 'Back to being a prince again. What do you think, Zoe? Is he ready for the cameras?'

'His top button's undone,' Zoe said.

'That's because it's hot,' he retorted but Elsa shook her head.

'No class at all,' she said soulfully. 'I don't know

what you modern day royals are coming to.' She carefully fastened his top button while he felt...he felt... He didn't know how he felt; he was only aware that when the button was fastened and she stepped back there was a sharp stab of something that might even be loss.

'There you go, Your Highness,' she said, like a valet who'd just done a good job making a recalcitrant prince respectable. 'Off you go and face the world while Zoe and I get back to our cats and our lobster pots.'

And she was in the car, turned and driving away before he had a chance to reply.

His first task was to get his breath back. To face the media with some sort of dignity.

His second task was to talk to the hotel concierge.

'I need some extensive shopping done on my behalf,' he said. 'Fast. Oh, and I need to hire a car. No, not a limousine. Anything not smelling of fish would be acceptable.'

Then he rang Prince Alexandros back in the Diamond Isles. As well as being a friend, Alexandros was Crown Prince of Sappheiros, and Alex more than anyone else knew what was at stake—why he was forced to be in Australia in royal uniform when he should be in theatre garb back in Manhattan.

'Problem?' his friend asked.

'I don't know.'

'What don't you know?'

'The child's been burned. She's dreadfully scarred.'

There was a sharp intake of breath. 'Hell. Is she…'

'She's okay. It's healing. But my idea of leaving her on the island… She'll have special needs.'

'You were never going to be able to leave her anyway.'

'I don't have a choice,' he snapped. 'You know I can't leave my work yet—I can't break promises. But there's a nanny. A good one. A Mrs Elsa Murdoch. She's not like any Mrs Elsa Murdoch I've ever met.'

There was a lengthy silence on the end of the phone. Then, 'How many Mrs Elsa Murdochs have you met?' Alexandros asked, with a certain amount of caution.

Uh-oh. Alex and Stefanos had known each other since they were kids. Maybe Alex had heard something in his voice that he didn't necessarily want to share.

'Just the one,' he said.

Another silence. 'She's young?' Alex ventured.

'Yes.'

'Aha.'

'There's no aha about it.'

'There's a Mr Elsa Murdoch?'

'No.'

'I rest my case,' he said. 'Hey, Stefanos, like me, you've spent so much of your life pushing your career…avoiding family. Maybe it's time you did a heads up and noticed the Elsa Murdochs of this world.'

'Alex…' He couldn't think what to add next.

'You want something more?' Alex asked. 'Something specific? If not…my wife's waiting for me. Not a bad thing for a prince to have, you know. A wife. Especially if that prince needs to care for a child with injuries.'

'This isn't a joke.'

'I don't believe I was joking,' Alex threw back at him. 'Okay, so this Mrs Elsa Murdoch… You want to tell me about her?'

How had he got himself into this conversation? He didn't have a clue.

'I'll leave you to your wife,' he said stiffly.

'Excellent,' Alex said. 'I'll leave you to your Mrs Elsa Murdoch. And your little Crown Princess. Steve…'

'Yes?'

'Take care. And keep an open mind. Speaking as a man who's just married…it can make all the difference in the world.'

Elsa lay awake far into the night, staring at a life she'd never envisaged. A life without Zoe.

She'd never thought of it.

Four years ago she'd been happily married, full

of plans for the future, working with Matty and her good friends and their little girl.

One stupid drunken driver—who'd walked away unscathed—and she was left with nothing but the care of Zoe.

Up until today she'd thought Zoe depended totally on her. Up until now she'd never really considered that the reverse was true as well.

Without Zoe…

No. She couldn't think it. It left a void in her life so huge it terrified her.

He'd backed off. He'd said he was leaving tomorrow.

Zoe's needed back on Khryseis.

She reran his words through her mind—she remembered almost every word he'd uttered. He hadn't backed off.

Zoe's needed back on Khryseis.

She was Zoe's legal guardian. But if it came to a custody battle between Elsa, with no blood tie and no means of giving Zoe the last operations she so desperately needed—or Stefanos, a royal prince, a blood relative, with money and means at his disposal, able to give her every chance in life…

What choice was there?

She felt sick and tired.

A letter lay on her bureau. She rose from her tumbled sheets—lying in bed was useless anyway—and read it for the thousandth time.

It was an outline of costs for cosmetic plastic surgery to smooth the skin under Zoe's chin and across her neck.

She'd sold everything she had. There was no money left.

Stefanos.

Not if it meant losing Zoe. Not!

Who was she protecting here? Herself or Zoe? Damn him!

She should be welcoming him, she thought. Knight on white charger with loaded wallet.

Not if it meant giving up Zoe.

To watch them go…

To watch him go.

Where had that thought come from? Nowhere. She did not need to think he was sexy. The fact that he was drop-dead gorgeous only added to her fear. She did not need her hormones to stir.

They were stirring.

She walked outside, stood on the veranda and stared into the dark.

Prince Stefanos of Khryseis. Cousin to Zoe.

A man about to change her life.

A man about to take her child.

Fifteen miles across the water, Stefanos was doing the same thing. Watching the moonbeams ripple across the ocean. Thinking how his life had changed.

Because of Zoe.

And…Elsa? A barefoot, poverty stricken marine biologist of a nanny?

He had a million other things to think about.

So why was he thinking of Elsa?

It was mid-morning when he arrived and they hadn't left for the beach yet. There was a tiny seeping wound under Zoe's arm. It was minuscule but they'd learned from bitter experience to treat small as big. This was a skin graft area. If it extended Zoe could lose the whole graft—an appalling prospect.

Elsa had found it while she was applying Zoe's suncream and now she was hovering between wait and see or ring the local medical centre and get it seen to now.

Only it was Sunday. Their normal doctor would be away. Waratah Cove had a small bush-nursing hospital, manned by casual staff over the weekend. Less experienced doctors tended to react to Zoe's injuries with fear, dreading under-treating. If she took Zoe in, she'd be admitted and transferred to hospital in the city. Simple as that.

And they were both so weary of hospitals.

Her worry almost made her forget Stefanos was coming—but not completely. The sound of a car on the track made her feel as if the world was caving in, landing right on her shoulders.

She hated this. She just hated it.

She tugged a T-shirt over Zoe's scarred little

body and turned to welcome him. And almost gasped.

This was a different Stefanos. Faded jeans. T-shirt. Scuffed trainers.

Great body. Really great body.

A body to make her feel she was a woman again.

She had to do something about these hormones. They were doing things to her head. She'd married Matty. His picture was still on the mantel. Get a grip.

'Hi,' he said, and smiled at the two of them and Elsa couldn't resist. She had to smile. It was as if he had the strength to change her world, just by smiling.

'Hi,' Zoe said shyly and smiled as well, and Elsa looked at Zoe in astonishment. Two minutes earlier the two of them had been close to tears.

Stefanos's smile was a force to be reckoned with.

'I thought you'd be at the beach,' he said, and then he looked more closely—maybe seeing the traces of their distress. 'Is something wrong?'

'We thought we wouldn't go to the beach this morning,' Elsa said repressively. Zoe loathed people talking about her injuries. She'd had enough fuss to last one small girl a lifetime.

Stefanos had never mentioned her scars. Maybe he hadn't even noticed. Or…not.

'Why not?' he said gently, and suddenly he was talking to Zoe, and not to her. As if he'd guessed.

'There's a bit of my skin graft come loose,' Zoe said.

Once again it was as much as Elsa could do not to gasp. Zoe never volunteered such information.

She'd had the best doctors—the best!—but almost every one of them talked to her and not to Zoe. Oh, they chatted to Zoe, but in the patronising way elders often talked to children. For the hard questions—even things like: 'Is she sleeping at night?'—they turned to her, as if Zoe couldn't possibly know.

So what had Stefanos done different?

She knew. He hadn't treated her as an object of sympathy, and he'd talked directly to her. Simple but so important.

'Whereabouts?' Stefanos asked, still speaking only to Zoe.

'Under my arm at the back.'

'Is it hurting?'

'No, but…it's scary,' Zoe said, and her bottom lip wobbled.

'Can I ask why?'

'Elsa will have to take me to hospital and they'll make me stay there, and I don't want to go.' Her voice ended on a wail, she turned her face into Elsa's shirt and she sobbed.

'Zoe,' Stefanos said, in a voice she'd not heard before. Gentle, yet firm. He squatted so he was at her eye level. 'Zoe, will you let me take a look? I don't know if I can help, but I'm a doctor. Will you trust me to see if I think you need hospital?'

He was a doctor?

There was a loaded silence. Zoe would be as stunned as she was, Elsa thought.

You still can't have her, she thought, her instinctive response overriding everything else, but she had the sense to shut up. The last thing Zoe needed was more fear.

Because, astonishingly, Zoe was turning towards him. She was still hard against Elsa but he'd cut through her distress.

'You're a doctor?'

'Yes.'

'But you're a prince.'

'People are allowed to be both.'

'My papa was a doctor,' she said. 'But a doctor of science. He studied shellfish.'

'Did Christos get his doctorate?' he said with pleasure. 'Hey, how about that. I wish I'd known.' Still he was talking to Zoe. 'Your papa and I used to be really good friends. He taught me where to find the best shells on Khryseis. Only I always wanted to find the pretty ones or the big ones and he wanted to look for the interesting ones. Sometimes he'd pick up a little grey shell I didn't think at all special and off he'd go, telling me it was a Multi-Armpit Hairy Cyclamate, or a Wobblysaurus Rex, or something even sillier.'

Zoe stared in astonishment—and then she giggled.

You could forgive a lot of a man who could make Zoe giggle, Elsa conceded. And…a man who could make her giggle as well?

'Will you let me see what the problem is?' he asked gently, and Zoe lifted her T-shirt without hesitation. Which was another miracle all by itself.

And here was another miracle. He didn't react. Zoe's left side was a mass of scar tissue but Stefanos's expression didn't change by as much as a hair's breadth. He was still smiling a little—with Zoe—and she was smiling back. His long fingers probed the scar tissue with infinite gentleness, not going near the tiny suppurating wound but simply assessing the situation overall.

He had such long fingers, Elsa thought. Big hands, tanned and gentle. She wouldn't mind…

Um…whoa. Attention back to Zoe. Fast.

'What sort of medical supplies do you have here?' he asked, still speaking only to Zoe, and Elsa held her breath. This was a question every doctor or nurse she knew would address to her, but this whole conversation was between the two of them.

'We have lots of stuff,' Zoe volunteered. 'Sometimes when I'm just out of hospital the nurses come here and change my dressings. It costs a lot though, 'cause we're so far out of town, so Elsa keeps a lot of stuff here and she's learned to do it instead.'

'Well, good for Elsa.' And, dumbly, Elsa found she was blushing with pleasure. 'Can I see?' he asked.

'I'll get it,' she said and headed for the bathroom—and even that was a minor miracle. For Zoe to let her leave the room while a strange doctor was examining her... Definitely a miracle.

She didn't push it, though. She was back in seconds, carrying a hefty plastic crate. She set it down and Stefanos examined its contents and whistled.

'You have enough here to treat an elephant,' he said. 'You don't have an elephant hidden under a bed somewhere, do you?'

Once again Zoe giggled. It was the best sound. It made her feel... It made her feel...

No. She would not get turned on because this man made a child giggle.

Only she already was. She was fighting hormones here as hard as she could. And losing.

It had been too long. You're a sick, sad spinster, she told herself, and then rebuked herself sharply. Not a spinster. She glanced across at the mantel, and Matty's face smiled down at her from its frame. Sorry, she told him under her breath. Sorry, sorry, sorry.

'You know, I'm sure I can fix this.' Stefanos's words tugged her attention straight back to him. 'Zoe, if you and Elsa trust me... I think all this needs is some antiseptic cream, a couple of Steri-Strips to tug it together—see, it's at the end of the graft so we can attach the strips to good skin on either side and tug it together. Then we can pop one of these waterproof dressings over the whole thing and you could even go swimming this morning. Which, seeing I brought my bathers, is probably a good thing.' He grinned.

And Elsa thought, I'm in trouble here. I'm in serious trouble.

But they were moving on. Stefanos rose and washed his hands with the thoroughness of a surgeon. Then he lifted Zoe carefully—being mindful of where her scars were without Zoe noticing he was mindful, Elsa thought. He sat her on the kitchen table and proceeded to do his stuff.

He was skilled. She just had to see those fingers gently probing. She just had to listen to him chat to Zoe, distracting her as he worked. He was so careful, so precise, and she thought of all the doctors who'd treated Zoe over the past four years and she thought this man was a blessing.

This man wanted to take Zoe away.

This man was Zoe's cousin—a prince.

This man was a doctor, with all the skills needed to take care of her.

She was a marine biologist with nothing.

He was applying the waterproof dressing now and he glanced over his shoulder to say something to her. And he saw her expression. She'd tried to get it under control but he could see—she knew he could see.

'There's nothing to be afraid of, Elsa,' he said gently and she thought, You don't know the half of it. Nothing to be afraid of? When he was threatening to turn her world around?

'I... You came here to talk,' she said, and it was really hard to get her words out.

'I came here to swim,' he said. 'Are there any other problems to sort before we swim? Nothing I can treat? Ingrown toenails? Snakebite? Measles?'

Zoe giggled again and wriggled down from the table. She was totally at ease now, completely relaxed in his company.

He couldn't take her away, she thought frantically. Zoe would always want her. Wouldn't she?

There's nothing to be afraid of, she told herself, but she knew she was lying.

There was everything to be afraid of. Everything she held dear.

But for now...it seemed they were going for a swim.

CHAPTER FIVE

THE swim was glorious, fun and deeply scary.

Glorious in that the weather gods had decided this was another day out of the box—brilliant sunshine but not too hot, the water cool enough to refresh but not so cold they couldn't stay in for as long they wanted, turquoise-clear so they could see everything on the bottom.

Fun because Stefanos made it fun. He twisted and turned under the water, teaching Zoe new tricks, tickling her toes on the sandy bottom, making her play as a child should play. As Zoe had been unable to play.

She'd been isolated for so long. She should be with other children, but there were so many complications. Twice Elsa had tried to send her to school but each time she'd ended up with a major infection and back in hospital.

So if it couldn't be a bunch of kids whooping and hollering around her, Stefanos was definitely next best. He was a fabulous swimmer and he knew how to make Zoe laugh.

Of course he was and of course he did, Elsa thought, with what she recognised as dumb and irrational resentment. She loved that Zoe was falling for Stefanos's charm, but she was also fearful of it.

She was fearful of falling for Stefanos's charm herself.

Because he was…gorgeous. She'd seen him yesterday in full royal regalia and thought he was gorgeous then. She'd seen him this morning in his jeans and T-shirt and thought he was just plain yummy. Now, clad only in his board shorts, she could hardly keep her eyes off him. Lean and tanned, every muscle delineated…

He was a doctor, for heaven's sake. He must spend his life indoors. Where had he got those muscles?

He was scaring her. Not only because of what he'd suggested yesterday—that he take Zoe away. Not only because of his effect on Zoe. But because of his effect on her.

Mathew had been dead for four years now. Her friends told her it was time to move on.

She'd never had the slightest urge to move on, until right now. And now…what her body was telling her, what her hormones were telling her, felt like a betrayal.

'Mathew, Mathew, Mathew,' she murmured over and over, and because Zoe was perfectly safe with her big cousin, because Stefanos's sole desire seemed to be to make the little girl laugh, she left them to it, stroking strongly out across the entrance to the cove.

She put her head down and swam as she never swam, for it wasn't safe to do this when no one was here to watch Zoe. She'd always gloried in swimming. It was her quiet time. Her time of peace. She was swimming now, hoping her head could settle, so her jumbled thoughts could somehow untangle, so she could find the strength to stand up to this unknown prince and his terrifying charm.

She lost track of time. She swam and swam and finally when she raised her head she realised Zoe and Stefanos were out of the water, standing on the beach and watching her.

And that felt strange too. That this man was watching her…

She caught a wave back to the beach, surfing in with the agility she'd always gloried in. The sea had always been her escape. It could be again, she thought. If the worst happened. If he took Zoe away…

They strolled down the beach to meet her. Her wave washed her into the shallows, she wiped her eyes and looked up to find Stefanos standing above her, smiling, holding out his hand to tug her up.

She nearly didn't take it, she was so disconcerted. But that'd be petty. Zoe was standing beside him, beaming, waiting for her to stand.

She took his hand, he tugged her up and she came up too fast.

She stumbled and he steadied her. Which was a tiny gesture—Prince steadies Elsa—and why the feel of his hands on her waist should have the power to totally disconcert her she didn't know.

'You're beautiful,' he said and she was disconcerted all over again.

'Do you…' She fought for breath and took a while finding it. 'Do you mind?'

'I'm only speaking the truth.'

'Right,' she said and headed up the beach fast. She grabbed her towel and disappeared underneath. At least here she could get her face under control.

Beautiful?

Matty had thought she was beautiful. Until then no one. After him no one.

She wasn't even wearing a bathing suit. Neither she nor Zoe did. They both wore shorts and T-shirts. It'd be unfair for her to wear pretty bathers when Zoe had to wear scar-covering clothes. And she had scars herself—nothing like Zoe's, but bad enough.

And besides, she thought grimly, she was mousy. She'd always been mousy and she always would be mousy. Mathew had thought she was beautiful because he'd fallen in love with her mind. He'd been academically brilliant and he'd loved that she could keep up with him. Her intelligence was a turn on.

But her body? Not so much that he'd ever said. Beauty was in the eye of the beholder and in Mathew's eyes she was his brilliant wife.

Matty.

Dammit, why wasn't he here? And…why was he starting to fade? It was terrifying that when she thought of him now the image that came straight to mind was the photograph on the mantel. Photographs were becoming the reality, and reality moved on, whether she willed it or not.

All this she thought under her towel. All this she thought while she rubbed her hair dry.

'Zoe and I think your hair will dry faster in the sun.'

His voice made her jump. They'd followed her up the beach!

You're not being paranoid? she demanded of herself, and she knew that she was.

'It's lunch time,' Zoe said, puzzled. 'You never take this long to dry your hair.'

And I never have a Prince of the Blood waiting to see when I'll come out from my towel, she thought, but what the heck, there was no choice.

She emerged. She wrapped her towel around her hair and she checked on Zoe. Another surprise. She was wrapped sarong-style in her towel.

'You're dry.'

'Stefanos dried me,' she said. 'And he was really careful of my scars.'

Once again, a jolt. Here was another adult with

the responsibility and skills to help her look after this injured child.

If he lived down the road she'd welcome him with open arms.

He lived on the Diamond Isles. Khryseis. A world away from her world.

'Lunch,' he said, smiling at her, and there was a trace of sympathy in his smile that said he understood her turmoil. He couldn't help it, he couldn't stop it, but he understood.

How could you understand? she thought. You're not having her. You're not!

What had he said? *There's nothing to be afraid of.* Did she believe him?

No way.

Lunch was the same as yesterday, only Zoe ate more without being prodded. Then Stefanos disappeared to his car and returned with a box.

Cherries! She'd seen them in the shops last week. They'd been twenty dollars a small box, and they'd still been hard, not fully ripened. These were almost the size of golf balls, deep burgundy, shining and luscious.

Stefanos was looking smug—deeply pleased with the fact that her jaw and Zoe's jaw had dropped to somewhere round their ankles. 'The concierge at my hotel knows someone who flies up here from wherever cherries grow,' he told them. 'They're hot off the plane.'

Twenty dollars wouldn't pay for transport from the airport, Elsa thought. How much had these cost?

'They're not to be wasted,' he said severely, and Zoe needed no further prodding. She popped one into her mouth really fast.

'They're not just for eating,' he told her, lifting two pairs of cherries, each pair joined at the stem, and looping them over Zoe's ears. 'Cherry earrings are my favourite accessory.'

'You wear them too,' Zoe said, and he promptly did.

A prince was sitting at her kitchen table wearing cherry earrings.

Her foundations were getting shaky.

'Have a cherry,' he said kindly. 'They go off fast, I hear.'

'Not in range of us, they don't,' she said and ate a cherry and then another. And then…why not?… another.

'I'm up to nine already,' Zoe crowed. Zoe was showered and shiny clean, her face was flushed with pleasure and she was popping cherries in with an enjoyment Elsa had never seen. For four long years, for operation after operation, this little girl had been cheated of her childhood. And now… Stefanos had arrived and joy was flooding in.

Without warning, tendrils of fear wound their way round her heart yet again. But this time it was different. It wasn't just the fear of Zoe being taken away. It was stronger. Maybe Stefanos could give Zoe a better life than she could. If he cared for his little cousin and loved her and made her laugh… What right did she have to stand in his way?

'You're not eating,' he said gently and draped cherry earrings on her as well. 'There. We're the cherry family—Mama Cherry, Papa Cherry, Baby Cherry.'

She smiled and ate another cherry but there were icicles forming inside. She'd only ever wanted what was best for Zoe. If this was what was best…

'Let me show you what else I have in my car,' he said, watching her face. He could see her terror, she thought. This man saw things she didn't want to reveal to anyone.

Maybe it was the man himself who terrified her the most.

'Presents?' Zoe said hopefully and he grinned.

'Exactly,' he said. 'Coming right up.'

'This is exciting,' Zoe said.

'It is.' She was desperately trying to match Zoe's pleasure. Outwardly succeeding. Inwardly failing.

And then he was back, carrying suitcases, one soft blue leather, the other pink.

Suitcases. A wave of nausea swept over her so strongly that she rose and made a move towards the bathroom.

Stefanos dumped the suitcases and stopped her.

'Elsa, no,' he said softly. 'I told you before, you have nothing to be afraid of.'

'You're taking Zoe away.' She hadn't meant to say it. To say it in front of Zoe was unforgivable, but her terror was too raw, too real for her to disguise it.

'I do need to take Zoe to Khryseis,' he said, still in that gentle, reassuring tone that must surely be a learned bedside manner. *Yes, we are going to elongate your ears and swap your legs for your arms, but trust me, I'm a doctor.*

'Trust me,' he said now, as Zoe rose, her panic matching Elsa's. 'I want to take you both to the Diamond Isles. Zoe is the Crown Princess of Khryseis. Khryseis needs Zoe, and Zoe needs you. So I need you both. Thus I'm asking if you'll both come home with me.'

It was important—really important—to get her expression right. Zoe was staring at her and she'd seen terror. Stefanos was Zoe's cousin. This was Zoe's life, not hers. She had to get fear off her face and show courage.

'You…you scared me,' she managed at last, and to her relief her voice came out calm. 'I saw the suitcase and I thought you might be wanting Zoe to go away today. She doesn't even have a passport.'

'It will take a few days to get the documentation through.' His gaze was holding hers. 'Zoe, I think I frightened Elsa,' he said, rueful. 'How can we stop her being scared?'

You could go away, Elsa thought, but she knew Zoe wouldn't say that. Zoe was entranced with her big new cousin, and why shouldn't she be?

Stefanos was a prince, Zoe was a princess, and he'd pulled Zoe onside simply by acting as if the two of them needed to reassure her. Prince and princess together.

'Hey, Elsa, it's okay,' he said and reached to take her hand. His hold was strong and firm and…reassuring? How could touch be reassuring? How could his touch warm her when she was so cold she was beginning to shake?

She should pull away.

She couldn't.

'Does Khryseis have a beach?' Zoe asked, and Elsa knew right then that this was a done deal. 'Elsa likes beaches,' the little girl told her cousin. 'We looked at Khryseis on the computer and Elsa said she bet there were more fish than we could count. And more starfish.'

'Starfish?' he said, bemused, and his hand was still holding hers. She should pull it away, but how could she? How could she find strength to pull from such a touch?

'The real name for starfish is echinoderms, or asteroidea,' Zoe was saying importantly. 'They have two stomachs. They use one stomach to digest food while the other stomach turns inside out to pull its food in. But the really cool thing is that if they lose an arm they can grow another one. If I was a starfish

I could grow another finger. And if you find just one leg of a starfish still joined to just a little bit of its body, a whole new starfish can grow. How cool is that?'

'Really cool,' he said, sounding stunned.

'It's what me and Elsa are working on,' she told him, sounding about twenty years older than her eight years. 'And the Internet says Khryseis has some really weird starfish.' She turned to Elsa, her eyes shining with small girl excitement. 'Elsa, can we go?'

No, she wanted to scream. No!

Instead she took a deep breath. She tried a tug on her hand but it wasn't released.

'Sweetheart, maybe we could work things out so you could go,' she whispered. 'I need to work.'

Zoe's face fell. 'I can't go without you,' she said, her bottom lip wobbling. 'I'd be scared.'

So would I, Elsa thought, but once again she held her tongue.

'I need you both to come,' Stefanos said. He was watching the two of them, focusing as much on Elsa as he was on Zoe. The pressure on her hand remained. Was he trying to warn her? she wondered. It didn't feel like that. It simply felt as if he was feeding her…strength. It was a crazy concept but it seemed the only one that would fit.

'That's why I've brought two suitcases,' he told them. Finally he released her hand. He'd set the suitcases on the floor and he flipped one open.

From the top he lifted a shiny new laptop computer. She'd seen these advertised. They were worth…a tenth of Zoe's next operation?

'This is for you,' he told her, setting it on the table. 'Whether you decide to come or not. You work from home. Why can't that home be on Khryseis?'

Because…

There was no because. She couldn't think of one, apart from the fact that the thought left her terrified.

She glanced at the mantel. Mathew's face smiled at her. Steadied her.

There must be a because.

Because my husband is buried here? Because this is where my grief is?

That wasn't a good because.

Because this guy in front of me makes my body react as I don't believe it's ever reacted?

Well, that was something she needed to dismiss. How weak a because was that?

Because I'd have no control over Zoe's life? Because people would stare at her scars? Because, as a royal, she'd be on display, and it could well destroy her?

Here at last were valid reasons, but before she could voice them Stefanos had lifted parcels onto the table.

'These are for you,' he said softly to Zoe. 'Because you're one of the bravest young women

I've met. Because I know how much your body's hurt over the last four years, and I know how beautiful you are, inside and out. I'm so sorry I wasn't here for you when your parents died but I am now. These are to make you even more beautiful than you already are.'

Zoe looked uncertainly at Elsa—and then tentatively unwrapped the top parcel.

It was a pink blouse. It had tiny buttons shaped like butterflies. It had soft puffed sleeves designed to reach Zoe's elbows. A tiny white mandarin collar was designed so the top buttons could stay open, but the collar itself would stay high. Just high enough to hide the scars.

And there was more.

Elsa had searched for clothes like these, as far as her budget could afford it. She'd even tried making them. That was a joke, trying to learn dressmaking from an instruction manual. To say her attempts had failed was an understatement.

But after one night Stefanos had found these. There were three pairs of trousers, capri style, like long shorts, one red and white, one a lovely soft blue and one a deeper shade of pink. There were four more blouses, each with the same soft high collar. There were hair ribbons to match, and pretty sandals and a couple of dainty bracelets. There was an exquisite lilac party dress with white lace and a vast bow at the back. It came with a lilac choker with stars embroidered in white.

Within minutes Zoe was surrounded by a sea of clothes. She looked up at Elsa and her eyes were shining.

'They're beautiful,' she breathed. 'Can I keep them?'

What sort of question was that? There was no way she could refuse this gift. She just wished, so badly it hurt, that she'd been in a position to give these to her herself.

'They might not fit,' Stefanos warned, casting Elsa a thoughtful glance and then directing his attention back to Zoe. 'I had to guess sizes, but I've organised a dressmaker to visit you this evening and let them out or take them in as you need. We can change anything too—she has my authority.'

'And my authority?' Elsa whispered.

'I hope you'll agree,' Stefanos said gravely and met her gaze and held.

What was she thinking? 'Of course I agree,' she said shakily. She hugged Zoe and managed a smile. 'They're lovely. Your cousin has been wonderfully generous.' She bit her lip. 'But you're not my cousin, Stefanos. I can't take the laptop.'

'It's part of a debt,' he said softly. 'I owe you so much.'

'You owe me nothing.'

'I loved Christos.'

'He was my friend too.'

'No,' he said, and suddenly he was almost stern. 'You don't understand. Christos was my family.

That I didn't know he was dead…that Zoe has been alone for so long…it touches my honour. I'm asking you to take this and it doesn't begin to repay the debt I owe you.'

It touches my honour… It was a quaint phrase. Old-fashioned.

He meant it—absolutely.

'I…' She took a deep breath. If they were going to talk about old-fashioned… 'Then it's my honour to care for Zoe,' she said, and she tilted her chin. 'Zoe is not related to me by blood, but I'm her godmother and her guardian. I won't let that go.'

'I'm not asking you to,' he said evenly. 'I'm asking for you to give Khryseis a chance. I'm asking you to come with Zoe—as her nanny as well as her guardian—and if you do this then you *will* be paid. I want you to help me introduce her to her birth-right.'

'And then come home without her?'

'No,' Zoe said. She'd been examining her pile of clothes with joy, but this wasn't a child who could be bought. She looked at the clothes with longing and then pushed them away. Suddenly panicking. 'I don't want them if I can't have Elsa.'

'You can have Elsa,' Stefanos said evenly. 'I'm asking you both to come.' He smiled at Elsa, ignoring her obvious panic, simply smiling at her as if he understood what she was thinking; she was being slightly foolish but he wasn't about to threaten her.

His smile lied, she thought desperately. This man was a prince, about as far from her world as it was possible to be. He was accustomed to having his charm work for him. He thought now that he simply had to smile and shower gifts and he'd get what he wanted.

'Do you know what a royal nanny earns?' he asked, and she caught her breath.

'I don't want to know.'

'Now that's just dumb,' he said. 'Knocking back a fabulous job because you haven't heard the terms? I rang a couple of friends last night. They have nannies in Europe and they kindly rang a couple of the top agencies and asked. What's the going rate for the best nanny in the world? they asked.'

And he gave her a figure.

She gasped. She stared across the table at him and he smiled back at her. 'That's what I'm offering,' he said softly. 'Starting today.'

She could be paid for doing what she loved? Caring for Zoe?

But this… This could never be about money. Because she did what she did for Zoe for love; for nothing else.

'Elsa, Zoe needs to come home anyway,' he said gently. 'I'm sorry, but it's not negotiable. I've also talked to people here in Social Services and to lawyers from your Family Court. I have more chance at success in gaining custody than you might think. The court would look at what Zoe stands to inherit. They'd look at the home I'm prepared to give her. The consensus is that she should have the right to learn about Khryseis. It's her heritage.'

He turned to Zoe and spread his hands. 'Zoe, your father was the Crown Prince of Khryseis and you're now the Crown Princess. If you agree, I'd like to show you the place where your papa grew up. I'd like to introduce you to an island that I know you'll love, to live in a palace that's exciting, to see what your father's life could have been if he'd lived. I'm asking Elsa to come as well, and I'd like you both to consider Khryseis as a place to live.' He glanced at Elsa and then glanced away. Her emotions were written on her face, she thought.

'I'll sign legal documents with international legal authorities,' he said, and now he was speaking directly to Elsa. 'We need Zoe for at least three months a year.'

'For ever?' Elsa whispered.

'Until Zoe's old enough to know whether she wishes to accept the Crown,' he said and suddenly he sounded stern. 'It's her birthright, Elsa, and neither of us have the right to take that away from her.'

She was close to tears—but she would not cry. Not in front of Zoe. Zoe was taking her cues from her—to disintegrate on her own behalf would be cruel.

And he knew what she was thinking.

'Hey, it's not so bad. You could think of it as a holiday.' He took her hands again. Strong and warm and sure. 'You've been on your own for so long, Elsa. Will you let me share?'

She would not cry. But the feel of his hands…

You've been on your own for so long…

That was what it felt like. Four long years of fighting to get Zoe the medical treatment she needed, fighting to keep her own career viable enough to put food on the table, fighting to forget the ache in her hip and to stop the grey fog of depression and loneliness taking her over.

A holiday in Khryseis. Three months a year?

If she said yes, she'd lose Zoe.

'You won't lose her,' Stefanos said, strongly and surely. 'I promise you that. I've spent the last eighteen hours finding out exactly what you've done for Zoe. The money you've spent. Your own money.'

Her eyes flew to his. Distress gave way to indignation. 'How did you find that out? Who are you to…?'

'To enquire? I have friends in high places, Elsa. So does Zoe now. In future she'll have the best medical treatment money can buy.'

Anger, fear, anguish… They were a kaleidoscope of her emotions. But they should be her emotions. Not Zoe's. This was Zoe's future and she must not deny her.

Her own terror had to be put aside.

'What do you think, Zoe?' she asked, feeling inordinately pleased when she got her voice right. 'Stefanos is offering us an initial three-month holiday on his island while we see what it's like. It's been…it's been a shock, but I don't think it's something we should be scared of. His island looks really beautiful on the Internet.'

'It's *your* island, Zoe,' Stefanos said, gently but firmly.

'So let me get this right,' Elsa said, opening the laptop to give her something to look at rather than Stefanos's face. He saw too much, she thought. He knew how scared she was and he was sympathetic. But still he was determined.

She couldn't afford to be seduced into doing what was wrong for Zoe.

Seduced? It was the wrong word but it was the one that popped into her head. Because… because…

Because he was too big and too male and too sexy and she'd been alone for far too long. It felt dangerous to even be in the same room as him.

Maybe *he* should be worried, she thought dryly. If he knew what this scary, ridiculous part of her was thinking…

Nanny jumps prince…

Whoa.

Well, at least that pulled her out of the fog, she decided, fighting an almost hysterical desire to laugh. Maybe she ought to focus on slightly more…realistic issues.

'Let me get this straight,' she said again, and watched him smile. How much of what she was thinking was obvious? To her fury she felt a blush start, from the toes up.

'Christos…Zoe's papa…should have been Crown Prince of Khryseis,' she managed, staring fiercely down at the laptop as if she was totally absorbed in its keyboard. 'How come the King wasn't his father?'

Stefanos nodded, still serious. 'Potted history? The Diamond Isles were principalities for hundreds of years,' he told her. 'Then the Prince of Sappheiros invaded the other islands and declared himself King. Subsequent armies kept the islanders under iron rule, and his line continued as long as there was a direct male heir. Six generations later, King Giorgos died without a son. The islands have continued supporting their own royal families, even though they haven't been able to publicly acknowledge them, and now they can take their rightful place. Giorgos's death meant Christos was heir to the throne of Khryseis. Under the old rule, men and women inherited equally. Therefore Zoe inherits after Christos. As her closest adult relative I'm Prince Regent until she can take the throne at twenty-five. Currently the island's being run by a council set up by Giorgos. They're corrupt and useless.

The only way for us to unseat them is for Zoe to come home and for us to take over.'

'Us?'

'I was thinking me,' he said, suddenly converting from history lesson to the personal. 'But in the long-term…' He smiled at her, considering. 'Maybe you can find a way to be useful as well.'

'Useful?' The concept made Elsa gasp. What was she letting herself in for? This man…this *prince*…was moving way too fast, and she had no idea where he was going. 'Like how?' And then as he paused as if he wasn't sure how to answer, she decided this was deeply scary and a girl had to set some limits.

'Can we get some ground rules in place?' she ventured, searching wildly for some way to ground herself. Employment as a palace nanny… What did she know of such a job? What did royal nannies do?

In the absence of a job description, maybe she ought to list her own.

'Ground rules?' he asked, quirking one eyebrow. Again he seemed to be on the verge of laughter, and the sensation made her feel crazy.

'No washing, no ironing and definitely no scrubbing the stairs on hands and knees,' she said wildly, while he and Zoe looked on with astonishment. 'No attending royal banquets and sitting at the bottom of the table where I don't know anyone. Neither will I wear a calf-length uniform with a starched collar and *Nanny* embroidered on the front. Nor will I curtsey or walk out of Zoe's presence backwards. No shoe shining, no…'

'But we do still need to go,' Zoe said, cutting into a tirade that was getting…well, more than a bit irrational.

Elsa paused. She looked at Stefanos's hiked eyebrows—both of them were hiked now. His lips were twitching.

Maybe she was being just ever so slightly over the top.

She struggled for calm. Hysteria wasn't what was needed, she told herself severely. Nor was treating this as a crazy joke. She needed to stay practical and focus on Zoe—regardless of whether or not Stefanos was laughing at her.

In her short life Zoe had faced her parents' deaths, and then more hospitals and doctors and paramedics and social workers than Elsa wanted to think about. Almost all of them talked over her head. It made Zoe mad, but usually she became quiet and passive.

Not now. She'd been listening to Elsa in astonishment, but with an attention more suitable to one twice her age. Now she turned to Stefanos and frowned.

'Elsa doesn't have to do all that stuff, does she?'

'No,' Stefanos said definitely. 'I think Elsa's been reading too many fairy tales.'

'But there really is a palace?'

'There really is a palace,' he said and smiled at her. 'And you really are a princess.'

He'd hooked Zoe, Elsa thought frantically. Just because he had a smile to die for.

Just because he was logical, thoughtful and he sounded as if he cared. Just because he was smiling at Zoe now with kindness and also the trace of a challenge, convincing her that this could be some sort of magical adventure.

He was glancing at her with a quizzical look that was kind as well as knowing.

How could he be kind? What did she know of the man?

What did she know about the island?

'What…what medical facilities are on the island?' she managed, trying valiantly to sound grown-up, sensible and in control. Or at least as grown-up, sensible and in control as Zoe.

'Zoe will have me to care for her,' he told her, matching her tone. 'And there's specialist backup in Athens.'

'There are no paediatricians on Khryseis?'

He hesitated. 'Education has hardly been King Giorgos's concern,' he admitted at last. 'In fact he's actively discouraged it. Even I haven't been able to work there. Giorgos wouldn't permit me to practice medicine on Khryseis, so I've built my career elsewhere.'

'There are no medical facilities at all?' she asked incredulously.

'There's one elderly doctor and a midwife. Up until now the fishermen have taken really ill islanders to Athens.'

'You're kidding me.'

'Sadly, no.'

'And…and now?'

'And now we go back to the island and think about the future from there.'

'You'll get more medical staff?'

'That's one of my first priorities. The island's not big enough to support a huge range of specialties but there will be good basic medicine with fast transfers to Athens at need.'

He hesitated. 'Elsa, you will be looked after,' he said, gently but strongly. 'You both will. So no, Elsa, you will not be asked to scrub stairs or polish silver. You'll be on the island as Zoe's friend and as her nanny, for as long as you wish to stay. I'll ask nothing more of you. This isn't a trap, Elsa. I promise you. No strings.' His face broke into another of his magical smiles. 'Our island's lovely, Elsa. Zoe. We can work things out. The three of us. Please?'

His smile caught her and held. Demanding a response. How could she resist an appeal like this?

And, despite her fears, a tiny trickle of excitement crept in.

She had no idea where this man was coming from—or where he was going—but his smile was mesmerising. And as well as that…

She and Zoe had eaten sandwiches for lunch almost every day for four years. She'd had to chop wood to cook and to heat their water. Wood-chopping jarred her hip so much that sometimes it was hard not to just give in. But there was never the choice of giving in.

But now…Stefanos was offering them a home in a palace on an island in the Mediterranean. He was offering her a well-paid job. She'd have no more money worries. No wood-chopping. Did he realise how enticing it sounded? This man might appear seriously sexy but right now it was the lack of wood-chopping that was more seductive.

'I do need to keep my research skills up,' she muttered, fighting to sound practical and reserved and wary.

'Of course. I see you doing the same things you're doing now. With Zoe.'

'Home-schooling?'

'We can get a tutor. Zoe, you'll need to learn Greek.'

'I already know Greek,' Zoe said proudly.

'You already know…'

'Christos spoke Greek to her as a baby,' Elsa told him, feeling a bit smug herself as she noted his astonishment. 'We figured it was part of who she was, so we've kept it up.'

'Elsa speaks it now too,' Zoe added, 'and we both read it. There are two old Greek ladies in Waratah Cove. We visit them once a week and talk with them, and Elsa does their shopping and says it's payment for our lessons. If we went away I'd miss them.' Her face clouded. 'And the cats. How can we go away without our cats?'

'Yeah, the cats,' Elsa said, as if it was a challenge.

He grinned at that. 'That's one more thing fixed. Zoe, open the blue suitcase.'

She opened it. Fascinated. To display cat food. Bulk cat food. A suitcase of cat food.

'So we're supposed to open the suitcase and come home when they need a refill?' Elsa said and she couldn't help sounding waspish.

'That's fixed too,' he said, his grin teasing her to smile with him. 'There's a guy who works round here tending gardens, doing odd jobs. I've arranged for him to visit every night at dusk, feed the cats, lock them up, then let them out at dawn. In perpetuity. And if any other stray comes along then he's to do exactly what you'd do. Take it in, get it neutered, tell it the house rules. He can even do your two Greek ladies' shopping if you want. Now... Any more objections?'

'My...my house?' Elsa stammered.

'I told you, he does gardens and odd jobs. He'll maintain this place as long as we want.'

'You found this guy when?'

'The concierge at the hotel earned his keep last night,' he said, and grinned again. 'He brought his wife in to help. His wife knows you and knows what you need. So there you go. Local knowledge and my cash.'

'Yeah, your cash,' she said, breathless. 'We can't take it.'

'See, what you don't understand is that you can,' he said. 'Zoe's a princess. You're nanny to a princess. Are there any other problems?'

'The medical facilities…'

'I'll be there and, as I said, there are fast flights to Athens. Until we get other medical facilities organised we can cope.' He took her hand again and held, and with his other hand he took Zoe's. 'Khryseis needs a team,' he said. 'A royal team. Prince Regent, Princess Zoe and Nanny Elsa. Do we have it?'

'Yes,' Zoe said.

There were no arguments left. The only one that was still swirling round and round in her mind was, I don't want to be a nanny to your prince.

But that was dumb. She glanced at the mantel where Matt still smiled.

Definitely it was dumb.

He glanced to where she'd looked. Saw what she'd been looking at.

Didn't ask a question.

'It'll be fine,' he said softly, and the pressure on her hand strengthened. Then, before she knew what he was about, he put his hand under her chin and tilted it—and kissed her. It was a feather-light kiss, quickly over, and why it had the capacity to make her feel…make her feel…

No. She had to stop thinking about how it made

her feel, because that was nonsense. But his hand was still under her chin, forcing her to meet his gaze.

'I will keep you safe,' he said, strongly and surely. 'And Zoe too. You've worked too hard for too long, Elsa Murdoch. Now it's up to Zoe and me to see you have some fun. Just say yes.'

And what else was she to do?

'I guess…yes,' she managed, but she didn't add, Yes, Your Royal Highness. Because that would be agreeing to all of it. The whole royal fairy tale.

Ridiculous.

CHAPTER SIX

Two weeks later they left Australia, luxuriating in first class seats on a direct flight to Athens, to be followed by a smaller plane to Khryseis.

'I'll be on Khryseis to meet you,' Stefanos had said in one of the scores of calls he'd made since then. 'But our people will take care of you all the way.'

They hadn't seen him since that fateful lunch. He'd had to leave. 'Things are chaotic,' he'd said. 'I need to get back to the island straight away but I promise I won't let that disorder touch you.'

It wasn't touching them now. They were in first class airline seats. They had a cocoon each, with every conceivable gadget, including one that turned the seats into beds at the flick of a switch. A hostess had already made Zoe's bed for her, with crisp linen and fluffy duvet, and she was fast asleep.

Elsa was staring out of the window and seeing what was probably Hawaii.

She was trying not to gibber.

She'd been on one overseas flight in her life. To Tasmania. She didn't remember all that many gadgets and duvets and cocoons on that flight. She remembered being served a packet of nuts and a warm beer.

She was about to be a nanny to a princess.

The princess was bone weary. Her little body still wasn't up to strength. The last weeks had been excitement plus, and Elsa had worried about the wisdom of letting her go at all.

'But it's imperative,' Stefanos had said in his deep, grave voice and, dumb or not, she believed him. If Zoe wasn't there he had no power to replace the council. He had no power to stop the corruption he told her was endemic.

So, once again, why rail against something she had no control over? Now, as Zoe snuggled into sleep, she thought with this level of luxury maybe her little charge could enjoy herself.

Maybe *she* could enjoy herself.

Amazingly, her hip wasn't hurting. Normally, sitting for more than a couple of hours made it ache unbearably, but her hip obviously decided it liked first class treatment, thank you very much, and it wasn't only her hip thinking it.

She was on her way to live in a castle. As a nanny. A nanny, she reminded herself. A paid servant. She'd get to eat in the servants' quarters, while Zoe ate in state. She'd use chipped pottery while Zoe swanned round in party dresses, using cut-glass crystal and silverware, attended by butlers and…and whatever else royalty had.

Um…this was Zoe she was talking about. Maybe she couldn't see that happening.

And tucked in her bag was a document, prepared by Stefanos's legal team, read from all angles by her local lawyer and then faxed to a team of international lawyers in Canberra for a final check.

The document said that if, at any time, Zoe seemed so distressed that it was damaging her mental or physical health—and that decision was to be made by a team of independent *Australian* medical experts flown out at Stefanos's expense—then Zoe's fare back to Australia would be paid immediately. And so would hers.

So. Maybe it'd work?

But…she was a marine biologist, not a nanny. Stefanos had promised her starfish.

Yeah, great. She shoved that thought as far back in her head as she could. She'd like to be rid of it completely—the ache to follow her own dreams.

But Zoe came first. Zoe was more important than dreams. And maybe those dreams could still be resurrected. If Zoe was unhappy they'd come home.

Catch-22. She didn't want Zoe to be unhappy.

'But we can make it a game,' she'd whispered to Zoe as she'd watched her little charge drift towards sleep. 'You being a princess in a castle.'

'With a prince,' Zoe had said sleepily. 'Isn't he nice?'

He is nice, Elsa admitted. Um...all things considered, he's very nice.

Which was why she had to remember that he was a prince and she was a nanny. A nanny with a sliver of a career left as a marine biologist, who could maybe be happy with starfish.

Certainly a nanny with no interest whatsoever in a prince. Even if he was as drop-dead gorgeous as Stefanos.

Especially if he was as drop-dead gorgeous as Stefanos!

She closed her eyes. Two seconds later the hostess was beside her. 'Can I make your bed up for you, ma'am? Here are your pyjamas.'

She handed her a pair of pink silk pyjamas.

There was a well-known Australian politician sitting in the seat diagonally in front of her—she recognised him from the newspapers. He was wearing blue silk pyjamas as he read the financial pages.

What a shame Stefanos wasn't with them, she thought. He'd look really cute in blue pyjamas.

See, she told herself sternly. That's what nannies are paid not to think.

What are nannies paid to think?

Not about lost careers. Not about lost dreams.

And not about drop-dead gorgeous Prince Regents.

* * *

Stefanos paced the palace balcony and waited for them, feeling ridiculous. The staff were beside themselves with excitement, so much so that he'd given in and done the dress-up thing again. He'd done it twice now, once in Australia at the formal reception and again today. Hopefully there wouldn't be too many more occasions where he had to feel so ridiculous.

But maybe there would be.

This whole situation was crazy, he told himself, for maybe the thousandth time since he'd heard the news of Christos's death. He was automatically Prince Regent—island ruler until Zoe turned twenty-five—but, although the Regency gave him some powers, the thing he wanted most was denied to him.

He wanted the island to be a democracy, but as Regent he had no power to change the constitution. Democracy would have to wait for Zoe to turn twenty-five.

Since he was a kid he'd dreamed of Khryseis being a great and wonderful place to live. But now…he'd fallen in love with his medicine. He was good at his job. His research was vitally important, and he loved what he did.

What could he do here but tinker round the edges, protect the islanders from the worst of the excesses they'd endured in the past, then—what?—try and remember his general medicine so he could treat the islanders' minor ailments until Zoe came of age? In what, seventeen years?

Then he'd go tamely back to the States and pick up where he'd left off? To a career that was waiting for him?

Yeah, and pigs would fly.

He had no choice. He had to care for the island. He had to care for Zoe.

And Elsa?

She needed care as much as Zoe, he thought. Elsa had stood up to him with the air of a battered warrior, a woman accustomed to having her world shift and accepting those shifts with as much dignity and grace as she could muster. He'd seen how much the thought of losing Zoe terrified her, but once she'd realised how needful it was she'd simply got on with it.

He had the feeling that even if he hadn't offered her a generous salary, she'd still be doing exactly what she was doing. Taking care of Zoe, no matter what life threw at her.

What had life thrown at her?

He needed to find out more about her—and her husband. Why was he no longer on the scene? She still wore a wedding ring.

Um…why was that relevant?

He should have found out. His enquiries had been professional. It had seemed wrong to pry.

But he wanted to know.

He did already know some things. For one… *She seemed loving.* For some dumb reason that phrase had been playing in his head since he'd met her. Her fierce devotion to Zoe was touching something in him that he'd learned to ignore a long time ago.

He didn't do emotion. Since he'd left this island as a teenager he'd been totally committed to his medicine. Yet here he was, not only realising he'd have to abandon the work he was passionate about but, in the stillness of the night, as he lay trying to find a way he could sort all his commitments, Alexandros's idle teasing kept rising up to taunt him.

Wife. Family.

No!

He remembered the horror of his father's death, and his mother's anguish as she'd insisted he take a scholarship to the US to keep him safe. He remembered grief and homesickness, and his mother's death had cemented his knowledge that love caused nothing but pain. Work had been his salvation then, as it could be his salvation now—whether or not it was the work he desperately wanted to do.

'If you please…' A delicate cough sounded behind him and he jumped a foot. The old palace butler moved like a cat. One of these days the old guy was going to give him a heart attack.

He turned and tried to look as if he hadn't had a fright. 'Yes?'

'I believe they've arrived, sir,' the old man said gravely.

He glanced out at the magnificent formal driveway. An ancient Rolls-Royce was proceeding in state down the avenue, the flag of Khryseis flying proudly from the grille.

The butler was beaming with pride and anticipation. That was what this was all about, Stefanos thought grimly. Giving the islanders back their identity.

Which was why he was wearing this ridiculous uniform.

But there were other imperatives hammering at him. Back in New York he had a surgical list still waiting. He couldn't let those kids down. He'd have to return before he could finally commit himself to this place.

The car had pulled to a halt and the driver stepped out. He must be eighty as well—half the retainers in this household were in their dotage—but, like most of the staff, he was also wearing the imposing uniform of the Khryseis royal household.

Since Giorgos's death, since the islanders had discovered they could revert to their own royal family, the excitement had been building. The Isle of Sappheiros now had its own royal family in its palace. So did the Isle of Argyros. Khryseis, the smallest of the islands, was last to revert to rule by its original royal family, and the islanders were looking to Stefanos to make this good.

And they were also looking to this one little girl, coming home. A child who must be protected.

At least he could share that responsibility, he

thought, once more feeling grateful for Elsa. Ruling the island might be his duty but with Elsa here he didn't need to commit emotionally. If he kept Zoe safe and her nanny happy, then that was the extent of his obligations.

The Crown Princess was loved by a woman called Elsa. Which meant the love bit could be shelved as not his business.

Elsa and Zoe climbed from the Rolls-Royce and if they weren't quite clutching each other they came awfully close.

'This is really scary,' Zoe whispered, and Elsa couldn't agree more.

It was a palace. A real, honest to goodness palace, vast and ancient. Turrets, battlements, spires and flags, vast entrance steps and Grecian columns, all set against a magical backdrop—sapphire seas, golden beaches, white cliffs with mountains in the background.

Internet pages they'd read had told them that Khryseis was the most impoverished of the three Diamond Isles, but once it had been fabulously wealthy. This palace backed it up. Elsa had never seen a building so fantastic. Or big.

'I hope we don't have to dust and hoover it,' she whispered to Zoe, and Zoe giggled. The tension eased.

Only then Stefanos strode out of the vast front entrance and the tension zoomed back again.

'Ooo er…' Elsa muttered, and Zoe clutched her hand and gave another shaky giggle. Striding down the great granite steps towards them, Stefanos looked like something out of history. Romantic history.

'He's a real prince again. Do you think he wears a sword?' Zoe whispered, awed.

'Hey, he is,' Elsa said as he got closer and they could see the great golden hilt emerging from its scabbard. 'Be good, Zoe.'

'It's only Stefanos. He won't hurt us,' Zoe said, and it was the child who was trying to reassure the adult.

Some nanny she made, Elsa thought. Telling her charge to be scared.

Actually, she wasn't a great nanny at all. She looked down at her scuffed trainers—she'd needed comfy shoes for the flight and these were all she had. For the last four years she'd lived in jeans and sweatshirts. If her royal duties demanded better clothes, they'd need to wait until pay day.

Zoe, however, looked beautiful. In her sparkly new clothes, her dark curls held back with diamanté butterfly clips, her pretty blue sandals adorned with butterflies, she looked every inch a child of royalty.

Underneath her carefully chosen clothes were scars which were still healing, but her new clothes hid them and gave her confidence. As this man coming towards them was giving her excitement.

'I'm going to be a princess,' she whispered.

'And I'm going to be a nanny,' Elsa whispered back.

'Stefanos said we could still look for starfish,' the child said, picking up on her nerves and, amazingly, trying to reassure her.

'He did, didn't he,' Elsa said and fought for a bit more backbone—the courage to pin a cheerful smile in place and turn to greet her employer.

What in the world was she doing here? And why did the sight of the man strolling towards her make her knees feel as if they were turning to jelly?

'Welcome to Khryseis, Princess Zoe.' Stefanos strode towards them and he greeted Zoe first. He took her hands and stooped to kiss her cheeks. It might be a normal Greek greeting but here, now, it seemed a truly royal gesture. Zoe looked suitably amazed.

'I'm not a real princess,' she told him, as if admitting a falsehood.

'You are,' Stefanos said gently. 'Your father was the Crown Prince Christos and you're his daughter. This is where you belong.'

'It's a really big palace.'

'It is.'

'Elsa says we might have to dust and hoover,' she ventured, and Stefanos turned to Elsa and his dark eyes lit with laughter.

'Welcome to you, too,' he said and it was her turn

to have her hands grasped and her cheek kissed. Was this the way royalty greeted nannies? 'I promise you no hoovering—and I'm so glad you decided to come.'

Whew. This was a formal gesture, she told herself wildly. He'd kissed her cheek and smiled at her. Why that had the capacity to make her insides melt…

She'd been isolated for too long. She was starting to feel… Like she had no business in the world feeling.

'Zoe was never coming alone,' she managed.

'No,' he said, but something in his tone said that such a concept wasn't unthinkable. 'She'll be so much happier with you.'

'She…she will.' It was really hard to breathe while he was smiling at her—while he was so close—but she had to start as she meant to go on. 'And thank you for making us feel right at home, by the way.'

'Sorry?'

'By wearing your casual gear,' she said, and managed to smile. 'It makes me feel I'll fit right in.'

His eyes met hers, laughter meeting laughter. But he couldn't respond how he wished. He was aware their conversation was being listened to, even if she wasn't.

There were only three staff members within sight, but every window was open and the palace curtains were inched back enough to allow the servants to hear. He'd deliberately not lined the staff up to meet Zoe, but the islanders' desperate need for a new royal family had to be met.

'Would you like to see your bedrooms?' he asked them both.

'Um…bedrooms,' Elsa said. 'Plural?'

'I want to stay with Elsa,' Zoe said urgently and Stefanos smiled a reassurance.

'I don't blame you. Come and see what we've organised. You'll need to meet a couple of people first. The housekeeper. The butler. We'll leave the rest of the staff for you to meet tomorrow.'

'Oh, goody,' Elsa whispered, and Stefanos smiled in sympathy.

'There's a photo shoot here after lunch,' he added apologetically. 'Christos was well loved on the island and there's huge interest and pleasure that his child is coming home. To ban all photographers would have had cameramen scaling walls, so I've permitted a representative from each of the island's media outlets.'

'You have more than one?' Elsa said, incredulous.

'It's not a complete backwater,' he said gently and she flushed.

'You have multi-media outlets and you have only one doctor?'

'I know—priorities that need fixing. They will be fixed, but I haven't managed everything in two weeks.' He took Zoe's hand and grinned down at her encouragingly. 'You want to see your bedroom? You have a four-poster bed with curtains.'

'Yes, please,' Zoe said breathlessly. She turned with him and they headed up the grand entrance steps.

Leaving Elsa to follow.

I'm the nanny, she told herself, trying not to feel bereft and hopelessly out of her comfort zone. Staying in the background is what I'm supposed to do.

Stefanos and Zoe reached the top step and paused, looking back to her.

They looked fabulous, she thought. Prince Regent and his Crown Princess. Zoe looked lit up like a fairy on top of a Christmas tree, holding her big cousin's hand with confidence.

'Are you coming?' Stefanos said gently. She met his gaze and realised that once again he'd guessed how she was feeling.

Zoe still needed her, she thought wildly. She wasn't being put out to pasture yet.

'I'm coming,' she called. The chauffeur was lifting their bags out of the boot and she grabbed the top one. The heaviest.

'Leave that to the staff,' Stefanos told her.

'I'm the staff,' she said determinedly and, to her amazement, he chuckled.

'I don't think so,' he said. 'I expect the staff to conform to a certain standard in their uniform. I need to tell you that your standard falls a long way short until we can get you outfitted as befits your status…as a friend of the Crown Princess.'

Then his tone became gentle and the laughter faded. 'You've worked hard already,' he said, looking down at her from the top step, and he spoke loudly and clearly enough for his voice to carry into all those open windows. 'You've cared for my little cousin—for our Crown Princess—with all the love at your disposal. It would be my honour to grant you a holiday for as long as you want. Your nominal title is nanny to Zoe, but my command to you personally—to you both—is to have fun.'

CHAPTER SEVEN

THEIR apartments were stunning—two apartments with an adjoining door. Rooms almost big enough to house a tennis court.

'They're built for the Crown Prince and Crown Princess,' Stefanos told them while Zoe and Elsa stared in incredulity.

'This is something out of a museum,' Elsa murmured. 'You know the ones I mean? This is the bed where Charles the First spent the night before the Great Wiggery Foppery of Seventeen Sixty-Two.'

'The Great Wiggery Foppery?' Stefanos asked, bemused.

'Or maybe it was the Great Gunfire Pirouette with Catherine Wheels,' she told him, desperately striving for humour in the face of splendour that was just plain intimidating. 'I'm Australian so my knowledge of royalty is distinctly hazy, but my grandma had a book on Bedrooms of the World. I read it when I was seven and I had chickenpox.

They all had descriptions like Queen Anne had dropsy in this very bed and threw up on this very pillow. And no, don't ask me what dropsy is.'

'Are we really going to sleep in here?' While Elsa was covering her nerves with nonsense, Zoe was awed into hushed delight.

'They've changed the sheets since the great dropsy plague,' Stefanos said gravely. 'I think it might be safe to sleep in them again.'

Zoe giggled.

Which was the whole point of the exercise, Elsa reminded herself. If she could keep Zoe giggling…

But for how long?

'We'll sleep in this one,' Zoe said, and proceeded to clamber up onto what was surely intended as the Crown Prince's bed. It was vast, with four golden posts, a golden canopy and rich burgundy curtains drawn back with gold tassels.

'Then Elsa will sleep in the other one,' Stefanos said, motioning through the open door to a bedroom almost as large and a bed almost as luxurious.

The giggling stopped. Zoe's bottom lip trembled.

'No,' she said. 'This is too big by myself. We sleep in the same room at home. Why can't we sleep in the same room here?'

'We can,' Elsa said. 'There's no need to worry Prince Stefanos, though. We'll fix it.'

'You've been sharing a room with Zoe?' Stefanos asked.

'I have.' She met his gaze with open defiance.

'So you had only one bedroom in that little cottage?'

'Zoe has nightmares,' she said. 'Even if we had ten bedrooms we wouldn't use them.'

'I'm not sure the staff will approve of a trundle bed in here. They're wanting Zoe to be real royalty.'

'So Zoe gets the four-poster and I get a trundle.'

'There needs to be some delineation.'

'I'm her friend and her guardian.'

'Yes, and her nanny.'

'So I am,' she said, figuring that here was a line in the sand—her first test. Zoe would not be made to suffer from the demands of royalty. 'So it's back to the trundle. Zoe will not sleep alone.'

'I don't like alone,' Zoe said, relaxing now she was sure Elsa was on her side.

'We'll sort it out,' Stefanos went on in a voice that said this issue wouldn't go away.

'If you think…'

'Leave it,' he said, and she met his gaze head-on. 'Zoe, take a look at the beach.'

Zoe looked—while Elsa met Stefanos's gaze and held. He smiled at her and she thought, Don't you dare. You smile at me and you think you can get away with murder.

The scary thing was that she suspected he could.

'Look at the beach, Elsa,' he said gently, and she tore her gaze away from his and looked.

The palace gardens led down to a wide stretch

of golden sand, a cove of shallow water and low, rolling waves.

'Wow,' Zoe breathed. 'Can we swim?'

'As soon as you're settled.' He hesitated, watching Elsa. Who forced her thoughts back to beds.

If he thought he could get his own way simply by smiling... She took a deep breath and started to form a cogent argument about trundle beds, but he'd moved on.

'Lunch is in half an hour,' he told them. 'We'll organise the beds later. Meanwhile, I'll leave you to get settled. The butler will let you know when lunch is ready, and he'll show you the way.'

'Can't we just come down in half an hour?' Elsa asked.

'You'd get lost,' he told her and there was that smile again. 'And now we have you both here we don't intend to lose you. Make yourselves at home and I'll see you at lunch.'

He went out. Elsa was left with confusion, an unaccountable fear and the knowledge that the room was bleaker for his going.

What was it about the man? In his presence she felt about the same age as Zoe.

This was crazy. It was just his uniform, she told herself. The fairy tale bit. He looked so...royal.

'Stefanos said we're getting our photos taken after lunch,' Zoe ventured, looking worried. 'Should I wear something pretty?'

'You look very pretty right now,' she said and gave the little girl a swift hug. A hug she needed just as much as Zoe. 'But maybe we can find you something even prettier. What about your new dress?'

They came down to lunch looking nervous. Zoe was wide-eyed with wonder, clutching Elsa's hand as if it were a lifeline—but she wasn't subdued, Stefanos thought, as he watched them walk down the stairs towards him. She looked like a little girl about to go to a birthday party where she didn't know anyone. It was a bit scary, but it might turn out to be fun.

Elsa, on the other hand, looked nervous in a different way. It was as if she was nervous of her royal surroundings. More. She was nervous of him?

She was still wearing jeans and sweatshirt. Zoe was in the most extravagant of the clothes he'd bought for her—her beautiful party dress. Beside her, Elsa looked subdued. She looked even more subdued when she saw him waiting for them at the foot of the stairs. It was this uniform, he thought regretfully. It was enough to scare *him*. After the media call he could take it off, but until then he had to be a prince.

So. He was a prince. Zoe was a princess. Elsa looked as if she didn't want to be here at all.

And she was still limping. He hadn't noticed when she'd arrived, but watching her coming down the stairs he saw it again. She was holding the balustrade with her spare hand and doing her best to disguise it, but she was being careful. The way she swung her left leg forward… There wasn't full movement in her hip and it looked as if coming downstairs hurt.

Last time he'd seen her he'd seen the faintest trace of a limp. She'd brushed it aside when he'd enquired, and he'd had so much on his mind then that to assume it was a temporary sprain had been the easiest option. Now, though… There was a lot he had to find out about this woman.

Like what was the damage with her leg.

Like why she was coming to lunch and a media call in faded jeans and sweatshirt. Looking scared. Up until now he would have described her as spirited and feisty. What was it about this place that was sucking the spirited and feisty out of her?

He glanced up at the massive chandelier above his head—two thousand crystals, the housekeeper had told him, and he didn't doubt it for a minute— and he thought, What's oppressive about this?

He smiled at them and Zoe let go of Elsa's hand and bounced down the last few steps to greet him. She gazed up at the chandelier and breathed deeply in small girl satisfaction.

'It's really, really beautiful,' she said.

'So are you,' he told her and she giggled.

He glanced at Elsa—and caught her unawares. There was a wash of pure, unmitigated pain on her face. It was gone as soon as it had come, quickly turned into a smile, but he knew he wasn't mistaken.

'We're hungry,' she said, a trifle too fast, and he thought she was still in defence mode.

'Excellent,' he said. 'In fact, more than excellent when you see what's in front of us.'

He led the way into the dining room and paused at the door, smiling down to Zoe again. 'This is a welcome lunch for you,' he said gently. 'Specially made by everyone who works here.'

And it was—a feast that promised a small girl's heaven. The delicate finger food looked as if it had been designed to tempt and tantalise a little girl's appetite. There were tiny cheesy biscuits in the shape of animals. Finger-sized sausage rolls. Chicken wings with tiny chef-hat wrappers around their tips so a small hand wouldn't get greasy. Strawberries and grapes and slivers of watermelon. Tiny chocolate cakes with a dusting of sugar. Miniature sponge cakes with the tops turned into wings and fixed in place with a mix of red jelly and cream. Petite eclairs with creamy custard filling.

Around them the room was a mass of fresh cut flowers, a wondrous fantasy feast of beauty and pure delight.

Zoe sat down and gazed at the table in awe. 'Elsa won't have to tell me to eat here,' she breathed.

'That's what we hoped,' he said and glanced at Elsa again—and got that look again. Raw pain.

'You don't approve?' he asked and she caught herself and managed to smile. But her smile was strained. She was having trouble disguising how hard it was to summon it at all.

'It's wonderful,' she said.

'So why do you look unhappy?' he asked gently.

'Elsa's a bit sad 'cause she hasn't got any pretty clothes,' Zoe said and popped a strawberry into her mouth—and then looked mortified. She swallowed it manfully and looked even more guilty. 'Is…is it okay to start?'

'Absolutely it's okay to start,' Stefanos said and handed over the sausage rolls. Zoe took two—and then looked at how small they were and took another.

'Thank you very much,' she breathed, and Stefanos glanced at the door. He knew at least six members of staff were behind there, holding their breath that she'd like their offering, that she'd be a kind child, that she could be a princess to be proud of.

She was all of those things, he thought. And it was thanks to Elsa.

Elsa, who didn't have pretty things to wear.

'So you don't have any dresses?' he probed and she cast him a glance that was almost resentful.

'I didn't bring any. And I'm not sad because of that. It's just…I'm just a bit overwhelmed.'

'You mean yesterday there was just you loving Zoe,' he said gently. 'And now there's me and a palace full of staff and an island ready to love her.'

'It's crazy to think like that,' she said, but she did.

'So back to the clothes,' he said gently. 'Can I ask why there's nothing but jeans?'

'I'm a marine biologist. Why would I need dresses?'

There was a loaded silence. Zoe ate two sausage rolls and a strawberry and then thought about what Elsa had said. And decided she might add her pennyworth.

'Elsa did have pretty clothes,' the child told him, considering an eclair. 'Only she got too skinny and they looked funny on her. We kept them for ages but then she said, "You know what, Zoe, I'm never going to be this size again; they might as well make someone else happy." So we packed them up and took them to a church fair. And Mrs Henniker bought Elsa's prettiest yellow dress and she looked awful in it and Elsa cried.'

'I did not,' Elsa said, fighting for dignity. 'I had hay fever.'

'You only get hay fever when you cry,' Zoe said wisely. 'Giving your clothes away made you really sad.'

The bond between these two was amazing. Up until now he'd thought it was Elsa who did all the giving. Suddenly a new view was opening up.

Zoe was eight going on thirty.

Elsa was…sometimes ninety. Sometimes a kid.

She was trying for indignant here but it wasn't coming off. Zoe had exposed her and she knew she was exposed.

'Why did you lose weight?'

'I stopped eating for a while,' she told him in a voice that said no more questions were welcome. 'I've started again.'

'We might need to buy you some clothes,' he said, and watched as vulnerability disappeared, to be replaced by indignation.

'You don't need to buy me anything. I like my jeans.'

'I like your jeans too,' he said—and he did. They were exceedingly cute. Mind, she could do with a bit more flesh on her frame. She was almost elfin. And that limp…

'What happened to your leg?' he asked, and got another scared look.

'Please…just leave it. I'm here to be with Zoe while she gets to know the country her papa came from. I intend to stay in the background. Can we leave it at that?'

He considered her gravely and shook his head. 'Zoe, what's wrong with Elsa's leg?'

He heard her gasp. He didn't look at her.

This woman had cared for Zoe for four years. If he'd known of Christos's death he would have been there for his little cousin. The responsibility was his, but he hadn't even known of Zoe's existence.

That hurt on all sorts of levels, and one of those levels was the fact that this woman seemed to have put her life on hold for Zoe—and it might be worse than that.

He'd watched her come down the stairs and realised this was no twisted ankle. She was protecting her hip—as she'd been protecting her hip two weeks ago on the beach but he'd been too preoccupied to see it.

'She hurt it when my mama and papa died,' Zoe said, not picking up on the undercurrents. She was back considering food. This meal was a huge success. He could practically hear the chef's sigh of happiness from here.

'Are you going to tell me how badly?' he asked Elsa.

'I broke my hip,' she said discouragingly.

'You were in the car accident with Zoe's parents?'

'Yes.'

'And your husband…' He hadn't put two and two together, but he did now, and he didn't like it.

'Elsa's Matty was killed too,' Zoe said, and she was suddenly grave and mature and factual. 'My mama and papa were in the front seat and Matty and Elsa and me were in the back. A great big truck came round the corner on the wrong side of the road and hit our camper van and our camper van started to burn. Elsa pulled me out but she couldn't pull anyone else out. We were both really, really sad. I was in hospital for a long time—I can hardly remember—but I do remember Elsa coming in a wheelchair to see me. She says my grandma came to see me too, but I can't remember that. I remember being in a bath a lot and crying, but Elsa was always there. And then my grandma got sick so Elsa took me home with her—and now we're living happily ever after.'

She was suddenly back to being a little girl again. Happy and optimistic. 'Only this is a better place for happy ever after, isn't it, Elsa?'

'There was nothing wrong with my beach,' Elsa said, making an unsuccessful attempt to glower, and Zoe giggled as if she'd said something silly.

'No, but our beach doesn't have cream puffs. These are really good. Can I have another one, please?'

'Be my guest,' Stefanos said and he handed her the plate—but his eyes were on Elsa. 'So why are you still limping?'

And once again it was Zoe who answered. 'Mr Roberts says she should have another operation. Mr Roberts came to see Elsa last time I was in hospital and he said, "When are we going to fix that hip, young lady?" And Elsa said, "When I have the time and the money, and like that's going to happen soon." And Mr Roberts said she had to get her pi…her priorities right and she said she did.'

'Zoe, don't,' Elsa said, looking desperate. 'Please, sweetheart, this is nothing to do with Prince Stefanos.'

'No, but he's nice,' Zoe said, as if that excused everything. 'Can I have one of those cakey things with wings, please?'

* * *

What would happen if she just got up from the table, walked right out of here, straight to the ferry, then on a plane back to Australia?

She had a return ticket. That was one of her stipulations about coming.

It was a first class ticket. If she traded it for economy she'd have enough to live on until she could start back to work.

Zoe didn't need her.

Only of course Zoe did. She looked happy and contented but she'd been here for less than a day. She was still clutching her. She was happy because this was exciting and Stefanos was kind. And the rest. Big and too good-looking for his own good—and did he know how sexy he looked in that uniform?

He was doing her head in and her head had to stay intact. She had to stay practical. She needed to find a role for herself here that wasn't tied to Zoe or Stefanos or the palace.

She could do this, she thought. She just had to stay detached from Stefanos and his dangerous charm.

This man was important to her only in his relationship to Zoe. He was good to Zoe. He made the little girl laugh. But he hadn't gained so much trust that Elsa could walk away.

She didn't ever want to walk away. Not from Zoe. The thought hurt on so many levels that the pain in her hip didn't even register in comparison.

'What are you thinking?' Stefanos asked, watching her quizzically from the head of the table. 'To make you look like that?'

'I…nothing.'

'I don't think I've been appropriately sympathetic.'

'I don't know what appropriate sympathy is.'

'Neither do I,' he said softly. 'But if it helped I'd find it for you.'

See, there was the whole problem. She had so much going on in her head—how to fit in here— what she was going to do with herself while Zoe settled—how she was going to make a life for herself after Zoe stopped needing her, as stop she surely would—and across it all was Stefanos's gorgeous smile, the way his dark eyes creased at the corners, the way he seemed to read her mind…

He left them for a while as she drank coffee. Urgent royal business, he said and that made her even more nervous. By the time he returned she was climbing the walls.

'You don't need me for this,' she said and pushed her chair back. 'Zoe, are you okay to do this photo thing with…with your cousin? I'll go up to the bedroom and unpack.'

'No!' Zoe was out of her chair in a flash, darting round the table to grab her hand. 'You have to come with me.'

Not so settled, then. Neither would she be, she

thought, if someone told her she had to meet the press.

'I've arranged for Elsa to come with us,' Stefanos told Zoe, and her heart hit her boots.

'Excuse me?'

'I've promised the press they can meet Zoe and you.'

'And me?'

'You're the woman who's been caring for our Crown Princess for the past four years,' he said steadily. 'The islanders would have taken Zoe to them in a heartbeat. All of us owe you a debt that touches our honour.'

He rose and held out a hand to Zoe, and the little girl hesitated for a moment and then gave him hers. It was that sort of gesture. Strong, sure, commanding. Royal.

'If Zoe's brave enough to have her photograph taken, surely you can,' he told her.

'Yes, but Zoe's a princess,' she said on a wail. 'Look at me. I'm not even a proper nanny.'

'You're not,' he agreed. 'You're our friend. And, as our friend…' He hesitated. 'Elsa, giving Zoe clothes seemed appropriate. For you, however, it seems almost insulting and I ask you to accept that it's not my intention to insult you. Nevertheless, I've made some fast phone calls and the owners of our two main dress shops are here already, setting out a selection of clothes. For Zoe's coronation you'll need evening wear and we can't get that here, but for now…it would please me if you could choose something more suitable than jeans and sweatshirt for your introduction to our island.'

She stared at him in stupefaction. 'You want me to buy clothes?'

'I want you to take the clothes that I will buy for you,' he said. 'This will be my pleasure.'

'To dress me?'

His eyes creased involuntarily into laughter. 'I don't think we're quite there yet.'

She stared at him, feeling a tide of colour sweep upward. 'Ex…excuse me?'

'Levity,' he murmured, obviously fighting to get back to being serious. 'You need to excuse me. But this is clothes, Elsa. No big deal.'

'I wear jeans.'

'Zoe says you don't. Not before the accident.'

'I'm a whole new me since the accident.'

'Then is it possible,' he said gently, 'that you can be a whole new you again?'

'I…'

'Please, Elsa.'

She stared down at her battered sneakers, her worn jeans. They were like her skin, she thought, yet another skin she was being asked to change.

Poverty-stricken single mother to royal child-minder.

Single woman to wife. Eager student to earnest professional. Married woman to grieving widow.

Skins, skins, skins. She hardly knew who she was any more. What harm could one more change do?

'Fine,' she said.

'Your gratitude is overwhelming,' he murmured, and there it was again—that hint of laughter.

'Did you like it when they told you that you had to wear a sword?' she demanded.

'I…no.'

'Then pay me the compliment of allowing that I feel the same,' she whispered. 'Thank you very much for providing clothes. I accept and I'm grateful. It's just…I've learned from past experience that it hurts to change direction. I'm doing my best to smile while it happens but you'll need to excuse me when my smile falters.'

She chose a simple green sundress. Zoe and Stefanos chose a whole lot more. Presumably the photographers and journalists had been told to wait, for Stefanos refused to hurry and was only satisfied when he—and Zoe—had decided she had enough clothes to make her…pretty.

Pretty was a strange concept. She'd stopped worrying about her appearance four years ago. Now, dressed in a lovely light sundress, with shoe-string straps and a skirt that twirled and swished as she walked, she decided there were definite upsides to shedding skins.

She felt…nice. Free. It was a novel experience, but it didn't stop her hanging back as she finally

followed Stefanos and Zoe to the palace media centre.

At the door Stefanos stepped back and motioned for Elsa to precede him.

No way.

She shook her head and dropped deliberately further back, and there was no time for him to react. The door was open. Cameras were flashing and questions were flying.

Zoe cast her a panicked backward glance, but Stefanos lifted her up and held her in his arms.

It was the best thing he could do, Elsa thought. Holding her in his arms. Zoe would feel totally protected.

The press was absolutely riveted on Zoe—their princess coming home. Which left her mind free to wander where it willed.

She kind of liked the way she looked in this sundress. And her new sandals were pretty.

Clothes maketh the woman? The man?

Her eyes flew back to Stefanos. She could see why he'd decided to wear his uniform, but it was more than clothes, she thought. He looked confident, sure, in charge. He was assuming the mantle of control of this country.

He had a job to do and he'd do it.

And he held Zoe as if she was his own. His body language was totally protective, and in his arms Zoe felt brave enough to venture shy answers of her

own, responses the media loved—responses Elsa knew would go straight to the heart of any islander.

The Prince and his little Princess. She watched them pose together, she watched Stefanos tease Zoe into laughter, and the weird sensations she'd been feeling since the first time she'd seen him standing on her beach were consolidating to something firm and definite and true. Her vision of Matty was fading still further—not disappearing entirely; she knew it could never do that—but fading to a place where he could be mourned without the constant piercing pain that had been with her for years.

She could be pretty. She could change her skin yet again with no betrayal of Matty.

What on earth was she thinking? Crazy, crazy, crazy.

A latecoming journalist jostled past her, nudging her out of her introspection. Hauling her back to reality.

Get back to earth fast, she told herself harshly. This is one of Zoe's fairy tales.

And maybe she ought to listen.

'And may I introduce Dr Elsa Murdoch?' Stefanos was saying, and she was suddenly being looked at by everyone in the room.

Doctor? She hadn't used that title since...

'It's Mrs...' she started but he wasn't allowing her to get a word in.

'Elsa—Dr Murdoch—was in the car crash that

claimed Prince Christos's life,' Stefanos said, and his voice was gentle and full of compassion. 'Also killed were Zoe's mother, Amy, and Elsa's husband, Mathew. Zoe still bears the scars, physically as well as mentally, and so does Elsa. Elsa is a world expert on…what did you call starfish, Zoe?'

'Echinoderms,' Zoe volunteered. Stefanos was still holding her tightly and she obviously felt confident enough to answer. 'Or asteroidea,' she added with aplomb.

'That's the one,' Stefanos said encouragingly. 'So, for the last four years, Dr Murdoch and Zoe have been conducting echinoderm—or asteroidea—research while they've gradually healed from their injuries. Dr Murdoch has cared for Zoe with total love and commitment, and for that this country owes her an enormous debt of gratitude.'

'Hey,' she said, startled enough to forget nerves and reply with spirit. 'That sounds like you're about to give me a gold watch and a pension.'

'You deserve much, much more than that,' he said, smiling. 'I'm hoping Dr Murdoch can stay here,' he told the reporters. 'I'm hoping she'll be a constant presence in Zoe's life. I need to be away from the island for a few weeks between now and Christmas—there are ends I need to tie off before I can stay here permanently—but Zoe and, I hope, Elsa, will be happy here for ever.'

And her tingle of humour and enjoyment disappeared, just like that.

Whoa. What was he saying? That she and Zoe would be staying, but he was leaving?

I need to be away from the island...

He was planning on coming and going at will? *While...what had he said?...Zoe and, I hope, Elsa will be happy here for ever.*

She stayed rooted to the spot while more questions were aimed at Stefanos. Was his work still important to him? How committed to the island could he be if he was returning to the States? Exactly how much time would he stay here and would he still play a ceremonial role?

'You know I'm a neurosurgeon,' he was explaining to the press, 'but of course there's work for me to do here now, medical as well as political. However, there are commitments to be honoured in the States before I can take on a permanent role.'

This was never in the contract, she thought wildly. He was leaving?

Stefanos was fielding the final questions. He was saying he'd be here until the coronation, and then he'd return by Christmas. He was intending to get the council sorted within the week...

She was no longer listening.

He was leaving.

He'd organised her to wear a sundress, while he wore a sword. The way she was suddenly feeling...

Maybe she needed a sword as well.

CHAPTER EIGHT

THE media session had taken its toll on Zoe. Jet lag and excitement had finally caught up with her. As the last of the reporters left, the little girl almost visibly drooped.

'Come on, sweetheart, let's get you up to bed,' Elsa said as Stefanos brought Zoe back to her. She carefully didn't look at Stefanos. The things she needed to say to this man couldn't be said in front of Zoe. In fact, maybe they needed a soundproofed room.

'I'm thinking you need a carriage, Your Highness,' Stefanos said grandly and scooped the little girl up again and carried her up the stairs.

Once again Elsa was left to follow. Her anger and bewilderment were building by the minute.

Stefanos was leaving. He was assuming she'd stay and take care of Zoe. In a place she didn't know. In a country she didn't know.

She was furious, but as she limped up the stairs

after them her anger receded, leaving her flat and deflated. Like Zoe, she was so tired…

She'd been tired for years, but this was worse. Jet lag? No. It was betrayal, and betrayal hurt.

She stopped at the top stair and thought, I don't want to go on. I don't want to watch Stefanos tuck Zoe into bed and make her smile. I don't want to see Zoe seduced into this life of media attention, of shallowness, of wealth, with only me to protect her.

Royalty had destroyed Christos's childhood— he'd told her that. Stefanos had left the island as well, and he'd left for a reason. How could she possibly assess the risks royalty posed for such a vulnerable child as Zoe?

Regardless, Stefanos was obviously intending that she take on the burden of protecting Zoe. That was what he'd said. For ever?

She didn't follow him into the bedroom. She made it to the top stair and sat. If Zoe needed her, Stefanos would come back for her, she thought, but the way the little girl's eyelids were drooping as he'd carried her, she doubted if she'd notice if Elsa wasn't there. And if she went in now she might explode. That he demand she drop the threads of her life in Australia on command, and yet manipulate her so he could still do what he wanted… That he could return to his old life in Manhattan and leave her to care for Zoe in a place she didn't understand…

There were weary chuckles from the end of the corridor. Stefanos was making Zoe laugh.

Bully for Stefanos.

She felt dizzy, as well as angry and confused and all the rest of it. Her hip hurt. She put her head on her knees and folded her arms over her head. This was jet lag and more. Desolation, homesickness, betrayal. The world could go away…

Footsteps sounded down the hall, approaching her on the stair and pausing. She opened her eyes. A pair of black Hessian boots was in her field of vision.

Stefanos.

'Jet lag too, huh?' he said and he was smiling again. She knew he was smiling. She could hear his smile.

'It's not jet lag,' she said without looking up. 'It's anger and disgust and deception thrown in for good measure. Zoe's your cousin. What do you mean by abandoning her?'

'I'm not abandoning her,' he said, sounding surprised.

'You're going back to Manhattan.'

'Only for a few weeks.'

'Why didn't you tell us?'

There was a pause. And then… Amazingly, an honest answer. 'Because I thought you wouldn't come if I did.'

'How very perceptive.'

He sighed and sat down beside her. 'I'm sorry. I

should have told you before, but I have an urgent surgical list to do before Christmas.'

'I had a paper on echinoderms to write up before Christmas,' she retorted. 'Believe it or not, it was important. Someone else is finishing it for me right now.'

'You're saying your echinoderms are more important than my surgical list?'

'You're saying your life is more important than my life?'

He hesitated. 'Elsa, I'm sorry. Of course I don't think that. But you don't understand.'

'So make me understand,' she flashed at him. 'Are there no other surgeons in New York?'

'I can't hand this over.'

'Why not?'

'I can't explain this while you're angry.'

'You don't have a choice,' she said wearily. 'From my point of view, you've conned me into bringing Zoe here. You've seduced the two of us, with your promise of palaces and lovely clothes and happy ever after. But what do I know of this life? How do I know Zoe is safe here? It was your assurance of safety and care that brought us here. How can you calmly say you're going away and leaving us when we've scarcely set foot in the place?'

She was staring downstairs at the massive chandelier below them. Wishing she wasn't in these clothes he'd bought her. Wishing she could wave a magic wand and be home with her beach and her starfish and even her disgusting fish-head cat food—somewhere where she knew the risks and could face them for her small charge; knowing exactly where she stood.

But it seemed that Stefanos wasn't backing down. He was hesitating over what to say to her but she could see that Manhattan was a done deal.

'Just explain,' she said wearily and for a moment she thought he wasn't going to say anything. And then he did.

'I work with overseas aid agencies,' he said slowly into the silence, as if he didn't yet know that he should admit it.

Aid agencies? What sort of aid agencies? What part of this could she believe? 'But you said you work in Manhattan.'

'I do. Patients come to me.'

'How?'

'Aid agencies send them,' he said bluntly, his tone implying he'd decided he might as well tell her and get it over with, whether she believed him or not. 'International aid agencies know what I do and they contact me at need. I intersperse these operations with my normal surgery—that way I can afford it. Mostly I treat people with head injuries from Africa. Neurological stuff. For children especially, as the brain continues to grow, scar tissue causes major problems. I work on techniques to remove the worst of the scar tissue without it reforming. I had to cancel some desperate cases when I realised I needed to find Zoe and get this place sorted. Those kids are still waiting. Now you're here, I need to go back, finish what I've promised and try to hand over my techniques to others to take them forward.'

'You cancelled…' She was staring at him in horror. 'You cancelled them for Zoe?'

'For the welfare of the whole island. If Zoe wasn't back here by the end of next week, then she'd forfeit the throne.'

She frowned, trying to keep up. 'But then you'd inherit.'

'You think I want it? I want to carry on my work.'

She swallowed. Hard. Trying to take this in. 'So… So you really are abandoning us?'

'No,' he said flatly. 'I can't. This place is a mess. Hell, Elsa, there's one doctor on the whole island and that's just the start of it. The local school only takes kids up to sixteen and then there's nothing. There's no infrastructure. The council needs replacing with good, solid people and they'll need support. How can I walk away and leave that to Zoe?'

'I haven't heard about this.'

'I keep it quiet.' He shrugged. 'My wealthy patients come to me in part because of my social position. To be honest, their fees pay for the other work I do, so I have to pander to them.'

'Honestly?'

'Honestly,' he said.

She stared at him. Said nothing. Stared at him still. Why did she believe him?

She did believe him. And if she did believe him…

She took a deep breath, summoned the words she needed and said them. 'I could help,' she said.

There was a loaded silence. He rose and stared down at her, as if she'd suddenly announced the arrival of aliens.

'You're kidding me,' he said at last.

'I don't say what I don't mean,' she said, and rose as well. 'Tell me what you need me to do and I'll do it.' She wasn't feeling very steady. She put her hand on the balustrade to support herself and suddenly Stefanos's hand was over hers.

'You can't,' he said softly.

'I can't help? How do you know I can't?' She tilted her chin. 'Sure, I don't know anything about this place, sure I was angry just then, but I'll get over it. You can teach me. If your work's so important, then I can try.'

The silence extended. She really was exhausted, she thought. If it wasn't for the balustrade and Stefanos's hand…

'Elsa, I'm starting to think there's nothing you can't do,' he said softly into the silence. 'There's no end to your generosity. Zoe's parents die and you abandon your career and take care of her. I arrive and tell you she's needed here and you upend your life and abandon your echinoderms and come with her. And now…your anger turns to an offer of help, just like that. If I said I had to leave tomorrow would you try and handle the council yourself?'

'Maybe I could,' she said and jutted her chin and he laughed, a lovely deep chuckle that had her confused. Veering towards anger again. If only she wasn't so tired.

'No, don't be angry, my lovely Elsa,' he said softly, and he placed a finger under her chin. 'I'm not laughing at you. Indeed, I never could. But no. Your generosity is amazing. Stunning. And, if I could, maybe I'd be tempted. But the island needs a ruler who knows it. Like it or not, I was raised here. I know the islanders. I know the problems. No, I don't want to rule here. I want to practice my medicine. I won't be able to practice the medicine I want here, but that's a small sacrifice in the scheme of things. I've already started a training scheme back in New York. I just have to hope my work keeps going. If you could bear me to be away for these few weeks it will make all the difference.'

'You should have told me.'

'I should have told you,' he agreed. 'Indeed, I'm starting to think I should have told you many things.' Then, as she pulled slightly away from him, his hands came to rest on her shoulders. 'Thank you, Elsa. I can't believe your generosity, and I will keep you safe. I will keep Zoe safe.'

'I know you will.' Unaccountably, her eyes filled with tears. Dammit, she would not cry. *She would not cry.*

But he was too big and too close and too male.

Matty, she thought, but it was a faint echo of a love that was gone. Only…why did it feel as if she was betraying him now?

'You're as exhausted as Zoe,' Stefanos said softly. She shook her head and tried again to pull away from him—and staggered on the staircase.

But she didn't fall. This man had promised to keep her safe and that was just what he was doing.

'That hip…' he said, holding her steady.

'It's fine.'

'It's not fine. It's on my list to do something about. But not now. Now's for sleeping.' And, before she realised what he intended, she was lifted into his arms and he was striding down the hallway, just the same way he'd carried Zoe. As if her weight was nothing.

'Put… What do you think you're doing? Put me down.'

'In a moment,' he said, not breaking stride. 'You need to go where Zoe's going.'

She wanted to struggle. She really did. But suddenly all the struggle was sucked out of her.

His arms were strong, he was big and capable and he was carrying her like a child. For Elsa, who hadn't been treated as a child since…well, since she was one, the sensation was indescribable.

She could melt into these arms, she thought. She could let herself disappear, stop struggling, let these arms hold her for ever.

Was this what jet lag did to a girl?

He was at her bedroom, pushing open her door with his foot. The interconnecting door to Zoe's room was open and she could see through. Zoe was asleep already.

She suddenly felt inordinately proud of herself, that she was a good guardian, or nanny, or whatever she was supposed to be. She'd checked on her charge, even when she wasn't exactly in control herself.

And then she realised that Stefanos was carrying her through to Zoe's room. And she saw why.

Zoe's vast four-poster bed had been moved closer to the door. Zoe was fast asleep in it. And on the other side of her massive bed was another bed. A matching four-poster. Velvet curtains, a vast canopy, eiderdowns and cushions…

The room had been turned into a twin room, with two beds that were so ridiculously enormous that she gasped with incredulity.

'Wh…'

'I know it's a bit crowded,' Stefanos said, smiling down at her in a dumb, indulgent genie sort of way that for some weird reason had her heart doing backflips. 'You'll just have to slum it.'

Slum it…

Matching four-posters…

'I'm probably going to have to pay out on workers' insurance too,' he said morosely. 'Do you know how much these things weigh? It took eight of us to get it in here.'

'You…you…' She could hardly get it out.

'Idiot?' he suggested, laughing down at her and her heart did another backflip.

'Definitely idiot,' she said, trying for asperity and failing miserably. 'I… Thank you.' She was so far out of her comfort zone that she could hardly make her voice work but there was something else she badly needed to say. 'And…at the press conference…thank you for calling me Doctor.'

'It's what you are.'

'Not since Zoe needed me. I've been her mama since then. If I called myself Doctor, everyone thought I was medical. It just confused things.'

'So you stopped being Doctor and started being Mama. As you'd stop being on holiday and start bossing councillors if I asked it of you. You know, you're one special lady.'

'I am not.'

He grinned and lowered her onto the bed, and when he let her go she was aware of a sharp stab of loss.

'You want some painkillers for your hip?'

'It's not hurting.'

'I'm very sure it is.'

'It's fine!'

'Right, then,' he said and smiled again. She could

hear his smile even when she didn't look at him. It was a smile that crept all around her, enveloping her in its sweetness. 'You want help to undress?'

'No,' she said and then, as she reran his question in her head, she found her voice. 'No! And…and don't think I'm not angry any more that you didn't tell me. I still am. It's just got to wait until morning.'

'That's my girl. What if I organise lunch tomorrow so we can talk about it?'

'I don't think…'

'I don't think you can think right now.'

He tugged an eiderdown from the foot of the bed and tucked it around her. 'You'd be more comfortable if you undress but I don't think I can help you there,' he said, his voice suddenly unsteady.

'No,' she said, and then couldn't think why she'd said it. Her voice didn't seem to belong to her.

'You'll be okay,' he said, looking down at her with all the tenderness in the world. As if he cared. As if he really cared.

'You'll be cared for here,' he said, echoing her thoughts. 'You and Zoe will be safe. We'll get that hip fixed. You can play with your starfish and live happily ever after.'

There was a lot to object to in that statement. He seemed to think he was reassuring her.

'I hate starfish,' she muttered.

'You hate starfish?'

'They don't do anything. They just blob. You move 'em and they just blob some more. I hate 'em.'

'You're studying them.'

'Doesn't mean I don't hate 'em.'

'You're done in, sweetheart.'

'I'm not done in. And I'm not your sweetheart.'

'You're not, are you? There's a complication to avoid.'

'Go away.'

'I will,' he said.

But he didn't. He stood gazing down at her and she didn't want him to go. She was half asleep, allowing images from the past—grief, pain, worry, even starfish—to be supplanted by this gorgeous Prince of the Blood.

Prince of the Blood. She wasn't actually sure what the term meant but she knew what it looked like. There was a Prince of the Blood smiling down at her right now, tucking in her eiderdown, looking gorgeous in his fabulous uniform. He was still wearing his sword!

'I love your sword,' she said.

'Don't encourage me,' he said. 'I'm starting to look in mirrors and swagger.'

'So you ought,' she whispered. 'Life should hold a little swagger.'

His smile softened. He stooped so his face was really close to hers and he placed a finger on her lips. To hush her? She didn't know and she didn't much care. It was enough that he was touching her.

It was suddenly incredibly important that he touch her.

'You've lost your swagger,' he said softly, almost as a whisper. 'Life's sucked it right out of you. Let me fix it for you.'

'I don't… You can't.' Matty, she thought desperately, but he'd faded even more. What remained was the memory of how grief felt, how loss felt, how she couldn't afford to fall…

'Elsa…' he said softly and as if in a dream she murmured back.

'Mmm.'

'Is it okay if I kiss you?'

Of course it wasn't. The idea was ridiculous.

But this wasn't real. It was a dream. And in her dream it was okay to kiss a prince. In her dream she could put her arms around his neck, link her hands and tug him downward.

In her dreams she could open her lips and wait for his lips to touch them.

In her dream he kissed her.

He kissed her.

Of all the dumb, stupid, complicating things to do, this must surely be the stupidest.

But she lay in her too-big bed, tucked under the vast eiderdown, looking up at him with eyes that were dreamy and close to sleep.

But not quite. She was watching him. She was smiling at him. And then her hands came up to hold him… He'd have to be inhuman to resist.

She was beautiful.

She was so different from any other woman in his world.

Slight and sexy, her sun-bleached curls were so fine they looked as if they'd float.

Her eyes were gorgeous in her too-thin face. A man could drown in those eyes.

She had eighteen freckles. He'd counted them when? Maybe the first time he'd seen her. How many times had he recounted? And her lips were so kissable.

What made Elsa's lips more desirable than any other woman's?

Because they belonged to Elsa?

And because she was responding.

Amazingly, she was tugging him down to her and there was no way he could resist these lips. This mouth. This woman. He sank so he was sitting on the vast bed, and he gathered her into his arms— and he kissed her with all the tenderness in his heart.

She melted into him. What had provoked him to ask permission to kiss her? He didn't know. All he knew was that the desire had become overwhelming. And when his mouth met hers…

He'd kissed women in his time. None like this.

She was warm and tender, close to tears and close to laughter, exhausted by jet lag and by fear of losing Zoe, intimidated beyond belief by her surroundings…and yet she was courageous beyond belief and she was melting into his arms as if she belonged here. She was kissing as well as being kissed. Her lips were demanding, opening, aching for him, and taking him as well as giving herself.

She felt right.

She felt like…home. Home and heart.

There was a ridiculous thought. And, as the acknowledgement of how crazy it was hit home, other realities slammed in.

He did not need to be attracted to this woman. This woman meant family.

He did not do family.

All this flooded through his consciousness like a shock wave, breaking the passion of the kiss, causing his arms to stiffen a little, causing him to break away…

Or maybe it was Elsa who broke away. He hardly knew. All that was certain was that she was still in his arms but the kiss had ended and he felt a flood of regret so deep it threatened to overwhelm him.

And Elsa's eyes were clouding as well, distancing herself from him, her arms untwining themselves from around his neck and pushing against his chest. Pushing him away.

'What…what do you think you're doing?' she whispered and he knew her confusion was at least as great as his.

'What do we both think we're doing?' he said ruefully and looked down into her face and saw fear.

Fear? Where had that come from? Surely she couldn't be afraid of him.

He was a prince in a royal palace and she was…a royal nanny.

He stood up as if she burned, taking a swift step back from the bed. If she could think that…

But… 'You needn't worry,' she whispered. 'I'm not thinking you're about to rape and pillage. I have a scream that can be heard into the middle of next week.'

'Good for you,' he said unsteadily.

'Don't patronise me.'

'I never would.'

She closed her eyes. It was a defence, he knew, but he never doubted for a moment that she'd sleep.

He stood looking down at her for a long moment, trying to think of what to say. Trying to think of how he could take this from here.

'Go away,' she muttered again.

Go away? It was the only sensible thing to do.

Of course it was the sensible thing to do.

Go away, he repeated to himself and it was a direct order, but only he knew how much effort it cost him to turn on his heel and walk out of the door.

If Zoe hadn't been asleep in the next bed…

Maybe it was just as well she was.

CHAPTER NINE

ELSA woke and sunlight was streaming in though the massive French windows of their bedroom. The crystals from the chandelier above her head were sending glittering sparkles across the room.

Zoe was sitting on the end of her bed, fully dressed in another of the lovely outfits Stefanos had bought for her.

She was cuddling a kitten. A small grey kitten with a white nose, white paws and a tiny tip of white on the end of his tail.

'Go say hello to Elsa,' Zoe said, and put the kitten down and watched in satisfaction as the small creature walked along the coverlet, crouched down and put a paw out to tentatively touch Elsa's chin.

'What…where did he come from?' Elsa managed, doing a speedy visual check of the room in case Stefanos was lurking behind the curtains. Not that she was afraid of Stefanos. Not exactly.

But she wouldn't put it past the man to lurk.

'Stefanos gave him to me,' Zoe said with deep

satisfaction. 'He said I must be missing my cats at home and he's mine to keep. His name is Buster.'

'Yours to keep...' Elsa said cautiously. This needed thinking about.

There were things like quarantine laws. It was easy enough, she knew, to get animals from Australia to Europe, but taking them the other way...

She'd just woken up and here was another instance of Stefanos's arrogance. He'd have planned this before last night, she thought. Before she'd known he was leaving. He'd assumed he could talk her round.

He had talked her round.

But something wasn't making sense. Zoe was up and dressed. She'd gone to sleep—what—at five or six p.m.?

She checked her wristwatch.

Eleven.

She sat bolt upright and yelped. Buster bolted for the far end of the bed, where his new mistress scooped him up and held him close.

'You're scaring him,' she said, reproachful.

'I'm scaring myself. How can it be morning already?'

'It's been morning for ages,' Zoe said. 'I woke up and waited and waited but you kept sleeping. And then I opened the door and there was a really nice lady sitting in the corridor and she said her name was Christina and she'd been waiting for me to wake up. She helped me have a bath—it's a really big bath, Elsa, you should see it—and she helped me with my clothes and then she took me down for breakfast and Stefanos was there. So we had a really yummy breakfast—strawberries, Elsa—and then Stefanos took me to the stables and gave me Buster. And I brought him up to show you but you were *still* sleeping, and Stefanos said we had to let you sleep for as long as you needed to, so we've been really quiet only we've just been watching.'

This was just about the longest speech Zoe had ever made. She sat back on the bed and cuddled Buster the kitten, and Elsa smiled at her in pleasure and wonder. The as-yet-not-met Christina must be good to have Zoe smiling after a bath. To be re-membering it with pleasure.

But there was another part of her that was saying uh-oh.

Stefanos was truly seducing them, she thought, watching Zoe's face flush with excitement. He'd already seduced her little charge. Zoe might be hugging her kitten but every time she said Stefanos's name her voice took on the hush of hero worship.

He'd given her strawberries for breakfast. He'd given her a kitten.

Bribery, she thought.

And what was he trying on her?

Seduction of another kind.

But…she kind of liked it.

Matty, Matty, Matty, she thought fiercely but it

didn't work. Wherever Matty was, however much she'd loved him, he was no longer protection against Stefanos.

'Do you want to get up now?' Zoe said. 'Stefanos wants to take you out to lunch. He said you both need to talk privately about boring stuff, so he asked if I'd mind staying here with Christina and Buster. And Christina thought she might show me the beach. If that's okay with you,' she added, but her tone said Elsa's agreement was never in doubt.

It couldn't be in doubt. Elsa inspected the request from all angles. There was a lot to consider.

Like going out to lunch with Stefanos. He'd suggested it last night. She didn't remember agreeing.

'He said to tell you it's a picnic. He said to tell you shorts are man…mandatory and swords are optional. I don't know what that means.'

'It means Stefanos is being silly,' she said, a bit too abruptly, and Zoe looked at her in astonishment.

'Don't you like Stefanos?'

'No. Yes! I don't know.'

'Do you want Christina to run you a bath?' Zoe said seriously. 'The bath is lovely. It's really, really deep.'

'I believe I can run my own bath,' Elsa said. 'Though I should take a shower. I hope your cousin Stefanos is taking one too. Preferably cold.'

'Why would he want to do that?' Zoe asked, astonished.

'I have no idea,' she said and summoned a grin. 'I know I'm being stupid. But I think it might be me who needs to take a cold shower.'

She went to shower—but then she changed her mind. This wasn't a place for denying oneself.

Her hip would definitely like a bath.

Back home she survived on tank water. Showers had to be fast of necessity.

Here she had a feeling if she wanted to stay in the bath all day, playing with the amazing selection of bottles of luxury…stuff? no one would say a word of protest. So she did. If not for a day, for almost an hour.

She might have used one too many bottles of smelly stuff, she conceded as she soaked on. She was fighting to keep an airway free through bubbles.

Finally, reluctantly, her conscience got the better of her. She wrapped herself in a fabulously fleecy white towel, used several more towels getting rid of the bubbles and padded back to the bedroom.

She opened her wardrobe and gasped. Yesterday she'd accepted two dresses and a couple of shirts and sandals. Some time during the night her selection had been augmented by…well, by enough clothes to keep a girl happy for a year.

This was really intrusive. She should be angry. But… She tugged out a lovely jonquil blouse and a soft pair of linen shorts. She held them up in front of her and any attempt at anger disappeared.

'If you need to change direction, then you might as well enjoy it,' she told herself, and thought she was about to go on a picnic with Stefanos and she had new clothes and she felt terrific and maybe changing direction wasn't bad at all.

He was leaving.

She wouldn't think about that. She'd cope. She always had coped with what life threw at her. And if life was now throwing bubbles and new clothes at her…and lunches with princes…a girl might just manage to survive.

She came down the staircase looking wide-eyed with apprehension, self-conscious in her neat lemony blouse, white shorts and new sandals—and very, very cute. She'd twisted her curls up into a knot. He liked it, he thought. He liked it a lot.

He'd like it better if he could just untwist it…

'Have you been standing there for hours waiting for me?' she demanded as she saw him.

'Hours,' he agreed, and grinned.

Did she have any idea how cute she was? Her eyes were creased a tiny bit from a lifetime spent in the sun, but that was the only sign of wear. Her nose was spattered with her eighteen gorgeous freckles. If he didn't know for sure she must be close to thirty, he'd have pegged her as little more than a teenager.

And she smelled… She smelled…

'Wow,' he said as she came close, and she grinned.

'Lily of the Valley, Sandalwood and Fig and

Anise. There would have been lavender in there too, but I couldn't get the bottle open.'

'Thank God for that,' he said faintly and then counted freckles again. 'Um… Don't you believe in cosmetics?'

'Pardon?'

'Most of the women I know wear make-up,' he said lamely, kicking himself for letting his mouth engage before head.

'Well, good for them,' she said encouragingly. 'Do you, too?'

'Do I what?'

'I've spent so much time in doctors' waiting rooms over the last four years that I've read enough cosmetics advertisements to make me a world expert. There's men's cosmetics as well. I'm sure princes use them. Fake tan's the obvious one. Does your tan rub off on your towel?'

'No,' he said, appalled, and she arched her eyebrows in polite disbelief.

'You'll need sunscreen,' he said, sounding lame, and the look she gave him then was almost scornful.

'Go teach your grandmother to suck eggs. I'm Australian. I put sunscreen on before my knickers.'

And then she heard what she'd said—and blushed.

It was some blush. It started at her toes and worked its way up, a tide of pink. She could feel it, he thought, and her knowledge that it was happening made it worse.

He loved it.

'So…so this is royal beachwear,' she managed, moving on with an obvious struggle.

He glanced down at his casual chinos, his linen shirt and his boat shoes. 'What's wrong with this?'

'Looks great for being a prince and lazing on a sixty-foot yacht on the Mediterranean,' she said. 'It's not great for rock pools, though. And that's where I hoped we'd be going. Somewhere rock pooly?'

She was defending by attack, he thought. But she was still blushing.

Last night he'd kissed her. Right now, all he could think of was that kiss. And how he could repeat it.

He may well get his face slapped, he thought. She'd been way out of control last night, exhausted and vulnerable. Right now…her defences were up and, even if he wanted to—okay, he did want to—she'd be sensible enough for both of them.

'The kitchen staff have set us up with a picnic basket,' he told her. 'There's a great little beach I know a few minutes' drive from here. I believe it even has rock pools.'

'What time will we be back?'

'Does it matter?'

'Yes,' she said, definite. 'I want control here. I should even be deciding where we're going.'

'Isn't it usually the guy…?'

'Who gives orders,' she finished for him. 'I'm sure it is, and if it's a prince then it probably works double. But *Sleeping Beauty*'s for wimps. I fight my own battles—and I set up my own defences. Can I tell Zoe four o'clock?'

'If you like.'

'I do like,' she said. 'You're on probation. After that kiss last night… I don't know why you did it but it scared me. I'm happy to have a picnic but let's make it quite clear this relationship is purely business.'

'Of course,' he said courteously but he was aware of a stab of disappointment.

He didn't know what was happening—but what he did know was that he didn't want to be on a business footing with Elsa.

'So why are we going on a picnic?' she asked as they headed out along the coast road. 'Aren't there urgent princely things you should be doing?'

There were urgent princely things he should be doing, but for now… They were ensconced in a Gullwing Mercedes—a 1954 300 SL. A car with doors that opened like wings from the centre. A car that looked like a weird seagull—a crazy, wonderful car. It had belonged to the King, but it had obviously sat in mothballs for the last fifty years. Finding it had been a highlight of the past two dreary weeks.

And now…it felt great. The sun was shining, they were cruising smoothly around the curves of the scenic coast road, the Mercedes' motor was purring as if it was finally allowed to be doing what it should be doing—and for the moment that was how he felt too. As if he'd got it right.

Beside him… A beautiful woman with freckles.

'So we're going to the beach why?' she prodded again and he shook off his preoccupation with Elsa the woman and Gullwing the car and tried to think of what she'd asked.

'I want to be private.'

'Not so you can kiss me again?'

'No,' he said, startled, and then thought actually that wasn't such a bad idea.

'Just as well,' she said, but her voice was strained. He glanced across at her and thought she'd come close to admitting that last night's kiss had affected her as much as it had him.

'So you want to talk to me,' she ventured.

'We need to depend on each other,' he said, trying to sound suitably grave and princely. 'Maybe it's time we got to find out a bit more about each other.'

'Without kissing.'

'Without kissing.' Hard to sound grave and princely while saying that.

'So you can figure whether I can take on this island?'

'No.' He grew serious then. 'I'm not asking that of you. It's my responsibility. But I did think—even before last night—that you deserve an explanation of who I am—of what's behind the mess of this island. So that while I'm away you have a clear idea of the background.'

He was manoeuvring the car off the main road now, turning onto a dirt track through what was almost coastal jungle. Once upon a time this had been a magnificent garden but that was a long time ago now. He parked the car under the shade of a vast wisteria draping the canopy of a long-strangled tree. As the car's batwings pushed up, the wisteria's soft flowers sent a shower of petals over their heads.

It was right to come here, Stefanos thought. Matters of state had to wait a little. This felt…right.

Elsa was gazing around her with awe and the beginnings of delight. A tiny stone cottage was also covered with wisteria. It looked ramshackle, neglected and unused.

'This looks almost like home,' she breathed. 'Without the termites.'

'You have termites?'

'My house is wood veneer,' she said darkly. 'Veneer over termites. So what's this place?'

'My home,' he said, and she stared.

'Your home? But you live in Manhattan.'

'Now I do. This is where I was brought up.'

She stared around her, puzzled. 'But a prince wouldn't live here.'

'I wasn't raised as a prince. My father scratched a living fishing. He was killed in a boating accident when I was sixteen. Accidents to the island's original royals are littered throughout our history—

never anything that could definitely be attributed to the King, but terrifying, regardless. After Papa died my mother insisted I go abroad. She sold everything to get me into school in the States. Christos left soon after, for the same reasons, only Christos's mother had a little more money so she was able to go with him.'

'So you left the island when you were sixteen? Alone?'

'Yes,' he said flatly. 'I had no choice. Mama was terrified every time I set foot on the island so she insisted I didn't return. She died of a heart attack just before I qualified as a doctor, and it's to my eternal regret I wasn't here for her. I hope...I hope she was proud of my medicine. I've always hoped that what I do was worth her sacrifice.' He shrugged awkwardly. 'Who can tell, but there it is.'

'So...' She was eyeing him cautiously. Sympathetic but wary. 'Why are you telling me this?'

'I want to tell you why I left the island and I want to explain how important my medicine is to me.' He hesitated. 'That's all. Dumb, really. But after last night...it seemed important that you know.'

'You can practice medicine here,' she said, still cautious.

'I can,' he said. 'I will. The old doctor here is overjoyed that I'll be joining him.'

'But...not practising neurosurgery?'

'I'd need a population considerably bigger than

this island to justify equipment, technology, ancillary staff. So no.'

'You'll be a good family doctor,' she said softly and he smiled.

'I hope so. If I'm not I'm sure you'll tell me. Now… lunch?'

'Yes, please.'

She climbed out of the car and gazed around her. It was a picture-perfect setting, a tiny house nestled in a tranquil little cove. She thought of Stefanos growing up here, using this place as his own private paradise.

He had it all. His career, his title, his good looks, his life.

So why did she feel sorry for him? It wasn't what he'd intended, she thought, glancing at him as he retrieved a picnic basket from the car. But suddenly… Suddenly she thought she hadn't had it too hard at all.

She'd lost Matty but she'd loved him and he'd loved her. Her own parents had died young but her best friend, Amy, had always been close. And then there'd been Zoe.

How hard must it be to walk alone?

How would he react if she told him she felt sorry for him? she wondered, and then she glanced at him again, at the sheer good looks of the man, the way he smiled at her, the teasing laughter behind his eyes.

All this and sympathy too? This man was too dangerous for words!

He suspected it was a picnic to surpass any picnic she'd ever had. Lobster, crunchy bread rolls, butter curls in a Thermos to keep them cool, a salad of mango and avocado and prawns, lemon slivers, strawberries, tiny meringues, a bottle of sparkling white wine…

'This is enough for a small army,' she gasped as he spread a blanket over a sandy knoll overlooking the sea.

'I doubt the royal kitchen appreciates the concept of enough. Do you think you can make a dent in it?'

'I'll do my best,' she said and proceeded to do just that.

She concentrated on eating, as if it was really important. It probably was, he conceded. She'd missed last night's dinner and this morning's breakfast, but she probably didn't need to concentrate quite as hard as she was.

She seemed nervous, and that made two of them. Last night had left him floundering, and quite simply he didn't know how to go forward. This was a woman unlike any other. A widow. A woman with a past, but a woman who was facing the future with courage, with humour and with love.

Quite simply, she left him awed. And now… He felt as if he were treading on eggshells, and he was already sure he was squashing some.

In the end it was Elsa who broke a silence that was starting to seem strained. 'So tell me about the island,' she ventured. She was lying on the rug looking out to sea. She was on one side of the rug, he was on the other and the picnic gear was in between. It was starting to seem a really intrusive arrangement. But it'd be really unwise to change it, he thought. No matter how much he wanted to.

'I'll show you the island,' he told her. 'When you've finished lunch I'll give you a quick tour. It's far too big to see in a day—but I do want to give you some impression of what we're facing.'

'We?'

'Hey, you offered to help,' he said and then smiled at her look of panic. 'But no, Elsa, relax. I meant *we* as in all the islanders.'

She managed a smile in turn. 'Not *we* as in the royal *we*? Not *we* as in, "We are not amused"?'

'No.'

'So there's still nothing for me to do.'

'There is.' He hesitated, trying to figure a way to say what needed to be said. He couldn't. But still it needed to be said.

'There are three things,' he said at last. 'Some time before I go back to Manhattan—before the end of the month—I'd like to take you to Athens. I want you to buy a dress for the coronation.'

It was such an unexpected request that she looked blank. It was left to him to explain—why he'd woken at three this morning and thought he had to do this. He'd fit it into his schedule somehow.

'I want you to have a gown that'll do justice to your role on the island,' he said simply. 'I want you to stand by Zoe's side at the coronation and look royal yourself. You're her guardian. I'll stand by her side as Prince Regent but you're guardian to the Crown Princess. You should be received with equal honour.'

There was a lengthy silence at that. Then, 'A dress,' Elsa said cautiously. 'You mean…not a nice nannyish dress with a starched collar and Nanny embroidered on the breast.'

'I had in mind more a Princess Di dress. Or a Princess Grace dress. Something to make the islanders gasp.'

'Yeah, right,' she said dryly.

'Yeah, right? That would be two positives? That means you agree?'

'That means there's no way I agree.'

'I wish it,' he said.

'Oooh,' she said. 'Is this insubordination?'

'Elsa…'

'Sorry.' She managed a shaky smile. 'It's an amazing offer.' She shook her head, as if shaking off a dream. 'But it's nuts. For one thing, you have way too much to do to be taking me shopping. How could you possibly justify putting off your surgical lists for something so crazy? And second… The clothes you've already arranged for me are bad enough.'

She faltered then, her colour fading as she realised what she'd said. 'I'm sorry,' she said again. 'I mean…they're lovely and I'm very grateful, but…I don't know how to explain. This is me, Stefanos. I might be changing direction but I'm still me. I don't do Princess Di or Princess Grace. Please. Let me keep being Elsa.'

'You can be Elsa in a couture gown.'

'Yeah, right,' she said again. 'But no. So okay, that's sorted. What next? What else did you want to talk to me about?'

'It would give me pleasure to see…'

'No.' Flat. Definite. 'You're royalty and I'm not. Let's move on.'

Uh-oh. He wasn't having much luck here, and the next one was more important. Maybe he should have voiced it first. Except when he'd thought this all through in the middle of the night, the thought of taking her shopping had distracted him. It was still distracting him.

Maybe now, though, he needed to get serious.

'It's not just shopping,' he said softly. 'I'd like you to see an orthopaedic surgeon in Athens. I want you to get your hip repaired.'

'Now?' she said, astounded.

'Now,' he said. 'You're in pain.'

'I'm not.'

'You are. The pin in your hip hasn't held. You need a complete joint replacement.'

Uh-oh, he thought, watching her face. Maybe he'd gone about this the wrong way.

She stood, staggering a little as she put weight on both feet, but she righted herself fast. Her eyes were flashing fire. 'How do you know,' she said, carefully enunciating each syllable, 'that the pin hasn't held?'

'I rang Brisbane.'

'You rang Brisbane.' The fire in her eyes was suddenly looking downright explosive. 'You mean you rang my treating doctor?'

He was suddenly in really dangerous territory. This woman might change direction at will but she was never going to be compliant or boring or...or less than the Elsa he was starting to have enormous respect for.

Respect? Respect didn't begin to cover what he was feeling.

'You wouldn't tell me what's wrong with your hip,' he said, trying to sound reasonable, but he was wrong-footed and he knew it. He'd wanted to sound caring and concerned and...maybe even magnanimous. Instead, suddenly he was feeling unprofessional and interfering and about the size of a rather small bug.

'So you just asked,' she said, and her anger was starting to make her stutter. 'You thought you'd just ask my doctor what was wrong with me. How did you do that? Did you say, "Hi, Doctor, this is a casual acquaintance of one of your patients.

Could you tell me what's wrong with her hip?"
Or… "This is Prince Stefanos Leandros
Antoniadis from Khryseis and I order you to hand
over my servant's medical records." Or…' She
paused for breath. 'Or, "This is Doctor Antoniadis
and I have a woman here who can't even get up
the stairs without limping so can you send me her
records—as one professional to another".'

'It wasn't like that. Elsa, I owe you so much.'
He'd risen to face her. Now he tried to take her
hands, but she wrenched them away as if he were
poison ivy.

'You owe me so much that you can't even grant
me privacy?' she demanded.

'I have to know what's wrong with you. Zoe
depends on you. We need to get it fixed before I
leave.'

'Before you leave… It'll take weeks. Months,
even. A week in hospital and at least a month in rehabilitation. When you get back from Manhattan,
when things are settled, when Zoe's happy, then I'll
think about it. Maybe. Possibly. But it's my
business. Mine, Stefanos.'

'Zoe will cope…'

'Zoe will not cope. I will not ask it of her. Now,
what's the third thing?'

'I don't think it's wise…'

'I don't think any of this is wise,' she said. 'But
ask me anyway.'

'It can wait.'

'I might not be speaking to you tomorrow. Tell me now.'

'It was just…' Hell, he'd messed this. He'd messed this so badly. He wanted to back off but she was waiting, breathing too fast, and he knew that not to finish it would make it even worse than it already was. The third request…

'It's none of my business.'

'So tell me and let me decide.'

He hesitated. But he did need to get to know this woman. Even as her employer, he should know her.

'I'd like you to tell me about Matty.'

'Matty.'

'Your husband.'

'You think I don't know who Matty is?' She seemed almost speechless.

'Of course you do. I'm going about this the wrong way but yesterday… I didn't even know how he died. I should have asked you about him and I'm so sorry I didn't. Matty was your husband and you loved him. He must have been really special.'

Speechless didn't begin to describe how she was feeling. What was it with this man? He'd brought her here for a picnic. He'd fed her lobster and wine—and then he'd talked of buying her ball dresses and phoning her doctor and now he wanted to talk about her dead husband.

Her head was hurting. Her hip was hurting.

She wanted to hit him.

Count to ten, she told herself. Come on, Elsa, you can cope with this.

Personally, Stefanos had overstepped the mark. The knowledge that he'd phoned her doctor and found out information was huge—it threatened to overwhelm her. But that was personal.

Asking her about Matty was personal.

This man was her employer. Nothing else.

So why not tell him about Matty?

It was too confusing. How could she tell him about Matty without betraying Matty? Yet how could the act of telling him about Matty be a betrayal? Unless...unless...

It was far too hard.

'Take me back to the palace, Stefanos,' she said wearily. 'I'm sure you have work to do.'

'But...'

'I have work to do too,' she said. 'If I can't help rule your island, then I'll just have to go back to starfish.'

'There are some great starfish...'

'How many times do I have to tell you—I hate starfish,' she snapped bitterly, irrationally, and shoved the picnic basket aside and lifted the picnic rug and shook it. And if the sea breeze just happened to be blowing in the direction of Stefanos...well, the gods must have meant him to get a face full of sand.

But his phone was ringing and he was retrieving it from his pocket. He didn't seem to notice she was throwing sand at him like a two-year-old having a tantrum.

Frustrated, she folded the rug nicely and gathered the gear together and waited for him to finish.

'Of course I can do it. No, you know I promised. From now on, this is what I do.'

'What?' she said as he snapped his phone shut.

'A two-year-old with croup,' he said. 'In the village near here. Would you mind if we stopped on the way back? Though…it'd mean you miss out on your rock pools.'

Okay, enough of the tantrums. She pulled herself together.

'My rock pools can wait. Of course they can. Croup? Are you working already?'

'Our island doctor has more work than he knows what to do with. I've told him I'll start helping at once. We'll get more medical staff here before I leave, but for now… He's stuck in a clinic on the far side of the island and the child's mother has newborn twins at home and isn't well herself. It's probably just reassurance. If you can wait…'

'Of course I can wait,' she said remorsefully. 'I'm not really a brat.'

'I know you're not a brat. You're…' He hesitated. 'No. Let's just go.'

The drive to the village was done in silence. Stefanos was feeling just about as low as it was possible to feel.

This morning it had seemed a good idea—

sensible, even—to take Elsa to the beach. He'd decided to show her he wasn't born a prince—that they had more in common than she thought. He'd offer her a beautiful dress, a shopping trip to Athens. He'd have to push to find time to do it but she needed some sort of gesture to show how much he appreciated her care of Zoe. And…it hadn't escaped his mind that watching Elsa buy a beautiful gown might be a whole lot of fun for him too. Time out for both of them.

The other things had been added because they were also starting to feel urgent. Every time he noticed her limp now he felt bad. And he needed to find out about Matty.

Okay, the last wasn't essential, but it seemed essential to him—more and more. He didn't fully understand why—it was simply the way Elsa was making him feel.

So he'd set his plan in place and, in doing so, he'd alienated her just about as far as he possibly could.

Good one, he told himself, feeling something akin to pond scum. Only pond scum might have more self-respect.

He knew the place he was going. He drove slowly through the nearby village and hesitated. 'Do you want to come with me? Would you mind staying in the car?'

'I'm happier here,' she said, motioning to the village street. 'I'll poke around and talk to people.

That looks a nice peaceful little park. If you take hours, don't worry; I'll be under a tree asleep.'

Once again she'd taken his breath away. He thought of the women he'd taken out before—colleagues, New York singles, women who were smart and savvy and stood up for what they wanted.

So did Elsa, he thought, but only when it was needed. Now…she'd made no fuss, she'd released him from any pressure and he knew instinctively that if it took hours she wouldn't fuss at all.

'Thank you,' he said.

'Stefanos?'

'Yes?'

'I might need a bit of money,' she said diffidently. 'I don't have any local currency and it's been so long since lunch… I might need an ice cream.'

And how good was that, he thought as he drove away. Without any more pressure she'd ensured she had enough money for phone calls and help if he really didn't come back for her.

Only she needn't doubt that. He'd definitely come back for her.

The old doctor was right—the little boy was suffering mild croup, easily handled at home. What was needed was reassurance and his mother got that in spades, just by Stefanos's presence.

'Our Prince,' the young mother said, over and over. 'Here in my kitchen.'

He smiled and cradled one of her twins and

shared a cup of tea with her. As the two-year-old slid into sleep, the young father came home, reacted with awe that Stefanos himself had come, decided his wife obviously needed more support if the Prince himself suggested it and, before he knew it, the children's aunt was unpacking a suitcase in the spare room, fast enough to also join the Prince in yet another cup of tea.

There was nothing to this family medicine, Stefanos thought with wry humour, though his house calls might well need to get a bit faster.

Could he be content with family medicine?

It had its own skills. He was out of date. He'd have to brush up on his general medical knowledge, but he would. It could give him satisfaction. If only…if only the work he'd been doing wasn't so imperative.

Elsa wasn't in the park, but he found her easily. She was standing in front of the butcher's shop, happily licking an ice cream cone, reading the literature in the shop window. With her gorgeous bare legs, her flyaway curls, her ice cream, she stood out like a sunbeam.

'Hi,' she said as he climbed out of his car to join her. Maybe he should get himself a less conspicuous car, he thought ruefully. These wings were crazy. The locals were staring at the car and starting to cluster.

'How goes your patient?' she asked.

'All cured.'

'Really?'

'I'm a fabulous doctor,' he said modestly. 'I prescribed one aunt and lo, the problem's solved.'

'Do they sell aunts in bottles?'

'Sure they do. Can we go?'

'Um…maybe. But have you seen this?' she asked, licking her cone with care.

Woman-cum-eight-year-old. She made him feel…

See, that was the trouble. He didn't know how he felt. *This* was something new, something frightening, something he didn't know what to do with.

'Is this beach far?' she asked.

'What beach?'

'Read the poster,' she said with exaggerated constraint.

He read the poster. It was handwritten, big and to the point.

Turtles hatching. Kemp's Ridley. Lagoon Tempio. Urgent assistance needed—now! Helena.

'Do you know where Lagoon Tempio is?'

'I…yes.'

'Can we go?' she asked. She took a final lick of her cone, decided against more and tossed the remainder in a nearby bin.

'You want to go to this beach?' he said cautiously, aware that the eyes of many people were on him.

'Yes.' To his astonishment, she was suddenly deadly serious. She wiped her hands on her hips and faced him square on. 'Please.'

He stared at the sign. It made no sense. 'Who's Kent Ridley?'

'Kemp's Ridley. Lepidochelys kempii. It's the smallest and most endangered of the world's sea turtles. And they breed together. All the females nest on the one night so hatchings are huge. If it's really Kemp's Ridley… I can't imagine it is, but please, Stefanos, I need to go.'

The sudden passion in her voice stunned him. The vibrant excitement. 'Didn't you tell Zoe you'd be back by four?' he said, astounded at the change in her.

'I told you I told Zoe I'd be back by four,' she said impatiently. 'I was scared you meant a spot of seduction. Stefanos, we need to hurry.'

There was a snort from behind them. The on-lookers were close enough to hear. This was a busy shopping street in the middle of the afternoon and every person here knew who he was. Maybe they didn't know who Elsa was—but they were surely interested.

She'd just made them a whole lot more interested. So many people spoke English these days, he thought.

'Elsa…'

'Okay, I know you didn't want to seduce me,' she conceded. 'You just wanted to ask me a whole lot of questions I failed to answer. But I wasn't to know that. So I'm safe but the turtles aren't. If whoever wrote this poster...Helena?'

'Helena's my mother,' a voice volunteered, and Elsa turned with eagerness.

'Your mother?' She'd slipped easily and fluently into Greek. 'Your mother is saving turtles?'

'They started hatching this morning,' a middle-aged man wearing a butcher's apron told her. 'My mother's excited, too. These turtles used to come here in large numbers—the mass nesting is called an arribadas, my mother says—but forty years ago scientists and tourists were coming to see so the King bulldozed the beach. It broke my mother's heart. But this year... This year they've come back. She wants me to help but I have my shop. I put her sign up in my window but it was all I could do.'

'Does she have helpers?'

'I sent my boy down to help her,' the man told her. 'But there are so many birds... My mother can only save a few.'

'Stefanos,' Elsa said and fixed him with a look he was starting to recognise.

'Yes?'

'As far as I know, there's only one known nesting ground and that's in Mexico. To have a Kemp's Ridley hatching ground right here, where I can help... There'll be a million predators feasting on them. Stefanos, we need a royal decree or something.'

'A royal decree?' he said blankly,

'We have to save those turtles.' She took a deep breath. Steadied. 'Stefanos, if you help me save the turtles, then I'll…I'll…I'll even let you buy me a Princess Grace dress.'

There was a ripple of stunned laughter through the crowd. More and more people were clustered around them now, with more arriving every minute. This was their Prince Regent. And the Princess's nanny.

'So what do we need?' he said simply.

'People. Lots of people.'

She was speaking with passion, and she was waiting for him to act.

People.

'The school,' he said.

'What about the school?'

He turned to the crowd. 'Is the school bus available?'

'It'll be taking the schoolchildren home,' someone told him. 'It should be back here in a few minutes.'

'Who's in charge of it?'

'My son,' someone else called.

'Okay,' Stefanos said. 'I'm commandeering the school bus. Can you tell your son that I'll pay him double the going rate to transport any islander and any child to Lagoon Tempio? There's as much ice cream as they can eat for a week for anyone who comes there.' He grinned at the ice cream vendor. 'I'll reimburse you, and I'll also reimburse you for closing the shop now. That goes for anyone who wants to help.' He glanced at the butcher. 'Phillip, can we set up a barbecue on the beach? If we're going to get people there we need to feed them. Can you contact the baker and Marios at the café? I'll reimburse you for anything anyone eats or drinks tonight. Portia…' he turned to another woman standing by a battered Jeep '…can you take Dr Murdoch there now? I'll pay you for your trouble. By the way, everyone, this is Dr Murdoch—a marine biologist who also happens to be the best thing that's happened to this island for a long time. Elsa, I'll organise things here. I'll phone the palace and ask that Zoe be brought down to join us.'

He smiled at Elsa. She was all fire and pleading and pure adrenalin, wide-eyed with excitement. He put his finger to his lips and then he placed his finger on hers. 'Let's do this together,' he said and he smiled. 'If only because I really want to see you in that dress. And I'm so sorry I upset you. Okay, everybody, let's go save some turtles.'

CHAPTER TEN

IT TOOK half an hour of phone calls and arrangements before he got to the beach himself—and when he did the sight before him almost blew him away.

Lagoon Tempio was a sheltered cove about fifteen minutes from the village. He'd heard stories about turtles hatching here in the past, but he'd only ever known it as a clear felled, barren stretch of land.

But gradually the land had been recovering. The beach was surrounded by thick vegetation again, a horseshoe cove protected from winds and tides, a perfect place for turtles to come to breed.

Because of the clear felling, it had fallen off most of the islanders' radar. Until now.

He looked down to the beach and there were people. There were so many people his heart sank. Uh-oh. Had he been guilty of overkill?

If Elsa was on a turtle saving mission, maybe bringing this many people here was hardly helpful. Maybe he'd done more harm than good.

He'd encouraged every islander to come,

thinking some would take up his invitation. Obviously everyone who'd heard of it had come.

But, even as he thought he'd created chaos, he emerged from the narrow track that led onto the beach—a track that looked as if it had just been created this afternoon by people pushing through—and he saw that he hadn't. Or Elsa and Helena hadn't let it happen.

The adults were in lines, forming corridors from the top of the beach to the water. They were standing like sentinels. Or maybe windmills would be a better description.

For overhead were birds. Hundreds of birds, many of which he didn't recognize—ocean feeders, migratory birds, birds who knew that here was a feast for all.

At the top of the beach were sandy mounds, and from each mound came a stream of hatchings. Tiny turtles, two or three inches across, struggling out of their sandy nests and starting gamely towards the water.

With the mass of seabirds above they'd stand no chance. But now… There were corridors of people from each mound.

He recognised Helena—she was in her eighties, one of the island's stalwarts. She didn't sound eighty. She was booming orders in a voice to put a sea captain to shame—but beaming and beaming.

Alone, she couldn't have saved more than a tiny proportion of these hatchings. But now…

Where was Elsa? Where…?

Finally he saw her, up to her waist in water, in the midst of a group of children. Then, as Helena called out to her, she was out of the water, darting up the beach, pulling people from one corridor to start another.

Hatchlings were coming from beyond the trees at the end of the beach. More mounds? Within moments, Elsa had more adults formed into more corridors. There were islanders arriving all the time and she was using them all.

With her new corridors in place she was off again, back into the shallows, whooping and yelling at the birds above and encouraging the kids to do the same.

Amazingly, Zoe was in there with them, whooping as if she was just one of the kids. The little Crown Princess was yelling and laughing and gloriously happy.

And so was Elsa. She was soaking, dripping with water, laughing at something someone said and then flying up the beach to lift a tiny hatchling which had turned the wrong way, lifting it with a base of sand and then setting it safely near the water's edge so it could meet the waves the way it should.

'Are you here to help?' she called out to him, and he realised he'd been spotted.

'Where do you need me?'

'In deep water,' she called. 'If you don't mind getting wet. I can't get protection deep enough.

There are so many turtles. For all the mounds to hatch together…'

'We need boats,' he said and lifted his phone.

'Yes, but meanwhile…'

'Meanwhile I'll do it.' He snapped a command into the phone, tugged off his shirt and shoes and headed for the water.

What followed was an extraordinary evening and night, and at the end of it hundreds—maybe thousands—of baby turtles were flippering their way into the deep, thanks to the islanders' turtle saving skills.

Elsa had moved constantly, working her corridor teams in shifts, making sure no one stayed in the water for more than twenty minutes, a miniature drill sergeant in action. She and Helena had formed a formidable team. Helena was frail, though, and she was almost weeping with joy to have this help.

By dusk Elsa had sent Helena home. 'You've done so much,' she'd told the old lady, and Helena had gripped her hands and wept openly.

'This is thanks to you. To you and your prince. I thank you.'

Embarrassed, Elsa had headed back into the water and stayed there.

As the afternoon turned to evening, as Phillip's barbecue faded to cinders, as the mass of turtle hatchling eased and finally it could be left to a dozen people taking turns, he finally dragged her off the beach. He made her dry herself, almost force-fed her a steak and an apple and watched over her while she ate.

'I should be back helping,' she muttered, impatient.

'You can be. But not now. Not until you've had a break.'

Someone had brought a vast mound of pillows and blankets. Zoe and a couple of other island children were lying cocooned in blankets, watching the flames, giggling sleepily to each other. He recognised one of the children as Phillip's daughter—a child about the same age as Zoe. They were lying side by side. It seemed Zoe was making a friend. She looked…happy.

So was Elsa. She was flushed and triumphant and glowing.

The scene was weirdly domestic. Family? In his mind was suddenly a piercing stab of what he'd once had. A longing…

'Did you see them?' Elsa said softly, speaking almost to herself. 'We saved thousands. They face so many dangers in the water but now… Thanks to Helena, they have a chance.'

'Thanks to you.'

'Helena was on her own,' she whispered. 'She's been watching the mounds. If one mound had hatched she would have had a chance to save some. She hadn't realized, or she'd forgotten, that Kemp's Ridley turtles lay their eggs in synchronisation so they all hatch together. There'll be another hatching

in twenty-five days—that's set as well. I've worked
it out—that's before your coronation so you'll still
be here. Kemp's Ridleys lay in synchronisation
twenty-five days apart. Isn't that amazing? Aren't we
lucky?'

She looked up at him then, and she smiled. 'But
it's you,' she said on a note of awe. 'You're a prince.
The islanders moved today because you asked
them to. If they'd thought about it—if Helena had
had the time to individually plead—then maybe
she'd have got half a dozen people to help her, but
you said come and they came. They came because
of you and I can't thank you enough.'

'There's no need for you to thank me.' He was
watching her and he was feeling…weird. She was
slight and feisty and sand-coated and bedraggled.

He'd hurt her today. He hadn't meant to but he
was starting to realise how he'd got it so wrong.
And why. She was tugging his heart strings in a
way he didn't recognise. Or maybe…in a way he
did but until now he'd been afraid to face.

'Do you know how rare these turtles are?' she
said softly. 'I can't believe it. They're so endangered. To have a breeding site on this island… I so
wish Matt was here.'

That set him back a bit. Pushed what he was
thinking to the side.

It didn't completely obliterate it, though.

Even if she didn't tell him about Matty… He
could compete with someone who'd died four

years ago, he thought, and then realised where his thoughts were taking him and thought who cared; they were going there anyway.

'This is wonderful,' she said softly into the firelight. They had the fire almost to themselves now. The children were nestled in their beds on the far side of the barbecue but the rest of the islanders had either gone home to rest or were back on the beach on their shift. 'I can stay here,' she said. 'I can do so much work here.'

'What about your starfish?'

She looked startled. 'What about my starfish?'

'Have you really lost your enthusiasm?'

She looked at him as if he were a sandwich short of a picnic. 'Enthusiastic about starfish?'

'According to Zoe, it's what you love.'

'I love Zoe.'

'You don't love starfish?'

'As opposed to Kemp's Ridley…' Her voice was awed. 'Kemp's Ridley turtles on an island where my Zoe needs to be. This is awesome.'

'But your research…'

'I can work around that, too,' she said. 'I've already handed over my initial starfish research—there were any number of students just aching to take it on. But if I can do this and keep Zoe happy… There's so much. Helena says there are plans for development of this beach. Something about moving the town's refuse station close by. She's worried.'

'We can protect this beach.' He hesitated.

'And…I hope we can get tourism going. The island's desperate for income.'

'It's hardly touched,' she whispered, looking out through the trees where the lights of a score of torches showed the turtles still had safe passage. 'It could be the best eco resort. Matt and I had such plans…'

There it was again. Matt.

Maybe this was going to be harder than he'd thought.

Maybe what was going to be harder? He knew. More and more, he knew. He watched her face and he thought he wanted this woman so much…

It was too soon. Way too soon. Stupid, even?

'Okay, we have that settled,' she said, not noticing his silence. 'I'll stay here and love Zoe and save turtles. You'll have to figure your own direction, but I have mine.' She rose and wiped her hands on her shorts—a gesture he was starting to recognise. 'Let's move on. If you'll excuse me, I have work to do.'

'I'd be honoured to help,' he said. 'And…I will be here long-term. I will be part of this island. Elsa…' He reached out and took her hands.

She stood, looking down at them in the firelight. The linking of fingers.

'Not a good idea,' she whispered.

'We could work this together.'

'Sorry?'

'It's just a thought.'

'I'm quite happy for you to help with the turtles any time you want,' she said and he knew she was deliberately misunderstanding him. 'But for now... Your patients and the islanders need you, and the turtles need me. Zoe needs me. That's enough for one girl, wouldn't you say, Dr Antoniadis?'

'Steve.'

'Prince Stefanos,' she retorted, still watching their linked hands. 'My employer.'

'I'm not your employer.'

'Why, what else would you be?' she asked and she carefully untangled their fingers. Separated their hands. Took a step back and looked at him with eyes that were carefully watchful. 'I need to go back to the beach. Will you stay here and watch over Zoe?'

'I'll go back to the water. Your hip must be hurting.'

'My turtles are important,' she said. 'They're my job. Let me have that at least,' she retorted and, before he could respond—before he even knew how to respond—she turned and headed back down to the beach.

Leaving him to try and figure where to take things from here.

He stared down at the fire—and then focused. Heading for the flames were three tiny turtles.

How had they made their way back here? They'd built this fire purposely far back from the beach, out of sight of the mounds, so the light couldn't distract the hatchlings from their course. Maybe these three had been distracted by a torch, had deviated from their course and ended up here. He scooped them up before they could get close enough to the fire to harm themselves.

'Elsa?' he called into the night and in seconds she was back. Looking straight to Zoe.

But Zoe slept on. Elsa's face slackened in relief, and he thought how much had she worried? How many infections, dramas had she endured during these four years of getting Zoe back to health?

'It's just turtles,' he said swiftly and she looked down at his hand. He had one hand cupped over the other but tiny flippers were peeking through. They felt weird. A handful of flippering.

'They were just…here,' he said, in case she thought he'd collected them from the beach, done something less than noble, he didn't know what, but he was starting to suspect she thought he wasn't exactly hero material.

Hell, he wished he could be.

'What in the world are they doing here?' she asked, opening his hands and taking them into her smaller ones with all the tenderness in the world. 'Hey, guys, the ocean's this-a-way.'

'I guess, if they walked far enough, the ocean is that-a-way,' he said.

'Yeah, but changing direction's easier,' she whispered. 'I ought to know. Come on, guys, I'll take you where you need to go.'

'What do you mean, changing direction's easier?' he asked.

She looked up at him in the firelight and shook her head. 'If you need to explain it, you can't do it,' she said. 'You just…follow your heart. Thank you, Stefanos, for saving my turtles. And thank you for giving me another direction. I'll make the most of it.'

'Your hip…'

'Has nothing to do with direction,' she said. 'Some things still hurt, no matter what direction you're travelling.'

CHAPTER ELEVEN

FOR the next three weeks she immersed herself in this new life and felt herself…unfurl. That was what it felt like, she thought. As if she was coming to life again.

For the last four years she'd been constantly worried, constantly battling for their survival. Here, Zoe's welfare was more than taken care of. It was Stefanos who inspected the little girl's grafts, who worried about her medically, who even told her to back off a little, she was fussing. Others cooked for her, cleaned… Elsa was an honoured guest, free to do as she wished.

And she was free. Zoe had made a friend her own age, Pip, daughter of Phillip the butcher, granddaughter of Helena, defender of the turtles. She was friends with every one of the castle staff now, she was happy and confident and more than content that Elsa do her own thing.

So Elsa was making her own friends. The turtle breeding grounds was a project which had her waking up every morning aching to get up and go.

The only problem was…in the moments when she'd sit opposite Stefanos at meals and watch his face as the palace secretary outlined what needed to be done that day, she felt…bleak.

He was doing the right thing, the honourable thing. But, for Zoe and for her, this new life promised excitement and freedom. For Stefanos… There was still a conflict that seemed to be tearing him apart.

She didn't know what was happening with his practice in Manhattan. The plan was to leave straight after the coronation and do what needed to be done and return. She tried to talk to him about it, but it was as if after their appalling picnic he'd decided he'd overstepped the boundaries; his life was separate, only overlapping with her need to be with Zoe.

Oh, his bleakness wasn't overt. Outwardly he was cheerful and confident and purposeful. It was only that she seemed to know this man; she seemed to sense how he was feeling.

His trouble was the one cloud on her horizon. Actually, no, sometimes it felt more than that, like a fog she could see rolling in to envelop him, but she had no idea what to do about it. The fact that sometimes she had an urgent desire to take him and hold him and love him… Well, that was just plain dumb.

And…she suspected it might not even help.

Meanwhile, the coronation was almost on them, and she'd made her promise. It was time to buy a dress.

Zoe's coronation dress was exquisite, stitched by hand by a team of dressmakers who smiled all the time they worked, who said what a pleasure it was to be able to do this, what a joy. So, 'Can't I get my gown made here as well?' she asked Stefanos, knowing how stressed he was and how little he could spare the time to be away.

But, 'It's my one bright day,' he said. 'I think I've worked hard enough to earn one free day.'

He surely had. What he'd achieved in these last weeks was little short of miraculous.

The island council had been reformed. Three councillors had been invited to stay on; five had been 'retired'. Stefanos had done it with tact but with an underlying ruthlessness that left her awed.

The governance of the island was now under the control of the council, with ultimate responsibility resting with Stefanos. The royal coffers were being used with a speed that made her blink. Advertisements were already appearing on the mainland, for teachers, for engineers, builders, nurses…

Unemployment on the island had been running at over fifty per cent. No longer. There were schools and hospitals to build, roads to repair, water mains to install, electricity to supply to the inland area…

'Giorgos and his predecessors have held on to our taxes for hundreds of years,' Stefanos told her when she questioned how the island could possibly afford what he was starting. 'Alexandros on

Sappheiros has split the royal coffers into three so there's more than enough to get things moving.'

He worked with a ruthless efficiency that left her awed. But still there seemed to be this aching need...

She heard him, late at night. Her balcony overlooked the sea and so did his. She'd walk outside to watch the sea and she'd hear him talking, discussing operations, questioning results, talking to colleagues about cases they needed his help with.

He was needed elsewhere. He was working frantically so he could leave, fitting in as much medicine as he could as well. He'd found a locum to work here while he was away, to leave him free.

And he'd come back. He'd promised that he'd come back. But he didn't want to. She heard it in his voice—that coming back would tear him in two.

And she couldn't help.

But first...her dress.

'I've organised a seaplane to pick us up and take us to Athens for the day,' he'd told her at dinner the day before.

Three weeks ago Zoe would have reacted to this proposal in fear. Now she simply looked up and said, 'Am I coming too?'

She'd been tucking into her dinner as if she had hollow legs. The difference in her health since she had been here was astonishing.

'I've asked Pip's mama if you can stay with Pip for the day,' Stefanos said. 'Is that okay?'

'Ooh, yes,' Zoe said, pleased.

'And Pip's mama says it's okay if Pip comes back here and sleeps for the night. Christina will look after both of you and you'll have Buster to keep you company. I thought I might take Elsa shopping in Athens for something beautiful to wear to our coronation, and I thought I might take her to dinner afterwards.'

From the start he'd been able to wind his cousin round his little finger and this was no exception.

'Elsa would like that,' Zoe said seriously. 'She says she doesn't like dresses, but she does really. And boys are supposed to take girls out to dinner.'

'Hey,' Elsa said, startled. Half laughing, half horrified. 'I'm here. It's not like you're talking behind my back.' But she was ignored.

'It'll be a date,' Zoe said in satisfaction. 'You have to kiss her on the way home.'

'Who says?' Elsa demanded.

'Pip's big sister went out on a date last week. Pip says when the boy brought her home he kissed her goodnight.'

'Pip's sister is eighteen,' Elsa retorted. 'I'm too old for that nonsense.'

'You're not,' Zoe said seriously. 'You're still quite pretty.'

'Gee, thanks.' She hesitated. 'Stefanos, it really isn't necessary.'

'You promised,' Stefanos pointed out. 'A bargain's a bargain. I've saved your turtles. Twice.'

He had, too. The second hatching, twenty-five days after the first, had been orchestrated so that, as far as they knew, every single hatchling had made it to the water. It was a fraught journey the turtles had before them, the sea was full of dangers, but Stefanos had done everything humanly possible to see they had every chance.

And the price? A snip. An agreement to buy a dress.

'Athens or nothing,' he said. 'It has to be special.'

'All right,' she said grudgingly.

'You're very gracious,' Stefanos said and he was laughing at her. Laughing!

At least the bleakness had lifted for the moment.

That conversation had taken place last night. And now…

Stefanos was waiting in the hall. A car was waiting to take them down to the harbour, to the seaplane.

In minutes she'd be climbing aboard an aeroplane with a prince…

'Are you coming or do I have to come up and carry you down?' he called from below in the entrance hall.

She went.

There was something about this day that made her feel…dizzy. Sitting in the seaplane across from Stefanos, she stared straight ahead.

'Are you okay?' he asked gently, fifteen minutes

into the flight, and she nodded but couldn't even find the courage to answer.

This was one day out. A shopping expedition for a dress, followed by a meal.

Why did it feel so overwhelmingly scary?

Stefanos smiled at her and retired to a medical journal. Medicine, she thought. He missed it so much. Or…he missed his own niche of medicine.

He was already busy helping the elderly doctor on the island with his workload. It wasn't the medicine he was trained for, but that was the medicine he was reading up on.

Finally they were there. Athens! It was all she could do not to sit with her nose squashed against the car window.

Athens. The world.

'Not a seasoned traveller?' Stefanos teased, and she flushed.

'Sure I am. I just like looking.' And then, as they swung off the road into a huge car park, she frowned. 'Where are we?'

'It's a hospital,' he said. 'I've arranged an appointment for your hip.'

'Stefanos…' She was almost rigid with shock. 'You've interfered enough.'

'No,' he said. 'Not enough. I know I handled this badly. I know I should have gained your permission before I accessed your records, but what's done is done. I'm sorry but if I'd told you about this appointment I was afraid you'd refuse to come.'

'You'd be right.'

'Then I'm justified.' He hesitated, but his look was stern. 'Elsa, this is only a doctor's appointment. I'm not chaining you to a bed and operating regardless.' He gave a rueful smile. 'Actually, that might be beyond even my level of intrusion. But I am one of only two doctors on Khryseis and before I go back to New York I need to know you're not doing permanent damage. This man's an orthopaedic surgeon. The best in Athens. You need to see him.'

'You still should have asked me.'

'I'm asking you now. This is my honour, Elsa, and it's also sense,' he said, stern again. 'I know I upset you—obtaining your medical history without permission—but it doesn't stop the need. I need you to do this—for you. It would be childish for you to refuse—no?'

'No.'

'Elsa… You *will* do this.'

She had no choice. He was right—she was being childish but it didn't make it any easier to swallow her temper. She followed him into the hospital, fuming.

He was recognised. Doors opened for him. The receptionist of this best-in-Athens-orthopaedic-surgeon practically genuflected.

'You can go right in, Your Highness. The doctor's expecting you.'

But, to her surprise, Stefanos didn't go in. He simply smiled at her, gave her a gentle push towards the door and settled his long frame into a waiting room chair as if he had all the time in the world.

She stared down at him, stunned.

'What?' he said, looking up. And then, 'He won't bite, Elsa. I thought, as he might want to examine you, I should stay out here. But if you're scared…'

The door was opening behind her. She wheeled round and an elderly doctor was smiling a greeting.

'Dr Murdoch. Come on in.' And then he smiled across at Stefanos. 'Steve. Welcome home. When are you coming home for good, my boy?'

'By Christmas.'

'But not to work in neurosurgery?' the older man said, looking suddenly concerned. 'I've heard you'll let that go. I had this young man working with me for a while as he was training and I was in the States,' he told Elsa. 'It was an honour and a pleasure to work with one so talented.' He turned back to Stefanos. 'But now…to abandon your neurosurgery… There must be some way you can fit that into your new life.'

'There's not,' Stefanos said. 'The island's far too small.'

'Could you work in Athens? There's a need here.'

'No,' Stefanos said abruptly. 'Please…leave it. It's Elsa we're concerned about here. Not me.'

'But what a waste,' he said softly. And then he turned back to Elsa. 'Well, then. What has to be has to be. Meanwhile, come with me, young lady, and let's see what needs to be done about that hip.'

* * *

He was, as Stefanos had promised, very good.

He examined her with care and with skill. He already had the X-rays from Brisbane—a fact that made Elsa gasp again with indignation but that shouldn't reflect on this kindly doctor. She let him take his time, carefully assess and then tell her what she wanted to hear.

'You're doing no real harm to the hip itself, but it does need to be repaired and it will give you pain until that happens.'

'So I can wait,' she said thankfully. 'Can you tell that to Stefanos?'

'You want me to call him in?'

'Yes, please,' she said, tugging on her shoes. 'Tell him and let me get on with my life.'

So Stefanos came in. He listened while the doctor outlined exactly what he thought.

'But you know this,' the doctor told Stefanos. 'You've seen the scans.'

'I'm too close to treat Elsa myself.'

'You are,' the doctor said gently. 'And you'd need first rate surgical facilities on that island of yours to be able to do it. You know, that's what you really need. A state-of-the-art suite of operating theatres. Cutting-edge techniques. All the things I hear you're doing in New York.'

'And an island like Khryseis would support that how?'

'I have no idea,' the doctor said sadly, and he turned to Elsa and smiled. 'This man tries to save the world and I wish I could help him. But of course he's right. We can only do what we can do. So let's do that, young lady. We need to get your surgery scheduled. When?'

'But you just said…'

'I said the operation's not urgent. That means it doesn't have to be done as soon as possible. The only way to keep you pain-free is to give you so much opiate as to risk addiction, and I suspect you made the decision some time ago to live with the pain. But, because it's hurting, you're not weight-bearing evenly. That will cause long-term back problems. There's tenderness already in the lower spine and I'm concerned there'll be too much pressure on the muscles around the lower verte-brae. So when can we schedule surgery?'

'We can't,' Elsa gasped.

'I can be back here in seven weeks,' Stefanos said, ignoring her. 'Can we schedule it just after Christmas?'

They left the hospital grounds without speaking. Elsa should have been furious. She tried to dredge up fury all the way to the shops. But instead she simply felt bleak. The cab stopped, Stefanos paid, she got out and looked around her—and she decided there and then to cheer up.

She was here shopping. For a gorgeous dress. This was obviously where the wealthy women of Athens shopped.

Indignation—and bleakness on Stefanos's behalf—would have to wait until later.

'What are we waiting for?' she said. 'Do you have the royal credit card?'

'I believe I do.'

'Then let's not let the little pet get cold,' she said and dived happily into the first shop.

It was as if her visit to the doctor had unleashed something in her that had needed to be unleashed for a long time.

Her exultation—dizzy bordering on hysteria— lasted until she was standing in front of a mass of mirrors wearing a gown that fitted her like a second skin, crimson silk, shimmering and lustrous, flecked with strands of glittering silver. The gown had shoe- string straps, the bodice clinging and curving around her lovely body, then falling in generous folds to sweep the floor. She gazed into the mirror in incre- dulity. She met Stefanos's gaze in the mirror and stared at him as if he were part of the same fairy tale.

Then she seemed to come to earth with a crash. She dragged her gaze from his—and lifted the price tag.

And yelped.

'We'll take it,' Stefanos said, and grinned as her mouth dropped open. He'd obviously put aside his bleakness as well. 'One gown down, half a dozen to go—dear,' he said.

'D…dear?' she spluttered.

'Sorry…' he said, and smiled.

The salesgirl was looking on with incredulous delight. 'You want more?'

'Maybe the others don't need to be quite so formal,' Stefanos decreed. 'But we do want at least three more. And what about some sexy lingerie to go with them?'

'Sexy lingerie!'

'It's in the royal nanny dress code,' he said, straight-faced. 'Don't tell me you haven't read it?'

'But I don't need…'

'You do need.'

'What about your Third World kids?' she demanded. 'Don't you need all your money for them?'

'They're not watching,' he said. 'Quick, buy.'

'Stefanos…'

'Tell you what,' he said with magnanimity. 'For every dollar you spend on your wardrobe I'll donate ten more to my Third World medical network. I can't say fairer than that, now can I? So if you refuse to spend, you're doing an orphan out of medical treatment.'

'Stef…'

'You want to start calling me Steve?' he asked, and suddenly his tone was gentle.

'No,' she said and then, more strongly, 'no. You're Stefanos. Prince Stefanos. And I'm the nanny. But I'm a nanny who won't say no to a dress or two.' Then she blushed. 'Or…or even lingerie. But, Stefanos…'

'Yes?'

'You know when you stayed outside while I saw the doctor?'

'Yes.'

'Step outside, Your Highness,' she said, smiling sweetly. 'In the interest of Third World aid, I need to discuss knickers.'

He'd booked them into a hotel. At first she was incredulous. The taxi dropped them outside the most lavish hotel she could imagine. She stared out at the ancient Grecian columns—how had they incorporated them into a modern hotel?—and then she gazed back at Stefanos.

For a moment she said nothing. And then… 'Ten times the cost to a Third World orphan?'

'You have my word,' he said solemnly. 'My orders are for you to have fun tonight. That's all I ask.'

'I'll wear my second best frock,' she said. And then, more cautiously still, 'I didn't think we were staying the night. I don't have a toothbrush.'

'I believe these things are obtainable for a small fee,' he said. 'Multiplied by ten, of course. And you did buy enough lingerie to keep you respectable— or maybe not respectable—for a month.'

She blushed. 'How did you know I bought…?' He'd been out of the shop. 'How…?'

'You gave me the receipt,' he told her. 'So I could multiply by ten.'

'Right,' she said and blushed some more. Then,

'Okay. So I'll buy a toothbrush.' Then she had another thought and her blush moved from pink to crimson. But somehow she made herself sound stern. 'But it's definitely separate rooms.'

'Separate suites,' he corrected her.

'Oh, of course,' she said and suddenly she giggled. 'This is ridiculous.'

'I have a feeling there hasn't been enough ridiculous in your life.'

'I don't need it.'

'You know, I'm very sure you do,' he said gently. 'And maybe the same goes for me. Maybe we both need a good dose of crazy.'

They ate by candlelight in the hotel restaurant, with a view over all of Athens. A view to die for. Food to die for.

A man to die for.

The set-up was so corny she half expected an orchestra to materialise at any minute and strike up with *Love Me Tender* or something equally soppy. And, just as she thought it, a pianist slipped behind a grand piano and started playing. Not *Love Me Tender*—but close. She was wearing her second best dress, which was a fantasy of Audrey Hepburn proportions. Pale lemon silk with tiny white polka dots. Tiny waist, huge skirt. Cleavage.

She'd twisted her hair into a casual knot, trying for Audrey's look. She thought she looked a bit scruffy for the Audrey look, but Stefanos's long, lingering gaze when he'd come to her room to accompany her downstairs said she didn't look scruffy at all.

She was still nervous. Stupidly nervous.

'Should we be talking politics?' she asked as the waiter brought them plate after plate of food she'd never tasted before but would taste forever in her dreams.

'No politics.'

'About Zoe, then.'

'No children.'

'About your medicine? My turtles?'

'Nothing,' he said softly. 'Just you.'

'Well, there's a boring night,' she said, feeling breathless. 'There's nothing to talk about there.'

'We could dance,' he suggested as the pianist started a soft waltz in the background.

'Right. And my hip?'

'Let me dance for you,' he said. He stood up and held her hands and tugged her to her feet.

'I can't.'

'You can. Take your shoes off and put your feet on mine.'

'That's ridiculous.'

'Not ridiculous at all. Trust me, Elsa. Dance with me.'

Then he took her into his arms—and waltzed.

He moved with the effortless grace of a panther, a dancer who knew every move and who knew how to take her with him.

She hadn't danced since she'd injured her hip. She'd hardly danced before then, but it didn't matter.

Her feet were on his. He was holding her weight so her hip didn't hurt, so she could move with him, as one with him, in this slow and lovely dance, as if she weighed nothing.

How had she got herself here? She'd agreed to buy one dress and now…she was being seduced.

Seduced?

No. This was payola for what she'd agreed to do. He was giving her a very nice time.

And if it was seduction… She didn't care, she thought suddenly. What did it matter if her employer seduced her? Employers did these things. Princes did these things.

Um…no. Elsa Murdoch didn't do these things.

'Did you dance with your husband?' he murmured into her ear…and the fairy tale stopped, right then, right there.

'Pardon?' She froze in his arms. Her feet slipped off his, and she could have cried. She was on solid earth again and the lovely dance had ended.

'I didn't mean…'

'To remind me of Matty? I'm very sure you did.'

But he was looking confused. As if he'd been in a kind of dream as well.

'I did dance with Matty,' she said, jutting her chin. 'We danced very well.'

'You loved Matty?'

'With all my heart.'

'And you grieve for him still?'

'I…yes.' What was a girl to say to that, after all? But something went out as she said it—a light, an intensity in Stefanos's gaze.

And its going meant grief. How could she say she'd loved her husband but she was ready to move on?

How could she think it?

'You'll dance again when your hip's healed,' he was saying softly.

'I won't,' she muttered, coming back to earth with a crash. 'I shouldn't.'

'Elsa…'

'I don't want to think about Matty,' she whispered. 'Not here. Not with you.'

They were alone on the dance floor. There were maybe ten or so tables occupied, but the lights were low, the other two couples who'd danced with them to begin with had left, and there was now just the two of them. The pianist had shifted from waltz music to something soft and dreamlike and wonderful.

There was nothing between them. Only a whisper of breath. Only a whisper of fear.

'Elsa…' he murmured, and her name was a question. His hands slipped from the lovely waltz hold so they were in the small of her back.

'Elsa,' he said for the third time, and he bent his head…and he kissed her.

It was a long, lingering kiss, deep and wonderful, hot and warm and strong, demanding, caressing, questioning.

It was a kiss like she'd never been kissed before.

She was standing in the middle of a dance floor, her arms around his neck and she was being kissed as she'd always dreamed she could be kissed.

She was being kissed as she'd wanted to be kissed all her life.

Matty…

Stefanos himself had pulled her husband into the equation. He was with her still—maybe he always would be. His kisses had been just as wonderful, but different—so different, another dream, another life. He wasn't stopping her kissing right back.

This was the most wonderful dream. Her hip didn't hurt, her worries about Zoe were ended, she wasn't responsible for anything, for anything, for anything…

He was lifting her so he could deepen the kiss, cradling her, loving her and she thought her heart might well burst, as she realised she was so in love with him.

In love with him.

She, Elsa, was in love with a prince. Wasn't Cinderella only in story books?

And, almost as soon as the thought was with her, the spell was broken. People were…clapping?

She twisted, confused, within the circle of Stefanos's arms and found the tables of diners were all watching them, smiling, applauding.

'It's Prince Stefanos from Khryseis,' someone called out in laughing good humour. 'With the Princess's nanny.'

Oh, right. She pulled back as if she'd been burned and Stefanos let her go to arm's reach. But he was still smiling. Smiling and smiling.

'Not the nanny,' he murmured. 'Elsa.'

'In your dreams,' she muttered and it was so close to what was real that she almost gasped. Not in his dreams. In *her* dreams.

'Stefanos…'

'I'm falling in love with you,' he said, simply and strongly and she gasped again.

'You can't. I'm just…'

'You're just Elsa. You're the most beautiful woman I've ever met.'

'You're kidding me, right?' she demanded. 'I have freckles.'

'Eighteen.'

'Eighteen?'

'Eighteen freckles. I love every one of them. Elsa, I've been trying to figure where we can take this.'

'Where we…'

'If we were to marry,' he said and her world stilled again.

'M…marry?'

'I didn't come prepared,' he said ruefully. 'I should be going down on one knee right now, with a diamond the size of a house in my pocket. But

I've only just thought of it. Alexandros said I needed a wife, and he's right.'

'You've had too much champagne.'

'No,' he said and then, more strongly, 'no! I know what I want, Elsa, and I want you.'

'Because Alexandros said.'

'I don't think I did that very well,' he said ruefully. 'Believe it or not, it's far less about Alexandros than about eighteen freckles.'

'Eighteen freckles are hardly a basis for marriage.'

'I believe you're wrong,' he said gravely. 'But we could work on other attractions. Do you possibly think you could love me? I know you loved Matty. I know you still love Matty. I'll always honour that, but…is it possible that I could…grow on you?'

'Like a wart?' she said cautiously.

'Something like that,' he agreed. He smiled and, chuckling, pulled her close.

But… But. This might be the magic she'd longed for but there were buts surfacing in all directions.

'Stefanos, no.' She tugged away again, trouble surfacing in all directions. They were being watched, she knew, but the piano was still playing softly in the background and maybe they were more private here than if they went back to their table.

'Will you be my wife?' he asked, solidly and strongly, and there it was, a proposal to take her breath away.

The *but* was still there. Forcing her hand.

'No,' she said.

'No?'

'I'm not changing direction again.' She stood, mute and troubled. 'Not…not while you don't know where you're going.'

'I do know where I'm going.'

'You don't.' She was frantically trying to think this through. To be sensible when she wanted to be swept away in fantasy. Only fantasy was for fairy tales and this was real. 'Stefanos, the problem is…you've committed yourself to staying on the island and you're making the best of it. But that's not what I want. You making the best of it.'

'It's not such a bad deal,' he said, puzzled. 'If it includes you.'

'I'm not the consolation prize.'

'I would never suggest…'

'No, you wouldn't,' she whispered. 'Of course not. You're too noble and too wonderful and too…' She hesitated. 'Too just plain fabulous. The problem is, Stefanos, that even though I'm falling in love with you—and I am—I can't see you tied even more to the island. Tell me…you're thinking… or you have been thinking…that maybe you can take some slabs of time away. Maybe you can do some teaching. Not when you're needed on the island, of course, but if we can get more doctors, if the politics are settled… You're thinking that, aren't you?'

'Yes, but…'

'But I don't think that'll make you happy,' she said. 'I think that's going to tear you further apart. For you'll lose your skills. You'll see others go where you want to go.' She hesitated. 'Stefanos, when Matty died and I couldn't do what we were doing with coral any more… I know it sounds simplistic and silly in the face of what you're doing but it was important to me and I couldn't just do a little bit. It would have eaten at me. I had to move on.'

'I think,' he said steadily, 'that in marrying you I would be moving on.'

'I won't be the cause,' she said. 'In no way.' She bit her lip. 'Stefanos, do what you have to do and then decide you want to marry me. If you were to do that…'

'I am already.'

'You're not.' She shook her head. 'I can't make you see. I don't even know whether I understand it myself, but in the bottom of my heart it does make sense—that I say no. That I say wait. That I say loving is…for when it's right.' She hesitated. 'Matty and I…'

'Matty?'

'You asked me about Matty,' she said. 'Maybe I do need to tell you. Just as we finished university Matty inherited his father's company. His mother sobbed and said he had to come home and run it. So he did—his entire extended family seemed to depend on him and it seemed the only right thing to do. He loved me so I went with him, but it almost destroyed us. For two years I worked on my research while Matty self-destructed. And in the end he handed the entire company over to his cousins. It left us broke. His family thought he was mad. But, you know what, Stefanos, the one thing I do know… When he was killed I thought of those wasted two years.'

'You're saying…'

'I'm saying I don't want the heartache of those two years again, Stefanos. Oh, I want you. I don't deny I want you—my love for Matty hasn't stopped me feeling more for you than I ever thought I could again. But I will follow my own drum and I won't watch you self-destruct while you follow someone else's.'

'So what do you propose I do?' he said bleakly.

'Work it out,' she said steadily. 'For yourself and for me. Please, Stefanos.'

He didn't understand. He was seeing her distress, but not seeing it either, she thought. Maybe he was only seeing what he wanted to see. The Cinderella bit. The fantasy.

Whereas what she wanted was more. Love at first sight? No. Love for ever.

All at once she felt tired. Weary of the pain in her hip, weary of worry, weary of the pain inside her heart.

It'd be so good to do just what she wanted, she

thought. To have the world magically transformed so she could sink into her prince's kisses and let herself have a happy ever after.

Stefanos.

He was fighting to change the world, she thought. He was fighting himself.

She didn't have the courage to stand by his side as he did it.

It was too much. Too soon. Too scary. It was yet another direction, but this one was so big, so terrifying that if she got it wrong it could destroy them all. And if she didn't get it right…if she wasn't sure, if she jumped with her heart before her head said it could follow…where would that leave them all?

Oh, but she wanted to.

She mustn't.

'I need to go to bed,' she whispered. 'You've paid me the most extraordinary compliment…'

'A compliment! It's so much more…'

'It is, isn't it?' she whispered bleakly, and she stood on tiptoe and kissed him lightly on the lips. A feather touch. A kiss he didn't understand. 'I know you don't follow what I'm saying—I hardly understand what I'm saying myself. I only know that…I don't know if I can face your demons with you, Stefanos. Maybe I need more courage than I have. Goodnight and thank you. And I love you.'

And, before he could respond, she'd turned and

fled from the dance floor. She didn't stop until she reached her suite, until she was inside with the door locked behind her.

CHAPTER TWELVE

ON A sun-kissed afternoon in early November the Crowns of Khryseis were bestowed on Zoe and on Stefanos.

Crown Princess Zoe of Khryseis was seated on a throne too large for her. Her dress was pure fantasy. She looked adorable. She looked very, very scared.

Only the fact that her cousin was standing right beside her gave her the courage to stay. Stefanos, Prince Regent of Khryseis, the Isle of Gold, had vowed to defend his little cousin, care for her and cherish her and take care of her interests until she reached twenty-five years of age.

Stefanos looked magnificent. Zoe looked exquisite.

Elsa was looking not too bad herself, she conceded, thinking what a waste, why spend all this money on her fabulous gown if her nose was about to turn red? But she was fighting tears, and Crown Princess Lily of Sappheiros glanced sideways at her and smiled and passed over a handkerchief.

'This is dumb,' Elsa whispered, embarrassed. 'I shouldn't be here in the front row with you. I'm not even royalty.'

'Hey, I've only been royalty for a couple of months now,' Lily said. 'And, from what I've heard, you're even closer to Zoe than Stefanos.'

Elsa sniffed. The Archbishop was watching Stefanos sign before his little cousin now. It looked so official. It looked like another world.

She could have been up there. Beaming and waving and being royal too. As Stefanos's wife.

Her reasons for refusing him were sounding weaker and weaker. It was just as well he hadn't proposed again, she thought. Any pressure and she might well cave right in.

'He's gorgeous,' Lily whispered thoughtfully, watching Elsa's face.

'He is.' She looked dubiously at the handkerchief. 'I need to blow my nose.'

'Go right ahead,' Lily said grandly. 'I came supplied with hankies in bulk. They're monogrammed with the royal crest.'

Elsa nearly dropped it. Lily giggled and suddenly Elsa was smiling again, albeit through tears. What was royalty but individuals doing the best they could? The vows that Zoe and Stefanos had just made... They weren't taking them away from her. Or no further than they already were. And she was right not to join them. Her doubts still stood.

The signing was done. The orchestra was starting its triumphant chorus, a blaze of sound proclaiming that Khryseis finally had its own royal family.

Stefanos helped Zoe to her feet. Zoe stood, looking out nervously at the vast audience in front of her.

Stefanos held her hand, stooped and whispered to her.

Zoe stared up at him, then out at the people in front of her. And then, at a signal from Stefanos, the music suddenly died.

Zoe took a deep breath. She turned back to Stefanos, as if for approval of something prearranged, and she looked straight at Elsa.

'I need my Elsa,' she said in a high, clear voice. 'Elsa, can you come up and walk beside me?'

'Quick, blow,' Lily muttered urgently. 'And your nose isn't even red. You're beautiful.'

He walked out of the cathedral behind them. Zoe and Elsa. His little cousin and her beautiful guardian.

Elsa's eyes were looking distinctly watery. He wasn't surprised. His eyes were feeling distinctly watery too.

Elsa should be walking by his side. It felt wrong.

He'd rushed it. He'd pushed her too hard, too fast, ripping her out of her comfort zone, asking the world of her and then asking her to extend that world.

Zoe was happy again. She'd been coached with

care and kindness, and she knew exactly what was expected of her today. Elsa had raised her beautifully, he thought. When she'd spoken her responses it had been with the gravity of one twice her age. So much of that was down to Elsa's care, her constant assurances that Zoe was beautiful, that the scars and the pain were only skin deep and what was underneath was beauty and joy.

If he'd got it right he could have been walking down the aisle with Elsa, with Zoe between them.

He'd messed it up—badly.

But he had time, he thought. He could try again.

Only Elsa was right. His doubts about what he was doing were still there.

Khryseis needed him.

His work in Manhattan was still calling.

Elsa had the courage to change direction and move steadily forward. He kept glancing back.

Elsa knew him better than he knew himself. And, knowing him, she had the sense not to want to be his wife.

'Isn't Stefanos beautiful?' Zoe was so close to sleep she could barely form words, but she'd stayed until the last speech had been made, she'd sat attentive and courteous, and Elsa was so proud of her she was close to bursting. But now she'd retired to Elsa's knee for a hug, the hug had turned into a cradling cuddle and it was clear the little girl just wanted to drift off to sleep.

They were watching Stefanos say farewell to the dignitaries. Stefanos as they'd first seen him, only grander.

'I don't have to be scared of being a princess when he's here,' Zoe whispered. 'I wish he wasn't going away.'

'Me, too,' Elsa whispered. For what the heck; there was no point in lying, not even to herself.

'Do you think he'll come and live with you and me for ever and ever?'

'He's said he will. Maybe not with us but near us.'

'That's good,' Zoe whispered, her whisper fading so that Elsa could hardly hear. 'But I'll miss him and miss him. And so will Buster.'

'And so will I,' Elsa told her and watched her close her eyes and drift off into sleep. 'I think I might miss him so much I might have to think about changing direction all over again.'

Only of course there was no time for direction changing. No opportunity. No chance.

A call came through that night. Stefanos needed to be in New York within twenty-four hours.

There were so many things to do, documents to sign, authority to delegate… He moved as fast as he could. Elsa woke at dawn to a light tap on her door and it was Stefanos, come to say goodbye.

She stood at her bedroom door in her lovely new lingerie, feeling shocked, bereft and stupidly frightened.

'You will come back?' she murmured. She must have sounded needy for Stefanos took her hands in his and tugged her into his arms before she could resist.

'Of course I'll be back. I'll be here by Christmas.'

He was as she loved him most, in his casual jeans, an old leather jacket slung over his shoulder, unshaven, a man in a hurry. 'Hell, Elsa, I wish I didn't have to go. But these kids… I can't knock them back.'

'I so wish you could work from here.'

'And we both know that I can't.'

'Of course.' The population of Khryseis could never support the medical facilities this man needed.

'You'll keep Zoe safe. And our turtles. And Buster.'

'I promise.'

'Christmas in Australia's hot, isn't it?' he said. 'You think we can do an Australian Christmas dinner?'

'Amy's Christmas Cake,' she said before she thought about it.

'Amy's cake?'

This was crazy. Standing in her bare feet, talking to a man she loved with all her heart about her best friend's cake.

'It's a berry ice cream cake,' she said. 'Amy was so proud of it—it was a tradition started by the women in her family who couldn't bear a hot Christmas pudding. She'd start a month before Christmas, finding berries, then building layer upon layer of berry ice cream, each layer a different flavour. By Christmas we might have ten layers. Then we'd turn it out and decorate it with more berries. She'd make a berry coulis to pour over. It was so big sometimes it'd last until well into January.'

'So you make it every year?'

'Not…' She hesitated. 'Not since Amy died. Berries are expensive.'

'I see,' he said gravely and took her hands in his. 'Then here's my royal decree. You use the royal card again to buy as many berries as you need—import them, grow them—whatever you have to do to get them, you get them, and make us Amy's Christmas Cake. And we'll eat it well into January.' He was smiling into her eyes and his smile might as well be a kiss. And…she felt like crying.

'Is there anything you want me to bring from New York?' he said, maybe seeing her need to be practical, to get over the emotion. As if she could.

'Come home via Australia and bring me my cats,' she said, trying desperately to joke. 'I miss them.'

'It's a bit of a detour.'

'You're the Prince Regent.'

'So I am,' he said and smiled his crooked, heart-flipping smile, then stood looking down at her for a long, long moment as his smile faded. A door slammed below stairs, someone called to him and he swore.

'I have to go. Will you say goodbye to Zoe for me? I can't wake her yet.'

'Of course I will. Travel safe.' She smiled. 'I was teasing about the cats.'

'I know you were.' He gave an almost imperceptible nod, as though her cats and his safety were inconsequential. As if there was something more important he'd decided to say. 'Elsa…'

'Just go.'

'I will,' he said, but instead he tugged her close and she had neither strength nor will to resist. He pulled her tight into his arms, against his chest, and he kissed her, hard and long and aching with need.

And then he put her away from him.

'G…go,' she managed.

'I love you,' he said, loudly and strongly into the morning.

But still he turned. And he went.

She wanted to sob. Or maybe something louder. She'd actually quite like to stomp a bit. Toss the odd pillow.

Yell.

But Zoe and Buster were fast asleep. She should be, too. What else was she to do?

She needn't worry about breakfast. It would be

on the table in a couple of hours, a choice of eight or so dishes, eat what you like and certainly don't worry about the cost.

She was Zoe's friend and guardian, only Zoe already had a friend. After Christmas Zoe would try the little school that stood just by the castle gates. What was a woman to do then?

Research her turtles and don't deviate. Become a world authority. Stay facing in the one direction…

Hope Stefanos could find a direction too, one that could fulfil his dreams, and hope with everything in her heart that his direction matched hers.

She loved him.

There wasn't a lot she could do about it. Flying out of the door wailing, *Wait for me, wait for me,* would hardly be appropriate or sensible or even possible.

So…. Go back to sleep until it's time for the royal day to begin.

Start making Amy's Christmas Cake.

Wait for her prince to come home.

It was a direct flight from Athens to New York. The details of his surgical list had been faxed through to him so he had a mass of reading to do on the way. He leafed through the first case and then the second—and then found himself staring sightlessly ahead. Superimposed on the printed pages was the vision of Elsa's tousled curls, her bare feet, as she'd opened the door to say goodbye.

More than anything else he'd wanted to sweep her into his arms, take her back to her bed and stay with her for ever and ever and ever.

She'd knocked back his proposal of marriage. He was trying to understand her reasons.

He'd spoken too early. One night in Athens hadn't been enough. Her hip had been hurting. He needed to have her healed and then take her away properly— a weekend in Paris, maybe. Or a month in Paris.

Or New York? There was his dream. Manhattan and Elsa. Or…more, he thought. Manhattan and Elsa and Zoe and Buster. His family—something he'd never thought he wanted, but now he had such a hunger for that he couldn't see past it.

But… He had to stay in Khryseis.

And that was the problem, he thought. Elsa knew better than he did that marriage to her would make things better for him. But she'd knocked back his proposal. He had to make things better himself.

'Excuse me, but are you Prince Stefanos of Khryseis?'

The man in the next seat had been glancing at him covertly since take-off. Small, a bit unkempt, wearing half-rimmed glasses and the air of a scholar, he'd been reading notes that looked even more dense than those Stefanos had been studying.

'I am,' Stefanos said warily, because admitting to being royalty was usually asking for trouble.

'So you're the one who seduced our Dr Elsa from her studies.'

'Pardon?' What the hell…? This man looked angry.

'She's brilliant,' the man said, ignoring Stefanos's incredulity. 'She has one of the most brilliant scientific minds in Australia. In the world. She and that husband of hers…the research they did on the preservation of the Great Barrier Reef was groundbreaking. If she'd kept it up it could have made her a professor in any of the most prestigious universities in the world. And then she just hands it over. Hands it over!'

'I don't know what you mean,' Stefanos said.

'Her work,' the man said impatiently, and then suddenly seemed to remember his manners. 'David Hemming,' he said. 'Professor of Marine Studies at… Well, never mind, it doesn't matter. All I know is that I've never seen such a generous act. She had all the research done. All the hard work. She was just starting to see the academic rewards and suddenly a letter arrives out of the blue saying she can no longer go on with her studies but she doesn't want her research wasted so here it is, take it and publish as you see fit, just take it forward. Well, I tell you there's at least eight international experts now who are international experts only because of Dr Langham's generosity.'

'Dr Langham?'

'We could never find her,' he said morosely. 'Only then we started hearing about starfish research—really interesting stuff—and dammit, there she was, only she was calling herself Elsa Murdoch. But, just as we were finding out what she was doing, dammit if she didn't do exactly the same again. Package it all up and pass it on. No honours for her. Just good, solid research that'll mean species will survive that were otherwise facing extinction. And now…'

He'd been building up indignation, incense personified, and Stefanos got poked in the chest with a pencil. 'And now she's off again. But at least it's turtles this time. Kemp's Ridley, by what I hear, and you couldn't get a better woman working on them. You know what? She sees the big picture. Already she's contacting international institutions, trying to broaden our understanding. If she's found this breeding site there must be more. She'll use that to make them safe.'

'How…?'

'Pure energy,' he said, stabbing Stefanos again. 'Only don't you let her give her work away this time. If she settles—if she's allowed to settle—then I'm guaranteeing those blessed turtles will be safe for a thousand years, such is the commitment she generates. So you might have seduced her to your island but you make sure she stays. Or I and half the marine academics in the world will want to know why not.'

And, with a final poke in the chest, he retired back to his notes.

Leaving Stefanos winded.

Stunned.

The vision of Elsa as he'd last seen her was still with him—beautiful, almost ethereal, a freckled imp with her glorious sun-blonded curls. With her face creasing from laughter to gravity, from teasing to earnestness, from joy to...love?

To loss.

If he'd met her when she was twenty, when life was simple, when she was free to fall in love, then maybe he'd have stood a chance. He knew that. For he'd looked into her eyes and what he saw there was a reflection of what he believed himself. That she was falling in love with him as deeply as he was falling in love with her.

Only life had got complicated. He'd thought it was complicated for him. How much more complicated was it for her?

She'd buried a husband. She'd said goodbye to two careers. She'd taken on a child so injured that she'd needed almost a hundred per cent commitment, and that at a time when Elsa was injured herself.

And along came Prince Stefanos, grudgingly changing direction this once. Hating the idea that he'd be handing over his work, his teaching, his skills, watching others take his work forward while he ceased to be able to contribute.

She knew his commitment was grudging. She had so much generosity of spirit herself that she must know it.

He'd enjoy family medicine, he thought, and doing everything else he could to help Khryseis, as a doctor and as the island's Prince Regent. He must. He'd immerse himself into it all, convince Elsa that he was content.

Only she knew him. He couldn't lie to her. And it wasn't entirely the work he wanted to do.

Khryseis wasn't big enough for the medical work he wanted to do.

But…

For some reason, the academic's words stuck. Hit a chord.

You know what? She sees the big picture.

Khryseis was one of three islands. Put together…

He needed to concentrate on these cases. He'd be operating hours after landing. He needed to read his notes.

But there were things happening in his head apart from his most pressing concerns. Major things.

The image came to him of the night he'd held the three tiny turtle hatchlings in his hand.

I guess, if they walked far enough, the ocean is that-a-way, he'd said.

Yeah, but changing direction's easier, she'd whispered. *I ought to know.*

Could he somehow change direction but get to the same place by another route?

There wasn't time to think this through now.

Those kids were lined up waiting for him. But he had six weeks to think.

How much did he want Elsa?

And Zoe. And Khryseis. And turtles and cats and Amy's Christmas Cake which, for some weird reason, was becoming a really big thing to look forward to.

How much did he want them all?

He lifted his third set of case notes and tried to read.

But all he saw was Elsa.

CHAPTER THIRTEEN

THEY coped without him.

It was a strange thing, caring for a child who'd been dependent for years but who was finally finding her wings. Zoe couldn't wait to get out of bed in the morning, to meet her new friend, to play with Buster, to be allowed to start school. Medical constraints, always suffered stoically, were now a nuisance to be ignored. She bounced around the palace with growing confidence and pleasure, and by Christmas there wasn't a member of the palace staff who wouldn't have given their right arm for her.

Zoe was gloriously in love with this new life.

So was Elsa. Sort of.

She and Helena were working through the issues with the turtles with cautious exhilaration. There was so much to be done. The turtles' habitat had been destroyed once, and only part of it had regrown. Turtles were crossing roads to dig their nests. There were threats everywhere, and this for a world endangered species. Making them safe was imperative. Extrapolating the research was breathtakingly exciting. She could make a difference.

There were so many things she could do.

But she wanted to be with Stefanos. Every morning she woke rethinking his proposal. Was she crazy? She'd turned down a man she could love with all her heart.

She knew it was more than that, but that was the problem. Her head knew things her heart didn't necessarily agree with.

'Will Stefanos be home for Christmas?' Zoe asked for about the thousandth time since he'd left and, for the thousandth time, she replied.

'He said he would be. He's phoning us as often as he can, sweetheart, and he doesn't seem to be changing his mind. And then he's going to stay with you while I have my hip fixed.'

'I don't want you to go away.'

She didn't want to go away either, but it was organised. The day after New Year she'd fly to Athens and spend a month in hospital.

She should be grateful. She was grateful. Zoe was happy and blooming. There were no money problems. She had work that truly interested her, and her hip was about to be treated.

So why was a part of her so miserable?

Happy Christmas, she told herself fiercely on Christmas Eve, as she helped Zoe hang her stocking in front of the vast fireplace in the great hall. Last year she'd used a sock in front of the fire-stove. This year the housekeeper had hand-stitched Zoe a gold and crimson stocking, with the most beautiful appliquéd Father Christmas and elves and reindeer.

It looked beautiful on the great mantel. But, despite the massive Christmas tree the staff had set up—or maybe because of it—it looked really alone.

'You should have a stocking too,' Zoe said as she'd said every Christmas since they'd been together.

'Stockings are for kids.'

'You never get presents.'

'Stefanos should be home. That'll be a present for both of us.'

'He should be here now,' Zoe said severely. It was almost bedtime on Christmas Eve. She'd counted on her big cousin coming today. 'He said he'd come.'

'Maybe he'll come in the night like Santa Claus,' Elsa said. 'Maybe we won't see him come if we stay up.'

'You think we should go to bed?'

'Why not?' She was weary of waiting, herself. She was riding an emotional roller coaster and didn't know how to get off. If Stefanos didn't come… He'd promised Zoe.

He'd promised her.

'Okay,' Zoe said, infinitely trusting. She tucked

her hand into Elsa's and tugged her towards the stairs. 'Let's go to bed and make it come quicker.'

He had so much to do he felt like Santa Claus, zooming across the world at midnight. Actually he was only flying from Athens to Khryseis on the seaplane, but he did feel a bit like Santa. He had so many gifts in his pack. He sat next to the pilot, gazed out at the blue-black sky and the stars hanging low and lovely in the heavens, and he felt that a little bit of magic was around.

He needed magic. In his pocket was a ring almost worthy of the woman he loved—the ancient ring of Khryseis, plaited gold with three magnificent diamonds embedded in its depths.

She wouldn't take it unless she accepted the rest of his sleigh load, he thought ruefully. A woman of principle was the woman he'd chosen to give his heart.

Would she take it? He'd done so much. If there was anything else he could do… Anything at all…

He had a mad compulsion to tell the pilot to turn the plane around. So much was at stake. The woman he'd chosen as his life's partner had knocked him back because of her principles. If he didn't get it right this time…

What else could he do?

The lights of Khryseis came into view and the plane started its descent. He could see the palace from here, lit up like a fairy palace. That'd be the staff celebrating Christmas, he thought. The whole staff—the whole island—was overjoyed to have their royal family in residence.

Or their royal princess and her nanny, he corrected himself. For a family required more.

Would she accept him now? She must. For years he'd scorned the idea of a family. Now it seemed he couldn't live without it.

He'd met one feisty, beautiful nanny and his world had changed.

'Coming in to land now, sir,' the pilot said, looking ahead at the palace lights. 'Seems someone's keeping the home fires burning.'

'I hope so,' he murmured.

'I think every person on the island hopes so,' the pilot said enigmatically. 'Welcome home, Your Highness.'

'Santa's been and Stefanos is home.'

Elsa woke to find Zoe bouncing up and down on her bed, the long-suffering Buster being bounced with her. 'Come and see, come and see, come and see. Santa's been, Santa's been, Santa's been.'

Despite the tumult of emotions she'd gone to bed with and woken with—*Stefanos is home*—she had to smile. Zoe had been just as excited last year when all she'd been able to give her were a couple of handmade toys she'd bought at a local market. This year should be fun.

Stefanos is home.

'It's humungous,' Zoe was saying. 'You should see. How can Santa have brought it down the chimney?'

Humungous? Nothing she'd stuffed in Zoe's stocking could be described as humungous. And…

Stefanos is home.

'Stefanos…' she said cautiously.

'He got home really late. Christina told me he snuck in after all the staff went to bed—almost morning. Elsa, you have to get up and see what Santa's brought me.'

So Stefanos would be asleep. That gave her breathing space. She'd have time to enjoy Zoe's stocking with her before she needed to face him.

It wasn't that she didn't want to see him, she thought, feeling really confused. Not exactly. There was a big part of her that ached for him.

There was another part of her that was just plain custard.

But he was asleep. Hooray. She threw back the covers, pulled on a robe and padded downstairs.

She'd never get used to the opulence of this place. The staircase was wide enough to fit ten people abreast.

'The king who built this place must have been as fat as a whale,' she told Zoe. 'Or he had ten kids to take by the hand every Christmas morning.' Zoe giggled and they were both still chuckling as Zoe hauled open the double doors to the great hall.

She stopped dead.

How long since she'd believed in Santa Claus?

When they'd gone to bed the Christmas tree was a decorator item, set up by the staff as a tasteful ode to Christmas. Now…whoever had come during the night had turned the tree into an over the top muddle.

The exquisite decorations and silver lights were still under there somewhere, but they were now almost hidden. Hung over the top of them were rows and rows of coloured popcorn, threaded together and hung in vast ribbons of garish colour. There were paper lanterns—every colour of the rainbow. Pictures of cats had been placed in tiny silver frames and hung as ornaments. There was a collection of motley socks hanging everywhere, all bulging.

'The socks have got apples in them,' Zoe said, awed, tugging her towards the tree. 'That one's a football sock and that one has a hole in the toe. And look at my present.'

She was seeing it. Stunned.

It was a trampoline, an eminently bouncy mat, built with a net canopy around it so a child could bounce without fear of falling.

For a child who needed to be encouraged to stretch scar tissue…for a child who loved bouncing…it was the best thing.

'And you have a stocking too,' Zoe said, deeply satisfied. 'Look.'

She looked. On the mantelpiece hung three stockings. Zoe's was bulging with nonsense gifts, a tin whistle, a boomerang—a boomerang?—a clockwork mouse…

More pictures of cats.

And there was a stocking labelled *Elsa*. A small parcel bulged in the toe, a document rolled and tied with a huge red bow was sticking out the end, and there were more pictures of cats.

The stocking labelled *Stefanos* was empty.

'We should have something for Stefanos,' Zoe said anxiously. 'Santa didn't come to him.'

'We have a couple of gifts in our room,' Elsa said uncertainly. 'We could sneak up and put them in his stocking before he wakes.'

'It's too late for sneaking,' said a low gravelly voice and she yelped.

The voice had come from behind the vast Christmas tree. Zoe darted behind in a flash.

'Stefanos,' she shouted. 'He's here. Elsa, he's here, sleeping behind the tree.'

'I always sleep behind the tree,' a sleepy voice murmured, full of laughter. 'For years and years. But I've never yet caught Santa Claus. Has he come?'

'He's come, he's come.' Zoe was squealing with excitement. 'And he's brought crazy socks. Elsa, he's here. Stefanos is here. Come and see.'

There wasn't a choice. She should have at least brushed her hair, she thought desperately, as she tried to organise her smile to be cool and welcoming. She walked cautiously around the tree, and there he was. He'd hauled a mattress downstairs, and a mound of bedding. He was lying back, smiling up at them, his blankets pulled only to his waist. Bare-chested.

Breathtakingly gorgeous.

Buster was on his stomach already, kneading his blankets with her soft paws and purring so hard you'd swear she'd recognised him. Zoe was snuggling down beside him, a little girl with everything she wanted in life.

'You've messed with our Christmas decorations,' she muttered before she could stop herself, and his grin widened.

'I threaded popcorn all the way from New York to Athens, and I made half my fellow passengers help me. The rest were on lantern duty. And then it still looked a bit empty so Santa had to resort to socks. And a happy Christmas to you too, Mrs Murdoch. Dr Langham. My love.'

There was a bit too much in that statement for Elsa to think about. She opened her mouth to reply and gave up and closed it again.

'No Happy Christmas?' he said, smiling at her evident confusion.

'Happy Christmas,' she managed, sounding winded. 'Why…why aren't you in your own bed?'

'I might have missed present opening. Have you opened your stocking yet?' He rolled out of bed. He'd gone to bed wearing boxer shorts. Only boxer shorts. What more could a girl want for Christmas? she thought as she watched him stretch and yawn; as she thought all sorts of things that surely a nicely brought up girl—a mature widow!—had no business thinking.

Had she opened her stocking? 'N...no,' she managed, annoyed that her voice squeaked. 'It's bad form to open gifts until the family's together.'

'Is the family together now?' he asked gently and he looked at Zoe cradling Buster and then he looked to her with such an expression that her heart did a double backflip. Landed on its back. Refused to start operating again in any mode she considered normal.

'I...I guess,' she muttered.

'No guessing,' he said, suddenly stern. 'You need to be sure. Zoe, I'm assuming you've guessed this very fine trampoline came squeezing down the chimney in the wee small hours especially for you. Would you like to try it out for size?'

'Ooh, yes,' Zoe said and flew with Buster to the trampoline, only to be hauled back by her big cousin.

'Buster,' Stefanos said firmly, removing the long-suffering kitten from her arms, 'stays on the ground.'

Only he didn't. Stefanos handed Buster to Elsa and then, when her hands were safely occupied and she couldn't fend him off, he kissed her. Just the once, but the look in his eyes said there were more where that came from. Just the once, but it was enough to light her world.

'It appears I'm needing to send out a royal decree for mistletoe,' he growled, his lovely crooked smile warming parts of her she hadn't known were cold.

'Honestly. Can't you people be depended on to organise anything?'

She managed a chuckle but it was a pretty wavery chuckle. She was too…thrown.

'Happy Christmas,' he said again, and then obviously decided mistletoe was not absolutely essential and he kissed her again, deeply this time, long and hard and so wonderfully that finally Zoe ceased bouncing, put her hands on her hips and issued a royal decree of her own.

'Yuck,' she said. 'And you're squashing Buster. Stop kissing and open presents.'

'Yes, ma'am,' Stefanos said and swept Elsa— and the slightly squished Buster—into his arms and deposited them both on the settee by the tree. Then he lifted the rolled document out of the top of her stocking and handed it to her, with such gravitas it was as if he was handing over royal title to his land and his kingdom for ever.

She looked up at him, wondering, but he was looking grave and expectant, waiting for her to discover for herself what it was. Slowly she unfastened the ribbon holding the roll of documents together. Buster pounced on the ribbon; she set both ribbon and Buster on the floor and then looked up at Stefanos again, half afraid to go further.

'Well, go on, then,' he said, in the same tone of impatience Zoe had just used. 'Read it.'

She read.

*… Transfer of title of Diamond Mine Number
Two on the Isle of Argyros, the income from
which to be used in perpetuity for the health
of all the citizens of the Diamond Isles…*

She stared up at him, confused. He smiled back
at her, and he didn't look confused in the least.

'I'm changing my direction,' he said softly. 'So
I'm hoping…if I head in the same direction as you,
can we walk together?'

'I…I don't know what you mean.'

He sat down beside her, took the documents back
and set them aside. His face was suddenly grave.
'Elsa, on the plane on the way to New York I met a
man who knew you. He told me about your research,
and you know what else he said about you? He
said… *She sees the big picture.* And he spoke in
awe. He meant you don't just look at the turtles on
the beach that need saving. You broaden your work;
you look at their survival internationally. And I
finally figured it out. It was like I'd needed a swipe
to the side of the head to wake me up, and I finally
got it. That's what I've been guilty of. Seeing only
what's before my eyes. Not thinking big. Seeing
only my work in Manhattan and how much it means.'

'But your work is important,' she said, confused,
struggling to understand.

'It is,' he agreed, still grave, laughter put aside
as he tried to make her see. 'Elsa, without conceit,
I can say my work changes lives. So when I knew

I had to work here I was gutted. I knew I had no choice—the islanders are my people. And then there was a new imperative. You're my people. You're my family, Elsa. You and Zoe. I want you so much—and it was such a shock to realise I ached for a family. I ached for you. I was so committed to what I was feeling for you, and to the needs of the islanders as well, that I'd stopped thinking big. It took one stray remark about how wonderful you were to make me rethink.'

'I don't think I'm following your logic,' she managed cautiously, trying to focus on his words rather than the joy and love she was seeing in his eyes. The joy and love that was building inside her. She didn't know yet what he was talking about but the smile behind his eyes said it was good.

'We're too small.' He had her hands now, holding her tight. 'But now I'm thinking big. Elsa, this document is a plan.'

'Something about a diamond mine?' she ventured. Good one, Elsa. Intelligence wasn't on the agenda this morning—nor was speed reading. All she was seeing was Stefanos.

'Absolutely it's about a diamond mine, my love,' he said and tugged her into his arms and kissed her again. Long and lingering and lovely. But then he set her back from him. There were still things that needed to be said.

There were things she didn't understand, and he had to make her see.

'There are six diamond mines on Argyros,' he said softly while she listened in wonder. 'Argyros is therefore the wealthiest of the Diamond Isles but it has no hospital. Nikos has been talking to me about setting up decent medical facilities there. It's the same on Sappheiros—Alexandros is already making plans for a hospital. And then, on the plane, I made myself see the big picture. Separately we're small islands. We each need good medical facilities but we don't each have the population to set up a major base. But together…'

'Together?'

'It's too big,' he said ruefully. 'To land this on you on Christmas morning. But I can't wait any longer. Elsa, I love you, I want you more than life itself, but I've already asked you to marry me. What I need now is for you to know I've changed. Everything's changed. Except my love for you. So…can I tell you what we've decided? The rulers of the other two islands and me?'

How was a girl to react to that? Her heart was starting to sing. Bubbles of happiness were floating to the surface and filling the room with joy. 'I'm…I'm listening,' she whispered, and suddenly so was Zoe, sitting cross-legged on her trampoline, watching with big, serious eyes. She really was much older than her eight years, Elsa thought, and then she thought that, whatever was coming—and already joy was starting to overwhelm her—it was appropriate that Zoe was here. To bear witness, she thought, and then she thought that was a dumb thing to think but she thought it anyway.

'Earth to Elsa,' Stefanos said, laughing softly and tightening his grip on her hands and she thought, okay, thoughts could come at some other time. Now was the time for listening.

'It's a medical scheme,' he told her, and in his eyes was jubilation, excitement, a man about to embark on a *Boy's Own* adventure. 'A medical centre second to none will be built, here on Khryseis, with satellite hospitals on the other two islands. Fast and easy transfer facilities. Every specialist we need. Together we'll care for the people of the Diamond Isles as they deserve to be cared for. It's what I dreamed of as a kid, as did Alexandros on Sappheiros, and Nikos on Argyros. Three Crowns, Elsa. Three Crowns finally come together to provide care for all.'

'One…one big medical centre?' She was struggling to take it in.

'State-of-the-art. And, with the islands being as lovely as they are, and the salaries we're prepared to pay, we don't expect any trouble staffing them as they should be staffed. We don't see islanders needing to go to Athens for treatment any more. We see mainlanders coming to us.' His hands moved to her shoulders, holding her, desperate for her to share his joy.

'Alex and Nikos flew to New York to work this through with me. For such a project, for something so wonderful for all of us, the diamonds on Argyros will be needed, but none of us can see a better use for them. We envisage offering our medical facilities worldwide. And more. There'll be resorts on each island that are half hotel, half hospital. Come here and be pampered and made well, and support our economy while you do.'

He was so exultant now his excitement was practically blazing. 'We've done the preliminary figures and the guys in suits agree with us,' he told her. 'It *will* work. And here's the tail, Elsa. Here's my huge joy. With the money raised we believe we can still bring people here from Third World countries. I'll be able to operate as I've been doing and I'll be able to teach. So…so what do you think?'

He paused then. He was still holding her by the shoulders, his eyes not leaving hers. But now…his excitement faded a little, giving way to anxiety.

He was asking what she thought? *He was anxious about what she'd think?*

'You'd be here,' she whispered. 'You'd be doing the work you love.'

'I'd be doing all the work I love,' he said, excitement giving way to gravity. 'I'll be ruling this island in Zoe's stead, caring for it as it must be cared for. I'll be doing the medicine I love—I'll be making a difference. And I'll be sharing my life with you.'

'With me.'

'And with Zoe,' he said, his eyes lighting with

laughter again. This much joy couldn't be contained for more than a moment. 'And our cats.'

'Cats,' she said cautiously, for she was starting to see a theme here. There were pictures of cats all over the Christmas tree. 'Cats, plural?'

'I made a few calls to Australia,' he said. 'I figured…well, I hoped you might be staying here long term, and the guy feeding your cats now has twenty-three on his list.'

'Twenty-three…' she gasped.

'It seems he's Waratah Cove's answer to the Pied Piper of Hamelin. He's taken them on as his mission in life.'

'Don't tell me you're bringing them here,' she managed.

Zoe said, 'Ooh!'

'That's not an ooh,' Elsa said, torn between laughter and horror. 'It's an Are You Out Of Your Mind?'

'I hoped you might say that,' Stefanos said, smiling into her eyes with such a look that she might, just might, be forced to forgive him twenty-three cats—or anything at all. 'So what I've done is give the guy a job in perpetuity, caring for them all. With one exception.'

'One…'

'A skinny little black one,' he said apologetically. 'I met him that first day when you guys were on the beach and I had to find you. It seems he's been pining for you—he's hardly eaten since you left and, to tell you the truth, I sort of fell for him. So he's on his way here as we speak. My love.'

My love. There was enough in those two words to be perfectly adequate, thank you very much— she hardly wanted more.

Only Zoe was made of sterner stuff. She darted across to the mantelpiece and was flying back, tipping the contents of Elsa's stocking at her feet.

'You have another present and I have six. Maybe I ought to open some of mine first.'

'If you don't mind, Zoe,' Stefanos said and lifted the tiny crimson box from where it had fallen. 'So far Elsa's just had paper. You have a trampoline and this is important.'

'Elsa has a cat,' Zoe said.

'Yes, but he's not here yet. So, as yet, she's giftless.'

'Okay,' Zoe said obligingly, grabbing the long-suffering Buster and squatting beside Elsa. 'But it's really small. Open it fast, Elsa.'

'Open it slow, Elsa,' Stefanos said, and watched as Elsa forgot to breathe and tried to make fumbling fingers operate the catch of the tiny box.

'Let me,' Stefanos said at last, and flicked the clasp. And there, resting on a bed of black velvet, was the most beautiful ring she'd ever seen. It was gnarled and twisted gold, burnished with age and history, with three magnificent diamonds set in its depths—diamonds to take a girl's breath away.

'It's the ancient ring of this island, worn by the ruling Princess of Khryseis for generations,'

Stefanos said softly. 'On her marriage. If…if you'd like to be married, that is. If you'd like to be my princess.' He took a deep breath. 'If you'd like to be married to me.'

'It's beeyootiful,' Zoe breathed, but Elsa said nothing at all. She couldn't.

She was so proud of him. She was so in love with him.

He was giving her another chance.

'You can always change it if you don't like it,' Stefanos said, anxious again. 'If you fancy emeralds, or something modern? When Zoe marries she'll inherit it anyway so it'd be good to have a backup. Anything you like, my darling, just say the word. I believe the only thing non-negotiable in this whole deal is who you get to marry.' And he dropped to one knee. 'If it's okay, that is. If you say yes. Elsa, will you marry me?'

She looked up from the ring. He was kneeling before her. Her prince.

'You're proposing in boxer shorts?' Elsa managed.

'I believe I was wearing a suit and tie last time I proposed. Look where that got me. Now I'm trying a different tack.'

'Zoe, if you run and get my camera, I wouldn't mind this moment being documented,' Elsa murmured—weakly—and Stefanos grinned but he didn't shift from where he was kneeling.

Zoe stared at them both as if they were crazy. 'He's asking you to marry him?'

'I believe…I believe he is. I…can you get the camera?'

'Yes,' she yelled and whooped in excitement and headed for the stairs. 'I want to be a brides-maid,' she called over her shoulder, and contin-ued whooping all the way up the stairs.

'So now,' Stefanos said, starting to look long-suffering. 'Elsa… My love…' But then he had to pause as the butler's long face appeared around the door.

'Good morning, sir,' he said. 'Happy Christmas. Welcome home. Will you be wanting breakfast?'

'Josef,' Stefanos said, in a goaded voice.

'Yes, sir?'

'You're a servant to the royal family, right?'

'Yes, sir,' Josef said, taking in the tableau in front of him and grinning.

'Then you no doubt know about summary be-headings, boiling in oil and the rest.'

'I have read my history.'

'Excellent,' Stefanos said. 'Then I command you to close that door and lean against it and let no one else in, for fear of blood-curdling retribution, for the next ten minutes. At least.'

'Yes, sir,' Josef said, and chuckled and closed the doors.

'Servants,' Stefanos said. 'You can't do anything with them these days. Now, where were we?'

'Exactly where we were two minutes ago, I

believe,' she said cautiously. 'You want me to come down on the floor with you?'

'I want you to hush,' he said. 'Elsa.'

'Stefanos.'

'Will you marry me?' he said again, and again the laughter was gone. Only love remained. Only the gravity of a promise to be made for ever.

And what was a girl to say to that? Well, the obvious one for a start.

'Yes.'

He blinked. 'Pardon?'

'Yes.'

'I haven't used all of my very cogent arguments yet.'

'I'm marrying you anyway.'

'And…why would that be?'

'I believe I love you. Are you sure I can't come down there with you?'

'If you must,' he said and tugged her down so they were kneeling face to face under the Christmas tree. 'Elsa, I love you with all my heart.'

'That's exceedingly fortunate because I love you too.'

'Really?'

'Absolutely. Of course I love you more in tassels and with your dress sword and boots, but I'm so far gone I'll even love you in boxer shorts. Are you going to kiss me yet?'

'You don't want to know how much I love you?'

'You can start telling me,' she said, and smiled

as an imperious little voice sounded from the other side of the door.

'They want me in there. I've got the camera. They really, truly want me.'

'Well, I guess you can't tell me how much you love me anyway,' she said, smiling and smiling, and maybe even crying a little as well as he tugged her into his arms and held her close. 'Because I don't think we'll know how much we love each other until the end of eternity.'

'Starting now,' Stefanos said. He sighed and called out, 'Okay, let her in, Josef. Let 'em all in. Bring on the world. The Prince and his affianced wife are ready to receive visitors.'

But not quite. As Josef swung the doors wide they were too busy to receive anyone. For Mrs Elsa Murdoch alias Dr Elsa Langham had changed direction yet again.

The future Princess Elsa of Khryseis was kissing her beloved prince as she intended kissing him for the rest of her life.

'Oh, yuck,' Zoe said in deep disapproval as she was finally admitted. She waited and waited and finally looked around for something to distract her. 'And why is Stefanos's stocking empty?' she demanded of Josef. 'Did Santa forget him?'

'I believe His Highness has his Christmas gift,' the butler told her, and smiled at the pair of them. 'I believe His Royal Highness has his family.'

* * *

The christening of Christos Mathew Romanos Antoniadis was an occasion of great joy for the island of Khryseis. The celebration was huge, made more so because it coincided with the opening of the Diamond Isles Medical Base, to be celebrated the next day.

The world had come to see, to celebrate this wondrous occasion and to welcome these three islands into the twenty-first century.

For the difference in these islands in the eighteen months since the old King had died and the new generation of royalty had taken power was nigh on unbelievable. Already the islanders were prospering, the glittering Diamond Isles finally succeeding in becoming the magical place to live that they'd always promised.

This medical centre was the icing on the cake— a symbol of all they hoped to achieve. The staff it was attracting had caused its reputation to go before it, and already there were mainlanders waiting to use it. Already the islanders knew that the network of medical centres could cope with their every need. What was more, the medical centre was only the start of the new order. On every island there was employment, optimism and joy.

And now, on this day, that joy was exemplified by the royal family of Khryseis, and this, the christening of their new little son.

Father Antonio performed the ceremony, and the shaky old priest who'd loved the islanders for all his life blessed this baby with all the love in his heart.

Afterwards Elsa stood on the magnificent lawns of the palace grounds, with her husband by her side, with her baby in her arms and she thought the joy she was feeling right now could never be surpassed.

Only of course it could.

Joy is to come...

Stefanos was standing with his arm round her waist, greeting dignitary after dignitary, accepting their congratulations, smiling with a pride as deep as it was joyful.

There it was again. That word... Joy.

Zoe wasn't with them. She and Pip had slipped away, up to the palace balcony to play with Buster and Spike. Elsa glanced up and saw them, two little girls with two cats, a Zoe who was so confident with her new family that clinging was a thing of the past.

Joy.

'Happy, my love?' Stefanos asked as the line of dignitaries finally came to an end.

'How can you doubt it?'

'So...' he smiled into her eyes '...where do we go from here?'

She smiled back at her beloved husband, and she smiled again at her sleeping son. 'Where, indeed?'

'Another baby?'

'Absolutely,' she whispered, gazing down at the perfection of her little son.

'More turtles?'

'Oh, yes.'

'Another cat or two?'

'Two's enough. I'm thinking of a puppy.'

'Is there room for a puppy with two cats?' Stefanos asked, startled, and she grinned.

'I think there's room for anything in our family,' she said. 'This is the Diamond Isles. Place of miracles. Place of wonder. Home of our hearts, and room for all.'

* * * * *

This season we bring you Christmas Treats

*For an early Christmas present Marion Lennox
would like to share a little treat with you...
Happy Christmas to My Readers,
from Marion Lennox*

An Australian Christmas is often a lovely mixture of traditional and cool. Our extended family is large, we eat outside at our beach shack, we continue to serve the traditional turkey and pudding, but in deference to the heat we add a few things. Like lobster and prawns to start—and Amy's Christmas Cake after pudding. The 'Cake' is huge—it goes back and forth from the freezer well after Christmas; a lovely, lingering treat for all.

Make it and enjoy, whatever side of the equator you come from. It's a tradition we're willing to share.

Amy's Christmas Cake

For each layer:

   500 g (or 1 lb) berries
     (any variety except strawberries)
     blended and sieved*.

   4 eggs

   ¾ cup (6 oz or 175g) castor/superfine sugar

   1 cup (250 ml or ½ pint) whipped cream

1. Cream yolks and sugar.
2. Whisk whites until stiff.
3. Fold in yolk and sugar mixture, and berry mixture.
4. Pour into ice cream maker. Churn until frozen.
5. Pour into large cake-shaped container to form one layer of the cake. Cover with plastic food wrap. Freeze.
6. Two days later do another layer with different berries. Continue until you run out of bowl, berries or freezer space.

To serve:

Blend and sieve another 250g (½lb) berries. Sweeten to taste to make a coulis. (I make this at room temperature and the sugar dissolves. If your room temperature is not Australian Christmas room temperature (ie warm), you might need to heat gently and then cool again before serving.)

Turn cake out. Decorate with extra berries.

Slice and serve, pouring a little of the coulis over the top of each slice. Enjoy.

*Note from author: Last Christmas I decided to make deeper layers, and overloaded an ancient food processor with deep crimson brambleberries. This resulted in a startling non-traditional décor for my kitchen that I advise you not to try at home.☺

JINGLE-BELL BABY

BY
LINDA GOODNIGHT

All the characters in this book have no existence outside the imagination
of the author, and have no relation whatsoever to anyone bearing the
same name or names. They are not even distantly inspired by any
individual known or unknown to the author, and all the incidents are
pure invention.

First published in Great Britain 2009
Harlequin Mills & Boon Limited,
Eton House, 18-24 Paradise Road, Richmond, Surrey TW9 1SR

© Linda Goodnight 2009

ISBN: 978 0 263 86976 7

Set in Times Roman 12½ on 13½ pt
02-1109-52189

Harlequin Mills & Boon policy is to use papers that are natural,
renewable and recyclable products and made from wood grown in
sustainable forests. The logging and manufacturing process conform
to the legal environmental regulations of the country of origin.

Printed and bound in Spain
by Litografia Rosés, S.A., Barcelona

Winner of a RITA® Award for excellence in inspirational fiction, **Linda Goodnight** has also won the Booksellers' Best, ACFW Book of the Year, and a Reviewers' Choice Award from *Romantic Times BOOKreviews* magazine. Linda has appeared on the Christian bestseller list, and her romance novels have been translated into more than a dozen languages. Active in orphan ministry, this former nurse and teacher enjoys writing fiction that carries a message of hope and light in a sometimes dark world. She and husband Gene live in Oklahoma. Readers can write to her at linda@lindagoodnight.com

Winner of an RWA* Award, Linda Goodnight is
a nationally bestselling, award-winning, and
RITA-nominated author. Linda loves to hear on her
website. Linda lives in Oklahoma. Readers can write to
her at linda@lindagoodnight.com

CHAPTER ONE

LESSON NUMBER ONE in birthing class: never drive a car cross-country alone. Especially during the ninth month of pregnancy.

But Jenna Garwood had never taken a birthing class.

For the tenth time in as many minutes, she cast an anxious glance in the rearview mirror, relieved to see that no one had followed her when she'd exited the interstate some miles back.

Since her escape from the Carrington Estate, she'd zigged and zagged from the east toward the west, careful to cover her tracks. After three days, she shouldn't be so worried. But the long arm of the Carrington family reached far and wide. And they didn't give up easily.

When she'd heard the plans they had for her unborn child, Jenna had done the only thing that made sense. She'd run.

She had always been weak, but the little girl beneath her breast had given her strength. After the humiliation and sorrow of the last two years, the baby had given her a reason to try again.

A moan slipped past a bottom lip raw from constant gnawing. She bent forward over the steering wheel to stretch the kink in her back wishing she hadn't spritzed the car's interior with eau de parfum this morning. The stench of dirt and oil intermingled with the honeyed notes of orange blossom rose from the floorboard like an unwanted visitor. Saliva pooled in her mouth. As she tried to focus on the road, she swallowed, regretful, too, of the hamburger she'd eaten for breakfast.

Somewhere in this empty Texas landscape, there had to be a quiet little town where she could rest… and hide…until the ache in her back subsided.

"Only a little farther, darling," she murmured to the hard ball around her middle. "Mommy's tired, too."

Tired was an understatement of monumental proportions.

Her back had hurt nonstop throughout the duration of her pregnancy but during the last twelve hours the discomfort had grown steadily worse. If it had been her belly instead of her back, she would have been scared.

In conjunction with long hours behind the wheel, stress was the likely culprit. She hadn't relaxed once since leaving the estate. Even sleep was accomplished with an ear to the door and her eyes half-open.

The stretching, pressing ache deepened. She really needed to find that town.

She reached for her handbag, a pink crocodile spy bag her mother had purchased for Jenna's twenty-second birthday six weeks ago. The purse, stuffed full of the very best cosmetics, a spa coupon, and a five-thousand-dollar shopping card, had been nothing short of a bribe and Jenna knew it. Unfortunately Mother never understood that monetary possessions had ceased to inspire loyalty in her daughter. Only one thing had her complete and utter devotion—the tiny person who, at this very moment, was causing a great deal of discomfort to Jenna's body.

As her fingers flipped open the purse flap, Jenna hissed a frustrated breath between her teeth. She no longer owned the elegant slider phone, complete with GPS and remote Internet access. Still fully charged and activated, she'd donated it to a bewildered but grateful soldier at an airport in Philadelphia. By the time the device had been located, it would be somewhere in the Middle East.

"Who would you call anyway?" Even 9-1-1 was fraught with difficulties. Though the Carringtons disdained public attention, choosing to deal with their scandals in a more discreet and private manner, Jenna would allow no chance of alerting anyone to her whereabouts.

She forced herself to breathe slow and deep. The tense, tense muscles in her back only grew tighter.

A flutter of panic trembled in her stomach. What if she went into labor out here alone?

She turned on the radio, praying for a distraction, while also pressing the car's accelerator. She needed to get *somewhere* fast.

A male voice, rich in Texas twang, came through the speakers to announce a fall festival at Saddleback Elementary School and a garage sale at 220 Pinehurst behind the Saddleback Pizza Place.

Saddleback must be a town. But where was it?

She gave the radio a pleading glance. "Can't you be a bit more specific?"

The pressure inside her body increased. A new and more insistent discomfort had moved around front to a spot low in her belly. Very low. She gasped and shifted sideways onto one hip. The pressure mounted, deeper, harder, stronger.

A guttural groan erupted from Jenna's throat. The sound was foreign, so different from her normal modulated tone.

From the radio pounded a driving beat of electric guitar and bass. The intensity echoed in her body.

The road ahead seemed to waver.

Fingers of iron gripped her abdomen. She was in trouble. Real trouble.

She blinked, panting, fighting the pressure. Sweat stung her eyes. Texas weather was cool, though not nearly as cold as a Pennsylvania November, and yet, Jenna was roasting inside the small blue economy. She reached for the air-conditioning controls and saw, with concern, how pale and shaky she'd become.

Before she could take another breath, a squeezing pain of epic proportions followed hard on the heels of the intense pressure.

"Oh no." She *was* in labor. Either that or her body was rupturing from the inside out.

Mouth open, panting like a puppy, she gripped the steering wheel with both hands and tried to stay on the road.

"Not yet, baby. Not yet. Let me find a hospital first." She squinted into the glare of an overcast sky, hoping for something, anything. A town, a house, another car.

Nothing but the endless brown landscape and an occasional line of naked trees.

The pressure mounted again, little by little, a warning that another power punch was on the way. Dread tensed her shoulders. "Nooo."

Her body poured sweat. So unladylike. Had Mother perspired this much with her?

She had to escape the pain. She had to. Perhaps if she stopped, got out of the car and walked a bit. Walking had helped in the past to ease the back ache. Even if walking didn't help, she could drive no further. She wouldn't take a chance of having an accident.

She tapped the brake and aimed the car toward the grassy roadside. Her belly tightened again.

With one hand, she grabbed for the rock-hard mound, moaning with dread. The terrible pain was coming again. She could think of nothing but the battle raging in her body.

Just before the agony took control, Jenna saw a flash of barbed wire and orange fence posts. The fence moved closer and closer.

And there was nothing she could do about it.

As his King Ranch pickup truck roared down County Road 275, Dax Coleman had two things on his mind: a hot shower and a good meal.

At the last thought, his mouth curled, mocking him. He hadn't had a good meal since the latest of a long string of housekeepers quit two weeks ago. Supper would be microwave pizza or scrambled eggs, the extent of his culinary gifts. His own fault, certainly. He wasn't the easiest man in Texas to live with. Just ask his ex-wife—if you could find her.

A snarl escaped him. He reached over to raise the radio volume and drown out thoughts of Reba.

As he rounded the last lazy curve before the turnoff to the Southpaw Cattle Company, a car in the distance caught his attention. Dax leaned forward, squinting into the overcast day.

The guy up ahead was either drunk, lost or having trouble. Dax took his foot off the accelerator. The car, a dirty blue economy model, was taking its share of the road out of the middle. It wove to the left and then back again as the driver began to slow.

With a beleaguered sigh, Dax tapped the brake. He wasn't in the mood for drunks. He wasn't in the mood for any kind of people, come to think of it.

For the last five years, all he'd really wanted out of life was his son and his ranch. The rest of the world could leave him the heck alone.

The car ahead slowed considerably and aimed for the side of the road. Maybe the fella was having car trouble.

After an afternoon of helping Bryce Patterson separate calves, Dax was too tired and dirty to play nice.

Still, he was a Texan, and the unspoken code of the country was rooted into him as deeply as the land itself. Out here, folks helped folks. Even when it was inconvenient.

Another car might not come along for hours and cell phone usage was spotty. He grabbed the plain black device from the seat next to a pair of dirty leather gloves and a pair of fencing pliers. Sure enough. Not a single bar of connection. He tossed the phone aside.

"Don't know what good the blasted thing is if it never works where you need it."

As he glanced back up, still grumbling, the dirty blue car wobbled off the road, onto the grass, and down a slight incline.

"Come on, buddy, stop. Stop!"

The car ahead kept rolling.

Five strands of brand-new barbed wire bowed

outward before snapping like strings on a fiddle. Orange fence posts toppled. Dax's fence posts.

"Blast it!" he ground out through gritted teeth and slammed the heel of his hand against the steering wheel. Somewhere in the back of his mind he was proud of holding back the expletives that tempted his foul-tempered tongue like flirty girls. A few years ago, he would have let fly with enough curses to make the grass blush, but with a mimicking boy dogging his boot prints, Dax had cleaned up his act. At least, that part of his act. Nothing much would clean up the rest.

Braking hard, he slid the truck onto the shoulder and bounded out into a comfortable November afternoon. The metallic slam reverberated over the quiet countryside, joining the rattle and wheeze of the car now captured in his barbed wire like a sad little bluebird.

"Hey, buddy," Dax hollered, as he approached the still-settling vehicle. "You okay?"

His question was met with the slow, painful screech of wire against metal, like fingernails on a blackboard. The driver didn't answer and made no effort to get out of the car.

Dax frowned, slowing his steps to assess the situation. Maybe the guy *was* drunk. Or maybe he was a criminal fixing to bushwhack an unsuspecting rancher. Dax considered going for the wolf rifle resting behind the seat of his truck but fought off the temptation. At six foot one and a hundred and eighty pounds, he could hold his own. Besides, he'd watched the car weave and wobble for a couple of miles. His gut told him something was amiss, either with the driver or the car. Maybe the guy was sick or something.

The car had been moving too slowly for any kind of serious injury so the accident was a by-product of another problem, not the cause. There had been no real impact other than the scraping entanglement with wire and the now-toppled fence posts.

"Blast it," he said again. No matter how tired he was, he'd have to get this fence back up in a hurry or risk having heifers all over the road by morning.

Slapping his Stetson down tight, Dax strode down the slight incline and across the narrow expanse of calf-high weeds toward the blue car. Other than a cloud of dust circling the tires and fenders, there was an eerie stillness around the vehicle.

Dax bent down to peer through the driver's side window. His gut lurched. The occupant was either a guy with really long hair or he was a woman. A real curse drifted through his head. He savored the word like chocolate pie. Women were a lot of trouble.

"Hey, lady." He tapped a knuckle on the glass while tugging the door handle with the opposite hand. "Do you need help?"

The woman was slumped forward, her head on the steering wheel. She was breathing, but her shoulders rose and fell rapidly as if in distress. Dax exhaled a gusty breath. Crying women were the second-worst kind.

Suddenly, the object of his concern arched back against the cloth seat. A cry ripped from her throat, scary enough to make him jump.

The sound shot adrenaline through Dax's veins. He yanked at the door. It was stuck. Strong from years of wrangling five-hundred-pound bovines, he yanked again, harder. The door gave way, digging up dead grass and dirt as it opened.

He reached in, touched the slender shoulder. "Miss. Miss, where are you hurt?"

She turned a narrow, haggard face in his direction. Her eyes were wide with fear. Dark blond hair stuck to a sweaty forehead and cheeks.

"My baby," she managed, the sound more groan than words.

"Baby?" Dax glanced quickly into the backseat, but saw no sign of a child.

The woman squirmed, her hands moving downward to her waist.

And that's when Dax knew. The woman with the wide, doe eyes and the teenager's face was in labor.

All the expletives he knew rushed to his tongue. Somehow he held them back, useless as they were to anyone but him.

"Talk to me, miss. How long have you been in labor?"

"The baby's coming."

The implication froze him solid. "Now?"

She managed a nod and then slid sideways in the seat, lying back against the opposite door. Her body rocked forward. She fought against it, battling the wave of pain he could see on her young face. Nature was taking its course.

Oh boy.

"I'm sorry," she said. "I'm sorry."

Sorry for what? Going into labor? Having a baby? The latter set his stomach churning even harder. He knew about that kind of woman.

But he had no time to ponder the past or the woman's cryptic statement. His brain shifted into warp speed. He had a dilemma here. A real dilemma. A strange young woman was having a baby in a car on his property and he was the only human being around to help.

Great. Just great.

"We need to get you to a hospital."

Her eyes glazed over and she made that deep groaning sound again. His pulse ricocheted off his rib cage. He'd heard this particular moan before from cows and mares. The woman was right. They were out of time.

"All right, miss, take it easy," he said, as much to calm his own nerves as hers. "Everything will be okay."

She nodded again, her huge eyes locked on his face, clinging to his words, trusting him, a total stranger. Dax got the weirdest feeling in his chest.

"How far along are you? I mean, is it time for the baby?"

"Two weeks away."

Close enough to know this was the real deal. Dang. Dang. Dang.

"How long have you been in labor?" he asked again.

Her body answered for her. Dax was smart enough to know that contractions this close could only mean one thing. Birth was imminent.

Think, Dax, think. What did he need? What could he do, other than wait for the inevitable?

"I'll be right back," he said past a tongue gone dry as an August day.

She managed to lever up, almost heaving toward him. "No! Don't leave. Please. Please."

Her pleading voice ebbed away on the wing of pain, but not before the sound hit Dax in the solar plexus. What kind of jerk did she take him for?

Guilt pinched him. Okay, so he'd resented the interruption to his afternoon. He'd wanted to drive right past. The point was he hadn't. He might be a jerk, but he wasn't a complete slimeball. Most of the time.

He touched her foot, hoping to reassure her. She was barefoot. A pair of fancy-looking silver shoes, complete with a perky bow, rested on the floor. He had the silliest thought that her feet were pretty. Slim and elegant like one of those ballet dancers.

What the devil was she doing out here alone?

"I need some things from my truck," he said. "It's right behind us. Not far at all. I'll only be a minute."

He loped to his Ford and dug out any- and everything he could find in the cab that might be of some use. There wasn't much, but he had an old blanket and plenty of water. A rancher could never be certain when he might be ten miles from the house and need water or a blanket. At least he could wash his hands and wrap the baby when it arrived. A bright-red bandanna on the floorboard caught his eye. Gavin had left it behind. Though the cloth was likely none too clean, he grabbed it anyway and drenched the soft cotton with water.

Back at the car, he leaned in to wipe the wet bandanna over the woman's damp forehead.

"It's me again," he said and then felt stupid for saying it. Who else would it be? The Seventh Cavalry?

The little mama made a small humming noise he took for gratitude. She must have been in between a contraction because her eyes were closed and her expression less tense.

As he straightened, he caught a whiff of some sweet-scented flower. Imagine, smelling like flowers at a time like this. She looked like a nightmare, but she smelled good.

He wondered one final time if he could toss her in the truck and get to the hospital in Saddleback in time.

Just as the thought flitted across his mind, her eyes flew open, distressed. "Oh, no. It's coming again."

She grabbed for his hand and squeezed with a grip that would have taken down a sumo wrestler.

"Easy now. Easy," he said, talking to her the way he would a first-time mare. What else could he do? He was no doctor.

All right, Coleman, he said to himself. You've delivered plenty of calves and foals. A baby can't be much different.

If he believed that he would have gone into the delivery room when Gavin was born.

"You're doing great. Long, deep breaths. Work with the pain, not against it." He didn't know where the advice was coming from, but she seemed to do better when he was talking. "Attagirl. You're doing good."

The contraction subsided and she dropped her head back again. Dax shared her relief. This baby-delivering business was hard work. His back ached from bending over the seat and his pulse pounded so hard against his eardrums, he thought he heard tom-toms.

Having long since tossed his hat aside, Dax wiped a sleeve across his forehead. Even with a cool breeze floating through the open door, he was sweating like a pig. But then, so was the little mama.

Drenched in sweat, her hair a wet wad around her face, she reminded Dax of a drowned kitten.

Pitiful-looking little thing. Somebody, somewhere was going to be real upset that she was out here alone on the Texas plains having a baby.

He wondered about the baby's father. About her family. She was young. Though her age was hard to discern at the moment, to an over-the-hill thirty-something like him she looked like a kid. She needed her family at a time like this, not some broken-down old cowboy with a bad attitude, who wanted to be anywhere but here.

She was a brave little thing. He'd give her that. Tough as a pine knot. She had to be scared out of her mind, young as she was, but she hadn't screamed or fought or carried on the way Reba had. She hadn't cussed him or the baby, either.

Dax tasted gall as the old humiliating memory thrust itself into his consciousness.

The little mama shifted slightly, emitting a murmur of dread. Another contraction must be on its way.

He gently rubbed her toes. She captured his eyes; a tiny smile lifted the corners of her mouth. Dax felt oddly heartened.

Here they were in about as intimate a situation as he could think of, and he didn't even know her name. What if something went wrong?

No, he wouldn't think of that. Even if his life was ruled by Murphy's Law, he was not going to allow anything bad to happen to this gritty little lady.

"Name's Dax," he said. "You feel like telling me yours?"

Something odd flickered behind pain-clouded eyes. She licked dry lips. Then her gaze slid away.

Before Dax could decide if her silence was fatigue or reluctance, the wave of nature took over again. As her shoulders rolled forward, straining, she whispered, "I wanted to be brave, but I'm so scared. Don't let anything happen to my baby."

The admission touched Dax somewhere in the cold lump he called a heart. "You're doing fine, little mama."

He wanted to say a lot of other encouraging things, to tell her how courageous he thought she was, but with the blood rushing in his temples and his gut twisting with anxiety at the huge responsibility before him, he just patted her pretty foot and muttered nonsense.

He didn't know how long he'd been there. Couldn't have been more than fifteen minutes though it felt like a lifetime when suddenly she gave one last heaving groan and it was over. She fell back against the car seat, her exhausted breathing loud in the quiet.

A baby, the smallest thing Dax could imagine, slipped into his waiting hands. He'd expected her to be pink and squalling the way Gavin had been. Instead, the tiny form was silent, limp and purplish.

His heart, already jumping and pumping to beat Dixie, rose into his throat. He glanced at the little mama and then down at the infant.

Please God, no. Not this.

CHAPTER TWO

THE BROWN-HAIRED BOY barreling across the yard of The Southpaw in cowboy boots and an open jean jacket lifted Dax's flagging spirits. The last few hours had been rough to say the least.

"Daddy!"

A swell of love bigger than his fifteen-hundred-acre ranch expanded in Dax's chest. He stopped in midyard and hunkered down. The sturdy little boy, smelling of pizza and backyard dirt, slammed into him. Small arms encircled his neck and squeezed.

Dax pressed the slender body to him, clinging to the thought that his son was alive and well. He didn't know what he would do if anything should ever happen to Gavin, a fact that had come home to him with a vengeance during these last few hours with the little mama.

Life was fragile. His thoughts flashed to the tiny newborn baby. Real fragile.

"Where you been?" Gavin was saying. "Rowdy had to stay a long time."

Dax looked up at the young ranch hand ambling lazily toward them, his usual crooked smile in place. Dax figured you could punch Rowdy Davis in the nose and he'd still grin. Sometimes the man's smirky cheer was downright irritating.

"Everything all right, boss?" Rowdy asked, clearly curious. "You were kind of short and not-too-sweet on the telephone. Had us worried some."

Short and not-too-sweet. Yep, that was him, all right. He'd simply told Rowdy to be at the house when the school bus delivered Gavin from kinder-garten and stay there. Then, he'd hung up, too wrung out to explain that he was at the emergency room fifteen miles away with a strange woman whose baby he'd just delivered.

"Boys, do I have a story to tell. Let's get in the house first. I could use a cold drink." Since playing doctor on the side of the road, his appetite was gone but he still wanted a cold soda pop and that hot shower.

Gavin wiggled back from his embrace. "A story about Wild Bill and the buffaloes?"

"No, son," Dax said. "Not that kind of story."

He rose, lifting the five-year-old up with him. Gavin looped an arm over his dad's shoulder and patted his opposite cheek. Dax felt that quivery feeling in the center of his chest. He didn't know what he'd done to deserve Gavin, but he was grateful. Without the boy, he would have given up on life long ago. As it was, he clung to the edges of hope, fighting off his own dark tendencies in an effort to give the motherless boy a decent upbringing. It wasn't easy. *Gavin* wasn't easy. And at times Dax no more understood the boy than he could understand Chinese.

A frown cut a deep gash between Gavin's black eyebrows. "It won't be scary, will it?"

Times like these. The boy was scared of his own shadow. Since hearing a ghost story at a fall party he'd been especially nervous.

"No, Gavin, it's not scary." He tried, but failed, to keep the annoyance out of his tone. The boy was skittish as a deer. The teacher had had to peel him away from Dax's side the first day of kindergarten. And Gavin had cried, an occurrence that both worried and embarrassed his father. A sissified kid wouldn't survive in today's mean world, but Dax didn't know how to change his child's disposition.

By now, they'd made the house and were inside. Dax tossed his hat at a heavy wooden end table, shrugged out of his jacket, and collapsed with an exaggerated heave onto a chair. The living room was enormous, compliments of his ex-wife who had insisted on a house big enough to entertain. Trouble was she'd done her entertaining while he was out working. He liked the house, though, liked the warm, golden-brown stone and wood fireplace and the wine-colored leather furniture.

He propped his boots on a squat ottoman. "You ever deliver a baby, Rowdy?"

Rowdy, who had ventured off to the kitchen, reappeared with a glass in hand. "What? Are you serious?"

Dax accepted the glass and gulped the icy drink in three long gulps. "Crazy afternoon. A young woman ran her car through my fence between here and Jake's windmill. I stopped to see what the problem was and she was having a baby."

Rowdy slithered into a chair, the grin forming a surprised O. "Man."

"Yeah. Tell me about it."

"Everything go okay? I mean, you delivered the baby and everything." As the reality of what Dax had done sank in, Rowdy leaned forward, elbows braced on his knees. "Holy smoke, Dax. Are they all right? The mama and baby, I mean?"

"The baby was kind of blue and not moving at first. I thought she was gone." Running a finger around the rim of the glass, he didn't mention how scared he'd been. The telling sounded a lot calmer than the actual event. "Then I thought about how calves are born with a lot of mucous sometimes, so I wiped her nose and mouth off with Gavin's bandana...." He patted the boy's knee. Gavin curled up next to him, listening to every word. "Just as I was getting ready to turn her upside down and swat her bottom, she let out a howl." Sweetest sound he'd ever heard.

"Man." Rowdy said again, seemingly devoid of intelligent comment. Dax understood. He'd been speechless himself at the time. As soon as the baby had cried, he'd wrapped her in the old blanket and made sure the mama was all right. Then he'd jumped behind the wheel of the car, forced the little economy onto the road and sped like a NASCAR racer to the emergency room.

"Where is she, Daddy? Why didn't you bring her home? I want to see her."

"She and her mama are in the hospital in Saddleback." He rattled the ice in his glass, shaking out a few more drops of cola.

Beneath a swatch of thick, dark hair a fretful frown puckered Gavin's forehead. "Are they sick?"

"The doc's going to check them over. But I think they'll be okay."

The child stuck his legs straight out from the couch and tapped the toes of his boots in a steady rhythm. "Noah's mama had a baby. They got to bring it home and keep it. Now he gots two brothers. But a sister would be okay, too."

Dax sighed. He and Gavin had this conversation every time one of the boy's schoolmates welcomed a new sibling. How did he explain to a five-year-old that his daddy wasn't the kind of man women wanted to have babies with?

"Is she from around here?" Rowdy's question gave Dax an excuse not to answer the boy. "The woman. Anybody we know?"

"No. Not even a Texan." He knew that for certain. Her buttery voice with its clipped syllables was upper-class Eastern, a Yankee. He'd stake his ranch on it. Even her clothes were different.

"What was she doing out here on a remote county road all by herself? Visiting someone?"

"Can't say." Though he'd been asking himself the same question. "We didn't exactly have a conversation."

"No, I guess not." Rowdy ran a thumb and forefinger along his chiseled jawline. "What did she look like? Is she pretty?"

Dax shot him a frown. His top ranch hand liked the ladies and had a new one on his arm every week. Women seemed to like him right back. Still, the question didn't sit well with Dax.

"She was a scared kid." Scared but tough and courageous. He couldn't get that out of his head or the thought of the tiny, mewling baby that had been born in his hands.

"I'm sad for her, Daddy, if she's scared. Can we go see her?"

"I told you she's all right." The words came out a little harsher than he'd intended. Gavin blanched and sat back against the couch.

Dax patted the boy's knee, letting him know the sharp retort wasn't aimed at him. Gavin was tenderhearted to his old man's hard-hearted, plain and simple. But Dax refused to feel guilty about wanting the strange day to end here and now. He'd done his part to help the woman. He'd played the good Samaritan. She was receiving expert care and the hospital would contact her family. He had a ranch to run and a downed fence to fix. He'd heard the last of the mysterious young mother and her baby. And that's the way he wanted it.

Jenna heard voices. She opened her eyes in a semi-darkened room that smelled of antiseptic and over-steamed food. She faced a wall and a wide pair of windows covered by blinds. The morning sun sliced through, shedding strips of pale yellow across a white woven blanket. Memory flooded in with the sunlight.

The pain, the car, a tall, gruff-talking rancher with gentle hands.

"Oh." Her hands shot to her belly. The baby. The man had delivered her little girl and brought them to the hospital. A mix of embarrassment and wonder filled her. She'd had her baby in a car with only a stranger to help. Mother would be mortified.

She shifted in the narrow hospital bed. Her body was sore and stiff, but not painfully so, a fact that surprised her. After the torture in the car she'd expected to be half-dead today.

She rolled to her side, eager to hold her new daughter.

The baby was gone.

A tremor rippled through her as the possibilities played through her head. The nurses had left the newborn here, at the bedside, in an Isolette. Jenna was positive.

Had the Carrington machine already discovered her whereabouts?

Fighting the stiff sheets, she sat upright, only to tumble sideways onto the pillow, light-headed and weak. Blood roared in her temples. She took deep breaths, waiting until the black dots dissipated.

For a long moment, she remained still, frustration in every breath. Had someone recognized her and called her family? Was her baby girl even now in the smothering bosom of the Carrington clan?

The heavy wooden door opened with a swish. Jenna braced to face her censuring mother, determined to stand strong for her baby.

When a nurse appeared, backside first, Jenna wilted against the pillow in relief.

"Everything looks great with your little princess," the woman said, rolling the Isolette into the room. "Doctor checked her all out, gave her the requisite medications and said she was perfect."

"I didn't know where you'd taken her." Her voice sounded breathless and scared.

The nurse, a young woman with a long, black ponytail, whose tag read Crystal Wolf, RN, gave her a sympathetic pat. "Sorry, hon, you were sleepin' like a rock, so I didn't want to disturb you. Not after what you went through. You ready for her? Or are you too tired? You look a little pale."

Jenna held out her arms. Color would return now that she knew her mother wasn't on the premises. "Yes, please let me hold her."

"She's a darling. So pretty with all that fine golden hair and her little turned-up nose."

Jenna thought her daughter looked like an alien. A withered old lady alien. "Will her head always be pointed like this?"

With a shake of dangly white earrings, the nurse laughed. She reached over, flipped the soft pink blanket back and gently massaged the baby's head with a cupped hand. "You do that every day and before you know it, the cone head will be gone."

"Thank goodness." Jenna gave a shaky laugh.

She'd read books and searched the Internet on the topic of parenting and felt competent to be a mother, but now that the moment was upon her, the idea of caring for another human being frightened her. She had no home, no job, and no one to help. For a person who'd never been allowed to do anything for herself, she had a great deal to learn—fast.

"Do you have a name for this little princess?"

A gentle smile lifted Jenna's mouth. "Sophie. Sophie Joy because she is the greatest joy I've ever known."

"Oh, hon, that's beautiful."

Sophie stretched, her tiny face screwing up in an adorable expression. Jenna's whole body seized up with an overwhelming love, a love so powerful tears filled her eyes. This was why she'd run away. This precious bit of humanity deserved to love and be loved for the right reasons. She deserved to grow up free from fear and the hovering, controlling influences that had stymied Jenna's life since birth.

Her family, particularly Elaine Von Gustin Carrington, would not control this baby's life the way they'd controlled hers.

People who envied her opulent lifestyle had no idea what it was like to live in an ivory tower surrounded by hired bodyguards and nannies and private tutors. They had no idea the sadness of a child never allowed to play outside or with other children who were "not like us." They'd never sat with their faces pressed against the window watching others play in the snow while wondering what it would be like to build a snowman with someone other than a hired nanny and a burly bodyguard.

The world considered her a spoiled rich princess, but they were wrong. Elaine Carrington's elitism and her kidnapping paranoia had made her only daughter a lonely child, a prisoner of her family's enormous wealth.

Which was exactly the reason Jenna wanted Sophie Joy to grow up in a normal home, in a normal town, doing normal things. She'd play with other children and go to a real school and maybe even join a soccer team if she wanted to. When she was a teenager, she'd hang out at the mall and have sleepovers and attend school dances with friends of her own choosing.

Sophie would have a childhood her mother had only dreamed of, a wish that sounded foolish to most people—even her late husband, though he'd pretended something far different in the beginning. Early in their secret relationship, Derek had nurtured Jenna's longing to be a regular wife living in the suburbs. But the Carrington money had followed her in marriage, corrupting the boy who'd claimed to love her, and the few weeks of normalcy had disappeared as quickly as his love.

In the end, her mother had been right about her fortune-hunting husband, and Jenna had gone home to the estate, broken. From Derek, she had learned a cruel fact of life—never trust a man, no matter how pretty his promises. Men were only interested in someone like Jenna for one thing. As Mother had so succinctly put it, "A trust fund makes any woman attractive."

She swallowed back the festering hurt. She might not be beautiful, but she refused to care anymore. All that mattered now was assuring Sophie the happy, uncomplicated life and freedom she had never known.

To do that, she could never go back to the Carrington Estate or even to Pennsylvania.

As she marveled at her baby's velvet skin, at eyelashes so pale and perfect, the pink rosebud mouth, Jenna made a silent promise. No matter what she had to do from here, her daughter would lead a normal life.

The nurse, whom she'd almost forgotten, patted her arm. In a pleasant drawl she said, "I'll be back in a few, Jenna. We'll get your vitals again and then you'll be good to go."

Jenna's head snapped up. "Go?"

Go where? She'd hoped to stay in the hospital a few days, to get her thoughts together and form a plan. To read the newspaper and make sure the world hadn't been alerted to her disappearance. To figure out where to go and what to do with a newborn.

"Sure thing. Unless there are problems, an OB stays twenty-four hours or less these days. Would you like for me to phone your family?" The young woman reached for the chart at the end of the bed, flipped open a few pages. A frown appeared between her black eyebrows. "Seems we didn't get that information when you arrived yesterday evening. Well, it was a hectic time. No problem. Someone from the business office will be in. They always extract their pound of flesh."

Jenna managed a weak smile at the woman's joke. She hadn't thought about the hospital bill or even about the records a hospital would keep on her and Sophie.

She'd given them her name yesterday and no one had reacted. But she wasn't surprised no one recognized her face. Due to her family's paranoia, their only child had been publicly photographed very little. Jenna found a certain irony in that. The fear that had made her life a prison might be the very thing that assured her freedom. Unless her parents had released her disappearance to the press, there was a chance no one here in this small Texas town would ever guess that she was one of *the* Carringtons, reluctant heiress to a staggering financial empire.

"Would you like for me to call Dax?"

Jenna blinked. "Who?"

"The rancher who brought you in. Dax Coleman. I thought you knew him."

A warm blush crept up the back of Jenna's neck. She hadn't remembered her rescuer's name. "No."

"Oh, well, I just assumed…" The nurse flapped a hand. "Never mind. My mouth is running away, though it's too bad about Dax. He seemed real concerned, and for a reclusive guy like that, well, we just figured the two of you knew each other."

Was the nurse asking if she and Dax knew each other in the Biblical sense? Did she think Dax Coleman was Sophie's father?

Her flush of embarrassment deepened.

"Mr. Coleman," she said in her most dignified voice, "was kind enough to render aid to a damsel in distress. But no, I had never before made his acquaintance."

The nurse, who was darkly pretty and not much older than herself, looked disappointed. "Well, then, that's really too bad. Dax could use a spark in his life after what happened."

Jenna refused to ask the obvious question. "You know him?"

"Sure. In a region this sparsely populated everyone knows everyone else. Dax is an old friend of mine. Or used to be." The nurse fanned her face with her fingertips. "He's still pretty delicious-looking, too, if you know what I mean. Don't tell my husband I said that." She laughed.

Delicious-looking? Jenna remembered a gravelly, rough voice and strong, calloused hands, though he'd been as gentle as could be with her and Sophie. As far as his looks, she could only recall intense green eyes and dark hair that fell in sweaty waves onto his forehead. A cowboy. She remembered that, too.

En route to the hospital, he hadn't said much. But he'd glared at her and Sophie in the rearview mirror every few minutes until Jenna became convinced she'd somehow angered him. At the time, she'd been too tired and shaky to wonder about her roadside rescuer. Now she did.

"You were lucky he came along," Nurse Wolf said. "Out here you can drive forever and not see a soul."

She almost had.

"Yes, I owe him a debt of gratitude," Jenna muttered, absently rubbing the side of her finger over Sophie's delicate cheek. She'd never been indebted to anyone before, ever. People were indebted to the Carringtons, not the other way around, but the cowboy, a total stranger, had been there for her and her baby when they'd had no one else. She wasn't likely to forget that.

"I'll be back in a few," the nurse said and started out the door.

"Nurse?"

The woman did an about-face. "It's Crystal. Please."

"Crystal," Jenna said, oddly pleased at the simple request. "Would you mind bringing me a newspaper or two?"

"Nothing newsworthy ever happens around here except church dinners and baby showers and school sports, but I'll bring you a paper."

The simple activities sounded like heaven to Jenna who'd never experienced a single one of them. "Thank you."

With a hand wave, Crystal sashayed out of the room, only to lean back into the room with a twinkle in her eye.

"Prepare yourself. A certain delicious cowboy is headed your way."

Jenna was sure her mouth fell open. "You're kidding."

But Crystal had already disappeared, leaving the door open.

Dax kicked himself all the way down the hall. He had no idea what he was doing here. He'd done the right thing already. He'd played the good Samaritan. He should be on the south side of the ranch right now fixing a water gap before snow or rain made the work miserable. But here he was at

Saddleback Hospital in the maternity ward, feeling as uncomfortable as if he'd stumbled into one of those ladies' lingerie stores.

But he was here. Might as well get this over with.

Stetson in hand, he used the opposite hand to tap on the open door, doing his level best not to look inside until he was invited.

"Come in," a feminine voice said. He remembered that voice. Soft and educated and worried. He'd dreamed about it last night. Imagine that. Dreaming about a woman's voice. And her bare feet. And the way she'd gazed at him with trust.

Blast it. That's why he was here. She'd haunted his dreams and he'd not been able to get a thing done this morning until he was certain she and her baby were in good shape.

According to the desk nurse the baby he'd delivered was doing well. Thank God. That should have been enough. He should have turned tail and headed for his truck.

But no. He had to see for himself that the brave young woman with the fancy voice was okay.

With a final inward kick, he stepped into the room.

His eyes went straight to the bed. Fluffed up in white sheets, the little mama looked small and flushed. But good. Real good.

Her dark blond hair, sweaty and uncombed yesterday, was clean and neatly brushed and lay across her shoulders in a soft wave. She was prettier than he'd thought. Her thin face was blessed with long doe-shaped eyes the color of pancake syrup and a mouth that tipped up at the corners.

The thing that really drew his attention was the bundle nestled against her breast. A small egg-shaped head covered with a pink stocking cap protruded from a matching pink blanket. He could see the curve of the baby's cheek, the tiny button nose, the rise and fall of her body as she breathed. Thank God she was breathing smooth and even now.

He allowed himself to breathe, as well, aware that he hadn't quite believed the child would be alive.

The little mama saw the direction of his gaze and looked down at her baby with an expression that punched Dax in the gut. Mother love radiated from her. The kind Gavin had never known.

His admiration for the girl-woman, whatever she was, went up another notch. She loved her baby. She'd be a good mama.

He shifted, heard the scratchy sound of his boots against tile. What now? He'd seen what he came for. Could he just turn around and walk out?

"Would you like to see her?"

The words startled him, breaking through his thoughts of escape. Crushing the brim of his hat between tense fingers, he stepped closer to the bed and cleared the lump out of his throat. "She okay?"

"Perfect, thanks to you." The doe eyes looked up at him, again with that expression of trust.

"What about you?"

Roses bloomed on her cheeks. "Very well. Again thanks to you."

He'd embarrassed her, made her recall the liberties he'd taken with her body. He wanted to apologize, but he never seemed to know the right things to say to women.

"Would you like to hold her?" The little mama stretched the bundle in his direction. The blanket fell away from the baby's face and Dax went all mushy inside. He remembered how Gavin had looked those first few days. All squished and out of shape but so innocent Dax had fallen in instant, overpowering love.

Dax stepped away from the bed. "No."

He'd been to the feed store earlier. He couldn't be clean enough to hold a baby.

"Oh." The little mama's face fell. He felt like a jerk, but didn't figure it mattered. Once he was out of here, he'd never see her again.

"Sophie and I are grateful for everything you did."

"Sophie? Pretty."

"I thought so. Sophie Joy."

Feeling oversize, out of place and like a complete idiot, Dax nodded. "I gotta get back to the ranch. Just wanted to check on you."

"I appreciate it." She reached out a slender hand and touched his arm. Even through the long-sleeved jacket, Dax imagined the heat and pressure of her fingers seeping into his bloodstream. His mind went to the softness of the skin on her bare feet. She was probably silky all over.

Something inside him reacted like a wild stallion. He jerked away. What the devil business did he have feeling attracted to a new mother, a woman young enough to be his…well, his niece or something. She was a kid. A kid. And he was a dirty old man.

Without another word, he spun away and hurried out the door, down the hall and out into the gray November where the Texas wind could slap some sense into him.

CHAPTER THREE

STUNNED, JENNA STARED as the cowboy retreated, turning his trim, anvil-shaped back toward her before charging out of the room as if a pack of dogs was after him.

"I don't think he likes us, Sophie," she murmured. Though she couldn't imagine why. He'd behaved the same way in the car yesterday, as though she'd angered him. Yet he'd helped her. And he'd come to visit her in the hospital.

"What a strange man."

He'd left so fast, the scent of a very masculine cologne lingered in the room like a contrail. Were all Texas cowboys so…reticent? Well, it didn't matter. She would likely never see the man again, and the truth was, Dax Coleman had saved her, saved Sophie, and she would be forever grateful.

Before she had time to ponder further, a woman entered the room. Dressed in a black pantsuit and white, round earbobs of the 1960s, the woman carried a clipboard and a stack of papers.

"I'm Alice Pernisky from the business office." She rolled an over-the-bed table in front of Jenna. "Let's put the baby in the bassinet while we take care of the paperwork."

Her no-nonsense style brooked no argument, so Jenna did as she said. She was worried enough about completing these forms.

"Let's take care of the birth certificate first." The woman pushed a paper under her nose. "The doctor has filled in the basics, but we'll need your complete information, your name, the father's name, and of course—" she allowed a thin smile "—the name you've chosen for your baby."

Heart thudding crazily, Jenna stared down at the form and wondered if falsifying a birth certificate was illegal. Ink pen hovering over the sheet, she considered long and hard.

After a few seconds, Alice Pernisky said, "My dear, if you don't want to put the father's name, that's fine. Just take care of the rest. We see more of that kind of thing than we used to."

Heat flushed from her toes to her head. They thought she was an unwed mother who had no idea who Sophie's father was.

"My husband died," she said, which was true, though Derek had been out of her life long before the car crash that killed him.

"I'm sorry," Alice said automatically, although Jenna did not think the woman believed her.

Would people always assume the worst if she didn't put Derek's name on the birth certificate?

Of course they would. This document would follow Sophie all the days of her life. And Jenna would not do that to her daughter.

Taking a deep breath, Jenna bent to the form and began to write. After the divorce, her parents had insisted she return to Carrington and she'd gladly done so. Derek had humiliated her enough. But now, his name might be the one thing that could keep her and Sophie from being discovered.

If she was going to start her life anew with Sophie, she would do it correctly. She would lie only if she had to, and pray her family wouldn't be able to trace her through hospital documents bearing only her married name.

As she handed over the form, another form appeared beneath. "Those are your release forms, your instructions on self-care, and of course your hospital bill. Do you have insurance we can file?"

Jenna gulped. Lie number one. "No."

"How do you plan to take of this? We take check or credit card, of course, and if need be, we can set up a payment plan."

"Cash. I'll pay cash."

The woman pulled back, startled. "Cash?"

"Yes." Accessing her bank accounts or using her credit cards would be too easy to trace. Until she and Sophie were established and on their own, she would not even consider such a thing. Maybe never. Cash was the only way.

Jenna reached for her handbag, aware of how out-of-place the designer crocodile looked in the hands of a woman without health insurance. As she withdrew the funds from her wallet, she had the absurd thought that Alice might think she'd stolen the bag, along with the money. What if she called the police?

Jenna's hand trembled as she counted out the correct amount and handed it over. She could feel the woman's curious stare and almost hear the wheels turning in her head.

When the last paper was signed and the woman left the room, Jenna felt light-headed with relief. Before putting her purse aside so she could hold Sophie again, she counted the remaining bills in her wallet. A quiver of worry drew her brows together. Never in her life had she needed to consider money. A Carrington simply grew up knowing there was plenty. Discussing personal finance was considered vulgar.

But she was no longer a Carrington. She was no longer one of Pennsylvania's old money debutantes with an endless supply of cash and credit cards. She was a single mother alone, scared…and nearly broke.

A tangle of nerves and hormones and uncertainty gathered inside Jenna a short time later as she leafed through two newspapers, including a national one, and waited to be dismissed from the hospital.

After careful scrutiny of each page, she sat back against the scratchy chair and let some of her tension ebb away. There was no mention of a missing heiress. At least, not yet.

She flipped to the classifieds of the local paper, the *Saddleback Sentinel,* and scanned the help wanted ads. After a couple of minutes, her lips curved in wry humor. If she could run a drilling rig or drive an eighteen-wheel truck, she'd be in business before nightfall.

"Looking for anything in particular?"

At Crystal's voice, Jenna jumped. The nurse stood in front of her with a wheelchair, smile curious.

The newspaper crinkled as Jenna refolded it and placed it on the nightstand. Part of her longed to confide in the friendly nurse and admit she needed a job. She opened her mouth to do just that but Sophie chose that moment to awake with a startled cry. All thought rushed to her baby.

"Is she all right?"

Crystal chuckled. "Yes, Jenna. She's fine. Baby's cry. Get used to it. Real used to it. I probably startled her with the noise of the wheelchair."

"Oh." Jenna fought down a blush and gingerly scooped her daughter from the Isolette. "Shh, darling, Mommy's here."

To her joy, Sophie stopped crying immediately. Her scrunched-up face relaxed as she blinked up at her mother. A swell of love ballooned in Jenna's chest.

"You two ladies ready for your free ride in a wheelchair?"

"Can't we walk?"

"Hospital regs, I'm afraid." Crystal patted the black seat. "Hop aboard the Wolf Express for the only free thing in this hospital."

With a smile at Crystal's humor, Jenna complied, jittery to think that in a few minutes, she and Sophie would be alone and on their own. She'd known when she left the estate that this would happen, but she hadn't expected it to happen quite so soon. She'd hoped to be settled somewhere before Sophie's birth, to have the trunk full of layette items set up and ready for the baby's homecoming. She'd even had fantasies of a job where she could keep Sophie with her. Instead, she was down to her last few dollars with nowhere to take her newborn daughter.

Crystal guided the wheelchair down the long, pristine hospital corridor and out the exit toward the parking lot.

"So what did Dax have on his mind?"

The question startled Jenna. She'd tried to put the rugged cowboy out of her thoughts. "I'm not sure."

"What did he say?"

"He asked if Sophie and I were all right and then he left."

Crystal chuckled. "He's not a big talker."

"I noticed."

"Hunky, though, huh?"

"I suppose." She really didn't want to talk about the cowboy. "I think I scared him off."

"Nah. He's just quiet. I don't think anything scares Dax Coleman except his ex-wife."

"He's divorced?"

"Yep. For years, but as far as I know, he's never dated again. Reba did a number on him, the witch."

Jenna, in spite of herself, tilted her head in question. "Was she?"

Crystal hitched one shoulder. "I never liked her much, though some folks think the divorce was Dax's fault."

He wasn't exactly Mr. Congeniality, but after the way he'd helped her, she felt compelled to take his side. "Outsiders seldom know the full story."

She knew that from personal experience.

"Too true. And Dax has always been one of the good guys. Or he used to be."

Jenna let the subject of the cowboy drop. Something about him unsettled her in the oddest manner.

Wheels clattered over the concrete parking lot as Crystal pushed her and Sophie into the weak sunshine. The fresh air felt good on Jenna's skin after the stuffiness of the hospital.

Holding her pink-wrapped daughter snuggled close to her body, a few free baby supplies compliments of the hospital stuffed between her side and the arm of the chair, she couldn't help thinking how different this dismissal would have been in Philadelphia. Surrounded by masses of flowers, a private nurse, and at least two burly bodyguards—one for her and one for Sophie—she would have been gently hustled into a waiting car driven by Fredrick, the family chauffeur, and driven home to the nursery suite especially commissioned and furnished by her mother. There, in the stark white nursery, a nanny would have whisked Sophie from her arms and taken over every nuance of the baby's care. If Jenna was lucky and made enough fuss, she might get to hold her child occasionally.

No, she'd made the right decision, even if she had no idea where she would go or what she would do now.

The wheelchair slowed. "Which way is your car?"

"Out to the left, I think. It's a faded blue." She scanned the parking lot, hoping she'd recognize the still-unfamiliar vehicle. Was it only four days ago when, in an effort to conceal her true destination, she'd taken the train as far as Baltimore and purchased the car from a classified ad?

"There." She pointed, gripping Sophie tighter as Crystal picked up speed.

When they reached the car, the nurse held the baby while Jenna dug out her keys and unlocked the door.

"Someone washed my car," she said in wonder, gazing into the backseat. Someone had even cleaned the interior, which now smelled of vinyl cleaner instead of dust and designer perfume.

"Interesting," Crystal commented. "Must have been Dax."

"Why would he do that?"

The nurse shrugged. "Don't know, but it sure is interesting. Visiting you at the hospital and washing your car. Maybe he has a thing for new mothers."

Shocked, Jenna's snapped around to stare at the nurse. Crystal burst into laughter. "Girl, you should see your face. I was only teasing."

"Oh." But Jenna got that fluttery feeling in her stomach again. What was it about the mention of Dax Coleman that stirred her so?

"Where's your car safety seat?"

"My what?"

"Texas has a child safety seat law. You can't leave the hospital with Sophie until you have one installed."

One more thing she hadn't thought of. "Where can I get one?"

Crystal studied her from beneath black eyelashes. "The hospital sells them. If you'd like I'll run back inside and get one for you."

"Do you mind?"

"Not a bit." She named a price and Jenna extracted the required bills from her wallet.

"Cute purse," Crystal said. "Is that real alligator?"

"Crocodile. It was a gift," she hurried to say, downplaying her ability to purchase such a bag. What she really wanted to say was, "Want to buy it?" The cost of the handbag would go a long way toward apartment rent.

"Wish somebody would buy me gifts like that."

"No, you don't," she nearly said to the nurse's retreating back. You don't want someone to try to control you with money and things and fear.

While Crystal was gone, Jenna thought of her dwindling resources, spirits ebbing lower and lower. Even during her short marriage, they'd always had her considerable bank account, a fact that had changed her average Joe husband to Joe Millionaire in a matter of weeks.

She tasted the bitterness of his betrayal on her tongue. Before her name was dry on the marriage license, Derek, who had sworn he was not at all interested in Jenna's inheritance, had begun flashing her credit cards, living the high life and leaving her at home when she refused to play along.

"Here we go, Jenna." Crystal reappeared to pop open the back door and installed the car seat in short order. She held out her arms. "Give me the princess."

Jenna complied, happiness replacing the gloom. She wasn't alone anymore.

As the nurse settled the baby and strapped her in, Jenna watched, learning. She wasn't stupid. She was just inexperienced.

"All set." Crystal slammed the back door. Sophie's little arms jerked upward but before Jenna could rush to soothe her, she'd resettled.

"Thank you for everything, Crystal." Jenna slid behind the wheel, uncertainty overtaking her again. What now?

"You are as welcome as summer." Crystal, holding the driver's door open, leaned in, her dark eyes soft with concern. "Honey, are you going to be all by yourself with this new baby? Do you have anyone to help you?"

"Oh, certainly, I'll have plenty of—" Jenna lifted a hand to wave off the suggestion that she had no one and then let the hand fall against the warm steering column.

"No," she admitted, suddenly needing to talk to this young woman who was kindness personified. "My husband died. I'm alone, looking for a place to start fresh. I thought Sophie and I would be happier somewhere new, away from the memories." She gave a pathetic little laugh. "So here we are."

That much was absolutely true.

Crystal draped an arm over the top of the car door, all her weight on one hip. "So that explains it. I knew something was not right, but bless your heart, all alone. That's awful."

The woman's compassion was almost Jenna's undoing. She fought back a wave of self-pity, and then, angry at herself, she refused to acknowledge the emotion. She'd chosen this route even if things hadn't gone quite as smoothly as she'd planned. Starting fresh was the best thing for Sophie, no matter how difficult the first few weeks might be. She could do this. She wanted to do this. For her baby girl and even for herself. Alone was better than lonely and utterly dependent, with your life mapped out before you were out of diapers. Now that she had Sophie, she would never be lonely again.

Stiffening her spine, she said, "Can you direct me to a hotel?"

After a moment's consideration, Crystal took a scrap of paper from her uniform pocket and scribbled on it. "There's a little B and B over on Second Street, not fancy but decent and clean. Terri Wallace runs it. We graduated high school together. Nice gal. Tell her I sent you. I put my phone number on there, too. Call me if I can do anything. Or just to talk. I can always use a new friend."

A friend. Crystal couldn't begin to comprehend how much the offer heartened Jenna.

"Could I ask one more favor?"

"Name it."

"I need a job." She swallowed her pride and said the rest. "In a hurry. Do you have any suggestions?"

The darkly pretty face twisted in thought. "Can't think of anything right off."

Jenna's hopes fell. She pressed her lips together in dismay. Maybe Saddleback wasn't the right town. Maybe she should drive on to Austin or even on to Los Angeles, where she and Sophie could get lost in the masses. But she was too tired and shaky from childbirth to drive that far today.

"Listen," Crystal was saying. "The county employment office is located here in Saddleback. It might be worth a try." She rattled off an address. "In a few days, when you're feeling rested, just drive down Main Street. When you see the boot store—you can't miss it, there's an enormous sign out front shaped like a big red cowboy boot—the employment office is right across the street. Shirley McDougal runs the place. Sweet as pie. She knows everyone and everything in Saddleback. Go talk to her. Tell her I sent you."

"I don't know how I'll ever repay your generosity."

Crystal patted her shoulder. "Just take care of Princess Sophie and give me a call when you get settled. We'll have lunch or something."

Still stunned by the kindness of strangers in this Texas town, Jenna could only nod, fighting back the tears that suddenly clogged her throat.

Crystal stepped back from the car, lifting a hand to wave as Jenna slammed the door, cranked the engine and pulled out of the Saddleback Hospital parking lot.

CHAPTER FOUR

TEN DAYS LATER, Jenna knew she'd recuperated as long as her limited finances would allow. Twice during that time, Crystal Wolf had stopped by the B and B, spreading her brand of Texas hospitality, but Jenna had been afraid to tell her new friend just how desperate things were becoming.

After a sleepless night of baby care and worry, Jenna now stared at a pile of unfamiliar forms at the county employment agency while the woman named Shirley cooed and hummed to Sophie. From the moment she'd started the paperwork, Jenna had been stumped. About the only thing she could fill out easily was her name. She'd finally scribbled the address of the Red Rose Bed-and-Breakfast as her residence, but she had nothing to put in the experience and reference forms.

"What kind of work are you looking for, Jenna, sugar?" Shirley asked, never looking up from Sophie's sleeping face.

"I'm not at all particular, but I would like to

secure a position where I could keep my baby with me."

"Hmm. Well, that leaves out the fast-food places. I send a lot of folks to them. The junior high is always looking for substitutes, though you'd have to leave this precious one with a sitter." She glanced up, brows drawing together over her black plastic glasses. "Don't suppose you have a degree in education or computers?"

Jenna shook her head, hopes tumbling. "No."

She'd spent one semester at Brown University under the watchful eyes of her grandparents. Unfortunately, neither they nor her ever-present bodyguards were as watchful as her mother would have liked. She'd met Derek there. Heads had rolled but Mother's fury had come too late.

"How about the medical field? There's always a need for that. Nurses, paramedics, lab techs…"

Again Jenna shook her head. An overprotected heiress was a useless human being.

Shirley studied her beneath thick blond bangs. "Do you have any training? Any experience at all?"

Jenna's hopes fell even further as she bowed her head to the application and didn't answer. She could plan a dinner party for fifty, direct servants and organize a charity auction; none of those skills appeared all that useful in Saddleback, Texas.

Even if no one recognized her here, she might have to move on. Yet, Saddleback's friendliness and easy pace drew her. She wanted to remain in this remote place where her daughter had been born and where people treated her as just another person.

Shirley pushed her glasses up with one finger. "You don't seem the type, but would you mind doing domestic work? We get a few calls for that."

Domestics? As in a maid? Or a cook?

An idea popped into her head. She and Mother had taken a gourmet cooking class from a well-known chef. She'd loved it.

"Could I possibly keep Sophie with me?"

"That would be up to your employer, but I think most people would be all right with a little one around as long as you did the work."

"Then," Jenna said, suddenly thrilled at the idea, "I am a fabulous chef and quite amenable to domestics."

Surely, cleaning a house couldn't be that difficult. She'd watched the maids dozens of times.

Shirley grinned. "My dear girl, I think I may have something for you. A family outside of town needs a cook and general housekeeper. Want to check it out?"

A renewed zip of energy had Jenna sitting up straighter. "Absolutely."

The woman returned a still-sleeping Sophie to Jenna's arms and then riffled through a set of files, pulling out a card.

"Here you go," she said, handing the information to Jenna. "I'll call and let him know you're coming for an interview."

Jenna was beyond delighted, though admittedly a bit nervous as she gripped the index card in her fingers. This was her opportunity to start life all over again, to make a life for herself and Sophie, to finally be her own person.

With held breath, she glanced at the name and address of her prospective employer.

The information she read froze the smile on her lips.

Southpaw Cattle Company. Dax Coleman.

Dax slammed the telephone receiver down, then looked around the living room to be sure no one was listening before letting out a curse.

Last night, he'd dreamed of the little mama and her baby. Again. Then he'd lain awake, staring up at the dark ceiling as he listened to a north wind rattle the trees outside and wondered if the fragile pair was all right.

They haunted him. He couldn't get them out of his head, a fact that infuriated him.

Now a phone call to the hospital told him exactly nothing. What had he expected? The day he'd visited her, he hadn't even thought to ask her name. He'd just asked for the mother and baby he'd brought into the emergency room. How stupid was that? All the receptionist would tell him was that mother and baby had been discharged, but unless Dax was next of kin, and she knew danged well he wasn't, no other information could be shared.

A distant relative of Reba's, the hateful old biddy had never liked him anyway. She'd enjoyed putting him in his place.

"Fine," he said to absolutely no one. The little mama and her baby were gone. They were all right. He could forget them. They were not his responsibility. He had enough of that to choke a horse already. End of topic.

No use fretting over a baby girl he'd never see again when he had his own problems to contend with. Shirley down at the employment office was sending him a new recruit this morning.

He laughed, a mocking sound. Good old Shirley had warned him she was sick and tired of finding him housekeepers only to have him run them off with his cranky-butted attitude. Her words. Cranky-butted. He could almost see her shaking her finger in his face.

He'd laughed when she'd said it. Now he wondered. Was he cranky-butted? Was he a bitter man with a bad attitude? Was that why Reba had walked out, leaving behind a new baby, a husband who'd adored her and an easy life?

He kicked a chair leg. Reba and her betrayal was not allowed in this house.

Dax snatched up the two empty glasses and a corn dog wrapper from the coffee table, toting them to the big, silver, step-levered trash can in the kitchen. Silly to feel nervous about interviewing a prospective housekeeper, but he needed to get this woman on board right away. Rushing home to meet Gavin's school bus each evening took a bite out of his productivity.

He trailed back through the living room, wiping a shirtsleeve over the fireplace mantel then grimaced to discover his shirt was now covered in dust. He batted at it and sneezed when the dust flew upward, dancing in the overhead light.

The doorbell chimed.

As he strode across the carpet toward the foyer, he noticed two of Gavin's miniature cars and a sock sticking out from under the couch—along with a dust bunny the size of a jack rabbit.

He gave up. He was a rancher. This was why he hired housekeepers.

With a final slap at his dusty shirtsleeve Dax yanked the front door open. His mouth also fell open as he looked down into a familiar face. A very young, slender and decidedly pretty face.

Blast it.

What the devil was the little mama doing on his porch? Please, please. Surely not to apply for the housekeeper position.

Hot on the heels of his plea was a thrill that rocked him to his boot tips. Double blast and a dozen other curses. A burned-out old cowboy like him getting palpitations over a teenager.

"Mr. Coleman?"

Given his wayward thought processes and after what they'd shared in her car, hearing her refer to him as Mr. Coleman was creepy. He should call the sheriff on himself.

"Dax," he growled, wondering why he was in such a weird mood. His gaze went to the pink bundle in her arms and stayed there. "How's the little one?"

"Wonderful. Perfect."

"Good."

They seemed destined to repeat the same sentences to each other. Blast it.

Finding his manners, though admittedly a bit rusty, he stepped aside and motioned toward the interior. "Want to come in?"

She came inside, moving past him with a grace and elegance that had him thinking of ballerinas and her pretty feet again. He caught a whiff of that flowery perfume he'd smelled in her car. As if his eyelids ruled his body, they dropped closed and he inhaled. Nice. Really nice.

"Dax?"

His eyelids flew open. Why had he invited her inside?

"Have a seat," he said, feeling about as awkward as a three-legged horse.

He peered out the door, craning his neck to look down the long, long driveway. Nothing but her blue car. Where was the real housekeeper? Please let her pull up soon.

"Are you expecting someone?" the little mama asked, still standing in the middle of his foyer and close enough for him to see the flecks of gold in her eyes.

He backed up a step.

"A housekeeper applicant from the employment office is on her way out."

The little mama turned bright pink. "Oh," she said. "That would be me."

She handed him a card bearing the logo of the county employment office and her name, Jenna Garwood. Dax's heart stopped. Jenna Garwood was the name Shirley had given him. Oh no.

"You?"

Her pink drained away. "Is there a problem? I can cook. I'm an accomplished chef."

Dax was already shaking his head. "I don't think so."

The last thing he wanted was this new mama who haunted his dreams to live here. She was probably a teenage runaway. He'd get arrested just for thinking about the way her eyebrows took wing at the ends and for noticing how full and pouty her lips were. She was trouble with a baby in arms.

"I need a mature woman to look after my boy."

"I can do that."

"This ranch is far from town. It gets lonely out here."

"I'm accustomed to solitude."

Getting desperate now, Dax pointed to the infant. "You have a new baby."

"I promise to keep up with my domestic duties

and care for her, as well. Mothers have maintained homes for millennia while rearing children." Her doe-eyes had widened, almost pleading. "I can do it."

Before he did something really stupid, Dax grumbled, "No."

The little mama—Jenna Garwood—drew up to her full height, which wasn't much, come to think of it. "May I inquire as to why?"

Inquire as to why? What kind of question was that? Finally, he blurted, "How old are you?"

The corners of her too-full lips tilted up. "I'm twenty-two. Why? Age has nothing to do with anything."

Oh, yes it did. He was thirty-four years old and she wasn't.

"A young girl like you—" he started.

"I'm not a girl. I'm a woman—with a baby to support."

Like he didn't know that.

"I know this isn't ideal. Not for me, either, but I really need this job, Mr. Coleman."

"Dax," he growled. And what did she mean, this wasn't ideal for her, either? What was wrong with his ranch? "I have a son. He's in kindergarten."

"I have a daughter. You delivered her."

Jenna Garwood did not play fair. Had she intuitively known he felt some kind of warped sense of responsibility for her and the baby?

The baby in her arms squeaked, squirming.

Dax felt a momentary reprieve from this miserable conversation. "She's awake."

That motherly Madonna sweetness moved across Jenna Garwood's face. "Will you hold her for a minute while I get the diaper bag from the car? She's probably wet."

Dax swallowed hard and made no move to take the offered baby.

"She won't bite." That precise, clipped voice chided him for being a coward.

Him? A coward? "Get the bag."

As if he was hypnotized, he reached out, awkward at first as he took the tiny bundle in his arms.

Jenna wasted no time heading for her car.

The front door snapped shut. The baby startled in that special way only newborns do. With fingers too big and thick to be handling an infant again, Dax peeled back the blanket and looked down into a face as pink and new as a rosebud.

His heart did a funny jitterbug in his chest. He remembered when Gavin was this small and helpless. He remembered how scared and alone he'd felt knowing he was the only parent with sole responsibility for another human being.

Did Jenna Garwood feel that way, too? There was dignity in her voice but a look of desperation in her eyes that he understood too well.

The baby mewed and made that squeaky, about-to-cry sound. Tiny, gossamer eyelids lifted. A pair of dark blue eyes snagged him as if he were a marlin and she were a giant hook.

With an inner groan, he knew he was in trouble. Big trouble.

He'd been in Jenna Garwood's shoes. He'd been alone with a newborn—alone and desperate.

And, though he was sure he'd live to regret his rash, emotional decision, he was going to hire her.

CHAPTER FIVE

JENNA MOVED IN that afternoon.

She had plenty of reservations about living on the remote ranch with a man she barely knew, but she and Sophie were out of choices. She was troubled that Dax Coleman hadn't wanted to hire her at first and then had suddenly changed his mind. Troubled and curious.

For those few minutes when she'd gone to the car for Sophie's diapers, she'd been certain he would send her away. She'd returned to the house prepared to beg and lie and make up references, only to discover that his attitude had completely reversed.

The perplexing rancher had been sitting in a leather rocking chair with Sophie cradled against his chest. For one moment, Jenna had remained in the foyer watching and aching with the knowledge that Sophie would not have a father to cradle her. She'd listened as Dax murmured softly to the baby in a way that turned Jenna's insides to warm honey.

When she'd made her presence known, he'd gone silent.

But she'd heard. And that moment had told her a great deal about Dax Coleman.

By the time she had driven to the B and B for her belongings, then returned to the ranch, Dax was nowhere to be seen. A slim, nice-looking cowboy who appeared amused with the world greeted her at the front door.

"Well, ain't you a pretty little thing?" His grin widened as his gaze slid over her. "Old Dax must be going blind."

Jenna blinked, startled and uncomfortable. What exactly did he mean? That Dax thought she was ugly? Not that it mattered one iota what Dax thought about her appearance. She had no illusions about her looks, but still, a woman didn't like thinking her appearance was the topic of dinner conversation.

A dry leaf swirled from beneath a fat oak tree in the yard and glided around her head. The weather today was colder and she was eager to get Sophie inside.

"I'm Jenna Garwood, the new housekeeper."

The admission sounded strange on her lips. She was some-one's housekeeper.

The ranch hand crossed a pair of muscled arms over his chest. "You sure are. I'm Rowdy Davis, Dax's ranch manager. He said you'd be coming back soon."

No wonder the man was behaving in such an insolent manner. His boss—and hers—wasn't here. For very realistic reasons, she trusted the rancher who'd rescued her and had expected him to be here. Rowdy Davis, on the other hand, made her nervous.

Clutching Sophie closer, she glanced around, suddenly feeling alone and vulnerable. All she saw was barns and fences and acres and acres of serenely grazing cattle. In the distance several cowboys rode horses across a field. They were so far away no sound carried on the wind except the occasional bawl of a calf.

Jenna licked dry lips. It wasn't every day a Carrington hired on as a domestic and encountered a leering cowboy. The man must be either out of his head with loneliness or the kind of guy who thought every female was fair game. Jenna suspected the latter. But she was a new mother with a baby in arms that grew heavier with every second. The opposite sex was the last thing on her mind.

"Where is Mr. Coleman?"

The cowboy got that look again as if he was holding back a laugh. "Gavin got a bloody nose on the playground so Dax went to pick him up."

"Gavin?"

"Dax's son."

Gavin. Of course. He'd mentioned a son.

"Come on in. I'm supposed to help you with your things."

The man pushed the door open and stepped to one

side. Finally, he was demonstrating some knowledge of etiquette. Miss Manners would have been aghast at his previous behavior.

Holding Sophie's diaper bag against her side with one elbow, she started into the warm foyer. The cowboy's body crowded the narrow space. Jenna slanted slightly to one side, hoping he'd get the message that with her load, and attired in a heavy woolen coat, she needed more room. He didn't budge. He didn't even offer to help. Her backside accidentally brushed against him. She jerked away, face hot, and moved across the stone-tiled entry to the carpeted area beyond.

When she glanced back, Rowdy remained in the doorway, grinning. Her flush deepened.

"I have a number of things in the car if you wouldn't mind getting them please," she said stiffly, hearing the haughty tone her mother reserved for servants. Hopefully, the man would get the message that she did not want to play his game—whatever it was.

Rowdy's dark eyes glittered and continued staring at her several beats longer before he said, "I'll get them in a minute. Let's get you and baby situated first."

Jenna felt flustered. She wasn't sure what to make of Rowdy Davis. He had done nothing wrong, but he looked at her in a way that was disconcerting, as though he knew her secrets, as though he knew something she didn't.

He was young and good-looking and a tad bit cocky. Maybe that was her problem. His confidence was the antithesis of hers.

The sooner he went on his way, the sooner she could relax.

"Would you mind showing me to my quarters?" she asked. "Then I won't trouble you any longer."

The corner of Rowdy's mouth hiked higher. "Sure thing, ma'am. Your *quarters* are this way." He emphasized the word. "And you aren't troubling me one little bit."

"Thank you," she said, mustering her dignity. "I should like to see them."

Still wearing a strange smirk, Rowdy led the way down a hallway to the left of the massive living/dining area. He ambled in front of her with a slow swagger as if wanting her to notice his lean, fit body and tight blue jeans. Purposefully, she focused her attention elsewhere.

The ranch home was lovely in a Western manner. Spacious and well-appointed in colors and textures that glowed with warmth and reflected light from a pair of large patio doors in the dining area. The ranch was so different from the old mansion she'd escaped, and its modern warmth drew her like a magnet. She could really enjoy tending to such a lovely place.

"Dax wants you to have this section of rooms," Rowdy was saying as he pushed open a door down a hall and to the back of the kitchen area. "This larger bedroom has an adjoining bath and opens into a smaller room intended as a nursery."

"Oh, this should do nicely. Thank you."

Rowdy chuckled again as if she'd said something amusing. She didn't understand his behavior. But then her experience with the opposite sex was limited to one cheating husband, her absentee father and a host of older male employees.

"Dax set up the crib already. Said you could arrange things any way you wanted."

Jenna stopped in the doorway and lowered the diaper bag to the floor. Still unaccustomed to the weight of a baby and a bag, her arm ached. "He bought a crib for Sophie?"

"Gavin's old crib was in storage. Dax just dragged it out of the shed and cleaned it up a little."

The kindness created a warm glow in her chest. After purchasing the blue car, she'd used her credit cards for the final time at a baby store. Then she'd stuffed as many items as possible for Jenna's care into the trunk and headed west. The layette included a folding travel bed—the best she could do in a small car—but a real crib was even better.

"I shall have to thank him."

Rowdy grinned. "Indeed, you shall."

A flush of embarrassment rushed up her neck. Enough was enough. "Mr. Davis, are you making fun of me?"

"We call it teasing around these parts."

"May I inquire as to the reason?"

"You talk funny. All citified and stiff. Kinda tickles the ears."

"Oh, I see." Was her speech the only thing he found amus-ing? Had she been imagining his insolent stares?

She moved deeper into the room, eager to settle Sophie and to explore her new living arrangements. Rowdy remained in the doorway watching her. "Thank you for showing me the rooms. I'm sure I can find my way around from here."

The ranch hand didn't seem to get the message. He slouched against the door facing, picking at the button on his sleeve.

Determined not to let him bother her, Jenna lifted Sophie to her shoulder and turned her attention to the room.

The suite was different than the rest of the wood and stone and leather ranch house. Here was an English garden, a room filled with lush, print fabrics and graceful furnishings in sage and antique white with splashes of rose and blue. The decor bled over into a sitting room and through to the nursery. Jenna loved it.

"This looks new. As though no one has ever used it," she murmured.

"I don't think it was used much."

Sophie made one of her squeaky noises and squirmed. Jenna patted the tiny back as she turned toward Rowdy. "But these rooms are the nursery. Didn't Gavin sleep here?"

"That was before my time, but I doubt it."

"Why ever not? The rooms are beautiful."

He shrugged. "I guess beauty's in the eye of the beholder."

His answer was no answer at all, but Jenna didn't press the topic. If Dax didn't like the look of an English garden, why should she care? Her job was to cook and clean, not question the tastes of her employer.

A little thrill ran through her veins. She had acquired a job and she would be able to care for her daughter. Like a normal person.

Grateful, she left Rowdy Davis standing in the door while she took Sophie into the taupe-walled nursery and laid her in the crib. As she placed a kiss on her daughter's velvet cheek, the soft scent of baby breath and formula filled her senses. She thought the smell was pure heaven.

She slipped out of her coat and draped it over the railing.

Someone, Dax she supposed, had neatly made up the baby bed and placed pretty quilted bumper pads around the inside. A quilt rack complete with a darling patchwork quilt in sage and taupe stood next to the bed.

Jenna adjusted her daughter's blanket and stroked the miniscule hand, lost in a love that brought a lump to her throat. Sophie looked tiny in the big crib.

"I was just wondering something."

Jenna jumped at the sudden intrusion of a man's voice. She hadn't realized Rowdy had followed her through to the nursery.

She turned slightly to find him standing at her elbow. "Yes? What is it?"

"What's a pretty girl like you doing out here?" He edged closer, overpowering her nose with his heavy-handed co-logne. "I can't believe any man would let something like you get away. You married?"

The question startled her like an unexpected spray of cold water.

"I'm a widow. Sophie's father died in a car crash."

"My sympathies." The words didn't quite match the expression in his eyes.

"Thank you." She swallowed and slanted away to fuss with the elephant mobile hanging above Sophie. She expected Rowdy to take his leave.

He didn't. Instead, he reached into the crib and drew a fingertip over Sophie's rose-petal cheek. Jenna had to restrain herself to keep from pushing his hand away.

"So you and the little darlin' here are all alone in the world?" He straightened, turning his probing gaze to her.

"We are making our own way quite well, thank you."

"Good for you. But if you should need a man, give a holler." His words were soft, suggesting something more than helping her unload her car. "I'm always glad to help out."

Jenna had no idea how to handle the man. Pretending a fascination with the little lamp atop the armoire, she moved in that direction. She could feel Rowdy's stare on her back. Maybe he was just being friendly, but his sly, unyielding grin made her uncomfortable as if he could see through her clothes.

Surreptitiously, she glanced down to check her buttons. Though her breasts were uncomfortably full and pushed against her smocked top, she was covered and decent.

"Rowdy!" A gravelly voice called from the front of the house.

Jenna turned toward the sound, a sense of relief flooding her. She was probably being silly but Dax's gruff voice was a welcome sound.

"Back here, boss." Rowdy aimed a wink in her direction and stepped to the doorway. "I'm showing the lady her quarters."

"Her what?" Dax appeared behind Rowdy, a scowl on his face.

"She talks prissified. Called her room *quarters,* like this was the Taj Mahal or something. Pretty little thing, though," he said as if she wasn't standing right there.

Dax's scowl deepened. "Where's her stuff? I told you to help her."

Rowdy pushed off the doorway, seemingly undisturbed by Dax's bluster. "I was just about to get it out of the car."

"Go on then. I'll help you in a minute."

"No problem. I can handle it." With a final flicker in her direction, Rowdy strode out of the room.

Dax's gaze followed him for a minute before he turned his attentions to Jenna. "Everything all right? You getting settled?"

Other than not liking his ranch hand, she was delighted.

"I haven't been here long enough to get settled, but your home is lovely." Although it needed a thorough dusting. "The English garden decor in here is wonderful."

"English garden?" Bewildered green eyes blinked around the room. "Is that what you call this stuff?"

His clueless response made her want to laugh. In his black cowboy hat, sheepskin jacket and a pair of scuffed boots, he didn't exactly fit the image of a man who would be comfortable in an English garden or a room filled with soft colors and ruffles and baby things. Perhaps a nanny had occupied this suite.

"Thank you for thinking of the crib."

"Might as well get some use out of it. Baby need anything else?"

Dax stepped to the crib and gazed down. His shoulders relaxed as though looking at Sophie melted the tension from him. When he reached down and placed his wide hand lightly on the baby's chest, something warm and tender moved inside of Jenna.

The notion puzzled her. She hadn't wanted Rowdy to touch her baby, but she felt differently with Dax. Maybe because those rough rancher hands had brought Sophie safely into the world.

"She breathes so softly," she said, moving to his side, intuitively understanding his reason for touching the newborn. Hadn't she done the same thing dozens of times over the past few days?

Dax turned his head, bringing his face close to hers. "Like a whisper."

Jenna stared into those green, green eyes, the funny, unsettled stirring coming back in full force. Dax made her uncomfortable, too, but in a far different way than she felt with Rowdy. He was short-spoken and puzzling, but she would trust him with her life. A tiny smile quivered on her lips. Indeed, she had already done that.

Dax looked at her for another long, curious moment before moving to the window. He pushed aside the taupe draperies and looked out. "Wonder what's keeping Rowdy?"

Footsteps thudded down the hall. "That must be him."

"Slow as Christmas," Dax grumbled, relieving his ranch hand of a giant carton and a suitcase.

"You wouldn't believe all the junk she crowded into that trunk. Women and their stuff."

Dax made a harrumphing noise in the back of his throat. "Typical."

Jenna wasn't sure what he meant, but from his

darkened expression she decided not to ask. She did, however, want to ask about the little boy.

As soon as Rowdy disappeared for another load, she did.

"Rowdy said your son had a bloody nose. Where is he? Did you take him to the hospital?"

Dax made a face as though the notion was ridiculous. "He's all right. I sent him to wash his hands."

A small boy poked his head around the corner. Except for a pair of cobalt-blue eyes, he was a miniature version of his father. "I falled off the merry-go-round. My shirt's all bloody."

"I told you to change clothes."

Gavin's face puckered. "I forgot."

The child looked so small and worried, Jenna crouched in front of him. "I'm Jenna. I'm going to be your new chef."

"I'm Gavin Matthew Coleman."

"A handsome name for a handsome boy. From all that blood on your shirt, I'd say you must be a brave boy, too."

"Noah said I was going to die. He's my friend. I was kinda scart."

Dax made an impatient noise. "No one dies of a bloody nose."

Jenna ignored the irritation in Dax's voice as she tilted the child's chin. Dried blood ringed his nostrils. "I think we need to wash your face a bit, too, and perhaps have a nice warm bath and change that shirt."

"We were about to do that," Dax said. "Go on, Gavin. I'll be there directly."

The boy lingered in front of Jenna. "Are you the new cooker?"

Jenna smiled. Obviously, Gavin was unfamiliar with the term chef. "I am indeed."

The child gave an exaggerated sigh. "What a relief."

Behind her Dax snorted. "Tired of pizza, sport?"

Jenna patted the boy's narrow shoulder. "I shall prepare a dinner fit for two kings. Now head for that bath. Kings must be well-groomed."

"You talk funny, but I like you," Gavin said and surprised her with a quick hug before darting out of the room.

"That's a first."

She stood, turning to look at the rancher. He wore a bemused expression. "What is?"

"Gavin is bashful. I've never seen him hug a housekeeper before."

"Then, I shall take that as a great compliment. He's a darling boy."

"And about that meal fit for two kings?"

"Yes?"

"It might have to wait until you go grocery shopping."

When she laughed, Dax Coleman did a strange thing. He slapped his Stetson on his head, turned on his boot heel and stalked out.

CHAPTER SIX

DAX STOMPED HIS BOOTS at the back door and watched clumps of dirt and unmentionable debris fall away. He should have stayed in the house and made sure the new housekeeper did all right with Gavin. Rowdy could have seen to the cow with the bad foot.

Might as well face the truth, Coleman. The new housekeeper with her big innocent eyes and sexy laugh scared you off.

Jenna Garwood stirred feelings in him that he'd killed long ago. And he didn't like it. Especially from her, a slip of a girl far too young for him to be noticing. Now she was going to be in his house and under his nose, smelling like flowers all the time.

What had he been thinking?

What kind of father was he that he'd leave his son alone with a stranger? He hadn't even asked for references this morning, which showed just how stupid he was. He might have hired Jane the Ripper.

Yet, he wasn't worried about his son in Jenna's

care. Not in the least. He'd watched from the doorway while she had filled the bathtub and tested the water with her delicate fingers. She'd told the boy he was brave and strong as Gavin related the bloody nose incident in a child's convoluted manner. And she'd promised to read him a bedtime story.

None of those things kept her from being a serial killer, but Dax simply knew his son was safe with the new mother. Now, it was Dax's job to make sure the new mother was safe from her employer.

As he pushed open the back door, the scent of cooking wafted from the kitchen. He had no idea what the new housekeeper had found to cook in those cereal- and macaroni-laden cupboards, but it sure smelled good.

He chuckled. Anything smelled good to a man who'd been eating his own very bad cooking.

As he entered the kitchen, Jenna shot him a tentative smile. She'd found an apron somewhere and pulled her hair back into a hair clip. She looked about sixteen.

That's the way he needed to think about her. She looked sixteen. A kid. He had never lusted after teenagers.

His traitorous brain registered ample womanly breasts and curvy hips. Her new-mother's body looked far older than sixteen.

Blast his eyes for noticing.

"Dinner in five minutes," she said.

He wanted to tell her the food smelled good and he was starving. Instead, he grumbled, "Where's Gavin?"

She pointed an oversize wooden spoon toward the living room. "Diligently practicing the letter *A*. *A* is for *apple* and *ant* and *aaa-choo,* you know."

Again that smile that gave him belly flips.

"Gavin," he hollered. "Come on. Wash up."

His son appeared, toting a pencil and a piece of wide-lined paper. "I finished my *A*."

Dax took the page in hand to admire the squiggly effort. "Looks good, sport."

The smell of flowers and bacon assailed him as Jenna peered over his shoulder. "Lovely job, Gavin. Your teacher will be very impressed."

Gavin beamed up at Jenna as if she'd given him a year's supply of ice cream. Any fool could see the little dude craved a woman's praise. Blast Reba for her abandonment. Leaving her husband was one thing. Abandoning her son was inexcusable.

"Put your work away and wash your hands for supper," he told the boy.

"I took a bath already," Gavin said as he stuffed the paper down into his schoolbag.

"Doesn't matter." Dax led the way to the back of the house with Gavin dragging his feet behind. By the time they returned to the dining room, the long oak table had been transformed.

The new housekeeper, or chef as she liked to say, apparently had discovered the fancy dishes

Reba had purchased and never used—dishes he'd never bothered to use, either. Two places were set with matching plates and silverware, along with dark green cloth napkins and gleaming stemware. A candlestick graced each end of the table—who knew where she'd found those?—and in the center was a slender vase poked full of backyard weeds arranged in artsy beauty.

"What's all this? A party?"

Jenna blinked in surprise. "No, sir. Dinner."

"Never seen such a fancy table for a mere meal." For a bachelor and his child who often ate in front of the television or at the bar, this was like dining at the Ritz.

"Shall I serve now?" she asked, hovering as if worried about pleasing him. The notion made him mad. All he expected was a meal, not subservience.

"Just put the food on the table." He scraped out a chair for Gavin and then for himself. "We aren't helpless."

Face flushed, she did as he said, sliding a steaming casserole in front of him. "You were right about the cupboards being bare. I'll have to rectify that tomorrow."

He eyed the dish with suspicion. "What is this?"

"A macaroni-and-cheese quiche."

"I like macaroni," Gavin said. A doubtful Dax scooped a helping onto both of their plates. Wasn't there some kind of rule that men didn't eat quiche? What *was* quiche anyway?

"And," Jenna went on, standing so close he could still smell perfume, "baked potato soup with herbed toast points."

Toast points? He eyed the toasted triangles arranged in a tidy circle on a serving plate. Some kind of green leaf adorned the center.

He had to hand it to the new cook, the food was pretty. Might as well find out if it was edible.

"Dig in, Gavin." He could have saved his breath because the boy had already shoveled macaroni into his mouth until he resembled a chipmunk. "Slow down, boy."

"It's good, Daddy." Though muffled, the words matched the pleasure on Gavin's face.

Dax took a bite. His taste buds shouted for joy. Whatever quiche was, it included bacon and to his way of thinking, anything with bacon was good.

"Could I get anything else for you?" Jenna asked.

She looked tired. Dax wanted to kick himself. She was a new mama, not much more than a week away from having a baby. She shouldn't be slaving over a stove.

"Sit down," he said.

"Is everything all right with the food?" She drew her pouty bottom lip between her teeth.

Dax frowned. He needed no reminders that she had a mouth made for kissing. "Sit down. Eat."

"I'm the chef, not a guest."

"I'm the boss. Sit. Eat."

Gavin's head volleyed back and forth between the adults, expression worried.

Jenna hovered between the kitchen island and the dining table, looking as anxious as Gavin did. The notion that both of them were getting nervous made Dax feel like a jerk.

"Sit," he bellowed.

Jenna dropped an apple-red pot holder and slithered into the farthest chair from him.

"There is no need to shout," she said with a dignity that turned his annoyance to amusement. Posture stiff and nostrils flared, Jenna Garwood had gone from scared chick to mad hen faster than a mosquito bite.

Dax scooted back from the table and rose. "You need a plate."

She started up. "I'll get it."

"Sit," he said again, this time in a gentler voice. "You've done enough."

He retrieved the plate and utensils and put them in front of her. She looked flustered and pink and tired.

He kicked himself again.

"You've overdone it," he said, taking up his fork. "I shouldn't have let you start tonight."

She flashed him a puzzled look.

"I'm perfectly well, thank you." With graceful fingers she filled her plate and began to eat.

"How's the baby?" He shoved a bite of something cheesy into his mouth and chewed.

Jenna delicately patted her lips with a green napkin. "She sleeps most of the time."

"Don't worry. It won't last. How often does she wake in the night?" He couldn't believe he was having this conversation.

"Twice so far. Nights are the hardest." She dipped a spoon into the steaming soup and stirred. "I'm having difficulty forcing myself to think clearly when I'm half-asleep."

"Yes. I remember the feeling."

"You do?" Her gaze flicked to Gavin, who continued stuffing macaroni into his face as if he hadn't eaten in weeks. It occurred to Dax that he'd neglected teaching his son some common manners.

He tapped Gavin's forearm. "Slow down, sport. There's plenty."

Gavin grinned. Soup dripped on his chin. Before Dax could reprimand him, Jenna handed the boy a napkin and silently indicated the drip. When Gavin successfully swiped the spot, she reacted as though he'd conquered Mt. Everest. "Splendid, Gavin." She clapped her hands once beneath her chin. "I can see your handsome face so much better."

Gavin beamed a hundred-watt grin. "You make good soup."

"Thank you. A chef appreciates hearty appetites." She tasted the soup, her gaze observing Dax above the spoon. "Did you get up with Gavin when he was a baby?"

He hadn't intended to go there. "Yeah."

Her unspoken question hovered like a housefly, annoying him. Where was Gavin's mother? Why hadn't she cared for her son? Well, he wasn't going to talk about Reba, especially in front of Gavin. The boy had enough questions without stirring up more.

"I think that's an admirable thing," Jenna said.

Dax scowled. He'd missed something. "What is?"

"For a father to dedicate himself to the care of an infant." She tilted her head toward Gavin. "You must have been a very special baby."

Gavin looked pleased. "Did your daddy take care of you, too?"

Something tightened in her face. He was certain Gavin wouldn't notice but Dax had. That she was bothered by the question gave rise to new concerns about the woman he'd hired to care for his son. Who was Jenna Garwood anyway?

"No, I lived in the city," she said a little too brightly before glancing down at her plate. Dax wondered what living in the city had to do with Gavin's question about her father.

When she looked up again, her smile was as fake as Reba's fingernails. "You are such a lucky boy. You live on a wonderful ranch with your dad and all these animals. Can you ride a horse?"

Gavin dropped his head and fiddled with a piece of toast. "Not yet."

"Horses scare him." The notion perturbed Dax no end, but he was trying to be patient. Everything scared Gavin. Horses, cows, loud noises, hoot owls. The boy jumped at shadows.

The new housekeeper was all sympathy. "How old are you Gavin?"

"Five. I'll be six February 17."

She waved a hand. "You have plenty of time to learn equestrian skills."

Gavin's fork paused over the cheesy casserole. "Huh?"

"Riding a horse," Dax said. Rowdy was right. She did talk funny. She was far too refined to be a housekeeper. "Equestrian refers to horses."

"Oh." The word was too much for the boy so he let it slide. "When I get big I'll ride. Daddy will get me an old broke pony when I'm ready. All I have to do is the say the word. Right, Daddy?"

Dax's mouth twisted. He'd said that very thing to Gavin a dozen times. "Right, sport."

"And you will become a wonderful horseman, I am certain." Jenna favored Gavin with a smile and reached for another toast point. *Toast points*. He was still tickled over that one.

While the heavy dose of over-the-top kindness floated around his kitchen table, Dax's brain was also shooting off all kinds of warning signals. Jenna Garwood had come into his life in a bizarre manner and, like her pretty little toast points, she no more fit on a ranch than he fit at that pink hotel in Hollywood.

Clearing his throat, Dax interrupted the pleasant

chit-chat. "Where you from, Jenna? I forgot to ask this morning during our interview."

Some interview. She'd handed him that soft little baby, looked at him with worried eyes, and he'd forgotten to use the good sense his mama had given him.

"I beg your pardon?" she asked, dragging her attention away from his son.

"Your application was a little short on details. I was asking where you're from."

"Oh." She had that deer-in-the-headlights look. Her hands fidgeted with the napkin. "I'm from back East." She hopped up from the table. "Let me clear away the plates and bring dessert."

Gavin whooped for joy. "Dessert! She made dessert, Daddy."

Jenna disappeared around the bar and into the kitchen. Dax shoved back from the table and stalked after her. She was going to talk to him and she was going to do it now. All the dessert in the world wasn't stopping him from finding out more about her.

Her back was turned when he entered the kitchen area. Busy dishing up something onto his fancy saucers, she pretended not to hear his approach. Incensed, he moved closer. When she still didn't turn around, he slammed a hand down on each side of her. She couldn't run now. He'd trapped her.

Leaning next to her ear, he growled, "Are you trying to avoid my questions?"

With a gasp, Jenna whirled around, eyes wide as those saucers. "What do you mean?"

Cripes. She was so near he could feel her body heat. And smell that tantalizing perfume. What had he been thinking to move in this close?

Sweat popped out on the back of his neck. He dug his fingers into the countertop and hung on tight. Regardless of the unwanted physical reaction to his new employee, he deserved answers.

"I need to know more about you than the fact that you cook weird food."

If such a thing was possible, she drew farther back, pressing into the counter behind her.

"Weird?" Her eyes widened some more, this time in dismay. Her pouty mouth turned down. "You didn't like it?"

Blast and be danged. He'd hurt her feelings. He tried again. "I didn't mean weird. Different."

"Different?" She still didn't look happy. And her too-near chest rose and fell as if she might cry.

"Different but good," he said, growing more unraveled by the moment. A smart man would back away from her lush body and her sweet eyes and her tantalizing mouth. A smart man would never have come in here in the first place. "Real good. You're a great cook."

She was beginning to brighten. He wanted her to smile again the way she'd been smiling at Gavin all through supper… Dinner… Whatever she wanted to call it. "I haven't eaten such a meal in weeks."

Actually, he'd never eaten such a meal, but he knew when to cut his losses and keep his mouth shut.

She relented a little and Dax thought he saw a hint of humor lurking in those eyes. Brown eyes. Like the color of honey. Sweet, warm, delectable honey.

Why didn't someone just shoot him now?

"I'm glad," she murmured, the softness of her breath brushing his lips. Temptation tortured him. If he leaned in the slightest bit, they'd be touching from chest to thigh. A little closer and he could feel the softness of her mouth against his. "I want to do a good job for you."

And he wanted to— With rigid self-control he reined his wayward wants and tried to remember why he'd come in here in the first place.

"You will. You are. It's just that—" What? What was it he wanted to know?

He wanted to know a lot more than he would allow himself to think about.

Oh yes. Now he remembered.

Slowly, he loosened his white-knuckle grip on the counter and pushed away, leaving enough space between himself and his cook so that she could walk away from this encounter at any time. He'd had no business trapping her against the counter that way. What was the matter with him?

"You'll be taking care of my son," he said.

"A delight I'm looking forward to."

There she went with her fancy talk. "Right, but he's my son. It's my job to protect him."

She got that stricken look again as if he'd slapped her. "I would never do anything to hurt Gavin."

He believed her, but common sense said he needed more information about his housekeeper. "Why are you here, Jenna?"

"I required employment. You offered me a job."

"I don't mean here at Southpaw. I mean here in Texas. You have a new baby. Where is your family? Why aren't you with them? Won't they be concerned about you?"

The sadness that overcame her was a punch in his gut. Her bottom lip quivered. She looked down at her clenched hands. "Sophie's father died in rather embarrassing circumstances. Humiliating for me anyway."

A gentleman wouldn't press but Dax had to. "Meaning?"

She hesitated. And then sighed.

"At the time of the accident Derek was...my husband was..." Color drained from her face while she struggled to say the words. She twisted her fingers until the knuckles whitened. Until Dax had the insane urge to take her hands in his and calm her obvious stress.

"Never mind," he said. "I don't need details."

She looked up, her voice a whisper. "Thank you. It's difficult to discuss."

He got the picture. Her husband had cheated on

her and died in the process. Either that or he was a criminal killed during the commission of a felony. The last thought gave him pause, but even if it was true he didn't believe for a minute that Jenna was involved. She might be running from something, but not that.

"How did you end up here?"

"I wanted to escape the memories and raise my daughter away from the gossip and the painful past. Texas was an accident."

Dax watched as she twisted her hands over and over again until the whiteness reddened. Whatever she'd left behind had hurt her badly. He knew that kind of pain and the need to escape. Jenna Garwood was a kindred spirit, someone who understood the hurt that came from loving too much.

His voice gentled. "How was Texas an accident, Jenna?"

"I thought I had more time to find a place and get settled before Sophie's arrival."

"But Sophie had other plans."

Her face went soft, full of love for her child. "Yes. Once she arrived, I had to find work and a place to live immediately. A baby changes everything."

How well he knew. But at least, he'd had the ranch and a job and plenty of money to take care of Gavin. He could hire help. Jenna was alone with a newborn to support and no place else to go.

But one thought nagged him. "You're not the type to do this kind of work."

"Not the type?"

"Too educated or refined or… I don't know how to explain it but it's pretty clear you don't fit."

A determined glint flickered through her eyes. "I will do whatever is required to care for my daughter. At this point in time, domestic work allows me to be with her while earning a living. That's important to me. Regardless of my background, I am more grateful for this job than you can ever imagine."

His respect for the tough little mama ratcheted higher. What an amazing woman. He burned with an irrational need to pull his housekeeper into his arms and promise to care for her and Sophie.

Dumb. Real dumb.

Yet he had plenty of money. He could assure they lacked nothing. He could support and protect and befriend. He could take care of them both while Jenna mothered her child and his son.

Don't be an idiot, Dax. Women are trouble. Remember?

Finally, to quiet the noise in his head, he muttered, "I'm sorry for all you've been through."

Her chin hitched higher. "Don't be. Sophie and I are delighted with our new environment. It is absolutely perfect. That is, if maintaining my employment and residence here will be a satisfactory arrangement for you and Gavin."

Dax's mouth quivered. She was really cute when she talked like that. Cute and sexy.

Blast his brain! He bit down on the inside of his cheek to punish himself. She wasn't sexy. She was a kid. A new mother in need of help.

But somewhere in the back of that blasted brain a voice laughed at his protestations.

Before he could blurt something foolish and regrettable Gavin came around the corner of the cabinets. A hint of cheese rimmed the boy's lips. He took one look at the adults and slapped his hands onto his hips. "Are you two gonna talk all day or eat dessert? A kid could starve around here."

CHAPTER SEVEN

"MISS JENNA, are you gonna read me a story?"

Jenna sat in the padded rocking chair next to the baby crib, soft lamplight glowing golden around her and Sophie. She glanced up at the small, dark-haired boy standing uncertainly in the door of the nursery.

"Come in, Gavin."

Clad in cartoon image pajamas, the child crept closer. "I got a book in my room."

Jenna's arms and back ached as never before but she couldn't refuse Gavin's request. After all, she was his employee. Caring for him was her responsibility. More than that, she felt an empathy with the child that she couldn't articulate. And she *had* promised a story.

"Do you mind if I bring Sophie along? She's having her dinner now." She dipped her chin to indicate the bottle in the baby's mouth.

He edged closer, hands behind his back, watching in fascination as Sophie's mouth tugged greedily at the nipple. "Is that all she eats?"

"For now. When she's older she'll take cereal and baby food."

"Babies don't got no teeth, do they?"

Jenna hid a smile at the atrocious grammar but intentionally emphasized the correction. "No, babies haven't any teeth."

"Can't you buy her some from the dentist? My Grandpa Joe got some there."

The inner smile moved outward. "She'll grow her own in a few months. Just wait and see." Assuming she and Sophie were still here in a few months.

So far her mother hadn't discovered her whereabouts, and on a ranch this remote, perhaps she wouldn't. Someday Jenna hoped to be strong enough to stand up against her parents, but she never had been before. Even now, with hundreds of miles between them, she went weak and shaky at the idea of going head-to-head with the formidable Elaine Carrington.

Sophie's bottle emptied with a sucking sound. Jenna lifted the baby to her shoulder and patted the tiny back.

Gavin remained at her side, one small hand resting on the arm of the chair.

"She burped," he announced. "Can she say 'Scuse me?"

What an adorable little boy. "Not yet, but when the time comes, I hope you'll help her learn your nice manners."

Gavin's chest puffed with importance. "I will. I promise. I know how to say 'scuse me." He turned his head and emitted a pretend belch and then whipped around with a proud grin. "'Scuse me please, ma'am."

Jenna laughed. "You are excused. Thank you very much."

"Gavin!" Dax's voice rang from the living room. "Time for bed."

One hand supporting Sophie's back, Jenna rose. "Your dad's calling. Let's read that story and get you tucked in."

"Okay!" Gavin took off like a Thoroughbred in the Kentucky Derby.

Jenna followed behind more slowly. Her body yearned for a hot bath and a long slumber.

As she passed through the living room, she paused. Her employer was kicked back in a burgundy recliner that had been drawn too close to the television. He had to know she was in the room, but he chose to ignore her.

Dax Coleman was a puzzling man. One minute he was brusque and crabby. The next he was kindness itself.

The encounter in the kitchen after dinner had shaken her in the oddest manner. Dax had been angry and demanding at first, and then some other emotion had flashed from him that had set her heart to thundering and her belly aquiver. The sparks had almost ignited her hair.

After Gavin's timely interruption, Dax had abruptly withdrawn. Yet their conversation had given her hope that she and her employer would get along. He'd even helped clear the table and put dishes in the washer, gruffly chastising her for overdoing.

Yes, *puzzling* was the word. For all his bluster, perhaps he was, as Crystal had indicated, one of the good guys. He just had a hard time letting anyone know.

She cleared her throat.

A commercial danced across the television screen. The furniture in this room was lovely if badly arranged. To see Dax's face, she had to walk around the chair and stand between him and the television.

"Gavin wants a story. Would you care to join us?" He was the boy's father. Most likely, they shared a bedtime ritual.

Dax squinted in her direction. At some point, he'd run a hand through his longish hair and it stuck up in front. His five o'clock shadow had deepened to a real need for a shave. The quivery feeling returned to her belly and this time she recognized it for what it was. Attraction. Crystal Wolf was right about this, too. Dax Coleman looked delicious. Rumpled, relaxed, and delicious.

Oh dear. The last time she'd been attracted to a man had resulted in disaster.

She pressed a hand to her stomach. Dax followed

the motion; a muscle in his jaw twitched before he abruptly turned back to the television.

"Tell Gavin I'll be in later to say good-night."

So that was that.

By the time she reached Gavin's room he had crawled beneath a blue dinosaur comforter and sat with his back bolstered by two fat pillows.

"Sit here." He patted the spot next to him. "I can hold Sophie if you want me to."

Jenna smiled. "You are very thoughtful, but I think I can manage." With Sophie in the crook of her elbow, she picked up a book with the opposite hand. Already she was learning that mothers need three arms. "Is this the story you want?"

"Yep." He propped his hands behind his head. "That's the one."

Jenna rested the baby along her thighs before stroking a hand over the book's colorful cover. "*Peter Rabbit.* I remember this from when I was a little girl."

"Did your mommy read it to you?"

Jenna's chest clutched. "No."

"Mine, neither. I don't have a mom." He said the words in a manner-of-fact tone, but Jenna sorrowed for what he'd missed. At least she'd had a mother on the premises, though Elaine Carrington was not one to dirty her hands with the day-to-day details such as story-reading. A Carrington daughter was a collector's doll to be taken out of the box in pristine condition, displayed briefly at meals or recitals, and returned to the care of servants, not to be seen or heard until the next time. Without the kindness of nannies she'd likely never have heard a bedtime story.

She was determined this would not happen to Sophie.

With a lump in her throat she began to read. By page three Gavin had scooted until his body pressed against her side, bringing with him the pleasant smell of soap and toothpaste. She circled his shoulders with one arm, displaying the book so he could see the pictures. He sighed his approval, leaned closer and grasped the book's edge with one hand.

When the story ended, he said, "I'm glad Peter Rabbit escaped, aren't you, Miss Jenna?"

"Indeed."

"But he shouldn't have gone in the garden. His mama told him not to. Right?"

"Exactly right. Children should always obey their parents." She almost choked on the words. She had always obeyed her parents until Derek.

She closed the book and placed it on the stand next to Gavin's bed. When she turned back, the little boy was looking at the baby in her lap. Tentatively, with surprising gentleness, he touched the top of Sophie's hand with one finger.

"Miss Jenna?"

"Yes?"

"Are you and Sophie going to stay here for always?"

"I don't know."

She could see the answer troubled him. "I hope you stay a long time."

"Why is that?"

"So Sophie can be my baby sister. Noah has a baby brother. I want a baby, too, but Daddy says no. He says we'd have to get a mama to have a baby and he's not ever getting us another mama. So if you stay, Sophie can be my sister."

The child's words were a revelation into the father. Whatever had happened between Dax and his ex-wife cut deep. So much so that he feared getting hurt again, a fear Jenna understood completely.

No wonder Dax Coleman appeared kind and angry all in one package.

The dark-haired boy touched her heart, too. He longed for siblings and probably a mother, as well. Rough and tumble, timid and gentle at the same time, Gavin would be an easy child to love. The notion brought an ache to her chest. Where was his mother? What could have been so terrible about her life here at Southpaw that she would leave this precious, handsome son?

Even though Sophie was little more than a week old, Jenna knew she'd miss her more than life if they couldn't be together.

"Are you ready to have the lights out now?"

"I didn't say my prayers yet."

"All right then. Say them."

Squeezing his eyes closed, Gavin clasped his hands together beneath his chin. Jenna listened as he recited the "Now I lay me" prayer and went through a litany of God blesses before proclaiming with a sigh, "Amen." His eyes sprang open. "Can I have a drink?"

To her surprise, Dax stepped into the room. "He'll do this all night if you let him."

Gavin batted thick black eyelashes. "I'm thirsty, Daddy."

Dax relented with a half chuckle, half sigh. "Go on then. Get your drink, but nothing else."

Gavin scampered off the bed and disappeared. Jenna could hear him rattling around in the bathroom next door.

Dax glanced toward the noise, the hint of a smile on his face. "You read good."

The comment came out of nowhere. "What?"

"*Peter Rabbit.* Read in your voice, he took on a whole different personality."

"Well, thank you, I think." She offered a smile. "You were welcome to come in."

How long had he been standing in the hallway?

"Didn't want to disturb you." He shifted and cast another glance toward the bathroom and the sound of running water and clinking glass. "I need to say something."

Jenna tensed. "Have I done anything wrong?"

He made an irritated sound and swatted the air. "No. Not you. Me. I came on too strong in the kitchen. I apologize."

Relief surged like Hawaiian surf. "You have every right to know about the people in charge of your son."

His mouth twisted. "Don't let me off the hook that easy."

"All right, then." She pointed a finger at him. "Consider yourself appropriately castigated."

Dax surprised her with a laugh. "Castigated. That'll teach me to behave."

Jenna found herself sharing a smile with her employer. He was really handsome when he smiled. She took the thought captive and stowed it away.

"Dax, you have my solemn promise. I will care for Gavin as I will Sophie. With everything in me. You must never, ever be concerned that I would give anything less than my best to your son."

He gave a curt nod. "Can't ask for more than that. He's all I have, you know. He's—"

"Everything." Jenna finished the thought for him, intuitively understanding the depth of his feelings—because she felt the same about Sophie. "Your child is everything."

"Yeah," he said, shifting from one boot to the other. "Everything."

That one spark of kinship ignited a glow in Jenna's heart. Dax Coleman loved his son the way she loved Sophie. And that was a beautiful thing to know about a man. He loved deep. He loved strong. And forever.

The revelation shook her. She'd only just arrived

and was the man's employee. She had no right to think of him as a…friend. As a man.

But she did.

Stunned by the emotion splashing around inside like a raft on the Colorado rapids, she stroked Sophie's sleeping face with one finger, thinking.

Dax's gravelly voice scraped across the silence, quiet and dangerously attractive. "She's a good baby, isn't she?"

"I think so, but I haven't been around babies much, so I have no one to compare."

He cocked to one side, resting his weight on a hip. The tension from earlier tonight had inexplicably dissipated. Puzzling man. Fascinating man.

"No nieces or nephews?"

Jenna shook her head and met his gaze. "I was an only child."

"Are your parents still living?"

She could hear the unasked question. If they're still alive, why aren't you with them? Wouldn't they want to know about their grandchild? She focused her attention on Sophie's fingers, lifting the tiny digits up one by one, unable to look her employer in the eye.

"No. They're dead." At least to her, but her pulse rattled at the lie. "Yours?"

"Dad's gone. Mom moved to Austin some years back to be near my sister, Karina. Once in a while they drive up here or I take Gavin to see them. Not as often as I'd like. Life's busy."

"What about Christmas? Won't you see them then?"

"I don't know yet. Haven't given it much thought."

The holiday was only weeks away. "Doesn't Gavin have a list a mile long?"

"Two miles." He smiled again.

"Who's Grandpa Joe?"

Dax chuckled. "Gavin's good buddy and my ninety-two-year-old great-granddaddy. He's in a care facility over in Saddleback, feeble as a kitten but sharp as a tack."

Gavin wandered back into the room. "Grandpa Joe is my best friend." He hopped onto the bed, his little body slithering beneath the comforter. Water glistened on his hair and around his mouth. He'd apparently combed his hair as well as having that final drink. "I'm ready. Tuck me in."

Dax stepped to the bedside and bent low, pulling the boy into a hug before settling him again with the covers tucked snugly beneath the small chin. "'Night, sport. Sleep tight."

"'Night, Daddy. Don't let the bedbugs bite. 'Night, Miss Jenna."

"Good night, Gavin. Sweet dreams."

Dax gave the child one final pat on the chest and straightened, turning for the door. Jenna, baby in arms, moved past him and started down the hall. As the light snapped out, she heard Gavin's voice one last time. "See, Dad? Having a mama in the house isn't so bad after all."

Dax knew he was dreaming, but the knowledge didn't stop the parade of emotions. In his dream, Gavin was still a baby and he was an exhausted, confused single dad, asleep in his half-empty king-size bed, wishing his wife would come home and help with the baby. And Gavin was crying. Demanding a bottle. Screaming for the mother that would never come.

Dax burrowed deeper into the pillow. Sometimes if he let the baby cry for a few minutes, they could both go back to sleep. After all, he was dreaming. The dream would end, along with the deep ache of regret and the incessant crying.

The cries grew louder.

Reba's mocking face flickered through the dream like a ghost. Ignoring her son's tears, she danced before Dax with a flowy scarf over her face, laughing as she looped arms with another man and flitted away with only a parting glance at her devastated husband and crying child.

The sorrow in Dax's gut turned to acid. He hadn't had this dream in years. He needed to wake up.

Thrashing against the tangle of covers, he fought off sleep and sat upright. A film of sweat covered his body, and his chest heaved, but he forced his breathing to calm. He'd long ago stopped loving Reba. Why had he dreamed about her tonight?

A mewling cry from the far back of the house was his answer.

A baby *was* crying. Gavin? He shook his head. No, couldn't be. The baby was Sophie. Jenna's pink baby doll was crying.

Still mired in a kind of half sleep with cobwebs in his brain, he threw his feet onto the floor and padded down the hall toward the sound.

The house was dark except for the glow of a three-quarter moon splashing pale whiteness across the carpet. Dax needed no other light to maneuver in his own home. Even the nursery, as little as he'd used those rooms, was familiar. The baby's room had two entries, one from inside Jenna's bedroom and the other from the hall. He quietly pushed open the hallway door and stepped to the crib.

Sophie squirmed within the tight confines of a soft, thick blanket, her cries frantic now. Dax bent low, scooped the bundle into his large hands and lifted her against his naked chest. She was a feather, a dandelion puff, so light and fragile.

As he started out of the nursery toward the kitchen and the supply of formula he'd seen in the refrigerator, the tile was cold against his bare feet. The cooled atmosphere of the house sent prickles over his flesh. He came fully awake.

His heart slammed against his rib cage. This baby creating a single spot of warmth on his chest was not Gavin. This was Sophie, not his child. She was not his responsibility.

The infant whimpered, her head turning this way and that in search of food.

Jenna must be dead tired not to have heard the baby cry. But what did he expect? He'd worked her like a field hand from the very first day, expecting her to clean house, care for Gavin, do the shopping, cook his meals, clean the kitchen and still have the energy to get up at two o'clock with a newborn.

He'd even sent her to town for groceries that second day. She'd come back all rosy and chattery, talking about how much fun she'd had—in the grocery store no less. Picking out cantaloupe and watermelon and showing off Sophie to everyone in the place. He remembered how that worked. Carrying a baby into the grocery store in Saddleback was the same as throwing a party with free food. Everyone came running. He smiled at the memory.

Jenna had reacted to the trip with unbridled enthusiasm, as if she'd never shopped for groceries in her life. She was the same way about everything, come to think of it.

The ranch house was starting to respond to her enthusiasm.

But the truth was Jenna had been at the Southpaw for nearly a week now without a break, working hard enough to drive her into exhaustion.

He was an inconsiderate jerk.

Working in the semidark kitchen, he heated the baby bottle with one hand while holding Sophie securely with the other as he'd done dozens of times with Gavin. "Let your mama sleep, Sophie girl. Uncle Dax will fix you right up."

Okay, so he wasn't her uncle, but he felt like one. He'd been with her from the get-go. Not that he dared let himself get too close. No use getting in an emotional tangle about a baby destined to move on. A woman like Jenna wouldn't be here long. Once on her feet, she'd find a better job. She'd move on to a city somewhere with people of her education and breeding. Even a fool like him recognized quality and class when he saw it. Reba had no class at all, and even she hadn't stayed—which told him a lot about his shortcomings.

Sophie squirmed and let out a howl. Dax grunted away the useless, self-despising thoughts. He wouldn't let himself get attached, but right now, only a heartless jerk could ignore the cries of a hungry infant.

The microwave beeped. Dax took the bottle, shook a drop onto his wrist, then slid the warm nipple into the seeking, rosebud mouth. The crying stopped instantly to be replaced by the small, humming sounds an infant makes at feeding time. He'd always liked that sound. Relieved. Contented.

Padding barefoot back to the nursery, he thought about snapping on the lamp but decided against it. No use disturbing Jenna. He moved to close the door between the nursery and the bedroom beyond. As he did, he caught a glimpse of Jenna in the moonlight, curled on her side, sleeping like a rock. Her hair was down, spread across the pillow in spiky shadows. He could hear the soft hush of her breathing.

She didn't even stir.

He'd looked in this room many times before when Gavin was tiny and always found it empty. There was something renewing, redeeming even, to have a mother there now, steps away from her child. It eased the tight hard knot in his soul the tiniest bit.

He feasted on the feeling for several seconds, experiencing a connection with Jenna Garwood that he couldn't explain or fully comprehend.

Then, quietly, he shut the door.

CHAPTER EIGHT

JENNA AWOKE WITH A JERK and sat straight up in bed. Daylight streamed through the window. From down the hall came the sounds of people moving around and the undecipherable rumble of conversation. She'd overslept.

Leaping from the bed, she rushed into the nursery. Sophie was gone, her covers tossed aside. The changing table was in disarray. Had she been crying? Had Dax, annoyed by the noise, been forced to tend his employee's child?

Heart thudding, she quickly dressed and headed for the kitchen. Heretofore, she'd risen at six to have breakfast on the table before Gavin's school bus rumbled to a stop at seven.

Things had been going so well up until now, but her mother regularly fired employees for tardiness. Would Dax do the same?

She rushed into the kitchen only to be drawn up short. Dax, barefoot and shirt front unbuttoned, stood over the stove turning bacon with a long fork.

Gavin sat at the table dressed for school, hair combed, his face washed and shiny. And Sophie lay in her carrier in front of the little boy. Gavin gently tweaked her onesie-clad toes and shook a rattle above her face. Her eyes, still unable to fully focus, crossed from the effort.

"I'm so sorry," she gushed. "Please forgive me."

Dax offered the long fork. "Save me quick before I create a disaster."

She grabbed an apron from inside a cupboard and tied it around her waist. "Aren't you angry?"

"About?" He offered the fork again. She took it, reached around him, turned the burner down and the range vent on.

"I overslept. This is my job." She poked at the bacon. The crispy strips of pork were nearly done. "I'm supposed to have breakfast on the table by now."

He shrugged. "You were tired."

Fatigue was never an excuse. Domestics executed their duties or found other employment.

"I can't apologize enough."

"You'd better not apologize again." His tone was low and dangerous.

Her pulse skittered. She turned her attention from the bacon to her employer. He was impossibly close, his broad chest naked, the stubble of unshaved beard roguish and attractive. This man who'd taken care of her hungry daughter, started breakfast, dressed Gavin for school and wasn't even upset to have done so.

Since that first night when she'd felt the tug of attraction, she tried to maintain a professional if friendly distance, but this morning, after his incredible kindness, she was especially aware of his appeal. He wasn't classically handsome like Derek but he oozed rugged, masculine sex appeal. And he didn't seem to know it.

She hadn't thought about her appearance in a long time but suddenly she wished she were prettier. Though she'd gained little weight with Sophie, she wished her body was toned and tanned and sexy. The thought made her want to cry. She'd never been sexy. If she had been, her husband wouldn't have found another woman before the ink was dry on their marriage license.

Sophie made a fussy sound. Before she could react, Gavin poked the pacifier into the baby's mouth. Jenna rewarded him with a smile and then went back to the bacon, lifting the strips out of the pan and onto a plate.

Enough thoughts of sex appeal. She was here to do a job, to provide for her child, not moon over her employer's pectorals. And she was already running late.

"Sophie must have slept through the night," she said, scuttling about the kitchen, quickly taking breakfast items from the refrigerator and cupboards. "I'm sure that's why I overslept. After her two o'clock feeding, I'm usually half-awake until the alarm rings at five-thirty."

Dax leaned his jean-covered behind against the counter and crossed his arms over the appealing chest, expression amused. "Not."

She paused, carton of milk in hand. "What?"

"Sophie didn't sleep through the night. Just her mama."

The milk carton plunked onto the table. "You mean?" Dax had gotten up with her in the middle of the night? "Oh Dax, I'm so—"

Before she could apologize again, he lifted a finger in warning. "Uh-uh. Careful there. A tired mama needs rest. I was already awake. No need troubling you. Sophie and I did all right."

The tension in her shoulders relaxed. He really wasn't angry. "I suppose my brilliant daughter recognized a true expert while I, on the other hand, am still a novice, struggling much of the time to get her diaper on frontward."

Dax grinned. Oh my. He was luscious when he smiled. The tiny lines of weathering crinkled white near his eyes and increased his craggy attractiveness.

Aware she was staring, she spun toward the counter where boxed pancake mix awaited. Thank goodness, she'd had the good sense and had spent enough time researching on the Internet to understand the value of prepackaged goods. She wondered if the Carrington cooks had ever been allowed to use such conveniences. Knowing Elaine, probably not.

"She's a greedy little kitten," Dax was saying. "She likes her bottle right on time." He bumped against her side. "Need any help here?"

"Would you mind pouring juice?" Beating the lumpy batter, she glanced at the clock. "Gavin's time is running out."

The boy piped up. "I could stay home, Miss Jenna. Help you out around here."

Batter sizzled against the hot pan, sending up a wave of scent and heat. Jenna and Dax exchanged amused glances.

"You're exceedingly gracious to offer, Gavin, but your education is far too important. May I count on your help on Saturday?"

Gavin's forehead puckered. "After cartoons?"

Dax, a cup of coffee to his lips, sputtered with laughter. Jenna giggled. "After cartoons will do nicely. Thank you."

She slid the hot pancakes onto a plate which she set in front of Gavin while simultaneously scooting Sophie's carrier out of the way. The baby once again dozed, undisturbed by the sights and sounds swirling around her.

"Eat, sweetheart," she said to Gavin. "The bus will arrive soon."

She spun back to the stove to drip more batter onto the pan. Cooking breakfast required perfect timing. Most mornings she worked for a healthier offering, including breakfast casseroles and fruit compotes. One day of pancakes and bacon wouldn't hurt.

Dax had just poured a tooth-decaying amount of warm syrup onto a stack of pancakes when his cell phone chirped.

He made a disparaging face before barking into the mouthpiece. "What?"

After listening for a minute, he said, "Will anyone die if I eat breakfast first?"

Then he tossed the telephone onto the table and went back to his pancakes.

The short comment was exactly the kind she'd come to expect of her employer. He didn't waste words, which made him all the more difficult to understand.

Jenna refilled his coffee cup. As she turned away, he caught her wrist in his long fingers. "Sit down. Your pancakes are getting cold."

The touch of Dax's hard fingers against her skin brought a strange hum to her nerve endings.

She'd learned not to argue about taking meals with the family. He was insistent. She had to admit she preferred meals with the reticent rancher and his shyly sweet son to being alone. Very slowly, she was getting to know the nice man behind the glower. Getting close was another, more troubling matter.

"May I please get a glass of milk first?" she asked, glancing down at the circle of fingers where he held her captive.

He hissed through his teeth, dropped her hand and attacked his pancakes with an almost angry force.

Jenna turned away in confusion. What was that

all about? Had he felt the staggered trip of her pulse against those thick, calloused fingers? Had he recognized the buzz of electricity racing through her blood and been repelled?

She had no right feeling attracted to her employer. She'd lose her job. He'd toss her out. Worse, she was no judge of men. Hadn't she learned a thing after the fiasco with Derek?

Drawing upon a lifetime of pretending everything was all right when it wasn't, she poured a glass of milk and sat down, intent on making normal conversation. Executing appropriate small talk was a fine art, her mother would say, and though she was less skilled than her mother, she could manage.

"Problems on the ranch?" she asked, indicating the discarded cell phone.

Dax glowered at the device, though Jenna wondered if the scowl was meant for her. "Rowdy can handle the situation until I get there. That's what I pay him for."

Rowdy. The thought of Dax's top ranch hand soured the sweet taste of pancakes. For more than a week she'd managed to avoid another encounter with the man, a run of good luck she hoped would continue.

"What's wrong? A sick animal?" Beyond the subtleties of preparing a lovely prime rib, Jenna knew nothing about cattle. Dax had told her a little about the ranch, enough that she was interested. For a woman who'd been sheltered from so much, she wanted to know everything about everything.

"We have an A-I crew here today. They're early." He forked a bite of syrupy pancake and stirred it around his plate.

"May I inquire as to what an A-I crew might be?"

His mouth twitched. "You may. Artificial insemination."

Jenna was certain she turned pink. "I never realized such a thing occurred in cattle."

"Just one select group of experimental cows."

"Experimental cows. How fascinating." Not that she had any idea what he was talking about, but she liked the rumble of that scratchy-rough voice. And she felt rather pleased to have drawn him out. Most mornings, he mumbled hello and goodbye and disappeared out the door. Evenings were somewhat better.

Apparently, she'd been asking the wrong questions because once he started talking about his experimental cows, he didn't stop. Some of the conversation about selective breeding of a certain pasture of purebred cattle went completely over her head, but she listened hard. Dax Coleman was passionate about two things: his son and this ranch.

During a pause, Jenna noticed the clock. "Gavin, you need to brush your teeth. The bus will be here in five minutes." When Gavin scooted away from the table, she turned back to Dax. "Now tell me more about Number Thirty-two and what made her special enough to win 'Supreme Overall Breed' at the San Antonio show?"

Dax pointed his fork at her. "Do you really want to hear this or are you just being your perky self?"

Perky? Was that a compliment?

"I'm learning the nuances of ranch life," she said. "Please continue."

Dax shook his head. "The nuances of ranch life, huh? Okay, you asked for it." He launched into a technical explanation that had her mentally galloping to keep up. Dax Coleman might be a rough cattle rancher but he was a very bright man.

By the time Gavin returned, dragging his camo schoolbag, they'd turned the topic to horses and winter wheat pasture.

"I had no idea there was so much involved in raising cattle."

"Most folks think you turn 'em out to pasture and forget about them."

She smiled. "I can tell by the hours you put in that there is more to the work than that."

Gavin sidled up to his father for a goodbye hug.

"See ya tonight, sport. Be good."

Then the little boy headed toward her. She zipped his coat before pulling him in for a hug. Gavin had won her heart the first night with his precocious charm and obvious need for motherly attention. He seemed to crave her hugs and she was quickly growing to crave his, as well. Gavin was a sweet and gentle child.

She inhaled his clean, school-ready scent before turning him loose.

"Miss Jenna," he said, rustling inside his school-bag. "I forgot to show this to you."

"What is it?"

He pushed a note in front of her, his face a picture of hope. "Can you make cupcakes for my snack? I told Miss Baker you could. You're a real good cooker."

The compliment brought a smile. Gavin was such a dear little boy with such eagerness to please. Sometimes Dax grew impatient with the child's anxieties, but they touched Jenna's heart. She understood, empathized even, with being afraid. She'd been afraid most of her life.

Thankfully, he'd volunteered her cooking skills and nothing else. The kitchen was the only place she felt comfortable, but so far Dax had not complained about her mistakes in other areas. Like the pink socks. She wondered if he'd noticed those yet?

She shot a quick, relieved glance at his bare feet. She wasn't certain what she'd done wrong yesterday with the laundry but she suspected Gavin's bright red T-shirt was the culprit. Next time she'd separate the colors.

"I would be delighted to bake cupcakes, Gavin. When do you need them?"

With a shrug, the boy bent to zip his schoolbag. "It says on the note. I forget."

Jenna perused the note. "Oh dear."

Dax leaned to peer over her shoulder "What?"

Jenna refused to acknowledge the tingle of awareness where he brushed against her. "Today is Gavin's snack day."

Gavin's hope melted down his face like candle wax. Dax took one glance at his son and his own expression hardened. To Jenna he said, "Forget it then. It's too much trouble. If I have time I'll run into town to the bakery."

"But I wanted Noah to see the baby," Gavin protested.

"Son, don't make promises that aren't yours to keep." His tone was unyielding, angry even, though Jenna couldn't comprehend the reason.

The boy's mouth quivered. "Miss Jenna likes me. I thought—"

A nerve twitched in Dax's jaw. "I'll send your teacher a note and let her know you made a mistake."

The dejected child dropped his head.

"Gentlemen, please!" Jenna slapped down her napkin and rose. "May I speak for myself?"

At the startled glances of both males, she proceeded. "Though I lack the tools for anything artistically decorative, I want to provide refreshments for Gavin's class. I was only lamenting the lack of a pastry bag and tips, not refusing the task. Okay?"

Gavin, bewildered and uncertain, blinked from

Jenna to Dax and back again. "Does that mean you'll bring cupcakes?"

In spite of themselves, the adults looked at Gavin and then at each other…and burst out laughing.

CHAPTER NINE

HUMMING A HAPPY TUNE, Jenna shoved at the enormous leather sofa parked directly in the path of the dining room and the gorgeous stone-and-wood fireplace. While Gavin's cupcakes cooled and Sophie watched from her musical swing, Jenna had decided to do something about this ill-arranged living room. As lovely as the design was, the furniture was not being utilized effectively and the result was an unattractive and less-than-comfortable space.

She could actually imagine throwing a wonderful party in this house, maybe for Christmas or New Year's Eve. She already had her eye on some fabulous holiday decorations at the local hobby store and later today, she planned to explore Dax's storage building for others. But first, this space needed rearranging to reach its full potential of design and beauty.

With a groan of effort, she managed to scoot the sofa a few inches. Straining with all her strength while murmuring about her skinny arms, she didn't hear the door open.

"What do you think you're doing?"

At the sound of Dax's furious voice, Jenna jumped and spun around.

He stood, stance wide, hair windblown, looking like a thunderhead.

A hand pressed to her thudding heart, Jenna said, "Dax. I didn't hear you come in."

"Apparently." He slapped both fists low on his hips, billowing out the sides of a sheepskin jacket. "Answer me. What are you doing?"

"Rearranging." She bit her bottom lip. This was the first time he'd objected to any of her changes. She'd washed and moved curtains, rearranged pictures, added touches of color and interest with items she'd discovered in boxes in the garage. She'd even added a Christmas wreath to the front door and bowls of apple-scented potpourri to the tables. Last night, he commented on how good everything smelled and she'd been giddy with pleasure.

Now he was angry. And she had no idea why.

"You have no business moving furniture."

"I'm sorry. I thought you wouldn't mind."

"Well, I do."

"All right then." She pushed at the end of the sofa, edging the heavy item slowly back into the former position.

"Stop!"

She did. "Do you or do you not want this divan back where it was?"

"I don't give a rat's…behind where the couch is."

She blinked at her bewildering boss, lost until he continued.

"You'll hurt yourself. Show me where you want it. I'll move it."

"Oh." He was upset for her sake? Her insides turned to mush. Dax had the most unusual way of showing kindness. She touched his sleeve, surprised to feel the rigid muscle through all that cloth. "You're not angry because of the change in furniture, are you?"

"Why would I get mad about that? The place never looked better."

She smiled, her confidence soaring. Since taking this position, Jenna had discovered something about herself. She was actually good at many things her mother would consider below her station. She was good at them and she enjoyed them, too. She was starting to believe in herself in a way she'd never dreamed possible.

She was also learning some things about her employer. He struggled to express his true feelings, hiding his tender side behind bluster. But the evenings when he listened to her read to Gavin or helped his son with his homework, or even during those times she'd caught him in the nursery talking softly to Sophie, she'd learned the truth he tried to hide. He *was* a good guy. And Jenna was starting to like Dax Coleman. A lot.

"The fireplace should be the focal point of this room," she said. "So if we move the sofa there—" she pointed "—and a chair here and here, we'll open up the space and draw the eye to this beautiful stonework."

Dax contemplated momentarily. "I see your point."

"And the Christmas tree will be positively glorious there." She moved to the side of the fireplace, lifting her hands above her head in imitation of a tree. "See?"

"Couldn't ask for a prettier tree." Then as if he hadn't meant to say such a thing, he gave a curt nod. "Let's get it done."

But just the small hint that Dax thought she was pretty soothed an ache in Jenna's mind.

Biceps bulging and with barely any effort, he moved the furniture as she directed. Once she reached to help and he swatted at her with a growl. She hopped back, laughing, more confident now.

"You don't scare me."

Green eyes danced. "Then why'd you jump?"

She tossed a throw pillow at him. He caught it with one hand and growled again. "Careful, lady."

"Or what? The big bad wolf will get me?" She laughed, feeling free and a little excited.

Dax started toward her. "He might."

A delicious shiver raced up her spine. She

grabbed another pillow, holding the square bit of fluff in the small space between them. Dax snatched the pillow away, advancing. With a squeal, Jenna wheeled away. Her heart thudded and her blood zinged. This was one big bad wolf she wouldn't mind being pursued by.

She glanced back. Dax loomed above her, arms raised, hands forming claws like a bear. He roared.

Jenna screamed and jerked to the side. Her calves encountered a table she'd just moved. She lost her balance and tumbled backward. Dax caught her upper arms and yanked. He was amazingly strong. She was propelled forward and slammed into his chest.

"Are you all right?" He glared down at her, green eyes glittering.

"You saved me." Teasing, she pitter-pattered a hand against his heart. "My hero."

She'd meant it as a joke, as part of the silly game they were playing, but as soon as she touched him, all frivolity fled. She was aware of her body pressed against his, aware that she liked the feel of his arms around her.

"Dax?" she said.

A muscle twitched below his eye. His nostrils flared. After a long aching moment in which Jenna thought—hoped—he might kiss her, his whole body tensed, he dropped his hold and took three steps back.

Without looking at her, he grabbed his hat and jammed it down on his head.

"Let me know if you need any more furniture moved."

He wheeled away and left her standing in the living room alone.

She was getting under his skin in the worst way.

Dax tied off the end of a barbed wire strand and shoved his fencing pliers into his back pocket. For the last two hours, he'd been riding this fence line with Rowdy, checking for gaps, fixing spots and thinking about his housekeeper.

Though his body was warm from his labors, his face was cold. The shiny whiteness of the clouds along with a stiff north wind hinted at a weather change.

He hadn't slept fifteen minutes last night. Instead, he'd lain there in the dark thinking of how close he'd come to stepping over the line with Jenna. He'd never wanted to kiss anyone so much in his life. To kiss her. To hold her. Just to be with her.

To make matters worse, at least for him, after taking the cupcakes to Gavin's school, she'd returned bubbling over with chatter and goodwill. If she'd been affected by the near kiss she didn't let on. A man could get a complex. Not that he wanted her to think anything about that moment in his arms. Maybe she hadn't noticed. Maybe she hadn't been affected. Wouldn't that be for the best?

Right. Good. She'd gone to Gavin's school and

had a great time. She'd forgotten all about his unfortunate lapse in judgment.

A shaft of wind slid down the back of his neck. He flipped his collar up.

From the way Jenna had behaved at dinner, you'd think she'd never been in a school building in her life. She'd been all giddy and thrilled to eat cafeteria food and have kindergartner's wipe snot on what he was certain was a very expensive skirt.

Something was going on with Gavin, too. Last night, he'd found the little dude playing quietly in the nursery. He claimed to be guarding baby Sophie so she wouldn't get scared. From a kid who'd always been scared of his own shadow, the gesture was a puzzle.

But then so was his housekeeper. A puzzle and a disturbance.

"Been meaning to ask you something, boss." Rowdy shot a cocky grin his way.

"Yeah?" Dax squinted toward the clouds gathering in the west. Maybe the wind would blow in some much-needed moisture. They'd been irrigating the winter wheat for weeks now.

"How's your new housekeeper working out?"

The question, given he couldn't get Jenna out of his head, caught him completely off guard. He gazed at the clouds another second before turning a squint-eyed gaze at Rowdy. "All right. Why?"

"Just wondering about her. She's single. Pretty. Curved in all the right places."

Dax studied his hand for a moment, not liking the direction of this conversation. "She's a new mother."

He stuck a foot in a stirrup and swung up into the saddle.

Rowdy looped a roll of wire over the saddle horn and guffawed. "You're getting old, Dax, if that's all you see."

Thirty-four sounded older every day, but Dax didn't much appreciate the reminder. And he sure wasn't going to tell Rowdy the truth.

"She's doing her job, cooks great food I've never heard of and looks after Gavin." The boy adored her, followed her like a pup hungry for her smiles and hugs. The behavior was pitiful if he thought about it, but he was glad to see Gavin happy.

Rowdy swung into the saddle and they urged the horses to a walk, examining fence line as they rode while keeping an eye out for strays. "What about you?"

Dax ruminated a beat. "What about me?"

"You know what I'm talking about. She taking good care of you, too?"

Dax didn't like Rowdy's implication, though he supposed no insult was intended. The young cowboy was comfortable with horses, cattle and women. Lots of women. Naturally, his roving eye would land on the only female within fifteen miles. What man with any juice in his veins wouldn't notice Jenna?

"She's a good employee."

Rowdy, holding the reins with a light hand, rose in his stirrups and twisted around, squinting toward a pond dam. "That's all?"

No.

"That's all." Dax heard the growl in his voice, felt the prickle of jealousy beneath his skin.

The saddle creaked as Rowdy settled in again. "Then I guess you won't mind if I stop by the house and pay my respects, maybe ask her out sometime."

Dax rubbed a sleeve across his face, more to avoid looking at his employee than to scratch an itch. What could he say without admitting that he was attracted to his too-young housekeeper? "She stays pretty busy."

"You can't work her 24-7, boss. Every woman likes a night out. Considering she had a kid, she's probably hankering to get away once in a while."

Dax bit down on his molars. Why hadn't he considered that?

As soon as the thought crossed his mind, he mentally kicked himself. He hadn't thought of it because he couldn't, no more than he could consider kissing her. Jenna was out of his league in more ways that one. "She's not your type, Rowdy. Leave her alone. There are plenty of girls in Saddleback waiting for you to call."

Rowdy didn't answer and they rode on, but Dax couldn't get the worry out of his head. He had no right to keep Jenna from having a life. She and that pink princess of hers needed a man to look after them, though she'd probably poison his potato frittata if she heard him say such a thing. Women were testy about that independence business nowadays. But Rowdy was probably right. She needed to get out, make friends, do things that young people do. Get away from the likes of him.

Maybe he should encourage a relationship between his housekeeper and his best ranch hand. Maybe if he did, he could stop thinking about her so much. About her fancy voice and her honey-brown eyes and kissable mouth. About the sweet way she catered to her baby—and his son. About her silvery laugh that caused a catch in his chest as though he couldn't quite breathe.

A cord of tension crept across his shoulders and up the back of his neck. He hoped he wasn't getting one of those headaches—blasted, debilitating things. They made him feel like some kind of sissy.

He kicked the horse into a trot and headed across pasture, leaving the other cowboy in the dust. The rush of wind in his face cleared his thinking.

He'd brought Jenna here to the Southpaw. She was his responsibility. Rowdy might be a good worker, but he was fast and loose with the ladies. Jenna deserved better than that.

Yesterday's near kiss was still on Jenna's mind as she bathed Sophie. She'd mulled over the incident off and on all day, finally coming to a conclusion.

She had overreacted. Considering his normal behavior at dinner last night, Dax had already forgotten. Either that or he hadn't been about to kiss her at all.

She heard the back door open. A glance at the elephant clock on the armoire had her frowning. Dax hadn't come in for lunch and the time was long past, though he often skipped the noon meal in favor of work. But someone was certainly here now.

A quiver of concern passed over her. Was something wrong? Worse yet, had someone else come into the house?

Lifting Sophie from her tub, she wrapped the slick little body in a soft, hooded terry cloth towel and went to find out.

Dax stood in the kitchen. He looked weary as he rummaged through the cabinets searching for something. Weary and masculine. She fought back the memory of those strong arms holding her.

"May I help you find something?" she asked. He'd tossed his hat on the counter along with his jacket. His hair was mussed, his shoulders tense. Body heat and cold air radiated from him.

"Aspirin." He rubbed the back of one hand over his eyes.

"Headache?"

He nodded, looking at her through bloodshot eyes with an expression of both embarrassment and suffering.

"I rearranged the cabinets," she said. "All medicines are now in the master bath out of Gavin's reach. I'll get the pain reliever."

Pressing Sophie's still damp body against her shoulder, she started in that direction. Dax followed. "I can manage."

She let him pass her in the hallway, noticing his usual cowboy swagger was more of a stagger. "Dax. You're sick."

She followed him into the master bath, squelching the hint of impropriety. "Go lie down. I'll get this."

He lifted one arm halfway then let it drop in surrender. "Thanks."

He staggered out of the bathroom. Jenna stared after him.

He really *was* sick. And she was worried. Dax was cowboy tough, almost stoic.

With Sophie in arms, balancing the aspirin and water was a trick, but she managed. By the time she entered the bedroom, Dax was sprawled, fully dressed on a massive brown-and-blue comforter. He levered up on one elbow to accept the medication, then eased back down. His eyes were barely focusing now and his forehead glistened with sweat.

Without giving the action much thought, she lay Sophie next to him and touched his forehead. His skin felt both hot and clammy. He shivered.

"Should I call the doctor?" she asked, growing more worried by the minute.

"No," he murmured. "Just close the blinds and keep Gavin quiet. I'll be fine."

"You aren't fine, Dax. You're really sick." Too sick to remove his dirty boots.

When she tugged them off, he didn't protest. Oh yes, he was definitely sick. She went into the bathroom and returned with a cool, damp cloth. Dax didn't open his eyes but as she placed the cloth over his forehead, he sighed.

"You might feel better undressed." Her face heated to say such a thing, but the man was miserable.

"Later." Voice weak, he lifted a weak hand. "Go."

Gathering Sophie, she did as he commanded, backing out slowly, her gaze on him as long as possible. What was wrong? What if something terrible happened to Dax? He wasn't one to complain and in fact, she'd noticed the way he shrugged off hurts such as Gavin's bloody nose and his own more recent run-in with an angry cow that had left him with a dislocated finger. With gritted teeth, he'd yanked the joint back into place, slapped some ice on it and never mentioned the accident again.

This was something worse than a dislocation.

Fretting, she dried and dressed Sophie and rocked her for a while. The presence of her daughter soothed her nerves. When Sophie fell asleep again, Jenna put her to bed and tiptoed across the long house to Dax's door.

Peeking through the crack she'd left, she saw a white rim around his lips and the frown of misery between his dark eyebrows.

When Gavin arrived home from school, she met him in the foyer with a finger to her lips. "Your daddy is not feeling very well, Gavin. We need to be extra quiet okay?"

Nodding sagely, the boy placed his schoolbag on the table and slid off his coat, taking special care to make no noise.

"Is it one of his headaches?" he whispered.

"Does your dad often suffer from bad head-aches?"

"I can't remember what they're called. Grains, I think. Yeah, that's it. Dad calls them his grains. They're bad."

"Migraines?" she asked, amused at the child's misunderstanding.

The little face screwed up in sympathy. "You get 'em, too?"

"No, sweetheart. Thankfully, I have never suffered with the malady but I have encountered it." Her mother had them at convenient times. Somehow she doubted Dax's were the same. "Will you help me keep Sophie quiet in the nursery tonight so your daddy can recuperate?"

"Yep, but I got homework. The letter *E. E* is for *egg*."

"Very good. Can you think of anything else that starts with the sound of *egg?*"

"Elephant. Like that clock in Sophie's room." He screwed up his face. "*Elephant* and *egg* and *egg-cited.*"

Jenna's lips twitched. "*Excited?*"

"Yep. The way I feel about Christmas. I'm getting a bulldozer and a dump trunk. We're having a party at school, too."

"You are?"

"Yep. Miss Jenna?" He pulled papers from his bag and carried them to the kitchen table. "Are you coming back to my school?"

"I have to ask your father about it, but I hope to." The day at Gavin's elementary school had been one of the most interesting and enjoyable times she could remember. She'd never been in a public school classroom. The sounds and smells and colorful decor had captivated her. She'd read with a group of children, listened to their adorable chatter, and after serving cupcakes had helped put them down on little mats for a rest. When the teacher had asked her about volunteering once a week, calling her a natural with the kids, she'd been flattered and promised to give the offer some thought. But the answer had to come from Dax. He paid her to be here at the ranch.

"Noah said you're pretty. He said Dad probably likes you." Head bent as he carefully traced the letter *E,* his voice innocent as a lamb, he said, "I told him yes. Dad likes you a lot. Maybe Sophie will be my sister now."

With a pang, Jenna patted his back and headed for the kitchen to prepare dinner. This was Gavin's obsession with having a sibling and nothing more.

She took the marinated beef from the refrigerator, pausing with one hand on the oven dial.

Did Dax like her? She hoped so. She liked her job, loved the beauty of this austere country and was falling fast for Gavin. Most of all, she was safe here. In the days since Sophie's birth, she'd traveled into Saddleback, shopped, had lunch with Crystal, all without hearing mention of the runaway heiress from Pennsylvania.

Her life here grew fuller and more fulfilling every day. She could easily think of Texas as home, and as long as she and her daughter were free of the smothering pressures of her former lifestyle, Jenna didn't care if she was a domestic forever.

As she prepared dinner, she helped Gavin with his work, praised as he practiced writing his name in a laborious hand. She couldn't help thinking this was what a normal family life should be.

When the meal was complete, she debated about disturbing Dax. In the end, she prepared a plate of the beef tournedos and covered it. Though he'd teased her this morning about serving him tornadoes for dinner, she'd looked forward to his reaction to the delicious recipe. But that would have to wait. When and if he felt like eating, his meal would be ready.

After dinner, Gavin asked permission to play

with his cars and dinosaurs in Sophie's room. Jenna adjusted the nursery monitor to keep an eye on both children as she cleaned the kitchen. When she poured dishwasher detergent into the holder inside the machine, she grimaced. A few days ago, she'd made the mistake of using laundry detergent. The result had flooded the tile with soapsuds. Gavin had been gleeful over the turn of events and Dax had laughed. She pretended to have accidentally picked up the wrong box, but in truth, she hadn't known the difference. She knew now.

Drying her hands on a dish towel, she checked the monitor again and heard Gavin's voice quietly telling the sleeping Sophie about an incident at school. With a smile, Jenna headed toward the master bedroom to peek in on Dax. As she approached the door, she heard him groan.

She pushed the door open. His covers were a rumpled mess. His hair shot in a dozen directions as though he'd yanked at it in agony.

"Dax?" she whispered.

Bloodshot eyes opened, then closed again, but not before she saw the pain. Needing to help, she went to Dax's office and searched the Internet. The World Wide Web had been her salvation during these days of learning to be a domestic engineer. She liked that term. Now, she searched until she found simple techniques for alleviating the pain of a migraine.

Back in Dax's bedroom, she wet another cloth

and replaced the warm one, then eased onto the edge of the bed. Without asking permission, she began to gently massage his temples.

His eyes fluttered open to look at her in glazed curiosity, but he was clearly in too much pain to say anything beyond, "That helps."

She continued the gentle, circular strokes, praying he would find relief. When he tugged at the neck of his shirt, Jenna said, "Would you be more comfortable out of these clothes? I would be happy to assist."

Well, perhaps not happy but willing. The idea of seeing Dax unclothed made her belly quiver.

His body tensed and she could see him holding his breath. Then he exhaled but didn't answer.

Bracing herself to do what was best for her employer, Jenna unbuttoned his shirt. He had a magnificent chest and shoulders. Any woman would notice. She had the craziest urge to smooth her palm over the curved pectorals and discover if they were as rock-hard as she suspected.

Her pulse hammered against her throat. Her fingers tingled at the touch of him. Foolish, silly woman. The man was ill.

With steely resolve, she pushed the sleeves over his shoulders and slid them down his arms. He grunted once. She paused, afraid she'd hurt him.

With the shirt discarded, Jenna drew a deep breath and reached for the silver belt buckle. A hand stopped her. Jenna's gaze flew up to meet his.

Nostrils flared, he grumbled, "I'll do this."

She nodded and backed toward the door. "If you need me…"

"In a minute."

Did that mean he wanted her to return? She stepped outside the room, checked the portable monitor in her pocket to be sure the children were safe, and waited.

She heard rustling and footsteps, then the give of the bed. Her heart beat in her throat and she felt flushed. An embarrassing situation, no doubt, but there was more to her discomfort than that.

"Jenna." The word was slurred.

She reentered the room, finding Dax in string-drawn lounge pants and nothing else. He'd replaced the damp cloth, covering his eyes. His chest rose and fell with the effort of his movements.

Jenna stepped to the bed and reclaimed her place on the edge. Determined to help this man who had helped her, she placed the baby monitor within her line of vision and as gently as she knew how, began to massage his temples again.

"Rest," she whispered. "Relax."

He inhaled deeply and exhaled on a sigh.

She massaged until her fingers numbed and her wrists ached but she refused to stop. Dax hadn't abandoned her when the going had been rough with Sophie, and she would not abandon him.

After the longest time, the tension eased from Dax's body. His breathing grew deep and even. The furrow between his brows smoothed.

With a tenderness that shook her, Jenna let her fingers drift down his temples, over the whisker-roughened jaw where she paused at the corners of his remarkable mouth.

Relaxed in sleep, he looked young and vulnerable. And incredibly male.

Stunned at the tender feelings he aroused in her, Jenna quietly eased off the bed and slipped from the room.

CHAPTER TEN

THE DAWN HAD YET TO BREAK when Dax entered the kitchen, drawn there by the scent of fresh coffee. He felt washed-out but infinitely better, the rampaging pain but a fading nightmare.

As bad as the dream had been, there had been a good part, too. Jenna. Even in the fog of a migraine, he'd been aware of her soft hands touching him, easing the throb in his temples, sliding his shirt from his body. Had he not been so ill—well, he had been. Otherwise, she would not have taken such liberties.

Yet he remembered.

This morning, Jenna was nowhere to be seen, but from the looks of things she was up and busy, probably tending Sophie. From what he'd gathered, she rose with the baby around six and never let up again until bedtime. He'd seen the fatigue around her eyes, felt a twinge of guilt for working her so hard, but she never complained and any suggestion that she ease up seemed to trouble her. He didn't know why. There was no chance of her being fired, though he figured she didn't know that yet.

After last night, when she'd tended him like a baby, her job was safe for as long as she wanted it.

He was embarrassed at his weakness, but she'd responded with such genuine care. This morning would tell the tale, though. He would know when he looked in her eyes if she considered him less of a man. Reba had.

He poured a thick brown mug full of steaming brew, dumped in two spoons of sugar and stirred. His housekeeper was still a mystery. In the back of his mind a nagging voice claimed she hadn't come completely clean about her reasons for being here. Sometimes she seemed to be looking over her shoulder. Other times she embraced the mundane business of life with the exuberance of a child experiencing things for the first time.

But Dax didn't care where she'd come from or why she'd chosen to stay here. He was simply glad she had.

She'd figured out Gavin faster than a flea hops and the little dude responded like a dry sponge. He was grateful, though his growing feelings for his housekeeper went deeper than gratitude. Every day he reminded himself that she was too young, too smart and pretty and refined. She was wise, too, as if she had an old soul.

With a grunt at his fanciful thoughts, he stepped to the sink and deposited the spoon there for later cleanup. The window over the sink looked out on the backyard and beyond to the barns and corrals and separating pens. The first shifting of dawn's white-pink light cast a halo over the peaceful, drowsy ranch.

The beauty had particular significance this morning now that the Coleman curse of migraines had run its course and he'd survived.

He loved gazing out at the land he'd purchased from the rest of his family. No one else loved the ranch the way he did. No one else could tolerate the long days and 24-7 demands of the cowboy life. Most of all no one wanted to live out here far from the rest of civilization.

Which brought him back to his housekeeper. She seemed to relish the place and even if the pleasure was an act, he'd take it. He'd found her in the horse barns one day, Sophie attached to her front like a baby monkey on some kind of sling thing. He'd been surprised to hear that she had equestrian skills as she called them and after watching her with the horses for a while, he'd believed her. He'd offered to let her ride sometime, refraining from actually offering to ride along with her. No use being stupid.

After Rowdy's comments, though, he was having second thoughts. As much as he liked his ranch hand, he didn't want Rowdy messing with Jenna. She was too sweet and tender and innocent. Rowdy was a rounder.

He sipped his coffee, sighed out his pleasure in such a simple thing as good coffee and sunrise, and leaned against the sink to watch. The silent sun shimmered just beneath the horizon, casting up hints of the coral and yellow to come. The morning sun was magical to him, bringing with it the promise of a new, clean day, uncluttered by yesterday's suffering.

He chuckled and shook his head. He was feeling poetic this morning.

From the corner of his eye he saw movement on the long, back porch and turned in that direction. A figure—Jenna—huddled beneath a blanket on the cedar bench he rarely used. Once, he'd planned for the backyard and patio to be a place for family and friends to gather, a place to watch his children play and grow. Those plans, like so many others, had died in their infancy.

After pouring a second cup of coffee complete with cream, the way Jenna liked it, he eased the back door open with his hip and joined her.

"Good mornin'," he said. Standing with legs wide he breathed in the crisp, clean morning. The air was still as death, though he knew the wind would get up later on. Winter encroached on the perfect fall.

"Good morning." Her voice was a soft melody, blending with the hush of daybreak. "Feeling better?"

He nodded. "Much. Thanks to you."

He watched her eyes, held his breath and waited for the disgust or disappointment he expected.

When none was forthcoming, Dax accepted the fact that Jenna Garwood was even more special than he'd originally thought.

"I'm glad."

He held out the mug. "Careful. It's hot."

Expression quizzical, she accepted his offering, wrapping both hands around the cup before sipping daintily. "Thank you."

"Enough cream?"

"Perfect." She started to rise. "I'll finish breakfast now."

The blanket slid away. He replaced it and guided her back down, adding a reassuring squeeze to the delicate bones of her shoulder. "Stay. Weekends are lazy. No rush."

Jenna settled readily and sipped again at the cup. Steam curled upward, wrapping her face in a mist, as if she were a genie who'd appeared to grant his fondest wishes. Ah, if only it were so. But Dax Coleman was the worst kind of realist, a man who barely believed in people, certainly not in pregnant genies. Though if he could believe in anyone, after last night he might believe in Jenna.

Fool that he was.

Turned sideways on the bench, Jenna drew her legs up close to her body and arranged the long ends of a robe and the fleece blanket over them. Her feet peeked out, pink and elegant the way he'd remembered. He hadn't thought about her feet, about those pink-tipped toes, in days. Funny how he wished for an excuse to touch the smooth, soft skin again.

She patted the empty end of the bench. "I'll share my space with you."

Dax hesitated, wondering if spending nonworking time with the housekeeper was a good idea. Considering his fanciful thoughts this morning, it wasn't.

Her mouth curved in a soft smile. "It's so beautiful out here. People should take the time to enjoy these moments."

Hadn't he been thinking the same thing? He eased onto the far end of the bench and leaned forward, letting the coffee cup dangle between his knees. The space between him and Jenna was limited, though, and her toes grazed the side of his thigh. He tried not to think about it but the knowledge that only a layer of denim separated his skin from hers lingered.

"I try to find a few minutes to come out here every morning," she said, her voice soft and dreamy.

He hadn't known that. "No wonder you look tired."

She smiled. "Do I? I'm not really. I'm—" She stopped and sipped at the cup again.

He swiveled his head sideways just enough to watch the thoughts and feelings flit through her eyes. Even in the semilight, her eyes shone with an inner strength and beauty that had him mesmerized. He didn't know when he'd begun thinking of her this way. Maybe he was still asleep with the remnants of the cursed headache impairing his mental function, but the woman was messing with his mind. As hard as he tried to remember she was hardly out of her teens, he failed more often than not.

And last night, she'd offered to undress him.

A white-hot blaze flared in his gut. He tamped it down, glad for the chill morning, though even the fiercest winter wouldn't have cooled the fire Jenna had started inside him.

This morning she was rumpled and uncombed, still in her robe, the likes of which he'd never seen. It was expensive; he knew that much from watching Reba spend like a queen, but even she had never had anything like this. Jenna's urgent need for a job didn't fit with the fancy clothes or the air of upper-crust breeding she wore like a princess. Had her cheating husband left her penniless? Had he taken everything and caused her to run away in shame, destitute?

"You're what?" he asked, picking up the conversation, wanting to know more than he should have, but not willing to ask the questions about her husband. Had she loved him? Did she still?

"Mmm, I don't know how to express it." Her shoulders lifted. "Grateful, I suppose."

He'd wanted her to say happy. How dumb was that? No woman had ever been happy here. Not his mother or his sister or his ex-wife. Too far from the city. Too far from civilization. Too far from friends and shopping malls.

"Different from where you're from, I suspect."

She made a small amused sound. "Oh, yes. Very different."

He couldn't help himself. "Is that a good thing or a bad thing?"

The early-morning quiet, the intimacy of Jenna in her housecoat and blanket, and him remembering the touch of her cool hands against his temples had him talking in ways he wouldn't normally have.

"A very good thing. A person can feel safe here. Free."

He wondered at the assessment, so different from Reba's. She'd felt confined and alone. Jenna felt safe and free. Though he wondered at how such a young woman could know otherwise, another hitch in the terrible knot beneath his heart loosened.

"Wide-open spaces, fresh air, can't beat 'em."

She inhaled deeply. "Just smell that, Dax. So clean and pure." She touched his shirtsleeve. "I smell winter."

Resisting the urge to put his hand over hers, Dax smiled and looked toward the horizon. She had a cute way of putting things.

"You probably smell rain blowing up from the Gulf. Anyway, I hope you do. Lord knows we need it."

"Do we?"

We. He didn't miss the pronoun. "Always need rain out here. That's why we irrigate."

"Ah." She tilted her head in acknowledgment. "What is that sound?"

Dax listened, hearing only the usual noises of a Texas dawn. "Birds, hungry calves bawling for mama."

"No, that other sound. The popping."

His lips curved against the rim of his coffee cup. He'd lived so long with the noises he hardly heard them anymore. "Oil wells somewhere. Could be miles away. Out here sound travels forever."

"We don't have those in—back East."

That tiny pause caught in Dax's thoughts. What was it about her past that she wanted to hide? Why didn't she want him to know her hometown?

He mentally rolled his eyes. *Get a clue, Coleman. Women like an escape route.* Last night meant nothing beyond an employee showing kindness. Get over it.

The back door groaned open. Gavin poked his head out. "Dad?"

Both adults turned toward the sound.

"Out here, son."

Dressed in flannel pajamas, his dark hair sticking up in horns all over his head, Gavin stumbled out onto the porch. "What are you doing?"

"Talking. Watching the sunrise."

Gavin's face screwed up tight. "Is it time to get up?"

"Only if you want to."

"Okay." He scratched at his underarm, clearly bewildered by the adults' behavior. "Dad?"

"What?"

"Is your grain better?"

"My what?"

Jenna chuckled softly and touched Dax's arm. They exchanged glances. "My grains. Your grains. Understand?"

The light dawned in Dax's eyes.

"Yes, son," he said. "My headache is gone, thanks to Jenna."

"And me. I was real quiet."

"Yes, you were," Jenna said. "You helped me with Sophie, too."

"Yeah." The dark-haired child stretched, yawning loudly. "It's cold out here. Dad?"

The adults shared another amused glance. "What, son?"

"Can Jenna come to my school again? She wants to, don't you Miss Jenna?"

"Yes, I do, but that's entirely up to your father."

"Why would I care if you went to Gavin's school?"

"They'd like me to volunteer one day a week."

"You want to?"

"Very much, but my first duty is here."

Duty. For some inexplicable reason, the word chafed like starched pants. "Gavin is part of that duty. But you have a life, too, Jenna. You aren't a slave here."

"I know, but I want to do the right thing."

"Volunteer. It will be good for both of you." Good for him, too, not to be thinking about her in his house every minute of the day.

She smiled. "Yes, I believe so, too."

Her smile touched a sore spot inside him. The chafing evaporated. Hadn't he been thinking she needed to get out more?

"This reminds me of something I've been meaning to discuss with you." Since the conversation with Rowdy, the thoughts hadn't let up. Along with a near kiss over a rearranged couch, thinking about her had probably given him the migraine. A woman had needs, even a woman with a new baby. Maybe especially then. He didn't want her getting dissatisfied and running off. Though anyone with half a brain would tell you that Dax Coleman no more knew how to make a woman happy than he could sprout wings and fly. But he had to try.

She was a good cook. Gavin needed her. Things ran smoother since she'd come. He needed to keep her happy.

That gnat of a voice buzzing inside his head said he liked having her around, too, but he swatted it. No use thinking the impossible.

"You want to discuss something?" Jenna tilted her head, one finely shaped eyebrow upraised. "Is it something I'm not doing correctly?"

There were lots of those but he wasn't going there. Who cared about pink socks or a fork down the garbage disposal when she served beef tournedos and salmon roulade—and he wasn't even a fish eater.

"You're doing great," he managed, though complimentary words came out of his throat like opening a rusted door.

That smile came again, tickling his stomach. Dax fidgeted, turning the warm mug in his hands. He wasn't doing this for her smiles. It was self-preservation, plain and simple. He needed a housekeeper who would stick around.

"No woman likes being stuck on a ranch all the time. You need to get out now and then."

Jenna went silent. He shifted a glance in her direction. What he saw troubled him. Gnawing that pretty lip of hers, she looked worried.

What did she have to be worried about?

The notion that she was running from something—or someone—came back to haunt him. He'd vowed to protect her and the little pink princess. He couldn't do much else but he could do that. If someone was after her, they'd have to come through him.

The vehemence of the sentiment stunned him.

"I just mean—" What did he mean? Rowdy said women needed to go out and have fun. If he wanted to keep her happily employed, he'd have to make that happen. Though not with Rowdy.

"I thought we might go to a movie," he blurted. "Dinner, too, if you want." He couldn't believe he'd said that.

"You want to take me to a movie?" she asked.

Dax swallowed. Could he handle spending more time with a woman who was already messing with his head? And exactly when had he starting thinking of her as a woman?

"I don't want you to feel trapped here. A night out is good for you now and then. I don't want to put any pressure on you, either. I mean, you're my employee so if you don't want to go, that's fine. Just feel free to go out on your own or with someone else any time you feel like it. Don't let the job stop you. That's what I meant." The last statements ground against him like a handful of rocks in his boot. He didn't want her going out with anyone. "Not one of the hands, though. These cowboys. You can't trust them." He was babbling.

Jenna looked at him as if the headache had caused more mental stress than she'd originally thought. Maybe it had.

Gavin, on the other hand, had come to life. With enough glee to start his own clown act, he began hopping up and down on one foot, slapping his arms. "Say yes, Miss Jenna. Dad will even spring for a Friendly Meal. Won't you, Dad?"

"Oh, Gavin, you charmer." Jenna pressed a hand to her lips and laughed.

Dax's shoulders relaxed. He grinned. "Yeah, I'm a big spender."

Jenna's amused gaze captured Dax's. "Then I

shall be delighted to accept your kind invitation. A movie and a Friendly Meal it shall be."

No matter how hard he tried to convince himself he was doing this to keep her happy as well as safely away from Rowdy, Dax realized one thing. He was in big trouble.

CHAPTER ELEVEN

A MOVIE. DAX WAS TAKING her to a movie.

Jenna couldn't keep the smile off her face as she dressed that evening. What did one wear to a movie?

She opened the closet and browsed, regretting the decision to leave her dress clothes behind. The only public movie she'd ever attended was a premiere in New York. Derek had insisted on going, and later she'd realized he was enamored of the starlet who had invited them. She had deplored the ostentatious glitz and posturing, preferring the privacy of their home theater.

A regular movie outing would likely be different. Most people—*normal* people—did not wear Versace gowns to a movie.

Which was fine with Jenna. She'd left the gowns behind with the rest of her life. From her knowledge of the people of Saddleback, she was certain a movie was not a black-tie affair.

The hangers scraped over the metal bar as she

sorted through the clothes she'd brought with her. Up to now she'd mostly worn her loose-fitting maternity outfits, but with her tummy regaining shape, she took out a pair of jeans, a long-sleeved top and a pink leather jacket. They weren't Western wear by any stretch of the imagination, but they would do.

She slithered into the jeans, a snug fit, and spritzed eau de parfum in all the right places before sliding the blouse over her head. In front of the mirror, she turned this way and that, casting a critical eye on her appearance. She might not be beautiful, but she knew how to put herself together for the best effect. A Carrington always kept up appearances.

Her hair had lost its trendy cut, but a few minutes with a straightener and some shine serum made it presentable. Humming, she slipped on jewelry and heels, then went to dress the baby for their first night out in Saddleback, Texas.

By the time she entered the living room to await the men of the group, her palms were damp with excitement.

Gavin appeared first, strutting through the house with his chest puffed out, his black-brown hair slicked down and dressed in perfectly creased jeans and a red button-down shirt. His boots gleamed with a fresh polish.

"My goodness. You look immaculate."

"Yeah," he said proudly, craning his neck to

one side. "Smell me." He pointed to a spot on his neck. "Right there. Daddy put me on some of his smell-good."

With an inward smile, Jenna inhaled loudly. "Wonderful."

If Dax smelled this delicious, she might swoon.

The man in question ambled down the hall into sight. Jenna's heart banged once hard against her rib cage. He was definitely swoonworthy.

"Everyone ready?"

"Yearning for that Friendly Meal," she joked.

"Yeah," Gavin sighed. "I love Friendly Meals."

The adults exchanged glances. For a nanosecond their gazes locked and a feeling of pure pleasure danced between them.

"No headache?" she asked.

He touched his temple. "Good as new."

She reached for Sophie's carrier, but Dax nudged her out of the way. "I've got the princess. You grab the diaper bag."

She did as he said, covertly watching her employer tap the baby's nose and make faces at her. Sophie, her usual drowsy self, let her eyes cross and then closed them as Dax draped a blanket over the entire baby seat.

Feeling happy in a way she had never dreamed possible, Jenna walked alongside Dax and Gavin out the door and to his truck.

She helped Dax position the car seat in the back with Gavin and smiled her thanks when he helped her into the cab, closed the door and grinned at her through the glass before jogging around to the driver's side.

Yes, indeed, being a normal, everyday woman was beginning to feel very, very good.

Dax sat across the orange plastic table from Jenna watching her and Gavin devour French fries with the same zeal. He'd tried to take them someplace nicer, but she'd insisted on the burger joint. He was sure she'd done so for Gavin's sake and he appreciated that, but she deserved a classier establishment.

Part of him wanted to be sorry he'd asked her out, but tonight he just wanted to laugh and have a good time. When was the last time he'd done that? He didn't even know. From the looks of Gavin, hanging upside down inside the indoor playland, he felt the same. His squeals of laughter mingled with those of a dozen other kids out for a good time on Saturday night.

Dax looked around the colorful dining area, raising a hand to acknowledge a person here and there. He knew most people in Saddleback but hadn't seen them all that much during the last few years. It struck him that the world was moving right along without him to the detriment of his son.

Reba had driven him into a shell. Jenna was bringing him out.

"You have ketchup on your face," he said, pointing.

She took a paper napkin and swiped. "Did I get it?"

"Here." He leaned across the table, took the napkin and cleaned away the drop on her upper lip. "Messy."

The smell of her perfume had driven him batty in the truck, and now he smelled those flowers again. He sat back but the scent lingered in his nostrils.

"You look pretty tonight," he said and then wanted to jam a handful of fries down his throat and strangle himself. He'd brought her out as a means of keeping her employed, not to admire how good she looked in those jeans and that pricey-looking jacket.

Right, and all his cows would jump over the moon at midnight.

Her smile took away the urge to hurt himself. "Thank you. I wasn't sure what to wear."

Women. From the curve of golden hair against her slim face to the silver dangling from her wrist and ears, Jenna was a knockout. "You look great. Perfect." Shut up, Dax.

A hint of pink crested her cheekbones. "What time does the movie start?"

Relieved at the change of subjects, he checked his watch. "Soon. We'd better round up the boy and head that way."

Jenna nodded and began piling discarded wrappers and cups onto the plastic tray before following him to the yellow-and-red tube slide.

"Gavin, come on, son. Time to go."

"He's having such fun."

"Yeah. I liked this stuff when I was a kid, too." An odd look crossed her face. "Didn't you?"

She shook her head. "I've never played on one."

As if she'd said something wrong, she turned away to fid-dle with Sophie. Dax studied her, baffled. She'd never played on a playground?

"Why not?"

"Oh, it's not important. Look, here's Gavin," she said a little too brightly as if they hadn't just seen the boy moments ago when he was dancing in ecstasy over a Friendly Meal toy.

Whatever troubled Jenna about the past, she didn't want to talk about it. Dax decided to let the moment slide. He'd suggested this outing for her pleasure and he wasn't about to mess things up if he could help it. But one of these days Miss Jenna was going to talk to him.

One of these days.

The drive to the movie was a matter of blocks. Once inside the small theater, Dax paid for the tickets. The smell of popcorn enticed Gavin, so they stopped at the concession stand, as well. Cheesy-looking Christmas garland looped from the ceiling, and the walls were plastered with colorful posters of upcoming holiday movies. A cheap, fake Christmas tree stood in one corner of the lobby, lights blinking in lazy cheer. Dax would swear it was the same tree from six or seven years ago.

Jenna stared around with a half smile as if thrilled with the decor. While he waited for the slowest clerk in Texas to fill his order, Jenna gazed around, watching the good folks of Saddleback mingle and talk.

Teenagers swarmed the lobby, holding hands and talking too loud over the video games. Dax thought of how Jenna belonged more with them than with him. Though he felt a little better to see she had a serene maturity they all lacked.

He watched her soaking it all in, an enchanted expression on her face, as if attending a two-screen theater in a tiny town was the coolest thing ever. That was Jenna. She had a way of making a celebration out of everyday life.

The clerk finally brought their order.

"Ready?" he said to Jenna.

She nodded, the light of excitement in her eyes almost too much to believe.

Balancing popcorn and sodas along with Sophie and her gear, they wandered down the semilit aisle to a row of seats.

Jostling elbows and baby carrier, they settled in and the movie started. The loud music startled Sophie who began to whimper. Jenna removed her from the carrier and rocked her back and forth until she settled. The baby scent mingled with popcorn and the distinctive smell of a movie theater. Dax kicked back and relaxed with his snacks. Might as well enjoy himself.

The animated Christmas film had Gavin giggling

from the get-go. Thirty minutes in, though, he had to go to the bathroom. When they returned, Sophie was fussing again and Jenna grappled in the dark for a bottle from the diaper bag.

Without giving the action much thought, Dax took the baby while Jenna found the bottle. When she reached for Sophie, he shook his head, taking the bottle from her.

"I got her," he whispered.

Jenna looked more grateful than he'd expected. His conscience tweaked. He'd wanted her to relax and have a good time, but here she was wrestling the fussy baby.

He slipped the bottle into Sophie's mouth. She latched on like a baby 'possum.

Maybe he should have gotten a babysitter, but he'd never hired a sitter and didn't know where to start. Besides, the children made for a good buffer, so the night out didn't feel like a date. It was more like a family outing.

The notion stuck in the center of his brain and wouldn't move until he examined it. Family. This was what he'd always wanted, the thing that was missing in his life, and tonight he felt as if he and Jenna and Gavin and Sophie belonged together.

He squirmed in the chair and tried to concentrate on the pink princess staring up at him as if he was some kind of hero.

When at last Sophie slept again, he handed her over to Jenna who in turn placed her in the carrier.

"Thank you," she whispered, leaning toward his ear. Her arm bumped his from shoulder to elbow. In the flickering light of animation, he saw her smile.

His stomach went airborne.

He reached for her hand and she gave it willingly.

He swallowed hard, pretended to watch the dancing elves and ignored the warning bells going off in his head.

It was only a movie, only a hand. Just that sentimental Christmasy feeling. No big deal.

Tomorrow things would return to normal.

The night air was crisp and quiet when the moviegoers returned to the Southpaw. A banana moon tilted overhead as though paying homage to the stunning spray of stars in the indigo sky.

Careful to cover her daughter against the chilled air, Jenna made her way to the door. Dax strode alongside with a sleeping Gavin slung over one shoulder.

She had never dreamed a night at a fast-food restaurant and a run-down movie theater could be such pleasure. She cast a sidelong glance at her companion. Dax was the main cause of her enjoyment. At the restaurant, he'd teased her about the amount of ketchup she'd dumped on her French fries and told her funny stories about his first few months of taking care of a newborn. Between the lines, she'd read the desperation and sorrow he must have felt. Knowing his struggle matched her own had made his humor all the more endearing.

Then they'd laughed at the funny Christmas movie, and he'd held her hand, such a simple thing, but her entire body had hummed in pleasure. She wondered what it would be like to go on a real date with him, a dangerous thought perhaps, given who she was and the things she'd kept from him. But just this once she wanted someone—a male someone—to see her as something besides a trust fund.

Everything with Derek had been a secret until after their elopement. Secret meetings and stolen kisses in the university library had meant nothing to him but money.

Dax shifted Gavin's lax body, holding on to the child with one strong arm while he maneuvered the house key and opened the door.

"Youth and beauty before age and treachery," he teased, voice quiet.

He stood to the side, holding the door with his back while she passed through with the baby. She recalled that first day when Rowdy had crowded her in the doorway and she'd been repelled. Not so with Dax. He could stand as close as he wanted.

Of course, he didn't. He padded down the hall with the sleeping Gavin while she headed in the opposite direction to change and settle Sophie for the night, chastising herself for trying to make something significant from the evening. Dax was being kind, asking her to join in an outing with his son. That's all there was to it.

Sophie was sound asleep, rousing only slightly as Jenna changed and swaddled her for the night. After snapping on the elephant night-light, Jenna returned to the living room, hoping for an opportunity to let Dax know how much she'd enjoyed the night out.

She wasn't disappointed. Dax came down the hall toward her, rubbing the back of his neck. When he saw her standing there, he offered a crooked grin. "That boy could sleep through a tornado."

She answered with a smile. "He had fun tonight."

"Yeah. We haven't done that much." He plopped down on the couch. "I like this new arrangement."

The comment brought back the memory of that day when she'd thought he might kiss her.

"Why?"

"Because it looks nice," he said.

"No, I mean why haven't you and Gavin gone out much?"

"Oh. Good question. I don't know."

She smiled and settled on the end of the sofa, wanting to sit near again but unsure if he wanted that. "Would you like something to eat or drink?"

He looked horrified. "Are you kidding?"

"Yes. Nothing like a Friendly Meal and popcorn to fill me up."

"Sorry about that. Next time—"

He stopped but Jenna caught on the phrase. Was he think-ing about a next time?

"I'm serious. I loved the Friendly Meal."

He looked dubious, but said, "For a skinny girl you can put away the fries."

"I just had a baby. I am not skinny."

His gaze roved lazily over her, not in an insolent way as Rowdy's had done, but with an appreciation that made her knees wobble.

"I had a good time," he said softly, capturing her eyes with his.

"Thank you for asking me. The evening was wonderful."

"Are you happy here, Jenna?"

What a strange question. "Happier than I've ever been in my life."

The admission came as naturally as breathing. She was happy here, living a dream, bringing her daughter up the way she'd wanted to be. Safe and free and normal.

Dax's nostrils flared.

Everything in her longed to travel the short distance down the couch to him. The memory of his almost kiss stayed with her and she saw it now reflected in his eyes.

"Jenna?" The whisker-rough voice sent tingles down her spine.

"Yes?" she whispered.

A beat of silence quivered in the air before Dax dragged a hand over his face and looked away. "I guess we should call it a night."

Jenna wilted with disappointed. When he said

nothing else, only stared at the cold fireplace, Jenna rose. "Then I shall bid you good-night."

Stiffly, she left the room, not daring to look back, lest he see the longing in her face and pity her. Or worse yet, dismiss her. She'd misinterpreted his kindness, for that's all this lovely night had been.

CHAPTER TWELVE

AT HIGH NOON the next Thursday, the tables at Lydia's Lunchbox were jammed with diners. Jenna stood in the crowded entry, soaking up the sights and sounds—the clink of plates and forks, the soft laughter and conversation, the drawling accents she found so entertaining. In the back corner, she spotted a hand waving at her.

"Over here, Jenna." Crystal Wolf had become the kind of friend she'd always wanted.

"This place is really crowded today," she said as she settled into a chair.

"Lydia's is the best place in town for a light lunch. Besides, Pam's Diner is closed until after the first of the year." Crystal peeled the blanket off Sophie. "I swear, hon, she gets prettier every time I see her."

Pride swelled inside Jenna. Her little girl *was* beautiful and she looked adorable today in her hot pink mouse cap with matching jumper and shoes. "Her pointed head went away just as you predicted."

Crystal laughed. "Of course. I didn't go to nursing school for nothing. You look great, too. Wow." The other woman looked her over. "What is going on with you? You look…radiant. If having a baby makes a woman look that good, I need to have five or six."

Crystal and her husband had been married for several years but hadn't started a family.

Jenna shook out a napkin and placed it on her lap. "You saw me at my very worst in the hospital. Anything has to be an improvement on that."

"Sure, but you look different today."

"Same old me," she said, although she wondered if that was exactly the truth. Since the night out with Dax, she'd felt buoyant, excited as though something new and wonderful was just around the corner. "Must be the Christmas spirit. I'm having such fun decorating the house."

The waitress arrived and took their orders. Jenna could care less what she ate. She was delighted with the new freedom to make her own friends and go where she wanted.

Crystal patted Sophie before taking up her own napkin. "Any more domestic disasters?"

Jenna laughed. She'd told her friend about the pink socks and flooded kitchen. "Let's just say learning to be a good housekeeper is an even sharper learning curve than caring for a newborn. If Dax weren't so sweet, he would have fired me the second day."

The waitress appeared with their order of chicken salad sandwiches and veggie slices. Crystal's hand paused over the julienne carrots. "Sweet? Did you just refer to Dax as sweet?"

"Well, maybe *sweet* isn't the right word." Jenna was positive her cheeks flamed. She reached for her glass of water. "He's been very supportive and kind."

"Mmm, I see." The woman's gaze was speculative. "Looks good, too, doesn't he?"

"I'd be lying if I said no. But Dax is more than good-looking, Crystal. He's such a man, so protective and helpful." She refrained from adding that she felt safe with Dax in a way she'd seldom experienced in her childhood or her marriage. Crystal didn't know about her past. "Do you know he wouldn't allow me to move the furniture? He was afraid I'd hurt myself."

"This is getting more interesting by the minute."

Jenna reached for another cucumber slice. "You once told me that Dax Coleman was one of the good guys. You were right. Going into labor in this town was the best thing that ever happened to me. I love my job. The ranch is beautiful. Dax's little boy is a treasure. I'm even volunteering at the school every Tuesday and I'm planning a Christmas party. You're invited, of course."

"Dax is having a Christmas party?"

"Let's just say he has tentatively agreed to this whing-ding, as he calls it." She scrunched her shoulders in excitement. "It will be so much fun, and Dax could use a bit of Christmas cheer."

"There's no doubting that." Crystal stirred her cup of herbal tea and laid the spoon carefully aside. "I'm very impressed by the way you've assimilated, Jenna. When I first met you, I wasn't sure how you'd cope."

Necessity was a fast teacher. "I love it here," she said, drawing in a deep, contented breath. "I'm happier than I've ever been in my life."

Jenna hadn't meant to add the last line but her friend already knew she'd suffered heartache. She just didn't know the real reasons.

"You look happy. You sound happy." Crystal studied her over a bite of chicken salad. "That's it. That's the difference I see in you today. You're in love with Dax."

Jenna nearly choked on a drink of water. She clunked the glass onto the tabletop and stared at Crystal. Blood rushed through her head like a hard rain.

"In love?" she croaked.

Crystal tilted her head. White earrings flashed against her dark skin. "Aren't you?"

"I—" Jenna blinked. Once. Twice. She lifted a hand to her mouth. "Oh dear."

"Honey!" A warm hand closed over Jenna's arm and gave it a shake. "That's fantastic. I'm so happy for you."

"No. I don't know." She floundered. "Dax doesn't…"

"Dax doesn't what? Know you've fallen for him? Or return the feelings?"

"Both." She gripped her friend's fingers. "Promise you won't say a word."

"My lips are sealed. But let me tell you, hon, Dax Coleman is carrying a load of hurt. He may take some time and effort, but I know one thing, when that man falls, he falls hard."

Yes, Dax was the kind of man who would keep a commitment. Hadn't she seen that in the way he'd wanted to be certain she and Sophie were safe and well after the unexpected birth? Maybe that's why he'd never recovered from the divorce. "Do you know what happened with his wife?"

Crystal's long hair fell forward as she nodded. "Everyone in Saddleback knows. She left him for another man."

"After Gavin was born."

"Yes, and to make things worse, the man she ran off with was Sam Coleman, Dax's younger brother."

Jenna's stomach dropped to her shoes. "Oh no. Poor Dax."

"Some thought Reba suffered from postpartum depression, but I never believed that. She was always wild and needed con-stant male attention. Sam wasn't her first lover. She'd been cheating on Dax for a long time. I guess everyone knew but him."

No wonder Dax had become so reclusive. He'd been as humiliated by Reba as Jenna had been by

Derek. More so. Both his spouse and his brother had betrayed him.

Jenna's conscience tugged. Wasn't it betrayal of a different kind not to tell him about her trust fund?

She fought off the worry, convinced she and Sophie were safe as long as no one knew who they were. Not even Dax.

She and Crystal went on talking, jumping from subject to subject. Crystal was a wealth of information about babies and housekeeping, Dax and the people of Saddleback, and the best places for Christmas shopping. Gaining this woman as a friend had been nothing short of a pre-Christmas miracle.

Finally, Jenna glanced at her watch. Gavin would be home soon, so the women reluctantly parted ways with the promise to meet again the following week.

All the way back to the Southpaw, Jenna mulled over the personal revelations that had come out over a chicken salad sandwich. She was falling in love with her employer, her res-cuer, a man with deep emotional wounds. Gavin, though he'd never known Reba, was wounded, too. He sensed his father's pain and overprotection. The insecurity had given rise to an inner fear and a timid nature. Jenna didn't know how she understood this, but she did.

Maybe love gave a woman insight.

Casting a glance at Sophie in the rearview mirror,

she smiled at the thought. What she'd had with Derek could never compare to this. She was almost ashamed to admit that Derek had been an escape route, a means to escape the prison of her life under Elaine Carrington's paranoid eye. What she felt for Dax and Gavin went deeper—all the way to the center of her heart.

The troubling conscience pressed in again. If she loved Dax, didn't he deserve to know the truth about her situation?

She bit down on her bottom lip, gnawing the skin in the same way the question gnawed away at her heart. Maybe she should tell him.

But what if she was being a fool again? What if her emotions clouded her reason? She'd thought she was in love before and look what had happened.

But this was different. Dax was different. She was different.

But Dax was not in love with her. He didn't even find her attractive enough to kiss, a fact that had been painfully clear the night of the Christmas movie. He was good to her and Sophie, but kindness did not translate into love. Her nanny was kind. Her bodyguards were kind.

She was an employee just as they had been.

By the time she had taken Sophie into the house and had returned for the shopping bags, she was convinced that keeping quiet was the best thing to do. Any decision she made affected her daughter, and Sophie's life would not be a repeat of hers. Until she could win love on her own terms, without the lure of the Carrington fortune, Jenna would keep her secret.

Bending, she reached into the backseat for the bags. The cold wind swept through the car, beneath her jacket and made her shiver. Paper and plastic crinkled as she hurried, eager to get inside the warm house. A masculine arm snaked from behind her and latched onto a bag. Her heart reacted happily. Dax must have seen her struggling in the wind and come to assist.

She spun around, smile ready. "Dax," she started but then the pleasure drained from her.

Rowdy stood, trapping her between the car door and the backseat, a grocery bag in hand.

"Sorry, darlin', if you were expecting the boss. It's just faithful Rowdy coming to your rescue. You don't mind some help with these bags, do you?"

Jenna swallowed back her disappointment and misgivings. "Thank you. I can manage."

She bent for another bag before realizing that Rowdy was probably staring at her backside.

"Old Dax would have my hide if I let a lady handle this alone. It's cold out here." He stood too close, that insufferable grin taunting her.

Jenna sighed and tightened her jaw. She was not going to let this guy get under her skin. "As you wish, then. I'll offer my thanks if you will please be so kind as to get out of my way. My daughter is already in the house and I don't like to leave her alone."

"Yes, ma'am," he said, though his tone mocked her as he backed off. "Lead the way. I'll bring the rest."

Aware of his eyes on her, Jenna hurried inside. Perhaps she was overreacting. Perhaps the cowboy was genuine in his offer of help. But he gave her the creeps.

Rowdy followed her into the house and though she would have preferred he leave immediately, she didn't want to be rude. She began putting the groceries in the cabinets.

"You wouldn't happen to have a cold drink for a hot man, would you?"

Jenna ignored the double entendre. There was no way he had worked up a sweat in this weather.

She took a can of orange soda from the refrigerator, handed it to him and went back to work. Rowdy leaned an elbow against the granite countertop and watched her.

"I've been meaning to ask you something, Jenna."

She slid a carton of eggs onto the refrigerator rack and shut the door. Cool air wafted out. "What is it?"

"A friend of mine is having a party Saturday night. I thought you might want to get out of here, have some fun."

"Thank you for the kind offer but I have a baby."

"So we hire a sitter. I know lots of girls."

She imagined he did. "I really can't."

"Ah, come on. We'll have fun."

"I—I already have plans." It was a lie worth telling.

"Cancel them."

The man wouldn't take no for an answer.

"I'd prefer not to." She started around him.

He grabbed her elbow. His face hardened. "So what's the deal? You and Dax have something going? Is that why you won't go out with me?"

She stiffened. "I beg your pardon?"

He laughed, though the sound didn't delight. "You sure are cute when you talk prissy. Come on, Jenna, throw me a bone. I'll show you a good time."

She tugged her arm, but his fingers bit into the flesh. "Please let me go."

"On one condition."

She sighed. "I really can't go out with you. Please. I have duties here."

"What kind of duties, Jenna?" He yanked at her, pulling her so close she could smell his breath. He'd been drinking. "What exactly does Dax pay you for?"

She went as cold as ice inside. "I do not appreciate the insinuation. Please unhand me."

"Sure thing, darlin'." He pulled her closer. "Just one little kiss and I'll be on my way."

"I don't think so."

"Well, think again, honey." And his face descended.

* * *

Dax wiped his boots on the mat, eager to get inside and tell Jenna the news. That mare she liked was going to foal tonight. But first he took extra care not to track unmentionable stuff onto the clean carpet and tile. She never complained, but she'd given him the evil eye a couple of times. He did not want to make his housekeeper unhappy.

Shaking his head, he chuckled to himself. Fancy-talking Jenna with her real fur house shoes and gourmet meals was quickly becoming more than a housekeeper. She was becoming a part of his life and of Gavin's. The Christmas decor that looked like something out of a magazine wasn't the only thing full of cheer in this once-somber ranch house.

As he crossed the foyer and living room, he heard her voice. She was probably on the phone inviting someone else to the Christmas whing-ding. His smile widened. She even had him looking forward to the invasion of his privacy.

Her tone rose higher. Another voice answered. A male voice. Stomach dropping like a brick, Dax stopped to listen. What was a man doing in the kitchen with Jenna?

A flash of memory made him shudder. Reba, half-naked, in the arms of his brother.

He bit down on his back teeth and shook away the image. Jenna was not his cheating, lying wife.

Yet the dread weighing him down wouldn't go

away. He started forward then stopped again to listen.

The pair in the kitchen were not murmuring love words. Jenna's voice sounded strained, frightened. Tension hummed in the air.

Adrenaline kicked in. Something was wrong.

He rounded the wall into the kitchen. His first vision was of Rowdy and Jenna, bodies pressed close. Their mouths were mere inches apart.

The memory of Reba in Sam's arms came again. Pain slammed through Dax, stealing his breath.

Stuck between Rowdy and the counter, Jenna twisted her face to one side. "Stop it, Rowdy. Stop it."

One hand came up to press at Rowdy's chest.

Dax shook his head, battling down the past to understand the present.

Jenna was not inviting Rowdy's attentions. On the contrary. She was resisting.

Relief replaced jealousy. Just as quickly a cold fury washed over him.

Fist clenched, he stormed into the kitchen. "You heard the lady, Davis. Back off."

Rowdy's grip loosened. Jenna jerked to one side, face flaming. She rubbed at her arm. Dax's fury turned white-hot. If she was hurt…

"Hey, boss." Rowdy turned slowly and raised both hands like a criminal. "Everything's cool here. No harm done."

"Doesn't look that way to me." Dax opened his

fist, clenched it again. He was half an inch from punching out his best cowboy. He flicked a glance at Jenna. "You okay?"

Still rubbing her arm, face the color of paste, she nodded. The anxiety radiating off her made him even angrier. Rowdy Davis might be a good hand, but he had no business coming into the house to harass Jenna.

Rowdy shifted backward one step, his eyes never leaving Dax's face. "I'll just be heading back to the barn then."

Dax wagged his head. "I don't think so. You're done here. For good."

Rowdy's mouth dropped. "You're not letting me go because of her, are you?"

"Yeah, I am. Get out, Rowdy, before I lose my temper."

The cowboy's mouth curled in a sneer. "Don't be stupid, Coleman. I'm the best manager around."

Dax was afraid his jaw was going to snap. "We don't need your kind here."

"What about her kind? What's the deal, boss? Why are you so jumpy about an unwed house-keeper with a brat in tow?"

Jenna's gasp drew Dax's gaze. If possible, she'd grown whiter. She pressed a shocked hand to her lips.

"She's a widow."

Rowdy laughed, an ugly sound. "Yeah, and I'm Santa Claus. Ho-ho-*ho*." The last syllable was aimed maliciously at Jenna.

Dax's restraint snapped. He drew back a fist. Before he could throw the punch, a soft hand caught his.

"Please, Dax. No."

Dax turned, incredulous. "You're defending him?"

"No. I just want him to leave me alone." Her voice quivered. "Gavin will be here soon. I don't want him to witness fisticuffs."

Jenna's concern was for Gavin, not for herself. The anger toward Rowdy increased until Dax trembled with the need for a physical release.

"Get your gear and get off my property, Davis, before I satisfy a powerful hankering to break your nose."

Rowdy postured for a few seconds, weighing his options. Apparently, he was smart enough to know when he'd lost. With a curse that Dax hadn't allowed past his own lips in years, the fired cowboy slammed out of the house.

He'd no more than cleared the room when Dax turned to Jenna. "How are you really? And don't say okay."

As she opened her mouth to reply, her lips trembled. That was his undoing. He folded her into his arms. She nestled against him, her soft breath puffing warm against his neck. Her body quivered.

So did his.

He stroked her back and murmured as he'd done the day she'd given birth. The reminder of that shared intimacy swirled inside him, provocative in a way that shook him to his boot heels. He recalled her strength and grit, her frantic concern for her infant. He recalled the way she'd looked at him as though he was the greatest hero ever.

With an inner groan, Dax squeezed his eyes shut.

A hero. He wanted to be a hero. Her hero.

He was a fool. A woman his own age had dumped him. What made him think Jenna, a woman years younger and with far more inner beauty and refinement, would think of him as anything but a worn-out old cowboy?

Yet, he went on holding her against his chest, feeling the thud of her heart so close to his that the rhythms seemed to be one.

A tangle of thoughts coursed through his head.

He wasn't falling for her. No way. It was inappropriate. She was his employee, a young mother, a *very* young mother. She thought of him as a protector, a friend, maybe even an uncle.

Yeah, that was it. An uncle.

"Dax?" Jenna murmured.

He smoothed a hand down the back of her head, over the soft hair, and filled his nostrils with her orange blossom fragrance.

He cleared his throat, thick with some troubling emotion. "Yeah?"

Jenna lifted her head from his chest and tilted her face up to look at him. "Thank you."

Her lips curved, drawing his attention.

He couldn't keep his eyes from a glance at her mouth. He'd thought about it, maybe even dreamed about it.

"Ah, Jenna."

She placed a hand against his cheek, the curved smile deepening. "My hero," she whispered. "Again."

With warning bells clanging like fire engines, Dax groaned, aware he should walk away now while he still could. He started to loosen his hold but Jenna held tight.

"Kiss me this time, Dax. Please." She tiptoed up, waiting.

The request was his undoing.

Just once, he told himself. Just this one time.

With his heart pounding in both fear and hope, Dax cupped her face and pressed his lips to hers.

CHAPTER THIRTEEN

JENNA TUCKED A BLANKET around the sleeping Sophie, kissed her velvet cheek and snapped off the overhead light, though she remained in the semi-darkness gazing at her daughter while she thought about the eventful day.

The scene with Rowdy had both embarrassed and unnerved her, but Dax's reaction had shaken her to the core. She still couldn't believe he'd fired his ranch manager because of her. More than that, she couldn't believe he'd finally kissed her. Kissed her in a way she'd never been kissed. Tender and ravenous and with such care, as if she were fragile crystal in danger of shattering.

She'd wanted him never to stop, but they'd both heard the front door open and the sound of Gavin's book bag thump onto the coffee table. With a wry twist of that delicious mouth, Dax had pressed his forehead to hers, given her a look that would melt steel, then gone to greet his son.

Jenna touched a finger to her lips, feeling him

there even now and foolishly wishing to repeat the pleasure. Dax Coleman, with only the touch of his mouth, had given hope to an impossible dream.

At dinner he'd been unusually quiet and thoughtful and Jenna wondered what he was thinking. Dare she dream that he was as stunned as she? For stunned she was. Stunned by the emotions roaring through her. Stunned to feel so complete in his arms. Stunned to be falling in love.

Could Dax possibly feel the same? Or was he instead filled with regret about a rash behavior?

All through the meal of beef medallions and pasta, he'd said little and afterward had left the house, using the excuse of a mare about to give birth. She'd wanted to go out to the barn with him to watch the miracle, but he hadn't asked and she didn't quite have the courage to impose.

Perhaps they both needed time to process what had happened. Her optimistic side believed he felt something special for her. He was certainly a better, braver, stronger man than Derek, but it was Derek's betrayal that kept her afraid.

Sensitive Gavin must have felt the tension between the adults because he'd been clingy and whiny all evening. She'd made a special effort to focus on him, finally bringing out the ingredients for baked dough ornaments. Working the dough with his hands and cutting the shapes seemed to ease his stress and by storytime Gavin seemed happier.

Still, when she'd put him to bed, he'd hugged her a long, heart-tugging time. After she flipped off the light and stepped into the hall, he'd called out, "Jenna."

Expecting a request for a drink, she'd said, "Yes, Gavin."

"I love you."

A perfect peace settled in her soul.

She loved him, too. She'd loved him since the first time she'd found him standing guard over Sophie's crib. With every day that passed, she loved him more.

With an ache for the little boy's hungry heart, she'd gone back into the darkened room for another hug. "I love you, too, Gavin." She'd kissed his forehead. "You're a very special boy."

Now, restless and too keyed-up to sleep, she padded down the hall toward the living room. The house still smelled warm and delicious from the cinnamon in the dough ornaments. Tomorrow they would be cool enough to paint and string with red ribbon for hanging on the tree.

The prelit, flocked spruce Dax had brought from a storage room filled a corner of the dark living room. She plugged in the lights, basking in the beauty she and the Coleman males had created. A lighted wreath sprigged with holly, along with swags of plush, snow-doused garland hung over the fireplace. More garland, flocked and sprinkled with tiny white lights, draped around fat red candles and down the sides of the mantel. Soon the stockings she'd been personalizing would be ready to hang.

At her parents' estate, she'd never been allowed to participate in Christmas preparations other than shopping. A designer had always been retained for the occasion. But Jenna had watched and longed for the day she could create a Christmas of the heart with her own special touches.

Touching a shiny red ball with one fingertip, she smiled softly. That day had finally come in a most unexpected manner and in an even more unexpected place.

She heard Gavin stir and tiptoed down the long hall to his room. He tossed restlessly and murmured, then settled again. She waited a moment longer before returning to the living room, where she went to the window and gazed out. A heavy frost lay over the brown grass and glistened beneath the moon. A Texas night could be so still, and yet she knew life teemed all around her.

The quiet snick of the door latch turned her around. Dax, shoulders hunched against the cold, came inside, filling up the room and her heart. Her stomach fluttered, foolishly happy. One kiss shouldn't mean so much, but to her, it did.

"Hey," he said softly.

"Hey." She'd never said *hey* to anyone in her life, but it sounded right in this place and time. Voice as quiet as his, she went on, "How's the mare?"

"Getting close. I thought you might like to be there."

The foolish happiness expanded. "I was hoping you'd ask."

He tilted his head, serious green eyes reflecting the spare light from the Christmas tree. "Were you?"

She nodded, staying still, not wanting to move away from the way he was looking at her. "Yes."

He breathed in through his nose and exhaled. "Smells good in here."

"Gavin and I made ornament cookies. With cinnamon."

"Bet he liked that."

"I think so."

"You've been good for him."

Jenna's mind stumbled on the past tense. Was he going to let her go? Or had the turn of phrase been unintentional?

The balloon of happiness deflated but filled again when Dax motioned toward her end of the house. "Get your coat. It's cold out."

"Don't you want something hot to drink first?"

"Later. The barn is warm enough, and as you know, babies don't wait." His face lightened at the reminder of Sophie's untimely birth.

She laughed softly. "No, they don't."

Feeling both unsettled and excited, Jenna hurried to her closet for coat and gloves, glanced in on Sophie, then slid the baby monitor into her pocket before returning to Dax.

He was in the kitchen, eyeing the pans of cookie ornaments with an unreadable expression. When he felt her approach, he said, "Ready?"

She nodded and they headed outside and across the glistening yard. The air was every bit as crisp and cold as the frost implied.

Dax took her elbow and guided them through the darkness toward a long, lighted horse barn. Neither spoke, and the only sounds were their soft footsteps and the pounding of her pulse against her eardrums. His touch, his nearness set her entire body a-hum.

She shivered once but otherwise ignored the cold. She felt invigorated, alive, her blood pumping through her veins with new strength and clarity. She was in love with Dax Coleman. In love.

She glanced his way. His face was in shadow but the shape was strong and masculine. She felt comforted and safe in this foreign world of rural Texas with Dax at her side.

Did he know what he had done to her? Did he have any idea how much he'd helped her grow and mature? She'd run away from Pennsylvania a scared girl. Today she was a woman.

He felt something for her, she was certain. But what? Gratitude? Responsibility? Did she dare to believe a man as handsome and honorable as Dax could really find her attractive?

"She's in the third stall," Dax said as he released her elbow to slide back the enormous metal door.

Jenna blinked against the bright, overhead light.

The barn, surprisingly warm, smelled clean and grassy with the overtone of warm animals. She liked this barn just as she liked the big, soft-eyed horses who resided here. When time permitted, she brought Gavin inside to pet the horses, hoping that exposure would lessen his fears.

She followed Dax inside stall number three, standing just inside while he approached the mother-to-be. Blanca, as white as her name implied, lay on clean straw with her back legs folded beneath her. Her massive chest rose and fell with the effort of labor. Jenna empathized.

"How ya doin', Blanca girl?" Dax asked as he knelt beside the mare and ran a hand over her glossy hip. He tossed a glance toward Jenna. "Ease on over here. She won't mind."

Jenna did as he instructed, crouching next to him.

"Look right there," he murmured.

Jenna's stomach leaped. She grasped the thick quilting of Dax's sleeve. "Is that the baby?"

"Yep. In good position, too, nose and knees first. We should have touchdown any minute now." There was excitement in his voice that matched the rising tide of energy inside her.

"I've never seen an animal born."

His mouth curved. "First time for everything. I'd never seen a baby born before Sophie."

Their gazes collided and held, the memory of that first day a bond between them.

"I'd never had one before, either."

"We did a great job, though, didn't we? Pretty special watching a life come into the world."

The mare rose slightly on her back legs and heaved. Both humans turned their attention to her as the foal's nose and knees inched forward.

"Amazing. So amazing," she muttered. "Do we need to do anything?"

"Not yet. Let nature take its course." He hitched his chin toward a box residing along the edge of the stall. "Unless she goes too long or has trouble, all we have to do is take care of the foal when he arrives. The kit is ready and waiting if we need it."

Jenna had no idea what was in the kit but was not surprised that Dax was ready for any eventuality. Any man who could help birth a baby by the side of the road could handle anything.

The mare rose slightly and strained.

Jenna gasped. "There's his head. Oh, Dax. Look, there he comes."

Dax, who'd been watching the birth, turned to watch Jenna. Instead of feeling self-conscious, Jenna laughed, happy, excited and filled with wonder as the tiny foal slipped onto the clean straw.

"Oh, oh, oh." Tears filled her eyes. In a voice of wonder, she whispered, "Is he okay?"

It occurred to her then that Dax may have felt this way the day Sophie was born. Anxious and awed and overwhelmed by the beauty of new life.

Dax's voice was soft, too. "Watch his mama work. She knows what to do."

Sure enough, the mare pushed to a stand and turned to her newborn, instinctively stimulating and warming him with her tongue. As she did so, Dax examined the foal, applied antiseptic to the umbilical cord and stepped away, motioning Jenna to join him.

Together they watched the mother care for her baby. When the foal struggled to stand, Jenna's whole body tensed with the effort. "Come on, baby. You can do it."

The spotted foal wobbled up. Jenna turned to Dax, realizing for the first time that she held his hand in a death grip. He smiled into her eyes. She smiled back. He took a step closer. She stood her ground. When his calloused rancher's hand slid beneath her hair and caressed her neck, she shivered. He looked pleased by her reaction. Slowly, he titled her face up and brought his down. Jenna's fingers roamed up the front of his open jacket, over the muscular chest and shoulders to twine in the hair at his nape. She breathed in and let her eyes fall closed as Dax's warm, supple mouth caressed hers.

Sensation washed through her. Desire and hope and love and the belief that this was right and good. He kissed her until her heart hammered in her throat and her knees quivered. When at last the glorious torture ended, he went on holding her in his arms. His breath came in soft rasps against her hair. He took one of her hands and pressed it to his heart. The powerful beat hammered against her palm.

Holding his beautiful green eyes with her gaze, she returned the favor, pressing his big hand to her chest. His nostrils flared and he smiled softly.

Without words, they communicated the flood of emotions rushing in and around them. The feelings were too new and raw to express aloud. At least for Jenna. She wanted to believe she wasn't being a fool and that Dax felt the same.

Behind her, the mare and foal rustled and moved about as the newborn searched for his first meal.

Jenna longed to stay in Dax's warm embrace but a sound from the baby monitor in her pocket ended the moment.

"I should go," she murmured, hearing the tremor in the words.

As he stepped away, Dax dragged a hand over his face and nodded. "Yes. You should. Go."

Jenna tilted her head, trying to gauge his meaning. Gone was the loving look of moments before. An anxious moth fluttered in her chest. What was he not saying?

Maybe he kissed women in the barn all the time. Maybe this meant nothing to him. Maybe she was still the gullible girl that had fallen for Derek.

"Dax?"

He heaved a great sigh. "I apologize. That shouldn't have happened."

He'd kissed her twice in the space of a few hours and it shouldn't have happened? She couldn't believe this.

What was going on inside that complicated head of his?

She stared, waiting with a fragile hope that he would explain.

He clenched his fist and averted his eyes.

Jutting her chin, she said, "No need to apologize. I'm a grown woman and, in case you didn't notice, I was not resisting."

Then with head held high, she rushed outside, the chill in her heart far colder than the December night.

Dax called himself ten kinds of fool and uttered every curse word stored in his memory banks. It was a good thing horses didn't speak English or the mare would have chased him out of the stall.

What had he been thinking to kiss Jenna, not once but twice? The first time he'd convinced himself was to comfort her after the ugly scene with Rowdy. He had no excuse for this second time. He should never have asked her into the barn. He should have left well enough alone. She was his housekeeper, not a girlfriend. His indecently *young* housekeeper.

At least Rowdy was close to her age. Dax had

no excuse at all. No excuse except for the fact that he was falling for her. One minute they'd been admiring the new foal, then he'd gazed into those warm brown eyes so filled with the same wonder he always felt at a birthing, and he'd seen a woman after his own heart. A woman who'd returned his kiss with a hungry innocence that turned his insides to jelly. His brain had shorted out. That's all there was to it. He had better self-discipline than to do such a thing.

Anyway, he used to.

No fool like an old fool, Coleman.

He kicked the side of the stall. Pain shot up his leg and he accepted it with a perverse pleasure. The mare turned her head to give him a censorious stare.

"Sorry, old girl." Sorrier than he could ever say.

He cleaned up the stall and after one last examination of mother and baby, he returned to the house.

The tree lights were the only light shining inside the house, and he stood in the entry for several seconds, thinking and admiring the beautiful display. He had erected the tree each year for Gavin's sake but the efforts had been halfhearted. A few ornaments. A few gifts. Gavin's stocking. Jenna had transformed the house into a Christmas wonderland and claimed she wasn't finished yet.

Shucking his boots, he headed for bed, stopping to peek in at Gavin. The night-light—a necessity for his anxious son—illuminated the room enough that he could see the twin bed. The covers were tossed and rumpled but Gavin wasn't there.

His heart leaped. "Gavin?"

He entered the room, flipping on the overhead light as he moved toward the pile of camouflage-patterned covers. Sure enough Gavin was gone.

Sometimes his son had nightmares and climbed into bed with old dad. Dax stepped to his own room and flipped on the light. Gavin wasn't there, either.

There was only one other place he could be.

With a quick stride, Dax crossed the long ranch house to Jenna's room. He dreaded opening the door and seeing her in the bed, but he needed to know that his son was all right. Just the thought of Jenna in a nightgown with nothing underneath drove his imagination wild. He had enough problems with seeing her in the full-length robe, her pretty toes peeking from beneath.

Like an embattled prizefighter, he shook off the fantasy. Jenna was off-limits. If he was any kind of man, she had to be.

As quietly as possible, he turned the knob and entered the nursery first. Sophie lay on her back, little arms flung up and out. His heart squeezed. Once upon a time he'd dreamed of having a baby girl to call him Daddy. And Sophie had no father to love and protect her.

He watched a moment longer, confident that the pink princess was breathing, and then moved to the connecting doorway. At the sight before him, he squeezed his eyelids tight and let the wave of sweetness take him, if only for a moment.

Forever, he would cherish the mental image of his little boy snuggled safely in Jenna's bed. Her body was spooned around his and her arms held him close, one hand on his chest and the other against his cheek as though reassuring him that she was there and all was well.

The noise on the monitor that had sent her scurrying away from the barn hadn't been her child, as he'd thought. It had been his. And yet Jenna had responded to Gavin's call as though she was his mother.

Dax dragged a weary hand over his face and heard the scratchy beard. Jenna disarmed him. Took away his resistance. Touched him to the very soul.

Ah, God, he loved her. He *loved* her.

He loved her enough to do what was right.

The problem was, he hadn't figured out exactly what that was.

CHAPTER FOURTEEN

"Blast this rain. Blast this wasted day." Dax stomped into the mudroom and bent to remove his boots. Water sluiced from his hat and rain slicker onto the tile. He shucked the hat and jacket, too, and took a towel from the overhead cabinet, breathing in the fragrance of fabric softener. That was another of Jenna's touches.

Frustrated, he ground his back teeth. He'd risen before sunrise, having slept little, and hurried out to check the mare and foal. Mostly, he'd hurried out to avoid Jenna and the whirlpool of confused emotions she incited. Now a cold December rain had forced him back inside.

Maybe he should have stayed in the barn all day.

But if he was honest, he missed having breakfast with her, missed seeing Gavin off to school, missed the few minutes of playtime with Sophie.

Jenna rounded the corner, carrying a laundry basket. Upon spotting him, she stopped dead still. Her eyes widened. One aristocratic eyebrow twitched.

It was a moment he'd both dreaded and longed for.

"Blasted rain," he grumbled, more to avoid the real issues than for conversation.

"You're soaked." She dropped the basket and dug more towels from the cupboard, handing him one and patting his drips with the other. "You're going to be sick."

Her ministrations felt too good, too…wifely.

He took the towel from her. "I got it."

She stood her ground, watching him. "You need to get warm and dry. I have fresh coffee."

"In a minute. I have to change."

"Clean clothes in the dryer," she said and left the room.

Dax stared after her for a few seconds, contemplating the psychology of women. If he lived to a hundred, he would never understand. She didn't seem angry. She didn't seem upset. She didn't seem anything. After his weird behavior last night, she should have tossed him back out in the freezing rain.

He made a self-mocking noise, glanced down at the pool of water forming around his bare feet and quickly undressed, letting his clothes drop to the floor.

He was standing buck naked in the mudroom while his housekeeper, the woman who was driving him crazy, was in the next room with only a wall between them.

He was chilled to the bone, but his traitorous male body reacted inappropriately anyway. Being a man was an annoyance at times. Jaw clenched, he scavenged in the dryer and sighed with appreciation as he dressed in warm, fragrant clothing.

Once Jenna had gotten the hang of doing laundry, the result was far more pleasant than his pitiful attempts. To his way of thinking, chuck all the clothes in at once and let 'em spin. Jenna's way was magic—and smelled good, too.

Out of long habit, he gathered up the mess in the floor, but the washer was already running, so he dropped them in an empty basket and went in search of that hot coffee.

Jenna wasn't in the kitchen. He wanted to be glad, but instead he poured a steaming mug and went in search of her. Might as well have a little talk, let her know she didn't have to worry about him coming on to her the way Rowdy had. Clear the air.

He found her in the living room, kneeling in front of the fireplace.

"What are you doing?"

She glanced over one shoulder, her hair catching on her mouth. His gaze went straight there as the thought of her kisses came slamming down on him. That puffy bottom lip tasted like sugar and cinnamon and pure delight.

"I thought a fire would be lovely," that mouth said. "And you need to warm up quickly. This is flu season."

His mouth twitched. "Afraid I'll get sick and you'll be stuck taking care of me?"

She studied him solemnly. "Actually, no. I don't want you to miss the Christmas party."

"Ah, yes, the party." He rounded the sectional and set his cup on the table to kneel beside her. Their shoulders brushed and enough electricity arced from his body to start the fire without matches. "Let me help."

She shifted to one side, breaking contact with him, and shoved a handful of crumpled newspaper into the fireplace. "I'm quite capable."

Ah, so she *was* upset with him but too dignified to say so.

Before his brain could engage, he grasped her hands and turned her toward him. "I apologized last night."

"How rude of you!" Color flared on her cheekbones.

Her abrupt words took him aback. He wasn't sure what response he'd expected but certainly not that one.

"Rude?" Since when was apologizing considered rude?

"A gentleman kisses a woman and then apologizes? What does that say to the woman?"

He blinked, baffled. This was a side of Jenna he hadn't seen.

"It says," she went on in that prissy, citified tone, "that he regrets kissing her. That somehow her kisses were unpleasant."

He blinked like a man staring too long at the sun. "It does?"

She nodded. "Isn't that why you apologized?"

"No. You kiss great. I could have stayed out there all night kissing you. You're amazing."

Her face softened. She pressed her fingertips to her chest. With wonder and hope, she whispered, "I am?"

Dax frowned, swallowing hard. She was confusing him. If he didn't shut up, he'd say something he shouldn't. But he couldn't let her go on thinking she'd done something wrong, either.

"I'm the offender here, Jenna. Not you. You—you're very special." He said the last on a rush of air, wishing the words back but thrilled with the joy that leaped into her expression.

"Oh, Dax." She took his chin in her small, soft fingers and held him captive. "What are you afraid of?"

All his resistance seeped out, as though her touch had the power to disarm every carefully erected defense.

"You," he said simply, quietly. "I'm afraid of you."

Her hand fell away. And oh, he wished it back. He wanted her to go on touching him, making him feel alive and real again in a way he hadn't felt in so long.

Bewildered eyes beseeched him. "I don't understand."

"I know you don't. I know." His throat tightened, full of emotion he shouldn't express. Yet he had to find a way to explain. She'd done nothing but make his life better. She deserved everything good.

Helpless to say anything yet, he pulled her head against his chest. The steady rhythm of his life force beat for her, and he didn't know what to do about it. She felt right in his arms and he wanted her there forever.

Her slender arms snaked around his neck. A wild flurry of hope rose inside him.

He tried to beat it back, tried to deny it existed, and still it fluttered there, as fragile as a new butterfly.

"Talk to me, Dax. Tell me what's going on." Her breath tickled his ear. He heard the hurt and confusion, but he also heard something else—determination and strength.

He realized that this woman-child who'd invaded his life was far stronger than he'd given her credit for. With grit and determination, she'd forged a new life for herself and her baby, taking on the role of his housekeeper when he knew very well that she'd never done this kind of work before. Yet, she'd persevered, and learning fast, had turned the Southpaw Cattle Company into a home filled with love.

He closed his eyes and inhaled her scent. Orange blossoms, she'd told him one day when he'd asked. He loved it. He loved her. She was more woman than his ex had ever been.

"Dax?" she murmured again. Only this time, she

brushed a soft kiss across his cheek as she leaned back on her heels. "Will you please talk to me? Tell me what's going on in that head of yours."

Talk. He wasn't much good at that. How did a man express his feelings and concerns without opening himself up to heartache? How did he do what was best for her and still keep his sanity?

He licked lips gone dry and turned toward the half-laid fire. "Let's get this fire going."

Jenna said nothing but remained there resting on her heels, hands in her lap. She was thinking, though he had no idea where her thoughts were taking her.

Horses and cows he understood, but he'd never quite figured out women.

Intensely aware of her beside him watching, he arranged kindling on the grate, scraped a long fireplace match along the stone hearth and lit the wadded paper. The flame started small but quickly grew to catch the dry pine.

He'd never been much into analogy, but building the fire reminded him of the woman by his side. He'd been as dry as this kindling. Then Jenna had come along, reminded him of his blessings and the joys of everyday living and started a small spark of hope and light inside him. Now that spark had grown into a flame that burned only for her.

He pivoted to reach for a hickory log. Jenna anticipated his needs, as she'd done for weeks now, and handed him the stick of wood.

His hand trembled the slightest bit as he finished laying the fire and sat back to watch the flames climb higher. Heat began to warm his face.

Jenna shifted away and then stood. Dax looked up. "Where are you going?"

Her mouth curved. "I'll be back."

"Promise?" Ah, man, he was a mess.

Her eyes twinkled. "Are you going to talk to me?"

As worried as he was about screwing up everything and causing her to leave, he still found a certain humor in the situation. "Are you going to nag me if I don't?"

This time she laughed. "What do you think?" And then she hurried out of the living room.

Dax set the fire screen in place, dusted his hands down the sides of his clean jeans and looked around the living room. The place was magazine beautiful since Jenna had rearranged furniture and accessories, added pictures and doodads to the walls and gone all out for Christmas. She'd added a pair of enormous floor pillows for Gavin to flop on when he watched TV. Dax took those now and fluffed them onto the rug in front of the fire, refusing to examine the reasons behind the action.

"Here we go, sir," Jenna said. He scowled at her. The term *sir* didn't sit too well, considering the battle raging inside him. He didn't need any reminders that she was his employee and that he was twelve years older.

Furry slippers snip-snapping against her heels, she came toward him carrying a tray which she deposited on the coffee table. The scent of cinnamon wafted up from a plate piled high with ornament cookies. The tray was jammed with paintbrushes, tiny bowls of colored frosting and red ribbon.

"Are you putting me to work?"

"This is on my to-do list today. I thought you might like to decorate some while you bask by the fireside. It's fun."

Bask by the fireside? Her words tickled him. "What about Gavin?"

"I saved a plate for him. He gets tired after five or six."

Well, decorating cookies wasn't the kind of thing he'd had in mind, but he had to admit her idea was better than his. Cozying up with Jenna in front of a fire could be a dangerous proposition.

"Sophie asleep?" he asked, taking up a paint brush.

"Midmorning nap. Crystal said some babies don't adjust to a schedule right away, but Sophie has. She's the most amazing baby." The light of mother-love warmed her face. Dax's insides squeezed with gladness for Sophie. His baby had never had that kind of female devotion.

A voice in his head said, "Until now," and the vision of Jenna curved protectively, lovingly around his boy rose in his mind.

Taking up a Santa-shaped ornament, he dipped

his brush in red frosting. "You gonna tell me about Gavin's nightmare?"

Brush and cookie in hand, she looked at him in surprise. "How did you know?"

"When I came in from the barn, I checked on him." He shrugged. "Always do. He was gone. You heard him on the monitor, didn't you? That's why you came inside last night."

Jenna tilted her head.

Yes, she'd come in for that reason, but also because he'd kissed her and then pushed her away. She was still pondering that turn of events.

"I'm not sure what he dreamed," she said. "But he was shivering and scared."

"Thank you for looking after him."

"No gratitude is required, Dax." Jenna dropped her gaze to the gingerbread boy. "I love him."

There, she'd admitted her love for one of the Coleman men. One down and one to go.

Dax didn't respond to the declaration, just went on painting Santa's hat with red frosting.

After a bit, he said, "You know I'm divorced."

The topic surprised her a little, but she was ready to hear the story from him. "Yes."

"Gavin never really knew his mother. She left when he was a few days old." He laid aside the paintbrush and drew in a deep breath. "She never wanted him."

"How horrible. He doesn't know, does he?"

"No. No. I'd never tell him such a thing, but he

has to feel it. Other boys have mothers and he has never even seen his. When he was three years old, he began to notice that baby horses have mamas. Baby calves have mamas. Even his dad has a mama. Now that he's started school, he talks about it more. He's more clingy and the nightmares come more often." He rubbed the side of his neck as though the worry gave him a pain. "I don't know what to do."

"His lack of a mother is not your fault."

"I feel as if it is. I wasn't the best husband in the world. Always working, constantly out in the barn or the fields or off to stock sales and shows."

He looked so sad Jenna couldn't stop herself. She put aside her decorations, reached across the table and touched the back of his hand. "You were making a living for your family. That's as it should be."

"Reba didn't think so. She wanted parties and travel and fun."

"Nothing wrong with those things."

"That's why I blame myself."

"You didn't understand my meaning. There is nothing wrong with those things in small increments, but they aren't a lifestyle. Or they shouldn't be." No one knew that better than her. "My husband was the same way. Life was a party." As long as she was paying the bills and didn't stand in the way.

"Did you love him?"

She lifted a shoulder. "I thought I did. Did you love Reba?"

He nodded. "Yeah. Too much, I guess."

The admission poked at Jenna like a pinprick.

"I need you to know something," he went on. "She started divorce proceedings long before Gavin was born." His Adam's apple rose and fell. "After I caught her in bed with my brother."

The stark pain on his face drove the breath from her lungs. She knew that kind of betrayal, too, although she'd never caught Derek in the act. The newspaper speculation had been humiliating enough.

"You must have been…shattered."

"Yeah. We had just found out she was pregnant. I was overjoyed—and too stupid to see what was going on under my nose. I thought she was finally ready to settle down."

"I'm sorry."

"You know the last words she said to me?" His jaw worked, his fist tightened beneath her fingers, and Jenna could feel the rage and hurt coming off him in waves. "She asked me if I'd always wonder for certain if the kid she'd given me was really mine."

Jenna had never been a violent person, but she wanted to slap a certain female named Reba. The woman was too cruel for words. "Do you?"

He shook his head. "No. Oh, I thought about it when she first left, but after a while I no longer cared. I believe he's mine by biology, but even if he isn't, he's mine in here." He tapped a finger to his breastbone. "I rocked him, walked the floor with him, diapered his bottom and spooned baby food into his bird mouth. With every new thing I did for and with my son, I loved him deeper. He's a trooper, a hearty little soul who survived a stumbling, bumbling daddy. I just wish I could have been a mama to him, too. How could she do that to him? How could she not love a son like Gavin?"

"I don't understand, either, Dax."

He turned his hand over and clasped her palm in his. "I know you don't. That's one of the things I— admire about you."

Jenna heard the hesitation in his speech. Had he almost said love? Her pulse quivered in her chest, a hopeful bird fluttering for release.

Dax had been badly wounded and now she understood that those wounds made him cautious. She wanted to reassure him that she would never hurt him that way. She wanted him to know that the longing to mother Gavin grew stronger every day.

But she didn't tell him. She couldn't. Yet.

Dax took up the paintbrush and cookie again. "This is supposed to be a fun rainy-day project. Didn't mean to get serious on you."

"I asked you to talk to me." The man needed a partner to share his heavy load. And she needed to be needed. For most of her life, she'd been nothing but an ornament like the ones on the massive

Christmas tree. Having Sophie and being a part of Dax's life had given her a sense of worth.

He turned the cinnamon cookie in her direction. "What do ya think of Santa?"

So he didn't want to discuss his ex-wife anymore. She understood. Derek wasn't her favorite topic, either. But she did want Dax to have some fun for a change.

She wrinkled her nose. "I thought Santa's boots were black."

Dax made a silly face. "Oops. I'll fix it."

When he leaned in to dip the brush in black frosting, Jenna dabbed paint on the tip of his nose.

"Oh, my goodness," she said with mock seriousness. "You have frosting on your nose."

"I do?" he asked in the same silly tone she'd used. All the while he swirled his paintbrush round and round in the frosting bowl. "Ever heard of face painting?"

Jenna dotted a gingerbread boy with white icing eyes. "Don't they do that at fairs and carnivals?"

Such events were below the status of a Carrington, but she'd seen the activity on television and had envied those lucky children their flowers and cartoon characters.

"And in living rooms on rainy days," he said.

Her gaze flew up to meet his. "Truly?"

He laughed and pointed the brush at her. "First time for everything. What do ya say, Jenna, want to launch my art career?"

She held up a warning finger. "Don't even think about it."

"Too late." Mischief filled his face.

"Dax," she warned, though the rise of energy inside her and the giggle she couldn't stop gave the lie to her warning.

"Ah, come on, Jenna. Play nice. Let me decorate your face. A few dots here, a blue stripe there. Gonna be fantastic." On his knees, he walked toward her, frosting near the drip stage.

"Don't you dare." She crab-crawled backward, but Dax kept coming, brush loaded with bright blue paint.

Like the villain in an old-time movie, he pumped his eyebrows. If he'd had a mustache, he would probably have twirled the ends, too.

Giggling, Jenna scooted back some more, though she couldn't escape—even if she'd wanted to.

Dax pounced. Jenna flung an arm upward to ward off the blue-drenched brush. Bits of cookie paint flicked loose. A laughing, halfhearted wrestling match ensued, but Jenna was no match for the big man's superior strength. In two seconds flat she was pinned to the floor, her wrists manacled above her head by one of his powerful hands while the other advanced toward her face with a glob of shiny blue frosting. Jenna switched her head from side to side, laughing so hard now that she could barely breathe.

When Dax saw that he couldn't paint a face in motion, he resorted to threats. "Take your punishment or prepare to wash sugar out of your hair."

She stilled but couldn't stop giggling as Dax moved closer with the brush. She'd never seen him playful. He was still a young man but the past and his load of responsibility weighed him down. He needed to laugh and feel young and happy again. And she was thrilled to be a part of the moment—even if it meant having her cheek painted.

But instead of dabbing her cheek, Dax stroked the brush over her mouth. The motion tickled, but Jenna stopped giggling. A tingle of awareness moved from her mouth into her chest and lower.

She became acutely cognizant of Dax's body pressing into hers in all the right places.

"You have the most gorgeous mouth," he murmured.

She tried to joke. "And you think it should be painted blue?"

A tiny smile played at the corners of his mouth as he slowly outlined her top lip with the fine-tipped brush. She shivered. He raised his eyes to hers and then went back to his beguiling work. With painstaking care, while she throbbed at his nearness, he outlined her bottom lip, then dipped his brush again and filled in every millimeter of her mouth.

By now her heart thundered in her ears. Though she tried to control her breathing, her chest rose and fell more quickly. Her tongue snaked out to moisten lips gone dry from nerves and drying sugar. As if she'd issued a command, Dax tossed the brush aside and leaned in to nibble at the corner of her mouth.

"Yum," he said, his breath stirring the sensitive tissues, making her yearn.

She tried to move, to turn her lips into his, but he backed away a fraction of an inch. His eyelids were hooded and sexy.

"Be still." The gravelly command raised goose bumps on her arms. Dax noticed and laughed softly. "I made this mess. I'll clean it up."

While Jenna thought she'd die if he didn't kiss her right then, she played his sensual game. His hot, enticing tongue followed the path of the paintbrush around her lips.

"Sweet as sugar," he murmured, the words flowing into her mouth from his. She smiled a little at the joke.

He nibbled her bottom lip. She let her mouth drop open slightly hoping he'd take the hint.

But Dax was not finished with his delicious torture. He went right on nipping and tasting, making soft moaning sounds that sent her blood racing and alerted every nerve ending in her body.

The taste of sugar mingled with the coffee they'd drunk and a taste that only belonged to Dax— manly, hot and yet cautious as though he was holding himself in check. She didn't want caution. She wanted him.

"Dax," she whispered in a shaky voice.

He raised his head and their eyes locked. The desire she saw there didn't surprise her, but the tenderness did. For all his gruffness, Dax had a way of making her feel cherished.

"I—I—" She longed to admit her love but there were other things she had to tell him first. And yet if she discussed her past, this beautiful spell would be broken. She couldn't bear if he was angry with her for keeping the secret. Not today when she felt more beautiful and special than she'd ever felt in her life. So in the end, she closed her eyes and said nothing. Dax didn't move and she could feel his gaze boring into her. His breath soughed gently and after a moment he shifted slightly, though he never released her hands. He held her captive with his fingers, his body and his lips. She wondered if he knew that he also held her captive with his heart.

Her lips dropped open and this time Dax took full advantage to devour the remaining sugar, caressing her mouth until she thought she might melt into the carpet.

He worked his way over her chin and jaw and to her ear where he puffed softly until she shivered, and then he kissed his way down her throat. It was then he loosened his hold on her wrists. With deep pleasure humming through her body, she laced her fingers in his thick hair and drew him closer.

Just when Jenna thought she would combust with desire, Sophie let out a howl.

Both adults froze. The only sounds in the room were the crackle of the fireplace and the pounding of their hearts.

Sophie cried out again.

Dax growled deep in his throat, and then he chuckled. The sound vibrated inside Jenna's chest. With a wry grin, he rolled to one side and helped her sit up. "Saved by the baby."

She hadn't wanted to be saved from Dax, but common sense would say to take things slowly. She pushed to a stand, using Dax's broad shoulder for leverage. Her knees trembled. "It's time for her bottle."

"Bring her in here." He shoved a hand through his hair, forking it up in all directions. "I missed playtime this morning."

Jenna studied him. He wasn't angry. A little frustrated perhaps, but not angry. Instead he wanted to spend time with her and Sophie.

How could she not love a man like that?

CHAPTER FIFTEEN

DAX LIFTED THE LID on the stew pot and sniffed. Steam and the aroma of chicken broth warmed his face. Jenna had gone into town for lunch with Crystal and a couple of other girlfriends, leaving the stew pot for his lunch. According to Jenna, they were revising a guest list for the Christmas party that seemed to grow larger each day. Not that he minded. If having a party made her happy, she could have one every day.

Taking a thick stoneware bowl from the shelf, he dipped it full of the Brunswick Stew, sliced a chunk of corn bread and settled in at the bar for lunch.

The rainy day had changed everything. He could no more explain it than he could explain why a woman like Jenna Garwood would choose to remain on the Southpaw with him and Gavin, but he felt more positive about life than he had in years. Hope was a magical emotion and he was filled with it.

As much as he'd wanted to make love to Jenna

that day, he now knew the timing had been wrong. They were still learning and growing together and each day was a discovery. Jenna in his kitchen. Jenna in his living room. Jenna dancing in circles to Christmas music with Sophie in her arms.

He loved sneaking up behind her when she was busy. He'd plant a kiss on her neck or her hair and she'd spin around, face flushed, to fall against him for a real kiss.

Sometimes at night when he crawled into the king-size bed, he let himself imagine what it would be like if Jenna was lying beside him. They'd talk about the day's events, laugh at things the kids had done, and then make love sweeter than any cookie frosting ever created.

He spooned the thick soup into his mouth and moaned with appreciation. His Jenna was a fine chef. *His* Jenna. Was she? Did she want to be? He thought she did but he had to be sure. *She* had to be sure.

She was in his house and in his heart. He wanted her in his bed, too.

Making love didn't scare him. Falling in love did.

They'd never spoken of age, but that rainy day in her arms had convinced him that Jenna was far more woman than girl. Part of him still worried that he was too old, too broken and too bitter to give a young, vibrant woman what she needed.

But hope had come to the Southpaw and Dax

clung to it like a drowning man to a bit of flotsam. For indeed, he'd been dead inside when Jenna Garwood and her baby had opened the door to his empty heart and made themselves welcome.

Though still convinced that she had secrets, he was afraid to ask. What if he didn't like the answers? What if he drove her away? For now, he couldn't take the chance. Maybe by spring, he'd be more confident—if he could keep his libido in check that long. Jenna deserved more than an employer who took advantage.

He slathered butter on his corn bread and bit down. Jenna had never before baked corn bread but when he'd mentioned a fondness for the Southern dish, it had appeared at the next meal, just the way he liked it with a touch of sugar. He took another bite and realized he was smiling.

She'd left the Christmas tree lights on and last night, she and Gavin had hung the elaborately quilted and personalized stockings on the gleaming wood mantel. The house was alive with her special touches.

Outside he heard the sound of a car and his heart leaped. Jenna must be back early. Forgetting all about his half-eaten meal, he shoved off the bar stool and hurried to the door. Though she'd only been gone a couple of hours, he missed her.

He yanked the front door open and paused. A long, sleek, black car pulled into his drive. No one he knew drove a car of that caliber, at least not out here in the country. This looked like something a government official would drive.

A sense of foreboding crawled up the back of his neck. He shook it off.

A uniformed driver complete with a flat cap like something out of a movie, exited the car and opened the back door. With a stiff bow, the chauffeur extended a hand to assist the occupant. Out stepped a dark-haired, middle-aged woman in a crisp tan suit. Nose high, she gazed around, taking in the brown landscape and finally coming to rest on him. She looked him over and then squared her shoulders and said something to the chauffeur. From the other side of the car, a burly man exited and came around to stand beside the elegantly clad woman. To Dax's way of thinking, the man looked like a cop—or a gangster.

Normally, Dax went out to greet his company, but something about this group bothered him. He didn't know them, but something didn't feel right.

The dark-haired woman and the burly man came toward the house. Dax stepped out onto the porch.

"You folks lost?"

"I think not." The woman's voice was high-brow and disdaining. "This is the Southpaw Cattle Company, isn't it?"

"It is."

"And may I inquire as to who you are?"

Both the phrasing and the accent sounded eerily familiar. "Dax Coleman. This is my place. And you are?"

"Elaine Carrington. May I come inside please? We have some business to discuss."

He couldn't imagine what business he could possibly have with a woman he'd never heard of but he motioned toward the house. "Come on in."

He led the way, taking note that the burly fellow followed but hadn't been introduced. The man cast a suspicious eye in all directions as they entered the foyer and passed into the living room.

"Have a seat," Dax said. He waited as politely as possible while the woman settled on the divan and then he perched on the edge of a nearby chair. The burly man didn't sit, rather took up residence at the end of the couch, his arms crossed over his chest.

What was this guy anyway? Some kind of bodyguard?

"I'll get straight to the point," the woman said. "I'm looking for my daughter, Genevieve Carrington."

Dax relaxed the slightest bit. For a minute there, he was scared she was going to mention Jenna. "Sorry, ma'am. I don't know her."

The woman's lips thinned. "That's not what my sources tell me."

Dax was stricken with an overpowering need to get these strangers off his land. "Well, your sources are wrong. So if you'll excuse me, I have a ranch to run."

"Just a moment, Mr. Coleman. I've spent thousands of dollars tracking my daughter. I know she's been here. I know she gave birth to a daughter—my grandchild—in the local hospital. I also know she took a position with your ranch—" her nostrils flared in distaste "—as a domestic."

Oh no. No.

Dax wanted to put a hand over her mouth and stop the flow of words but instead he sat frozen like a plastic snowman.

Mrs. Carrington opened her black leather bag and withdrew a paper which she handed to Dax. "This photo was taken shortly before her husband died."

Before he even looked down, Dax knew who would be smiling out at him, but his heart dropped anyway.

"Jenna," he said. "My housekeeper's name is Jenna Garwood, not Carrington."

"So she is here. Thank God." A world of tension left the woman's body. "Garwood was her married name. Where is she? Where is my granddaughter? We need to get them back to Pennsylvania under medical care right away."

Dax's pulse jumped. "Is Jenna sick?"

"Of course she is. What person in her right mind would run away from her family estate in the ninth month of pregnancy and leave behind a multimillion dollar trust fund?"

His ears buzzed. He could have sworn she said Jenna was rich. "If that's true, why did she come to work here?"

"My point exactly. Jenna is the sole heiress to a vast fortune. Since her husband's death, she has not been well. I blame myself for not getting her the help she needed sooner. Haven't you ever heard of postpartum depression? Hormonal psychosis? Our physician believes this is likely the culprit, and now that she has delivered the baby, the danger increases. So please, Mr. Coleman, tell me where my daughter is so we can take her home where she belongs."

Dax ran a shaky hand over his face. He couldn't believe this. He was living in a nightmare. Jenna, his love, the woman he wanted to keep forever, obviously didn't feel the same. She'd had plenty of chances to tell him who she was, and she hadn't.

He felt as if his heart would burst right out of his chest. What an idiot he was to think a woman like Jenna could care for him. He'd known from the beginning she didn't fit in his world. She was too young, too classy. The warning signs were all around him, and yet he'd shut them out.

The rumble of a car engine sounded, growing closer. His gut knotted to the point of nausea. He had to get out of here before he did something he'd regret forever. Call him a coward, but he couldn't look into Jenna's eyes without losing his cool. It wasn't so much that she hadn't told him, it was that she hadn't trusted him. And more than that, her mother was right. Jenna was a blue blood. She shouldn't be scrubbing floors for a Texas rancher.

"That's Jenna's car," he said, somehow managing to force the words past the knot in his throat. "If you'll excuse me, I'll leave you to your reunion."

With a curt nod, he took his hat and coat and exited out the back way.

They had found her.

The moment she turned down the graveled drive into the Southpaw, Jenna went weak all over. Though she didn't recognize the black luxury sedan parked next to the house, she recognized the Carrington style.

She tapped the brake, blood roaring in her head as she contemplated the best mode of action. If the visitor was, indeed, Mother, she'd already spoken to Dax. By now, he'd be wondering what kind of crazy person would run away from a fortune. Worse yet, he'd be wondering why Jenna had kept such a secret from him even after their relationship had begun to flower.

Now she wondered the same thing. She should have told him. She should have explained about the years of living an overprotected life with a neurotic mother whose fears controlled her every movement.

The memory of her miserable childhood stiffened her spine. She was an adult. Her mother could not force her to return home.

She pulled into the garage, gathered Sophie into

her arms and let herself in through the back door. She could hear the clip of her mother's voice speaking to someone.

Holding her baby close, knees trembling, she moved quietly down the hall and through the house until she stood in the entry between the dining and living rooms.

"Hello, Mother." Jenna's voice sounded cool, but her insides wobbled.

"Jenna, darling." Elaine rose and reached toward her. Jenna remained aloof and on guard, but an unexpected surge of emotion struck her. Tears pressed at the back of her eyelids. As damaged as their relationship was, she'd missed her family.

Elaine moved forward to touch the white blanket surrounding Sophie. "Is this our little Rose Elizabeth?"

The moment of weakness fled. Her mother had insisted Jenna name her baby after two matriarchs of the Carrington family, considering her choice far more fitting than anything Jenna suggested. Elaine had even preenrolled Sophie in an elite private school under that name and against Jenna's wishes.

"Her name is Sophie Joy."

Elaine drew back, startled that her will had been questioned, but as "befitting one of her station," she quickly masked her real feelings.

"Sit down, darling. You look terrible." She glanced at Parm, head of Carrington security for as long as Jenna could remember. "Don't you agree, Parm? She's clearly been ill."

Parm inclined his head, agreeing as always with his employer.

"I've never been healthier, Mother."

"Don't try to hide the truth from me, darling. I know when something's wrong." She tilted Jenna's face upward and studied her as if she were a painting. "If you would only have told your father or me how distraught you were over Derek's death and—well, that other distasteful affair, we would have gotten you the help you needed."

Leave it to mother to consider death and adultery as equally distasteful. "The situation with Derek was only one of the reasons I left. I don't expect you to understand. But I do expect you to get in your car, return to the airport and go home."

"Not without you and my granddaughter." Elaine smoothed the back of her skirt and reseated herself. "You're ill. You have been for some time."

"You want me to be ill so you can control me. And Sophie."

"Don't be ridiculous. Genevieve, darling, do you have any heart at all? Don't you realize the terror and despair your father and I experienced when we realized you were gone? We thought our worst nightmare had finally come to pass." She paused, pressed a pampered hand to her heart and closed her eyes. "I wept for days, waiting for the ransom call, certain some vicious monster had stolen my only child."

Jenna's conscience pricked. The Carringtons feared kidnapping above all things. "I left a note."

"A note could have easily been forced from you at gunpoint. Even Parm was deeply concerned that something untoward had occurred."

Jenna swallowed. "I'm sorry, Mother. I never meant to worry you."

"Don't you see, darling, your behavior has been unbalanced, a danger to you and my grandchild."

"I'm a good mother."

"Your love is not in question, but your emotional health is. Now that I'm here I see for myself how desperate the situation is. You look dreadful, exhausted, weathered like a common street urchin. And those hands, your once-beautiful hands…" Her mother's voice trailed away as she stared at Jenna's chipped fingernails.

"I work for a living."

Elaine placed the back of her hand against her forehead as if a migraine was coming on. "Clearly another symptom of how ill you are. Our kind do not work for a living. We serve others in charitable duties. Jenna, child, as difficult as it may be for you to think rationally, consider the things you've done. You engaged in an ill-begotten alliance with a gold-digging philanderer and got yourself pregnant. That alone shows very poor judgment. Then only days before that baby's birth, you disappeared, putting both your child and yourself in jeopardy. Anything could have happened. Dear heavens above, you gave birth to the Carrington heir on the side of the road. You could have died. Don't you understand how terribly ill you must be to have done such a dangerous thing?"

Jenna's heart sank lower than the Texas sun. She had never looked at the situation quite this way. Was Mother right? Had running away been the sign of a mental illness?

"I'm sorry, Mother," she said again and heard the voice of a little girl who had always apologized and obeyed. Five minutes in the company of her mother and Jenna was a child again. Growing more confused and uncertain by the minute, she felt herself weakening.

Perhaps she should go home. Perhaps she wasn't well. Sophie deserved to grow up in a healthy environment. She reached down to smooth the soft cap of blond curls and stared into her baby's eyes. What was the right thing to do for Sophie?

Elaine touched her shoulder, though Jenna hadn't seen her leave the chair. "Come on, darling. Let's get your things and leave before that cowboy person returns."

Like a remote control doll, Jenna rose, clutching Sophie to her breast. "I have to say goodbye."

Elaine took her elbow. "I don't think that's a good idea. Mr. Coleman was very upset."

She blinked. "He was?"

"There's no predicting what he might do now

that he knows you're an heiress. Extortion, black-mail. Anything is possible."

Something clicked inside Jenna's brain. "Dax isn't like that. Dax is—" A flood of emotion rushed through her at the thought of everything she'd shared with the Texas rancher.

Here on the Southpaw with Dax, she'd changed from a frightened runaway to an adult with the strength and good sense to run a household, nurture her child as well as his, and turn a lonely house into a lively, beautiful home filled with love. Thanks to Dax, she'd learned that her value and worth had nothing to do with a trust fund. Here she loved and was loved for who she was inside.

Suddenly she knew her mother was wrong. Neither depressed nor mentally ill, Jenna Garwood had become a woman in control of her own life. And she wanted that life to be here, on the Southpaw with Dax if he'd have her. "I love him."

Elaine's head snapped back. "Don't be a fool again. You know what happened the last time a man discovered your trust fund."

Jenna shook her head slowly from side to side as hope returned, a gentle salve to her wounded soul. "He didn't know. He didn't know and he loves me anyway."

He'd never said as much but she knew now. Dax loved her and Sophie. His love was there in every-thing he said and did.

She wouldn't go back. She would not allow the

Carrington money to ruin Sophie's childhood the
way it had ruined hers. She'd run away for Sophie's
sake, not to cause her harm, and no amount of psy-
chological manipulation by her mother would
change her mind.

Right then, she knew what she had to do.

"Mother, I love and respect you, but I am a grown
woman. I am not returning to Pennsylvania."
Regardless of what happened with Dax, she could
not go home again. "If you wish to be a part of my
life and Sophie's, you'll do so under my rules."

Elaine's mouth dropped open. Parm snapped
to attention but Jenna knew he wouldn't stop her.
He couldn't.

"Now if you will excuse me, Sophie and I have
some unfinished business to attend to." With a song
in her heart and head held high, she went in search
of Dax. Somehow she would make him understand.

CHAPTER SIXTEEN

DAX SAW HER ROUND the corner of the barn and come toward him across the dead grass, purpose in her stride. The hood of her coat had fallen and her hair blew away from her face. The cold air tinged her cheeks with rose, giving her an invigorated, healthy look. She was carrying the baby bundled in a thick blanket. As she drew near, he could see the excitement emanating from her like heat from a summer sidewalk.

He knew. She was coming to tell him goodbye. She was heading back to the fancy life where she belonged.

Dax hurt so bad he didn't have the strength to cuss. He was breaking in half, shattered at the thought of losing this woman that he'd known all along he shouldn't fall for. And yet he had.

When Reba left, he'd been furious and bitter. But with Jenna, he was simply broken. She'd done nothing but make his life better. She'd driven out the bitterness and replaced it with soft smiles, lobster croquettes and Christmas decorations. And the best kisses a man could fantasize about.

Ah, man, he loved her. Maybe if he'd told her and held her and promised her the moon…ah, what was he thinking? She could buy the moon for herself. She didn't need him.

"Dax?" she said, coming to a halt at his side. He should be angry, but he couldn't muster the energy. He looked down into those brown eyes and fell apart. Dropping the wrench he'd been using to hang the metal gate, he pulled her and Sophie gently into his embrace.

"I'll never forget you, Jenna," he said, memorizing the scent and silkiness of her hair and the curve of her body. Long after she was gone from his life, he wanted to remember. "Gavin will miss you. I hope you'll keep in touch. For his sake."

She stilled. "What about you? Will you miss me?"

He squeezed his eyes against the question. Jenna wasn't normally a cruel person.

"Yeah," he answered raggedly. "I'll miss you, too."

Jenna's body began to tremble. Dax held her tighter. Soft weeping filled his ears. Gripping her upper arms, he put her a little away from him. Tears flowed down her face and dripped onto Sophie's blanket.

"What? Why are you crying?"

"Because I think you love me."

So that was it. She knew he'd fallen hard, and tenderhearted Jenna felt bad about hurting him. But Dax refused to lie about something as precious as love.

He tilted her chin. "You stole my heart the day we brought Sophie into this world. And every day since then I've fallen more in love than I ever dreamed possible."

More tears gushed from her eyes, down her cheeks and into the corners of her mouth. It was all he could do not to kiss them away.

"What would a beautiful angel like you want with me? But I don't regret one moment we spent together. And if I could have one wish in this world—" He stopped, too emotional to go on.

Still weeping softly, Jenna turned her face into his palm and kissed him. The sweetness of that act nearly brought him to his knees.

"Tell me your wish."

He shook his head. "No. I won't put any more guilt on you. Go home with your family and be happy, Jenna. That's what I wish for you."

The baby had grown restless while the adults talked and let out a whimper. Thinking this was the last time he'd get to hold her, Dax took Sophie and rested her against his shoulder. She settled instantly and if possible Dax's heart broke a little more. He'd fallen for this baby girl as surely as he'd fallen for the mother.

Jenna smiled through her tears and gripped the lapel of his work coat.

"I *am* home with my family, Dax."

He wasn't sure he understood. "Aren't you going back East with your mother?"

Her face crumpled again. "Do you want me to?"

"No!" he shouted.

Sophie jumped and started to cry. Dax patted her back and made a shushing sound until she settled again.

"I mean," he said more quietly, "I want you to do what's best for you. I won't stand in your way." Even if it killed him. "But tell me one thing, why weren't honest with me from the start?"

"I'm sorry. I wish I had been." So did he. "But I was so very afraid."

"Of me?"

"Yes, and of my own inadequacies. Mostly I feared being found by my family and having Sophie taken away."

"I don't understand."

"I know you don't. Unless you've lived in a gilded cage, you can't imagine what it's like. All my life, I've been nothing but a trust fund baby, controlled, overprotected, and only accepted for my fortune. The one time I tried to break away, I chose a man who claimed to love me until he had his hands on my money. And then I was nothing. Nothing."

"You thought I'd care about your blasted fortune!" The idea infuriated him.

"Derek did."

"I'm not him."

"Exactly. You didn't know and you loved me anyway. You saw me and accepted me for who I am in here." She tapped her chest. "Do you know what that means to me? For the first time in my life, I'm a normal person, living a free, happy life. That's what I want. That's what Sophie deserves. Don't you see? I could never subject my daughter to that smothering lifestyle where she never really knows someone else's motives. I want her to have confidence that she can do things for herself, that she can earn her own way, that she's beautiful and special for herself, not her money. I want her to grow up where she was born, surrounded by the simple life and good people of Saddleback."

Wonder and hope began to warm his frozen blood. "You want to go on as my housekeeper? You? A woman who could buy this place and hire a dozen servants?"

Her eyes flashed fire. If he'd been kindling, she would have incinerated him.

Hands on hips, she said, "For a smart man, you can sure act dumb. If that's all you want from me, tell me now and I will leave. Because I don't want to be your housekeeper."

"What do you want?"

She slashed at the tears that had begun again. "I want to love you every day of my life. I want to be your partner and your friend and—"

Before she could finish, he used his free hand

to yank her against him. His heart banged against his rib cage like hail on a tin roof. "And my lover and my wife?"

She raised her face to his, eyes red-rimmed but glowing with joy. "Yes!"

With a fierce groan of relief, he kissed the lips he craved. For the rest of his life, he'd remember the feel of the December chill seeping through his clothes, the smell of wood smoke in the air, and the taste of her salty tears…mingling with his.

EPILOGUE

CARS LINED THE YARD and driveway of the Southpaw Cattle Company. Jenna's Christmas Eve party was in full swing and she was so excited and happy she could hardly think straight.

The house was full of friends and Dax's family, who'd driven up from Austin for the holiday. She'd been a little nervous about meeting them, but they seemed to like her and were taken captive by Sophie. Even now, the baby, dressed in a red velvet Mrs. Santa suit, was being passed from person to person.

"The house is gorgeous, hon," Crystal said, coming up from behind with a mini quiche in one hand and a glass of wassail in the other.

"So are you." The darkly pretty nurse had chosen a body-skimming dress in Christmas red, a color that suited her perfectly.

"Joe can't keep his hands off me." Crystal giggled and waved at her husband, a quiet guy as blond as Crystal was dark.

"Who can blame him?"

"Same with your man. Look at him over there by the canapés, watching your every move. I think he could gobble you up in one bite."

Jenna blushed, tingling with anticipation at what was to come before this night was over. Dax had gone cross-eyed when she'd slid into the barely silver one-shouldered dress and strappy stilettos. "I think I just might let him, too."

Crystal's eyes widened and she laughed. A pair of snowflake earrings danced against her dark skin. "You two are perfect together. I'm thrilled for both of you."

Jenna's heart beat a happy rhythm. "Me, too. The day I crashed my car into Dax's fence, I never dreamed how wonderfully my life would work out."

"You seemed so lost and scared that day, but gritty and determined, too. I knew you were gonna make it. But I have to admit things turned out better than I thought." She sipped her steaming wassail and then whispered, "But the Gucci purse should have given me a clue."

"I'm sorry for keeping that from you."

Jenna had shared the truth about her wealthy family with Crystal, but she was still determined to live a normal life and put the trust fund money to use for others less blessed.

"Trust me, girl. I totally understand." She hunched her shoulders and grinned. "Well, sort of. The emotional part anyway, but money and Crystal are soon parted. Oops, I see that hunky husband of mine coming my way. Bet he wants to find a dark corner and make out." She popped the remaining quiche into her cherry-colored lips and waved two fingers. "Ta-ta."

Heart glad, Jenna waved and continued her journey through the partygoers, stopping to chat with first one and then another. Gavin's teacher was there, looking cute and young in a Santa hat. Her little girl was twirling in circles to *The Nutcracker* music playing softly through the sound system.

Talk of the weather and Christmas, politics and children, and lots of laughter mingled with the clink of glasses and the smells of pine and cinnamon. It was a good party. People seemed to be enjoying themselves.

But the best was yet to come.

Gradually, she made her way to Dax's side. He was deep in conversation with another rancher about an upcoming stock show in Fort Worth. As soon as he saw her, Dax said to the other man, "'Scuse me, Jake. There's a beautiful woman wanting my attention."

Jake clapped him on the shoulder. "Talk to you later, then. Great party, ma'am."

Jenna smiled her thanks as he moved away.

Dax slid an arm around her waist and nuzzled her ear. "You smell good. Look good, too."

"Ready for our surprise?"

"Can't wait." He stroked the sensitive flesh on

the back of her neck. "I'm sorry your parents chose not to come."

With Dax at her side, she'd talked again with her mother and hammered out a fragile truce. Though Elaine would never fully understand, Jenna hoped to build a workable relationship with her family. She loved them. She just couldn't live with them anymore. When they'd been invited to the wedding, however, they'd refused, certain Jenna was making another mistake. She'd been disappointed, though she'd expected the response.

"Someday, they'll realize. But until they do, I refuse to let them ruin tonight."

"I love you." He kissed her cheek.

"I love you, too."

"Come on, then. Let's find our boy." They glanced around the crowded room and located Gavin easily. Reindeer antlers poked up from his dark head. He'd insisted on wearing a brown suit and antlers in honor of Rudolph who, he was convinced, would be stopping at the house later tonight.

"You painted his nose." Dax said, eyes twinkling.

"He asked."

"I wasn't complaining. I was remembering. You. Me. A lot of sugary frosting." He nuzzled her ear again and whispered. "Very soon, I'm going to paint you all over, just so I can clean up the mess."

She gave him a sultry look and twitched one eyebrow. "Ready when you are, cowboy."

His pupils dilated until the green irises were but a rim around the edges. "How about now?"

She laughed, feeling beautiful and sexy and desirable. Dax had done that for her, given her the confidence to be a woman. "How about you get the real party started and we'll save the good stuff for later."

"As my lady wishes." He executed an elegant bow and led her to a roped-off area in front of the crackling fireplace. Guests assumed she'd been protecting the white rug, but she and Dax had other plans. Dax's family already knew and when they spotted Dax and Jenna, they moved into action.

Within minutes, the houselights came down and the glow of the tree, the candles and the fireplace filled the vast room with a festive, romantic glow. A hush came over the guests as they turned in curiosity.

Holding Jenna's hand, Dax stood with his back to the stone fireplace, surrounded by flickering candlelight as he spoke. "Friends and family, Jenna and I have a surprise for you tonight. You've come to celebrate Christmas with us, but we also invited you here for another, more personal reason." He glanced her way and she smiled, certain she radiated enough love and joy to light the darkness all by herself. "Jenna Garwood, this gorgeous, classy, incredible woman has agreed to be my wife."

A murmur of excitement rushed through the

crowd. Dax held up a hand to quiet them. "And all of you are invited to our wedding which will take place—" he glanced at his watch for effect "—right now."

The excited murmurs started again as the minister from Dax's church stepped forward. Dax's sister had control of the sound system and the music changed to gentle piano by the O'Neil Brothers. A swish of recorded wind and wind chimes set a mood of peace, and hushed expectation settled on the room. As the minister began to speak and gentle strains of "I Wonder as I Wander" added background, tears filled Jenna's eyes. For indeed, she had wandered a very long distance to find her rightful place.

Dax turned to face her and spoke his words of love and commitment. His voice trembled with emotion that she knew was not nerves but his heart speaking to hers. He slid the diamond band onto her finger and then it was her turn.

She was too full of feelings to tell him everything, but she spoke from her heart, and when a tear slid down her cheek, he bent to kiss it away. A collective sigh went up from the guests.

The ceremony ended and the minister said, "Ladies and gentlemen, I present to you, Mr. and Mrs. Dax Coleman. May they always be as happy and committed as they are this moment."

Applause sounded. The photographer they had hired to capture their party and wedding snapped photo after photo. Gavin, his antlers quivering, pulled away from his grandmother and rushed to hug Dax's legs. "Does this mean Jenna is my mom now?"

Tugging Jenna down with him, Dax crouched to meet his son at eye level. "Yep. What do you think about that?"

Gavin threw his arms around his father's neck. "I think all my Christmas wishes just came true."

As the melody of "I'll be Home for Christmas" began to play, Jenna joined the embrace of her new husband and son, thinking how prophetic both the song and Gavin's words were.

All her Christmas wishes had come true, as well, and she was truly and forever home for Christmas.

* * * * * *

This season we bring you
Christmas Treats
For an early Christmas present Linda Goodnight would like to share a little treat with you…

Creative Way to Give Money
Teenagers love receiving money as a gift, but let's face it, handing over an envelope of money is kind of boring. There are many great ideas for giving money creatively. I stumbled onto my idea quite by accident. As I browsed the department store, I spotted a small, inexpensive snow globe that doubled as a two-sided photo frame, and an idea was born. I inserted the teen's photo on one side of the globe and a carefully folded twenty dollar bill on the other side and wrapped the globe as I would any other gift. When my granddaughter opened the gift and turned it over, there was Andrew Jackson's green face smiling through the falling snow. She loved it, of course, and can reuse the snow globe photo frame for other pictures. Don't have a photo of the teen? Go to MySpace or any of the popular online communities. Chances are you can lift one there as I did.

Edible Craft for Kids
Simple, edible crafts are just the thing to get your child involved in the Christmas celebration. One tasty and fairly healthy treat is made with pretzel

rods. I've seen a number of variations, but the simplest one is pretty to look at, very tasty, and kids can make these themselves with only a little supervision. Take the fat pretzel rods and dip one end in melted almond bark/candy melt, the flavor of your choice. (I like the chocolate best, but the white chocolate and butterscotch are good, too.) Let them cool a minute and then roll in a plate of colored sprinkles, sugars, or crushed candies. The resulting product looks pretty standing in a festive cup and your child feels as if she/he has really done something special. These are great for your child to make and take to school parties, too!

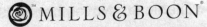

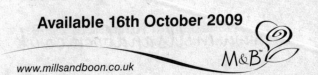

millsandboon.co.uk Community

Join Us!

The Community is the perfect place to meet and chat to kindred spirits who love books and reading as much as you do, but it's also the place to:

- Get the inside scoop from authors about their latest books
- Learn how to write a romance book with advice from our editors
- Help us to continue publishing the best in women's fiction
- Share your thoughts on the books we publish
- Befriend other users

Forums: Interact with each other as well as authors, editors and a whole host of other users worldwide.

Blogs: Every registered community member has their own blog to tell the world what they're up to and what's on their mind.

Book Challenge: We're aiming to read 5,000 books and have joined forces with The Reading Agency in our inaugural Book Challenge.

Profile Page: Showcase yourself and keep a record of your recent community activity.

Social Networking: We've added buttons at the end of every post to share via digg, Facebook, Google, Yahoo, technorati and de.licio.us.

www.millsandboon.co.uk

2 FREE BOOKS
AND A SURPRISE GIFT

We would like to take this opportunity to thank you for reading this Mills & Boon® book by offering you the chance to take TWO more specially selected books from the Romance series absolutely FREE! We're also making this offer to introduce you to the benefits of the Mills & Boon® Book Club™—

- **FREE home delivery**
- **FREE gifts and competitions**
- **FREE monthly Newsletter**
- **Exclusive Mills & Boon Book Club offers**
- **Books available before they're in the shops**

Accepting these FREE books and gift places you under no obligation to buy, you may cancel at any time, even after receiving your free shipment. Simply complete your details below and return the entire page to the address below. You don't even need a stamp!

YES Please send me 2 free Romance books and a surprise gift. I understand that unless you hear from me, I will receive 5 superb new stories every month including two 2-in-1 books priced at £4.99 each and a single book priced at £3.19, postage and packing free. I am under no obligation to purchase any books and may cancel my subscription at any time. The free books and gift will be mine to keep in any case.

Ms/Mrs/Miss/Mr_____ Initials _____

_____

Surname _____

Address _____

_____

_____ Postcode _____

Send this whole page to: Mills & Boon Book Club, Free Book Offer, FREEPOST NAT 10298, Richmond, TW9 1BR